The Energy Chronicles
Book 1

Energy – The Awakening

To Tracy

You give so much and ask for nothing in return.
My heart is yours, forever.

Copyright 2011 – MJ Schutte
All rights reserved

Books by MJ Schutte

The Energy Chronicles
Energy – The Awakening
Birth of a Wizard
Guardian of Magic

The Magic Chronicles
Princess
Witch
Lost

facebook.com/mjschutte

instagram.com/authormjschutte

Chapter 1

LILIAN CRAWLED AROUND the tree, trying to be as quiet as possible. She held her breath as she looked behind her. Her dress was covered in mud, but she didn't care, as long as she stayed hidden. She turned her head forward again and looked straight into a pair of muscular legs. She scrambled to her feet but a strong arm circled her waist and lifted her off the ground.

The man pulled her close to his chest.

A deep voice growled softly, 'Where are you going, little one?'

Lilian pounded her tiny fists against the thick, muscular arm around her waist but it was like hitting an oak tree.

'Please put me down. Please!' she shrieked.

The man ignored her and started walking towards the river. Lilian pounded her fists even harder on his arm.

'Put me down, you big ox!' she yelled.

Again, there was no reaction from the man so Lilian decided to change tactics.

'Please put me down,' she pleaded in a sweet voice, 'I promise to walk beside you and not be any trouble.'

Still the man ignored her and kept walking. As they reached the river, Lilian was still begging and pleading.

'So, I should let you go?' he snarled and proceeded to walk into the river. When he was waist deep, he unceremoniously dumped Lilian into the cold water. She barely had time for one last scream before her head disappeared under the water.

Brighton waited with a grin on his face for Lilian to surface. Although he knew she had swum around his legs and already surfaced behind him, he didn't turn around. It wasn't that he saw her; instead, he sensed her presence behind him. He decided to act concerned. He reached down and felt under the water for her. It always made her feel special when he was concerned about her.

'Lily!' he called.

He waited a few moments.

'Lily!' he shouted louder.

'Yes?' came the voice from behind.

'Lily! I thought you were drowning!'

'Were you worried about me?' she asked in a sweet voice.

'Of course I am! You scared me half to death!' Brighton complained.

'Well, that's what you deserve for finding me again and dumping me in the water,' she scolded him, folding her arms across her chest. She tried her best to look angry.

'You were dirty from crawling through the mud. Besides, the game is hide and find, not hide, find and then run away. Once I find you, the game is over but you always try to run. It was time to teach you a little lesson,' he said waving his finger at her.

'Yes, father,' Lilian said sarcastically, rolling her eyes.

She looked down at what used to be a white dress. Although the water only reached up to Brighton's waist, it came all the way up to her chest so she couldn't really see much. At thirteen winters, she was a petite girl who still carried a slight bit of baby fat in her face. She had long, flowing, blonde curls that reached halfway down her back. Although she spent a lot of time out in the sun with Brighton, her skin was fair and unblemished. Her big eyes tipped by long, black eyelashes were a deep, cobalt blue and sparkled like sapphires.

Brighton was the complete opposite. At sixteen, he was tall and muscular. From age fifteen, he was already the tallest man in the village. He was just starting to grow a beard and some hair on his barrel-like chest matching his almost black hair. His skin was well tanned and there was not a hint of fat on his body.

Brighton and Lilian were playing hide and find in the woods near the village where they lived. Like every other time they played this, Lilian would go hide and then Brighton would find her. She never understood how he was able to do that. No hiding spot was ever good enough. The day before, she climbed to the top of the big oak tree in the middle of the woods thinking this was the perfect hiding place. She was still marvelling at her own genius when she saw Brighton at the top of the tree next to hers, waving at her with that silly, big grin on his face.

'Take off that dress so I can wash it otherwise your mother might just break off my arm and give you a hiding with it,' Brighton said.

Giggling a little Lilian made her way to the shallow water and started unbuttoning her dress.

'I don't think anyone could break your arm off. It's as thick as a tree stump,' she said.

Brighton lifted his arm and flexed his muscles, making a scary face. That brought fits of laughter from Lilian.

'You're not supposed to laugh. I'm trying to be scary,' he complained.

Lilian laughed even harder. She couldn't imagine Brighton being scary. He was always gentle with her.

Brighton took off his shirt and tossed it onto the dry, smooth rocks next to the river. Lilian slipped out of the dress and held it out to him. Brighton didn't notice; he was staring upriver to where the crossing was. A sense of danger washed over him for just a moment.

'Here's the dress Bri,' she said.

She was the only one that called him "Bri".

'Now go lie down on a warm rock so your vest and undergarments can dry,' Brighton instructed as he took the dress from her.

Lilian found a nice smooth spot and lay down in such a way that she could still see Brighton. He was furiously trying to wash out the mud stains from her dress. Lilian watched the muscles in his arms and chest flexing and suddenly had a strange feeling stirring in her stomach. It was as if a thousand butterflies were fluttering around inside her. Her eyes travelled upward to his face. This was not the first time she had this feeling while secretly watching Brighton. She asked her mother about it but, as usual, her mother did not have time for answering "silly questions".

Brighton held up the dress. It was still very dirty so he dunked it in the water and tried again to get all the mud out. He did this a few more times until the dress was somewhat clean.

'That's better,' Brighton declared, 'It would have been easier with soap but this will have to do for now.'

Brighton hung the dress over a branch and walked over to Lilian. He shook his legs making drops of water fly everywhere.

'No Bri!' Lilian shouted, 'I'm almost dry!'

'Sorry, you're so small I didn't see you there,' Brighton teased.

'That's not funny!' Lilian complained.

'Ok, I'm sorry,' he said quickly in a serious tone.

He knew Lilian didn't like it when he teased her about her size, but sometimes he just couldn't resist. Lilian was frowning at him, she looked very angry so Brighton decided to make it up to her.

'Do you want me to brush your hair?' he offered.

Her frown disappeared instantly, her anger forgotten.

'Yes please,' she purred as she sat up and turned her back towards him.

Brighton knew his offer would have the desired effect. He produced a hairbrush from his pocket and started working on the tangled mess of blond hair. Although it hurt a little to get the knots out, she did not complain for fear he might stop. Brighton always said she was pretty whenever her hair was neatly brushed out.

'How come you have a hairbrush with you?' Lilian asked.

'To brush my hair,' Brighton replied.

'But you have short hair. It does not need brushing,' she said.

'Ok then, to brush your hair,' Brighton admitted.

Lilian smiled to herself, thinking *He is always so thoughtful.*

*****

Thomas watched the two children from across the river.

Brighton is not really a child anymore he thought.

As big as an ox and probably that strong.

Sitting on a rock, deep in the shadows and behind some undergrowth, he was certain that Brighton and Lilian could not see him.

'Ok Brighton, let's see if yesterday was just a coincidence,' Thomas muttered to himself.

He gathered his thoughts and carefully started scouting the area for life with his mind. It was part of the talent he inherited from his ancestors. Just like them, he was able to feel other life forms around him. Lately he had been keeping his feeling for life to a minimum for fear that the Dark Ones will find him again, but yesterday he was certain Brighton sensed him while he was scouting the clearing where the goats grazed everyday. Thomas did not fear the Dark Ones, technically, he was one of them, but he did not want anything to do with them or their ways anymore.

His feeling reached the other side of the river and like before, he was able to detect Lilian but not Brighton. Even more disturbing was that Brighton's head snapped up immediately. Thomas was sure Brighton was looking straight at him.

'Impossible,' he muttered.

He retracted his gift but still Brighton kept staring in his direction. Thomas didn't move.

*****

'What's wrong, Bri?' Lilian asked dreamily when Brighton suddenly stopped brushing her hair.

The hot sun and rhythmic stroking had almost put her to sleep.

'I thought I saw someone on the other side of the river,' Brighton said.

'On the other side? It is too far to see anyone there. I think you finally lost your mind,' Lilian teased.

The joke seemed lost on him as he kept staring across the river.

'Come, let's go check on the goats. We can hang your dress up there to dry.'

Brighton retrieved the dress, picked up his shirt, took Lilian's hand, and started towards the clearing.

Walking hand in hand with Brighton used to be the most natural thing in the world for Lilian but lately it's been pure joy.

She loved the way his big, strong hand wrapped around her tiny hand made her feel safe.

He was truly the largest man she had ever seen and probably the strongest she thought.

Brighton looked down at Lilian as they walked.

'Your hair looks nice like that. It makes you look very pretty,' he said a bit awkwardly.

Lilian blushed and stuttered a thank you.

As they continued through the woods, Brighton stole quick glances at Lilian.

Although quite small for her age, she was growing into a very beautiful young woman.

He loved the way her long blonde curls swayed when she walked and how her deep blue eyes seemed to shine in contrast with her fair skin.

They reached the clearing and Brighton stepped behind her, put his hands on her hips, and lifted her up to sit on his shoulders.

'Count the goats for me please?' he asked.

Carefully she counted as if it was the most important job in the world.

After double-checking her tally, she said, 'There is one missing.'

'No, she is at the house. She will be giving birth soon, remember?' Brighton reminded her.

'Yes, now I remember.'

They spent the rest of the afternoon lying in the sun making up stories of all the great adventures they would go on together.

All too soon, the sun touched the top of the mountain and Brighton knew it was time to go home.

Once the sun disappeared behind the mountain, darkness came quickly in these parts.

This did not scare him, he was far more worried about his mother's reaction if he got home too late.

The village was nestled in a relatively flat spot deep in the mountains. The only way to and from the little village was through a narrow pass to the east.

As far as everyone knew, there were no passes north,

south, or west. It didn't really matter though as this was effectively the western edge of the known world. The mountains stretched from the great sea in the north, all the way down to the great sea in the south. Nobody had ever crossed these mountains and returned. Some people claimed that there is only darkness beyond the mountains, but Brighton thought it to be a cruel attempt at scaring little children.

He could not imagine why anyone would want to leave here. This was the perfect place to live.

The town was surrounded by forests with a single path leading towards the east. It was only about half a day's travel in any direction before you would reach the mountains. The town itself was little more than a random collection of wooden houses with some footpaths leading between them. Everywhere in the forest there were small clearings.

Brighton brought the goats out to one of these clearings everyday. The grazing was much better than close to town. The village was small, only a few hundred inhabitants. The mountains protected them from the winter cold to such an extent that it hardly ever snowed.

Although the official name was Clareton, everybody here referred to it as "Four Mountains" since it looked like the four mountain peaks surrounding it guarded the village.

Brighton sat up.

'Someone is coming,' he said slowly.

A few moments later Thomas appeared.

Instead of heading into town, he went straight towards Brighton and Lilian.

'Isn't he your cousin?' Lilian asked.

'No, he's my mother's uncle or something like that. I'm not really sure.'

When Thomas was close, Brighton got up and walked over to greet him.

'Hello, Thomas,' Brighton said to the old man.

'Good day Brighton, good day Lilian,' Thomas greeted back.

'What brings you out this way?' Brighton enquired.

'I was looking for lemons on the other side of the river,' Thomas said.

Brighton looked down at the obviously empty knapsack and frowned.

'But I couldn't find any,' Thomas quickly added.

'Next time I'll go with you,' Brighton offered.

'Brighton knows where the best lemon trees are,' Lilian boasted.

'Thank you,' Thomas smiled, 'but that's not why I came to greet you. On my way back, I saw a little white goat in the woods. I thought I recognized it as one of yours.'

Brighton looked at the goats grazing in the field and saw the white one was missing.

'I'll go find her,' he sighed.

He turned to Lilian, 'Lily, please take the rest of the goats home and tell mother I'll be along soon. I have to go find that naughty goat. She is probably after those sweet, blue flowers that only grow close to the oak trees.'

'But I counted them and they were all here,' Lilian quickly defended.

'I know. She must have wandered off after that,' Brighton smiled.

'Shall I wait for you at your house?' she asked.

'No, that's not necessary,' Brighton replied.

A little disappointed, Lilian walked towards the goats and looked for the big ram. She knew that she only had to take the rope around his neck and lead him home for all the other goats to follow.

Brighton thanked Thomas and headed for the woods.

Thomas called after Lilian, 'Wait for me, I'll help you with the goats.'

She would have preferred to walk home with Brighton but since that wasn't going to happen, she was happy for Thomas' company.

To Lilian he looked as old as the biggest oak in the woods. He had long white hair and many wrinkles on his face. Although he walked without a limp or any difficulty, he always had a thick walking stick with him.

She liked him; he was always kind to her and quick to make a joke.

'I don't really need the help but would like the company,' Lilian said when Thomas reached her.

'I know you might not need help but maybe I do,' Thomas replied, 'Have you seen how old I am?'

Lilian put her hand over her mouth to hide the giggle escaping her lips. When she could control her voice again, she said innocently, 'Old? I didn't think you were more than a hundred winters.'

'Oh, what I would give to be that young again,' he teased.

This time Lilian couldn't hide her giggling.

If only you knew how true that was, Thomas thought to himself.

*****

Brighton headed straight for the spot where he knew the little white goat would be. Although darkness was falling quickly, it would be easy to see her completely white goat so Brighton wasn't worried about finding her. He reached the place where the blue flowers grew and looked around. It only took him moments to spot the goat and he started towards her. As he took the first step, a sense of extreme danger washed over him.

Brighton stopped and carefully looked everywhere.

Very slowly, he moved forward.

After a few steps, he spotted the danger.

Just past the goat, under a berry bush, a black panther was hiding. Black panthers were by far the most dangerous predator known to man.

Worse than that, they were highly aggressive.

He froze again and strained his eyes in the near darkness to get a better look at the animal.

He didn't really know what to do. Leaving the little white goat seemed cruel but he wasn't about to get into an argument with a black panther either. He was pretty sure he already knew what the outcome of that would be.

It was very uncommon to actually see a black panther. They normally hid during the day and hunted at night. Brighton had never seen one before so he decided to get a closer look. From the stories he'd heard, they moved like ghosts through the night and were faster than lightning.

The goat was still happily grazing, completely unaware of the danger only a few paces behind her. What little breeze there was, pushed from the goat to the panther so she couldn't even smell the danger. The panther wasn't stalking the goat as Brighton originally thought. Instead, it was lying on its side.

Strange Brighton thought. The panther was one good leap away from the goat and still it did nothing.

He realized then that the panther wasn't watching the goat; its eyes were fixed on him.

Stranger still, Brighton did not see any threat in those black eyes.

He thought he saw pain and a plea for help.

Relaxing a little Brighton slowly moved closer and squatted about an arm's length away from the panther.

He realized that this could be very dangerous but his curiosity got the better of him.

'What's the matter?' he asked softly.

Slowly he reached out and touched the panther's big black head.

A soft, throaty growl came from the animal. Brighton gently stroked its head hoping this will keep the animal calm and establish a bit of trust. With his other hand, he pushed the berry bush branches away a little. He instantly saw what was going on.

She was giving birth.

Brighton had seen a number of goats give birth so he was familiar with the sight. He pushed the branches further away and moved around to take a better look.

'This is not good,' he said to the panther.

He knew that in a normal birth, the head should appear first but instead he saw two hind legs. Every time a goat gave birth this way, the little one was long dead before they could free it from the mother.

Brighton didn't know how long the baby panther was stuck this way in the birth canal but he was certain it could not survive.

'I'm going to help you get the baby out,' Brighton explained to the mother, 'It's dead but if we don't remove it you will also die.'

He took hold of the small legs and gently pulled.

At first, nothing happened but as Brighton increased his pulling force, the small body started to move. The mother was clearly in agony but still made no threatening move towards Brighton.

Finally, he was able to pull the baby free. A quick check revealed that the little one was not breathing and Brighton could not feel a heartbeat. He wiped away most of the blood anyway and placed the baby next to his mother's head.

'I'm sorry,' Brighton said stroking the small lifeless body.

'It was a boy.'

Sadness washed over Brighton. He continued stroking the baby for a little while before deciding there was nothing more he could do. Besides, it was time to get the goat home.

Just before he removed his hand from the little body, he thought he felt the chest move. He pressed down a little harder and again the chest rose and fell as if the little one was breathing. Brighton put his hand between the front paws and felt for a heartbeat.

Very faint but still, it was a heartbeat! The little chest rose and fell, again and again.

'Your baby is alive!' Brighton exclaimed, almost beside himself with excitement.

'You need some milk and your mother is too weak to feed you,' he said to the little one.

Looking around he spotted the goat. From a nearby bush, he picked a round leaf slightly bigger than his hand. Cupping his left hand, he fashioned a makeshift cup in it with the round leaf. Next, he went to the goat, who had decided that this was as good a place as any to sleep for the night and got her to stand up.

In no time, his makeshift cup was half-full.

When he returned to the panthers, the little one was struggling to get on his feet. It was far too weak for that but he still tried.

'You're a little fighter,' Brighton told it.

He dipped his finger in the milk and pushed it into the baby's mouth. One taste of the milk was enough, the little panther started suckling on Brighton's finger. Brighton poked a small hole in the side of his makeshift cup with a twig and held it in front of the baby.

Eagerly the baby started drinking. Brighton continued to fill up the cup and feed the little panther until it didn't want any more milk.

He then offered mother panther some milk, which she gratefully accepted. Before she finished drinking the baby was fast asleep in Brighton's lap. He sat with the two panthers for a while longer and then said, 'I'd better get home, Mother is probably furious by now.'

He placed the sleeping baby next to its mother, gathered up the little white goat in his arms, and started walking home. He looked back at the panthers. The big cat's eyes were fixed on him again but this time he saw no pain. Instead, he saw the eyes of a grateful mother.

*****

It was close to midnight when Brighton got home.

Through the window, he saw a candle still burning in the kitchen.

'I think I'm in trouble,' he whispered to the goat.

He put her down with the others and went inside.

Before he took two steps into the kitchen his mother flew into his arms and hugged him so tight he thought she was going to squeeze the life out of him.

'Oh Brighton, I was so worried,' she cried.

'Sorry Mother,' he said sheepishly while hugging her back.

Stepping back, Clarissa asked irritably, 'Where were you?'

'Uh....Didn't Lily tell you?' Brighton stuttered.

'Yes, she said you had to go get the white goat but that was ages ago.'

'Well.....um.....I had trouble finding her.'

Brighton decided not to tell his mother about the panthers. She would only give him a lecture on how dangerous they are and he didn't want to ruin the good feeling that was inside him.

'You're hiding something,' Clarissa accused.

'How do you....I mean...I'm not hiding anything!'

'A mother knows these things. You were always bad at hiding things from me and even worse at lying about it,' his mother smiled.

Brighton tried to change the subject.

'I have to get cleaned up. Any chance I could twist your arm for some supper?'

Clarissa smiled at him. It seemed he was always

hungry these days.

'I made some stew and fresh bread earlier. It's probably cold now,' she replied.

'Let me go wash then I'll come eat. Dish up for me please?' Brighton asked as he headed outside to where the water barrel was.

'Hurry up,' his mother instructed, 'it's late and I want to get to bed.'

'Yes mother,' he said rolling his eyes.

Suddenly he turned around and put his big arm around Clarissa.

'I'm sorry I got home so late,' he apologized.

Chapter 2

THE NEXT MORNING Brighton was up long before the sun. He was still not going to tell his mother about the panthers but could not wait to show Lilian.

As soon as it was light enough, he headed out with the goats. When he got to the clearing he sat down to have some of the previous night's bread and stew.

He frequently looked up and scanned the area towards town to see if Lilian was coming. The excitement was almost too much for him and the wait agonizing.

After a while, he thought of quickly going to where he left the panthers but then worried that while he was gone Lilian might arrive. He settled down to wait some more.

It was halfway to midday before Lilian finally came.

She was wearing a pristine white dress and white shoes.

Instead of shouting for Brighton as she usually did, she walked right up to him and said, 'Good day, Brighton.'

Brighton looked at her quizzically and asked, 'And who might you be?'

'It's me, Lilian,' she replied seriously.

'It can't be,' Brighton teased, 'The Lily I know has a mop of tangled hair and would never wear such a fancy dress. I don't know who you are but you're certainly not my Lily.'

Lilian clenched her fists and shouted at him, 'You big monkey!'

She turned around and stormed off towards town.

'Wait!' Brighton called out. 'Lily, please wait!'

He chased after her and quickly caught up.

When he took her by the arm, she stopped but did not turn around. Brighton stepped in front of her and looked down into her blue eyes. She had tears running down her cheeks.

'What's wrong Lily?' he asked.

'Nothing,' she sobbed.

'Looks like something to me,' he countered.

He went down on one knee, wiped a tear from her cheek, and said softly, 'Please tell me?'

She looked away and said shyly, 'I spent hours making myself pretty, and all you can do is tease me.'

Brighton almost laughed. *Is that all* he wanted to ask but decided against it. She was already upset, no point in making it worse.

'I'm sorry Lily. Give me another chance please,' he said instead.

When she didn't answer he said, 'I promise to tell you that you look pretty.'

'No!' she shouted, 'I want you to tell me the truth.'

'Ok, ok,' he said quickly. 'I will tell you the truth.'

'Promise?'

'Yes, I promise.'

Lilian thought about it for a moment and then stepped back two steps muttering something about boys and stupid.

She slowly turned a few times so that Brighton could get a good look. The flowing, white dress hugged her body perfectly, the white shoes matching the dress. Her blonde curls were brushed out and neatly held back with a pink ribbon. Six tiny pink bows decorated her hair halfway down and six more at the bottom.

'So? What do you think? You promised to tell the truth!' she demanded.

Brighton was speechless for a moment. He always thought Lily was quite a pretty child but now she looked more like a woman, an exceptionally beautiful woman.

'Uh ... You're pret ... I mean .... um.'

He could feel his face going red.

'You are very beautiful, Lilian,' he finally stammered.

Her heart skipped a beat.

'Thank you, Brighton.'

Lilian could tell Brighton was serious.

He only ever called her "Lilian" when he was serious.

Her heart was beating so fast she feared it might fly right out of her chest. He said "beautiful". Not "nice" or "pretty" but "beautiful" and she knew he meant it. How she wished he would scoop her up in his strong arms and kiss her right now.

'What's with calling me "Brighton"?' he asked, still staring at her.

'You're making me uncomfortable,' she said.

'What? Oh, sorry,' he said quickly turning his eyes away.

'Let's go sit on that fallen tree and we can talk a while,' she suggested.

Without a word, Brighton turned, took her hand, and started walking.

'So?' he asked.

'So what?' she replied.

'So what's with calling me "Brighton"?' he asked again.

'Calling your boyfr...uh...friend silly nicknames is for little girls. I am a lady now and I shall act like one.'

'Boyfriend?' Brighton asked with a sly smile.

'Well ... you are a boy and you are my friend. That makes you my boy friend. Not like boyfriends and girlfriends who kiss all the time, but my friend who also happens to be a boy.'

'Oh,' was all he could think to say.

'Where did you get the dress?' Brighton asked after a while.

'I made it,' she answered.

Suddenly he remembered about the panthers.

'Lily I have.....'

'I prefer Lilian now.'

'What? No. I don't care how pretty or grown up you are; you will always be my Lily.'

She decided not to argue. She liked being "his Lily".

'What did you want to say?' she asked.

'I have to show you something,' he said, barely containing his excitement.

'Ok, show me,' she said.

Brighton grabbed his knapsack and said, 'Come with me, it's in the woods.'

They walked south to the edge of the woods where Brighton turned to Lilian.

'You can't go in there with that dress and those shoes. Take it off and leave it here,' he instructed.

She lifted her chin and declared, 'A lady does not get undressed in front of a boy.'

Brighton folded his arms and leaned back against a tree.

'Well, you will ruin the dress and shoes in the woods so it's your choice. Take it off or stay here.'

Lilian was in two minds. This was not lady-like but she desperately wanted to see what got Brighton so excited.

Her curiosity won the battle very quickly. She took the dress and shoes off and left them on a rock.

'Ok, ready,' she said standing in her vest and undergarments.

'Follow me and stay quiet. This could be dangerous,' Brighton warned.

They walked in silence to the spot where the blue flowers grew under the oak trees. Lilian knew better than to ask Brighton where they were going. He never gave away a secret.

When they got to the place, Brighton whispered, 'Stay behind this tree until I call you.'

'Ok,' she whispered back.

Brighton slowly rounded the tree and walked to the berry bush. Mother panther was still lying under the bush, her eyes fixed on him. She let out a low growl and the little one appeared from under the branches where he was hiding. He charged up and launched a mock attack on Brighton's shoes.

When Brighton saw they remembered him and there was no danger he called out to Lilian.

'Come slowly towards me.'

She came around the tree, saw the small panther, and froze. Before Lilian could speak mother panther was up on her feet, the hair on her back standing up, a deep menacing growl coming from her throat. Her eyes were fixed on Lilian, her tail flicking through the air.

'Stand still,' Brighton said quickly.

Lilian stood dead still, not that she was able to move anyway, she was frozen with fear. Brighton walked over to the big cat, the small one still playing around his feet.

Carefully he touched her head and said, 'That is Lily. She is my friend just like you are my friend.'

The big cat seemed not to take notice, still staring at Lilian and growling. Her body was shaking. She was far too weak for this but very determined to protect her young.

Brighton walked to Lilian and put his arm around her.

'See,' he said addressing the cat, 'she is my friend.'

For a few moments more it looked like mother panther might attack but then she suddenly sank down to the ground. Brighton was unsure if she accepted that Lilian would do them no harm or if her fragile strength just gave way. Either way, he was glad the danger seemed to be over.

He walked over and sat next to her.

'Come closer,' he said to Lilian.

She shook her head.

In a small voice Lilian said, 'It's a black panther.'

'Yes I know,' Brighton replied.

'They are dangerous,' Lilian whispered.

''Yes I know,' Brighton said again, 'but this one is my friend. I helped her give birth to the little one last night.'

The small cat was still trying to play with Brighton, but for the moment, he ignored the little one and stroked the big cat's head. Deciding that this was no fun, the small cat looked for something else to play with.

He spotted Lilian. Far quicker than seemed possible for the baby that he was, he charged at Lilian's legs in a playful attack.

A small whimper escaped her lips. Just before the little one reached Lilian, he stumbled and crashed into her legs. This brought a small giggle from Lilian and she started to relax a little. After a few moments, she plucked up the courage to reach down and stroke his head. This brought another menacing growl from mother panther.

'Easy girl,' Brighton said soothingly while stroking

her head.

Lilian bent over to pick up the little cat but Brighton quickly snapped, 'Don't!'

'She might think you're trying to take him away and that won't be good for us,' he explained.

'First walk over here slowly and come say hello to the mother, maybe then she will allow you to pick up her baby.'

Lilian slowly approached the dangerous animal. Careful to keep Brighton between herself and the predator she reached out with one hand and gingerly touched the animal's head.

'Sit down and stroke her,' Brighton said.

Still very unsure, Lilian sat next to Brighton and started stroking.

The big cat seemed to accept that Lilian was a friend and visibly relaxed. Behind Lilian, the small one was trying to get to one of the tiny pink ribbons in her hair.

'Now you can pick him up,' Brighton said.

Lilian turned, picked up the baby, and put him in her lap.

'Bri, have you seen his eyes?' Lilian asked.

'No. Why?'

'Look,' she said turning the cat's head towards Brighton.

His eyes were completely white.

Brighton looked at mother panther's eyes and said, 'Her eyes are black.'

'Seems a bit strange,' Brighton murmured as he took a closer look at the little one's eyes.

'White as the moon,' he said.

Brighton slowly wagged his finger in front of the little one's nose.

'He is certainly not blind. He follows my finger easily.'

'I know what we'll do, we'll ask old Thomas about it. He seems to know a lot about animals,' Brighton said.

They sat in silence for a while, Lilian playing with the small cat and Brighton stroking the big one.

'Let's name them,' she said.

'Why would they want names?', Brighton asked and then added, 'They are not pets, they are dangerous predators!'

'I know, but I still want to name them,' Lilian replied.

Brighton smiled at her.

'Ok, but as long as you think of the names. There is a reason I have never named the goats.'

'Why?'

'Because I can't think of any good names,' Brighton shrugged.

The little one had calmed down and was trying to find a comfortable spot in Lilian's lap to have a nap.

When he finally settled she stroked his black fur and said, 'He feels so soft. We will call him Velvet.'

'You can't call a boy Velvet,' Brighton complained.

'Mmm, maybe you're right', Lilian mused.

She leaned over a little and stroked mother panther's fur.

'Her coat feels the same. We will call her Velvet', she declared.

'Yes, that's a good name for a girl,' Brighton said.

Lilian looked at the sleeping baby in her lap.

'He looks very mischievous. We will call him Mischief.'

Brighton nodded his approval with a smile.

*****

Brighton picked up his knapsack and pulled out four slices of bread and some cheese wrapped in a cloth. He always brought more lunch than was necessary so that he could share with Lilian. Brighton's mother knew this but didn't mind. They had more than enough food for the two of them and she often remarked that it wasn't going that well with Lilian's family. He handed Lilian two of the slices of bread and a slice of cheese.

'Tell me if you want more,' he said.

Lilian's mouth was already too full to speak so she just nodded.

He turned to Velvet.

'I have something for you too, girl.'

'Velvet,' Lilian said past the piece of bread in her mouth.

He shot a sideways glance to her and repeated, 'I have something for you too, Velvet.'

Reaching into the knapsack, he pulled out a large piece of raw meat.

At the smell of the meat, Velvet's ears perked up.

'Here you go,' Brighton said and placed the meat in front of her.

She did not immediately start eating as Brighton expected but instead let out a low growl. Instantly Mischief was awake and made his way over to the meat. He tore off a small piece and started chewing. Only then did Velvet start eating.

'That's odd,' Brighton remarked.

'What?' Lilian asked.

'A goat will suckle on its mother for days before it can eat solid food. The cub...uh...Mischief is a day old and he is already eating meat.'

'You can't compare a goat to a black panther,' Lilian giggled.

'No, I suppose not.'

Brighton made a mental note to ask old Thomas about that. It just seemed strange to him. As Brighton was on his last mouthful of bread, he got that strange feeling of danger washing over him again. His head snapped up and he stared through the undergrowth. Nothing moved but he was certain there was something there. He noticed that Lilian and Velvet were still calmly eating but Mischief had stopped and was also staring in the same direction.

'This is happening too often,' Brighton muttered.

'Come, it's time to go,' he said to Lilian as he got up.

'But I want to stay a while longer,' Lilian complained.

'Someone is coming and I don't want them to see Velvet and Mischief,' Brighton said.

Lilian shoved the last of her bread into her mouth, gave both the cats a quick scratch behind the ears, and followed Brighton.

'How do you know someone is coming?' she asked.

'I heard them,' came the reply.

Lilian cocked her head sideways and listened but could only hear birds.

They walked back to the clearing without encountering anyone.

'Are you sure you heard someone?' Lilian asked.

'Yes,' was all Brighton said, looking very worried.

He never told anyone he could feel danger, not even Lilian.

He still felt it, someone, or something very dangerous was close by. He was pretty sure Mischief also felt it.

They retrieved Lilian's dress and shoes. As she was getting dressed, Brighton looked over to the east side of the clearing, the side from where he felt the danger.

A black robed figure was standing at the edge of the woods.

'Hurry, we have to go,' Brighton urged Lilian.

'But the goats...'

'We'll come back later to get them.'

Brighton grabbed her hand and started walking towards town with long strides. Lilian had to run to keep up.

'Bri, what's going on?' she whimpered.

Brighton gestured towards the robed figure.

'That man is dangerous. It's best we get away from him.'

'What man?' Lilian asked.

Brighton stopped and looked.

Nobody.

'There was a man,' he said sheepishly.

'Well, now he's not there. Let's go back to Velvet and Mischief,' Lilian pleaded.

'I think we'd better get you home. I will come back for the goats later.'

'But Bri....' she started.

'Don't argue with me please Lilian. I don't want you to be in any danger and that man I saw is very dangerous,' Brighton said a bit more harshly than intended.

Although very disappointed, Lilian didn't argue further. It gave her a warm feeling all over to know Brighton was that concerned for her safety. They started walking again, a bit slower this time. As they reached the path that lead to town Brighton stopped and looked back.

The robed figure was almost in the middle of the clearing and moving towards them with incredible speed.

'Get behind me,' Brighton snapped.

The man reached the middle of the clearing and opened his arms. A line of black smoke as thick as his arm came from his right hand and raced towards Brighton and Lilian. Brighton turned, grabbed Lilian, and covered her with his body. When he looked back the line of black smoke was just reaching them.

The moment the smoke touched his forehead it recoiled as if in pain. The smoke tried again and again it recoiled.

'What's happening?' Lilian screamed in fear.

Brighton looked at her.

'I don't know but it's time to do something about it.'

As he said it, he felt a shockwave going through his body. He looked around again and saw a bolt of pure white light racing towards the robed figure. The bolt hit the man square in the chest and sent him flying backwards at least ten paces.

The black smoke was gone in an instant.

'Let's go before he decides to try again,' Brighton said to Lilian.

She had tears running down her cheeks and could barely stand.

He bent down and said, 'Tell you what, hold on to my neck and I will carry you home.'

Lilian gratefully threw her arms around his neck and clung onto him for dear life. She wrapped her legs around his waist and buried her face in his neck.

'What happened?' she asked through her tears.

'I don't know,' Brighton said.

'What was that white light that you threw at the monster?' she tried.

'I didn't throw anything,' Brighton said. 'I don't know where that came from.'

'It came from you,' Lilian said in a small voice.

Brighton managed a small smile and said, 'I really don't know Lily.'

'But....' she persisted.

'Lily, I don't know. Please stop it now. I am just as scared and confused as you,' the young man pleaded.

She pulled her head back and looked him in the eye.

'How can you be scared of anything? You're as big and strong as...as....as the biggest oak in the woods,' she said.

'Oh really?' Brighton chuckled, 'That big and that strong?'

'Yes,' she confirmed.

Before Brighton could answer she continued.

'And also very kind. You always share your food with me and you helped Velvet and Mischief. Only a very kind person would do that.'

'Thank you, Lily,' Brighton said a bit self-consciously.

They walked in silence until they reached the village

and Brighton put Lilian down. She took his hand as they walked through the streets towards Lilian's house, which was on the northern edge of town. Brighton and his mother stayed just outside of town on the south side closer to the clearing where Brighton took the goats to graze everyday.

This early in the afternoon, the town was deserted because everyone was in the fields tending to their crops or busy working in their vegetable gardens.

Almost everyone.

Four young men were sitting outside one of the cottages when Brighton and Lilian walked past. They were all slightly older than Brighton but not nearly as big.

Garth, the leader of the gang saw them and shouted, 'Look at the two love birds holding hands in the street.'

The others hooted and howled with laughter. Brighton ignored them and Lilian pulled a face.

Garth snarled at her, 'One day that ox won't be with you and then you and I are going to have some fun.'

Brighton stopped, slowly turned his head and in a low, quiet voice said, 'Touch her and it will be the last time you ever touch anything.'

Garth went white as the moon and the other three, John, Brent and William fell silent instantly.

Brighton and Lilian resumed walking and Lilian said, 'They are scared of you.'

'I don't know why,' Brighton said, 'I've never laid a hand on any of them.'

'The way you just spoke even frightened me a little,' Lilian told him.

'Yes, that must be why they are so scared of me,' Brighton laughed.

'They don't like you very much, but don't worry, everybody else likes you. Especially me,' Lilian purred.

'Thank you, Lily,' Brighton replied. 'I think everyone likes me because we give them food.'

'Why is it that you and your mother always have so much food while everyone else is struggling?' she asked.

'I don't know,' Brighton said honestly, then added, 'Our crops just seem to flourish and our goats have lots of babies. I can't tell you why.'

'Well, I think it's good. If it wasn't for you and your mother a lot of people would go hungry in this village,' Lilian declared.

'Yes, I suppose so,' Brighton sighed. 'We have too much food for two people and rather than letting it go to waste we give it away.'

'See, I said you were kind and I was right. I think you learnt it from your mother,' Lilian speculated.

Brighton just smiled at her. He often wondered why they had such good fortune while everyone else seemed to struggle so much.

As they passed Thomas' cottage Brighton stopped.

'I'm going to see whether old Thomas is here. You go home,' he said.

'Ok,' Lilian said.

For once she didn't argue because she already had plans to make another dress tonight. When she found the white material in her mother's closet yesterday, she also came across the prettiest pink material.

'A hug?' she asked.

Brighton bent down to hug her but instead she planted a kiss right on his lips, turned around, and skipped off towards her house, the ordeal of earlier completely forgotten.

A little puzzled, Brighton walked up the path to Thomas' house. He knocked and stepped back.

That was strange he thought as he waited.

It took only a few moments for Thomas to open the door.

'Ah, young Brighton,' Thomas exclaimed. 'What a surprise. Don't just stand there, come in. Would you like some lemon juice? A biscuit perhaps? You should like them, your mother made them for me.'

'No, thank you,' Brighton said. 'I just came to ask a quick question. I don't mean to bother you for too long.'

'It's no bother, young man, I'm actually very happy for the company,' the old man beamed.

'Well, in that case I will have some juice with you,' Brighton said, following Thomas into the kitchen.

*****

Lilian saw her mother pacing outside the house. This was never a good sign and Lilian had an overwhelming urge to turn and run back to Brighton. She wished her father, Markus, was home but she knew that was unlikely this time of the day. He worked in the field until it was too dark to see. She felt sorry for him; it seemed that no matter what he planted his crops always failed.

Martha spotted her and shouted, 'Stop dawdling Lilian. Come here!'

Lilian slowly walked up to the house.

'Where were you?' Martha demanded.

'I.....' Lilian tried.

'Never mind, go inside,' the older woman snapped.

When Lilian did not move immediately, Martha pushed her through the door. Lilian shrank away from the touch. She new her mother's hands would be dirty and now there was probably a big brown mark on the back of her pretty, white dress. Lilian was sure that Martha never washed her hands, not even when she was preparing supper.

Her eyes took a moment to adjust to the gloomy light inside. A man was sitting at the kitchen table. He wore a black robe that had a neat round hole in front, right on the chest. Lilian froze.

It can't be she thought.

It was the black robed figure from earlier, she was sure of it. He was tall and thin with long white hair. His deep-set black eyes and thin dark lips contrasted his white skin giving him an evil appearance. A scar ran down his left cheek.

Although the man spoke in a soft voice, it was deep and menacing, like when the thunderclouds came rolling over the mountains.

'Come closer little one,' he said.

Lilian couldn't move.

The deep voice rumbled again, 'Come closer, don't make me wait.'

Martha was beside herself with fear.

'Do as he says before you bring more trouble to this house,' she shrieked. Another shove on the back and Lilian was suddenly standing right in front of the man.

'I am Seth. What is your name?' he asked.

She managed to squeak out 'Lilian' in a small voice.

His hand shot out and touched her forehead. Lilian yanked her head away but not before a sharp shooting pain went through her entire body.

'You're quite a find,' the man whispered to himself.

Lilian did not dare say anything or even move a muscle.

'Where is the boy that was with you earlier?' he asked.

Lilian did not answer.

'I will not ask twice,' Seth threatened.

Lilian did not like him and certainly was not going to tell him where Brighton was.

Instead of answering him, she asked, 'How did you get here so fast?'

'I ran,' he growled. 'Now tell me where the boy is!'

'At his house,' she lied.

'Show me,' Seth demanded.

He grabbed Lilian behind the neck and marched her out of the house.

'Which way?' he growled.

Lilian pointed down the street. Seth set a brisk pace down the street still keeping a tight grip on Lilian's neck. When they passed Thomas' house Lilian was relieved to see that Brighton was not still standing outside.

They reached Brighton and Clarissa's home. Seth simply pushed the door open and entered.

'Where is the boy that lives here?' he demanded from a startled Clarissa.

'He is not home yet. Who are you?' she demanded.

'Where is the boy?' Seth repeated.

'I told you already,' Clarissa snapped back.

Looking at Lilian she asked, 'Who is this rude man?'

'Seth,' was all Lilian managed before he slapped her so hard across the face it knocked her clean off her feet.

'Lilian!' Clarissa shouted. She tried to get around Seth to see if Lilian was all right but Seth grabbed her by the throat and threw her clean across the kitchen. Lilian watched in horror as he lifted his hand and from his palm, black smoke appeared. It shot across the room and slammed into Clarissa's head.

Clarissa's first reaction was shock and then the pain came. More pain than she had ever experienced. Her body twisted so violently that Lilian heard her spine break. Clarissa's eyes and ears were bleeding. She tried to scream but no sound came.

Please let me die, she thought.

'Oh, you want to die?' Seth mocked.

The smoke disappeared. Seth crossed the room and grabbed Clarissa by the throat again. He jerked her up so that her face was almost touching his and whispered, 'I will be more than happy to help you die if that is your wish, but I do prefer the feeling of flesh under my hand rather than killing you from back there.'

He turned to Lilian.

'Come here,' he ordered.

Fearing that she might get the same treatment as Clarissa she immediately did as he said.

'Look into her eyes,' he instructed.

Lilian looked down at Clarissa. She saw the life draining from the woman's eyes.

Seth let go of the lifeless body, walked to the door, and said, 'Come.'

Lilian sank to her knees next to Clarissa's lifeless body. She could not believe what she had just witnessed. The black smoke slammed into her head.

Chapter 3

THOMAS PLACED TWO mugs on the small table and filled both with lemon juice. The biscuits were already on the table.

'Help yourself, your mother made them,' came the offer.

'Yes, you said so, thank you,' Brighton said as he took one.

Thomas also took a biscuit and shoved the whole thing in his mouth.

'You have a question for me?' he said with crumbs flying everywhere.

Brighton decided to jump right in.

'This morning I saw a black panther and her cub, about a day old.'

He didn't want to tell Thomas what really happened so he thought to change the story a bit.

'The cub was eating meat. Is that normal?' he asked.

'Yes, that is quite normal for a black panther,' Thomas confirmed.

'Something else, the cub had completely white eyes. Have you ever seen that?' Brighton pressed on.

'How close were you to these panthers?' Thomas asked.

'Um...not that close,' Brighton stammered.

'You must have been very close if you could see the colour of the cub's eyes. They are extremely dangerous animals you know,' Thomas admonished.

Brighton shifted uncomfortably in his chair. He hated telling lies but he did not really want anyone to know what actually happened.

'Don't worry young Brighton, I won't tell anyone you're playing with black panthers,' Thomas chuckled.

He thought for a moment and then said, 'To answer your question: No, I've never seen any animal with white eyes. Perhaps it's blind?'

Before he thought it through Brighton answered, 'No, he followed my finger easily. He is not blind.'

'Your finger? You were a lot closer to these animals than you're letting on,' Thomas said.

Brighton knew he said too much, he needed to tell the truth.

'Ok, I'll tell you what happened but please promise not to tell anyone,' he pleaded.

'You have my word,' Thomas said solemnly.

'I found the mother last night giving birth but it wasn't going well. The cub was coming out hind legs first. I helped release it from the mother,' the young man sighed.

'How did it survive?' Thomas asked.

'I don't know,' Brighton answered. 'At first I thought it was dead but then it started breathing and by this morning when Lilian and I went there, it was running around like nothing was wrong.'

'Incredible,' Thomas gasped.

'While we were sitting with the two panthers Lilian showed me Mischief's eyes. They were completely white,' Brighton added.

'Mischief?' the old man frowned.

'Yes, that's what Lilian named the cub. The mother is Velvet,' Brighton smiled.

'How sweet of her, Lilian is a very special child,' Thomas mused.

Remembering the kiss from earlier and seeing her in that white dress Brighton muttered, 'Not so much a child anymore.'

Thomas looked at Brighton closely.

'You love her,' he stated.

'Well, yes. She is my best friend. Actually, she is my only friend. She is like a sister to me,' Brighton said a bit defensively.

'I don't mean like that young man. I mean you're in love with her, yes?'

Brighton's face instantly went red and it felt like his ears were burning.

'I......uh.....well......Can we rather talk about the panthers please?' he pleaded.

'As soon as you answer my question: Are you in love with Lilian?' Thomas pressed.

'She is a child,' Brighton defended heatedly.

'And you're an adult?' Thomas countered.

'No, I mean Lily is so much younger than me. She doesn't even have...um....like some of the other girls. She has no......'

'Breasts?'

Brighton stared at his feet and wished the earth would swallow him.

'Yes, those,' he said softly.

Thomas poked Brighton in the chest with his walking stick.

'What does that matter?'

Brighton did not answer because he could not think of

one. Thomas was right it didn't matter. All that mattered was that he did love Lilian.

'I know she is slow to develop but there are many winters ahead of you both. Enjoy your time together now and don't be too hasty with any decision pertaining to matters of the heart. The age difference seems big now but when you're twenty one, she will be eighteen. Not that much different is it?' Thomas smiled.

'No, I guess not,' came the muttered reply.

'Be patient young Brighton and enjoy your youth. All too quickly you will be old like me,' Thomas sighed.

'But how will I know if she loves me?' Brighton asked.

'He who knows the heart of a woman will be king forever,' Thomas said cryptically.

'What does that mean?' the younger man frowned.

'It means you will never know if she loves you. You will just have to guess,' Thomas replied.

'I think Lily loves me,' Brighton said confidently. 'She kissed me just before I came here.'

'If that is the case then I am very glad for you, young man. I never found love, hopefully you will,' Thomas smiled.

He reached for the cup of lemon juice. Brighton didn't like lemon juice all that much, but he didn't want to seem rude so he took a sip from his mug. He was not prepared for the shock that followed. It was all he could do to swallow the small sip. He nearly spat it all over the table.

'Dear angels, that is horrible,' he muttered.

'It's an acquired taste,' Thomas laughed.

'Don't you dilute it?' Brighton asked with a pained look on his face.

'No, I like it this way,' Thomas replied.

'How can you drink it like that?' Brighton frowned.

'A lifetime of practice,' Thomas said with a wink.

'How many winters? A hundred? I don't think I'll ever get used to it,' Brighton exclaimed.

'More like five hundred,' Thomas said, closely watching Brighton's face.

Brighton looked up expecting to see a smile on the old man's lips but instead Thomas' face was dead serious.

'Five hundred winters?' Brighton gasped. 'How old exactly are you?'

'Five hundred and sixty three,' Thomas said matter-of-factly.

'You're jesting!' the young man accused.

'I wish I was, but it's the truth,' Thomas sighed.

Flabbergasted Brighton asked, 'How is that possible? Are you a magician or a sorcerer?'

Thomas said softly, 'Everyone knows magicians only exist in bedtime stories designed to scare little children. No, I'm not a magician, sorcerer or a warlock or any of those mythical things. I am something much worse.'

'Then what are you?'

'I'll tell you but first I must have your promise that you will not share this information with anyone, not even Lilian.'

'You have my word,' Brighton said solemnly, mimicking Thomas' words from earlier.

'I inherited a gift from my ancestors. Well…uh…some call it a gift, others call it a talent, some, like me, call it a curse,' Thomas revealed.

Brighton leaned forward.

'What is it?' he asked wide eyed.

'Perhaps I should start at the beginning then you might understand better. Around a thousand winters ago, maybe slightly less, two babies were born. A boy and a girl…' Thomas started the tale but Brighton interrupted.

'Brother and sister?' he asked.

'No, they were unrelated. These babies were gifted in the sense that they could steal or leech energy from other living things,' Thomas continued.

'Energy? What do you mean energy?' Brighton

enquired.

'All living things have energy. You eat some biscuits or bread and this is transformed into energy. You use this energy to live. In basic terms, this is the life force in you. Do you understand?' Thomas explained.

'I think so,' Brighton said.

For a moment it looked like Thomas might offer more but then changed his mind. Instead he continued with the tale of the two babies.

'These babies didn't have to eat or drink. They had a talent for stealing energy from other living things. The two of them grew up and were drawn together because of this talent. They eventually got married and had eight children. They became known as the Dark Father and Dark Mother and their children call themselves the Supremes. Their descendants are called Dark Ones,' Thomas said.

'Call themselves the Supremes?' Brighton asked. 'Surely you mean called. They must be long dead if they were born a thousand winters ago.'

'No,' Thomas answered. 'They still live. This talent for stealing life force or energy kept them young. The Dark Father and Dark Mother had to touch other living things to steal their energy but the talent was much stronger in their children. They could do it over great distances.'

'Over great distances?' Brighton frowned.

'The Supremes don't have to physically touch another living thing. They can steal energy from far away. If you have the talent, you can see it happening. For those who are ungifted this happens without them even knowing,' came the explanation.

Brighton thought of the man in the clearing and the smoke that attacked them.

'What does it look like?' he asked.

'I've only seen it once but I will never forget it. Many winters ago, when I was still living in Zedonia…'

'What is Zedonia?' Brighton interrupted.

'It's a city where the Supremes live. Now stop interrupting or I will never finish.'

'Sorry,' Brighton mumbled.

'As I was saying, when I lived in Zedonia an uprising against the Supremes started. The Supremes have ruled like a royal family for many winters and some people thought it was time for a change. Nobody elected them as the rulers, they simply decided that they were better than everybody else was and took control. Because of their dark talent, nobody could stand against them. Many winters later a group of brave men decided it was time for a change and challenged the Supremes to meet them in the open for a battle. The victors earn the right to rule the land. The Supremes live in a cave inside a hill in the middle of Zedonia. They are very seldom seen but on that day seven of the eight came out to meet the brave warriors,' Thomas continued.

Brighton started interrupting but Thomas cut him off.

'Don't think that they are barbarians because they live in a cave. It's actually a series of caves and rumoured to be the most luxurious accommodation anyone has ever seen. The Supremes force ungifted people to work in the caves as slaves. Apparently, there are marble floors and golden ceilings everywhere. The walls are decorated with gold, silver, precious gems and the finest tapestries in the land. I've never seen it but have heard many stories about it. It is simply called The Palace. Anyway, the seven Supremes came out of the palace and met the warriors in the centre of town. Before anyone could speak, Seth, the oldest Supreme, stepped forward, raised his hand and something that looked like black smoke seemed to appear from his palm. The smoke, about as thick as his arm, shot out towards the leader of the warriors and slammed right into his head. There was nothing the poor man could do; he was dead in a heartbeat.

The smoke did not go away. It slammed into the next man's head. He did not die instantly like the first one but fell to the ground, his body twisting in pain. Seth smiled and looked at the crowd. With a flick of his wrist, the black smoke left the man's head and retracted back into Seth's palm. Seth spoke only briefly, before the seven Supremes retreated to their caves. He said, "Nobody will challenge us!" That was the last time any of the Supremes, except Seth, were seen outside the palace.'

'How long ago?' Brighton asked.

'Many winters. I was young back then,' Thomas replied.

'How did the smoke kill the warriors?' Brighton asked.

'It wasn't really the smoke that killed them; it was Seth that simply sucked all the energy or life out of them. The smoke is merely the link between the Supreme and his victim,' Thomas offered.

Brighton fired off another question, 'How come the first man died instantly, but not the second? Did Seth get tired or weak?'

'Not at all,' Thomas replied. 'When a Supreme or a Dark One steals energy it makes them stronger.'

'Oh I see,' Brighton said wide eyed, suddenly wondering how much of this was true.

Thomas did not notice the dubious look in Brighton's eyes so he continued.

'A Dark One can choose how fast he steals your energy. It can be instant, which kills you immediately or slower which is excruciatingly painful. I am a descendant of the Supremes. I am a Dark One,' Thomas confessed.

'So you can make that black smoke and steal energy from other people?' Brighton asked.

The old man merely shook his head.

Brighton was confused.

'Earlier you said you inherited this gift and now you tell me you're a Dark One but you cannot steal energy?' he frowned.

'I can take energy from someone, but I have to touch them. My talent is not strong enough to establish a link over any distance, no matter how small,' Thomas tried to explain.

'So, if you touch me now, I will die?' Brighton asked.

'Again, no'. Thomas said.

Brighton frowned, 'This is confusing.'

'There are two reasons for this. First the obvious one: A Dark One chooses to steal energy, it does not happen automatically when we touch someone. We can control it. Only in extreme cases do we lose control of the gift.'

Before Brighton could speak, Thomas went on.

'Any living thing has instincts of which the most basic is survival. When a Dark One's life is in danger his instinct for survival will take over and try to steal energy from any available source. This is the only time it will happen automatically. It is a bit like breathing. You don't have to think about it, it just happens. Do you understand?' Thomas said.

Brighton just nodded. It was all starting to sound like a bedtime story to him.

'Secondly, I cannot feel you. My talent is blind to you.'

'Feel me? What does that mean?' Brighton said slowly.

'Another part of the talent is a sort of sense or feeling. If you're going to steal energy, you need to know where it is first. All Dark Ones have this ability. Again, it's something we control. At the moment, I'm not using it but if I wished, I could cast a sort of sensing blanket over the village and tell you where everyone is. Every person's energy is slightly different. If a Dark One sensed your energy once he will remember the feeling of it and recognize it next time,' Thomas explained further.

'Show me,' Brighton demanded.

'And what will that prove?' Thomas asked. 'I could tell you that Lilian is at her house and you will have no way of knowing if it's true.'

'I'll go look,' Brighton persisted.

'And maybe she leaves before you get there, then it looks like I lied. Besides, it's too dangerous,' Thomas said, shaking his head.

'Why is it dangerous?' the youngster frowned.

'Because other Dark Ones can find me when I use my sense. That would be bad. This is why I hardly ever use it these days,' the old man explained.

'What do you mean?' Brighton asked.

'It would be bad if they find me. Not good. Bad,' Thomas repeated with a bit of sarcasm in his voice.

Ignoring the sarcastic tone, Brighton asked, 'What do you mean they can find you, if you use your sense?'

'When a gifted person uses his sense to scan for life, other gifted people can feel it,' Thomas answered.

'How do you know that your sense is "blind" to me?' Brighton asked next.

Thomas thought for a moment and decided he needed to tell Brighton about the previous day.

'Yesterday, you and Lilian were playing at the river. I was on the other side of the river where you and Lilian could not see me. I scanned the surrounding area with my gift for life. My sense reached you and Lilian but strangely, I could only feel her energy. It was like you were not there although I could see you with my eyes,' he said.

'Is this…..' Brighton started.

'Wait, there is more. You immediately looked up and straight to where I was hiding. It was like you knew I was there,' the old man added.

'I remember,' Brighton said pensively. 'I was brushing Lily's hair and suddenly had the feeling someone was watching us. Is this normal?'

'Normal? A person should not be able to steal energy from other people. A person should not live for five hundred winters or more. No, young man, none of this is normal,' Thomas shouted angrily.

That's not what Brighton meant with the question but after that reaction, he decided not to ask again.

Thomas took a deep breath and in a softer tone said, 'I'm sorry. None of this is your fault. I should not be shouting at you.'

'I take it you don't really like this talent of yours very much,' Brighton said carefully.

'It's not the talent itself. It's how the people who have it use it. We are no better than regular or ungifted people are. Why should we live forever?' came the sad reply.

Brighton asked his next question carefully, 'Do you steal energy from the people in the village?'

He was expecting Thomas to shout again but instead the old man sighed deeply and said, 'About sixty winters ago I stopped. I had the face someone barely past their thirtieth winter although I was more than five hundred winters old. I came to live out the rest of my life in Four Mountains. I started aging like everyone else and life was good. At first the people here distrusted me but slowly I became part of the community and now I'm just old Thomas.'

'How did you know we call you that?' Brighton asked wide-eyed.

Thomas laughed. 'I may have this cursed gift but I also have normal eyes and ears like everyone else.'

'Sorry,' Brighton stammered.

'Don't be. If everybody knew just how true that nickname is. They think I'm seventy winters old when I'm almost five hundred and seventy,' Thomas chuckled.

Brighton started laughing with Thomas.

'Yes, it is actually quite funny,' he said.

'If you stopped using your talent sixty winters ago and back then you were thirty, that would make you ninety now,' Brighton worked out.

'Yes,' Thomas said.

'You said seventy,' Brighton prodded.

'Yes,' Thomas said again.

Brighton thought for a moment and said, 'You started using your talent again, didn't you? You're stealing energy from everyone here.'

Thomas didn't answer but by the look on his face, Brighton knew he had guessed correctly.

'Why?' he asked.

'Because of you,' Thomas said softly.

'Me!' Brighton gasped. 'What did I do to you?'

'You did not do anything! It's because of who you are. Actually, what you are,' came the reply.

'What do you mean?' Brighton asked curiously.

'Roughly sixteen winters ago I was gathering lemons in the woods close to the foot of the eastern mountain one day. I heard something in the bushes and instinctively used my talent to sense what it was. I detected a single life form, a woman, coming towards me. When she appeared out of the bushes, I was surprised to see her clutching a baby. Somehow I did not sense the baby. I tried again but still could only detect the woman's energy with my talent. I thought perhaps my talent was failing since I hadn't used it in so long but something about that baby nagged in the back of my head,' the older man replied.

'And that baby was me,' Brighton said in understanding. 'You were curious about me so you started using your gift again to live longer. You wanted to see what I would become.'

'Correct,' Thomas confirmed. 'I brought you and your mother to town and introduced her to everyone as my niece and her baby.'

'Do you know who my father is?' Brighton asked.

'It would be better to have that conversation with your mother,' Thomas said with such finality that Brighton didn't even think to press the issue.

Thomas drained his mug and poured more lemon juice.

He looked at Brighton's cup and saw that it was still full.

'Shall I dilute that for you?' he asked.

'Please,' Brighton said gratefully. 'My throat is dry but I don't think I can drink the juice just like that.'

Thomas chuckled while he emptied half the juice out the window and added water.

'Try that,' he said.

Brighton sipped and nodded his head.

'You must have a few questions,' Thomas prodded.

'Yes,' Brighton confirmed. 'Why is it that your talent is so much weaker than that of the Supremes? You're a descendant of theirs, it should be the same?'

Thomas scratched his chin.

'How do I explain that?' he mumbled.

He saw his full mug of juice and got an idea.

Pointing to the mug he said, 'Let's say the juice in the mug is the gift.'

'Ok,' Brighton replied, a little confused.

'At the moment the cup is full and the juice is very strong,' Thomas said.

He drank half the juice and filled up the cup with water.

'Is the juice still as strong as before?' he asked holding it up.

'No, it's diluted with water. It's only half as strong,' Brighton said.

Thomas drank half of the diluted juice and filled up the cup with water again.

'And now?' he asked.

'You diluted it again so now it's half as strong as before, a quarter of the original strength,' Brighton said.

Understanding washed over his face.

'Oh I see!' he exclaimed excitedly. 'When a gifted person and an ungifted person have a child the talent gets diluted because it's only coming from one parent.'

Thomas confirmed the summation with a broad grin.

'How diluted is your talent?' Brighton asked.

'Very,' Thomas said. 'I am only a very distant descendant of the Supremes, many generations removed. I am a descendant of Danika, second daughter of the Supreme Raina.'

'What will happen if two gifted people have a child?' Brighton asked.

'The talent will be stronger in the child than the parents. It's like taking the water out of the lemon juice and adding more juice to it again, but it is forbidden. When the Supremes realized that this would be the case, they made a law that no two gifted people may ever have a child. This ensures that the Supremes will always be the strongest,' Thomas explained.

'Who can steal energy without touching their victim? With the black smoke, in other words?' Brighton pressed on.

'Only the Supremes and their children. Each of the Supremes took a spouse when they were all still very young to ensure that the talent will not die out. They did not know at that time that they would live forever. When they realized this, they killed their spouses and seven of the eight never had children again. However, this was many winters on when their grandchildren were already grown up and had children of their own. The Supremes were worried that their descendants would rise up against them but Seth, the oldest, theorized that if they can control the gifted, the gifted can control the general population and thus the Supremes can become the rulers of all mankind. His plan worked. It was a bad time. Dark Ones would simply pick a person off the street and kill him right there just to prove their dominance. When energy flows that quickly out of the body, it burns the skin. The Dark Ones enjoyed leaving black imprints of their hands on their victims for everyone to see, mostly on the victim's chest. It did not take long before the Dark Ones ruled through fear and intimidation. From time to time there would be talk of rebellion but the Dark Ones always managed to suppress it. The Supremes grew tired of this and that's when they decided to put an end to it, once and for all. Since that day in Zedonia I told you about earlier, there has never been any talk of rebellion again,' the old man said.

'You said seven of the Supremes never had children again. What about the other one?' Brighton asked.

'You don't miss much, do you?' Thomas observed. 'Seth has a taste for young woman. He is the only one that still leaves the caves to satisfy his urges. Sometimes these young women fall pregnant.'

Brighton thought for a moment then asked his next question:

'How did you steal energy from other people? Just walk up to them, take their hands, and steal it?'

'Casual contact, walking in town brushing against people. Shaking someone's hand as a greeting, that sort of thing. That is actually where the custom of shaking hands as a greeting originated. It's a means of touching the victim so that the Dark One can take some of their energy without them knowing,' Thomas replied.

'That's clever,' Brighton marvelled. 'If you just took my hand I would wonder why but shaking hands as a means of greeting is the most natural thing on earth.'

He thought for a moment and then a frown creased his forehead.

'But doesn't it hurt? You said to take the energy slowly means excruciating pain for the victim,' he asked.

'Only if you take all their energy. If you take a small

portion, they shouldn't notice and it leaves no mark. Let's say there are a hundred people each with a hundred lemons. If I take one lemon from each person, they won't miss it all that much because they still have ninety-nine left. I, on the other hand, will have a hundred lemons,' Thomas offered.

'I understand. You don't take all the energy from one person but rather little bits from a lot of people.' Brighton said.

'You learn quickly,' Thomas smiled.

'Can you take energy from me?' Brighton asked.

'I honestly don't know,' Thomas answered. 'But I don't think so. If I can't sense your energy I don't think I can steal it'.

'Try,' Brighton said holding out his hand.

Thomas shook his head, a determined look settling in his eyes.

Brighton did not back down.

He sat forward, grabbed Thomas' hand and said, 'Try!'

Thomas squeezed Brighton's hand, waited a moment and said, 'There, I tried. I can't.'

He quickly pulled his hand from Brighton's grip.

'You're lying,' Brighton accused heatedly.

When the old man said nothing Brighton tried a different tactic.

'Just try,' he pleaded. 'You said you can control it and it won't kill me.'

Thomas sighed and slowly held out his hand to Brighton.

'Take my hand,' he said softly.

Chapter 4

LILIAN OPENED HER eyes but couldn't see anything.

Am I dead, she wondered?

'Get up,' a deep voice rumbled.

Slowly a few images started to appear. She was lying on the wooden floor. A kitchen table, a chair, and a man sitting on the chair came into focus.

'Next time I will not stop and you will die,' he said.

Lilian slowly sat up. She looked around. Clarissa's dead body was right next to her. Lilian scampered away quickly.

'You killed her!' she screamed at Seth.

Ignoring her accusation, he got up, walked to the door, and said, 'Come.'

Remembering what happened last time she did not react she immediately jumped to her feet and rushed over to the door. Her muscles protested, but it was nothing compared to the pain the black smoke caused.

'You learn quickly, that's good,' Seth said.

Lilian followed him out of the house.

She noticed it was almost dark. Instead of turning towards town and going back to her house, Seth took course towards the east. Lilian followed silently. She was frantically trying to think of a plan to get away from Seth. Running wasn't an option. She was sure he could run faster than she could and she saw how fast the black smoke could move. Nothing could outrun that.

She walked a little slower until Seth was fifteen paces or so ahead then quickly slipped behind a tree.

'If I have to turn around to fetch you, you will be sorry,' his voice came from up ahead.

Lilian quickly ran to catch up.

How did he know? flashed thought her mind.

Panic started to rise in her. She walked right behind him until they reached the clearing where the goats were. As they were crossing the clearing, she started to lag behind again.

'Mister, my legs are tired. I can't walk anymore,' she tried.

Seth lifted his hand slowly. Lilian did not need any more motivation. She ran again to catch up. Noticing the goats, she got another plan.

'Would you mind if I took the goats home quickly?' she asked.

Seth lifted his hand towards the goats. The black smoke shot out and briefly touched every goat. In a blink of an eye, all the goats were dead. Lilian started crying softly. She was desperate to get away from this monster.

'Mister, I......'

'Shhhh,' Seth interrupted.

Lilian fell silent. The moon was full providing more than enough light to follow the path.

Maybe when we stop to sleep I can sneak away, she thought.

Seth continued on through the woods towards the eastern mountain with Lilian following closely. He did not stop as Lilian expected and by the time they reached the foot of the mountain, she was exhausted. She had trouble keeping up with the pace. Her legs felt like lead and her muscles protested with every step. Seth kept going at a steady pace up the mountain towards the pass.

Lilian had never been this tired in her life. She mechanically put one foot in front of the other. Seth didn't seem tired at all. He simply kept walking at the same pace.

Step after step they climbed higher until Lilian's legs simply gave way.

Her whole world went black.

When she opened her eyes again, she was flat on her back with Seth standing over her. She knew the black smoke was coming but she was too tired to care.

'Good,' that deep voice rumbled.

'Don't go anywhere,' he mocked. 'I'll be right back.'

Lilian watched him disappear into the woods. She knew now would be a good time to run but her legs simply wouldn't respond. Just lifting her hand to wipe the sweat from her eyes took almost all the energy she had left.

Seth returned holding two little rabbits. He placed them just outside Lilian's reach.

'Hold out your hand towards them,' he instructed.

Still lying on her back, she reached for the rabbits.

'Now feel them,' he said.

'Too far,' she whispered.

'I did not say touch, I said feel.'

Lilian did not understand. The black smoke slammed into her head but only for a moment before it retracted back into Seth's hand. She felt the last of her energy slipping away.

Closing her eyes, she waited for death. She became aware of a tingling in her outstretched hand and opened her eyes. There was a thin line of black smoke between her palm and the one rabbit.

Seth was watching silently.

Lilian started feeling better. Energy seemed to flow from the rabbit through the black smoke into her.

All too soon it stopped.

Lilian wished for more. It made her feel good. She looked at the rabbits. One was watching her, with fear in his eyes; the other was dead.

Sitting up she asked, 'What happened?'

'Your talent woke up,' Seth answered.

Seth saw confusion in her eyes.

'You're a Dark One,' he explained.

'What's that?' Lilian asked.

It was Seth's turn to be confused.

'You don't know?' he frowned

'No,' Lilian said with a shake of her head.

'Strange,' Seth mused, mostly to himself.

'What's a Dark One?' Lilian repeated.

Seth ignored the question.

'We need to keep going. I am uncomfortable out here,' he said.

'I'm tired,' Lilian complained.

'Take the rabbit's energy,' Seth instructed.

'What?' Lilian gasped.

'Put out your hand, establish a link, and drain its energy,' Seth snapped irritably.

'That's ridiculous. I can't do that,' Lilian said.

'You just did. Why do you think the one rabbit is dead,' he sneered, his patience running out quickly.

'You killed it,' she accused.

'You did,' he corrected.

Lilian knew in her heart that this was true. She didn't like it but couldn't deny it.

'Hurry up,' Seth said.

'No,' Lilian said defiantly but when Seth raised his hand she quickly said, 'Ok, wait, I'll try.'

She looked at the little rabbit.

'I'm sorry. I have to do this,' she whispered to the small animal.

She held out her hand and instantly a thin line of black smoke snaked across to the rabbit. As soon as it touched the rabbit, Lilian felt the tingling in her hand again. Energy flowed from the rabbit through the link into her body. Lilian could feel her strength growing but felt terrible for killing the rabbit.

'What is this black smoke that's attached to my hand?' she asked.

'It's an energy link,' Seth answered.

'There are more animals in the woods up ahead,' he went on. 'Come, we will both replenish our strength.'

Lilian got up without a word and followed Seth. She didn't look at the rabbits again. Although she felt guilty for killing them, it gave her an idea. If Seth could steal her strength through the link and she could do that to the rabbits, it made sense that she could do it to him.

She was going to kill him.

*****

Brighton took Thomas' hand.

'Do it,' he said.

Thomas frowned deeply and slowly muttered, 'I can't.'

'Do it!' Brighton shouted.

'You misunderstand young man,' Thomas said softly. 'I am trying but I can't feel anything. It's like you have no energy in you.'

Brighton sat back, confused.

'Technically that means I'm dead, doesn't it,' he said.

'Technically, yes, but that's quite obviously not the

case. No dead man can crush another man's hand,' Thomas said looking down at his hands.

Brighton also looked down and saw he had the older man's hand in a death grip. He quickly let go.

Thomas rubbed his bruised fingers.

'You can probably crush rocks with that grip,' he tried to joke.

'Any idea why you can't feel my energy,' Brighton asked.

He wasn't in the mood for jokes.

Thomas shook his head.

Brighton looked out the window and saw that it was dark. He desperately wanted to continue the conversation but struggled to make sense of what he already learned. He knew more talking would simply mean more confusion.

'I should get home. Mother hates it when I'm late for supper,' he said.

'Ok young man. Give Clarissa my regards,' Thomas replied.

He wished Brighton would stay longer so they could talk more but also understood that the young man had a lot to think about.

'May I return tomorrow so we can talk more?' Brighton asked.

'Anytime,' Thomas smiled.

Brighton left without another word.

*****

Walking home Brighton's mind was a mess of confusing thoughts. He was still no closer to making sense of it all when he got home. Deep in thought, he walked into the house.

'Mother,' he called to Clarissa.

He couldn't see anything in the dark room.

'Why haven't you lit a candle?' he asked.

He noticed a few glowing embers in the fireplace.

Holding the candle close to the glowing coals, he blew a little. A small flame jumped up, just enough to get the candle going. Brighton used the candle to light two more above the fireplace.

Light filled the room.

'Mother, where are you?' he called as he turned around.

He was not prepared for the scene that greeted him.

He rushed over to Clarissa's still body, fear welling up fast.

'Mother?' he whispered as he knelt next to her.

He knew she was dead but could not quite accept the fact yet.

Brighton cradled her head in his lap. Sadness and rage fought inside his mind. He looked down and noticed a black mark on her neck. He leaned closer and saw that it was in the shape of a hand.

Rage won the battle in his head.

Brighton screamed as dozens of pure white bolts of light shot from his body. It hit the walls and the roof of the house and instantly set everything alight.

Brighton got up and walked out of the burning house leaving Clarissa's lifeless body behind. He headed straight back to Thomas' place. The old man will provide answers even if Brighton had to beat it out of him.

Brighton was certain a Dark One was responsible for this. He resolved find them and kill them all starting with Thomas.

*****

Lilian made sure she was a few paces behind Seth before she lifted her hand. She summoned her talent.

The energy link slammed into the back of Seth's head.

Lilian felt the tingling in her hand. Energy started

flowing into her through the link.

I did it, she thought.

Did you now? popped into her head.

The energy flow stopped. Although the link was still there, she didn't feel any more energy flowing into her. Instead, she felt her own strength fading. She immediately understood that Seth had reversed the link and that he was now killing her.

She quickly severed the link.

Seth turned around, smiling.

'I was just....' Lilian stammered.

'Trying to kill me?' Seth finished.

Before Lilian could think of an answer, Seth spoke again.

'Good. You're a fighter but also very clever.'

'You're not angry?' she asked.

'No,' he smiled

'I'm confused. You try to kill me, then stop and show me a way to save myself. When I try to kill you, you are pleased?' Lilian frowned.

'Yes,' Seth replied.

'Are you going to kill me now?' she asked in a small voice.

'No,' came the answer.

'Do you ever give better answers than just "Yes" and "No"?' she asked angrily.

'I answered your questions. If you want better answers then ask better questions,' Seth smiled.

Lilian thought for a moment and said, 'While I was connected to you a random thought popped into my head. Why did that happen?'

'Did you now?' Seth said slowly.

'That's not a proper.....' she started but slammed her mouth shut quickly as she realized the truth.

'The thought came from you,' she said.

Seth smiled. 'Indeed a very clever child. When you are linked to someone, it is not just energy that travels through the link. Thoughts travel too,' he explained.

'So you can read the other person's mind?' Lilian asked.

'Not quite. You simply hear the thoughts the other person has at that moment. You cannot see their memories.'

'Why aren't you angry that I tried to kill you?' was Lilian's next question.

'Only one of your siblings ever tried to kill me. He was stupid and kept trying even after I reversed the link. None of the others were ever brave enough to try. You realized you could not win and broke the link. A very good decision,' Seth smiled.

'Siblings? I have no siblings,' Lilian said.

'You have many,' Seth corrected.

'What happened to the one who tried to kill you?' Lilian asked.

'I killed him. My talent is much stronger than that of my children, grandchildren or their descendants. When two gifted people battle, the one with the stronger talent will always win,' he explained.

'Am I your daughter?' Lilian asked through trembling lips.

A small nod confirmed Lilian's suspicion.

'How do you know?' she asked.

'I recognize my own talent in you,' he answered.

He turned and started walking again.

'Come,' he instructed.

Lilian followed Seth immediately.

She realized that for now she couldn't do anything about the situation, she would have to be patient.

Chapter 5

BRIGHTON BURST THROUGH the door.

Thomas was standing at the table squeezing lemons.

Brighton lunged forward, his fist flying straight for Thomas' face.

The old man moved like lightning. Brighton's fist found only air causing him to over balance. He crashed into the wall with such force it made the roof shake.

'You seem upset, young man,' Thomas said calmly from the other side of the room.

Brighton got up and lunged for Thomas again. Again, he found only air and crashed into the other wall. Thomas had moved around the table and now had his thick oak walking stick in his hands.

He held it square in front of him in a defensive position. Brighton approached more carefully this time. His fist flashed through the air again. This time it made solid contact with the walking stick.

Thomas had tried to use the stick to deflect the blow but the thick oak snapped like a twig under the force of Brighton's rage. The deflection tactic only worked partially.

Instead of hitting Thomas in the face, Brighton's fist slammed into the old man's shoulder, snapping bones with a sickening sound.

Somehow, Thomas kept his balance and was able to move away from the hail of fists coming his way.

His right arm was useless.

'Brighton!' he shouted. 'What's gotten into you?'

'Mother is dead. The Dark Ones killed her,' Brighton said through clenched teeth.

'Clarissa is dead?' Thomas gasped.

Brighton lifted his fist again but Thomas made no defensive moves this time. He simply stood waiting for the final blows.

Just before Brighton let his fist fly, he thought he saw genuine sadness in the old man's face.

Brighton hesitated for a moment and the rage suddenly drained away.

He dropped his hands.

'What happened?' Thomas asked softly.

'I don't know but I'm certain a Dark One killed my mother. There was a black handprint around her throat,' the young man whispered.

Pain washed over Thomas. He knew most of the bones in his right shoulder were crushed. Slowly he sank to the floor.

'Thomas!' Brighton exclaimed as he realized what he had done.

'You broke more than just my walking stick,' Thomas managed through the pain.

'Oh no,' Brighton whispered, hands in his hair.

'It will heal,' Thomas lied.

He knew he would never use his arm again.

Brighton kneeled next to Thomas.

'What can I do?' he asked.

'Help me to my bed,' Thomas whispered.

Brighton gently picked the old man up but the pain was too much and Thomas' world went black.

*****

Thomas woke up. Light was streaming in through the window. He tried to sit up but a dull pain in his right shoulder reminded him what had happened. He looked around the room.

He was alone.

Gently he reached over with his left hand and touched his right shoulder. He braced himself for the pain but it never came. Next, he tried to move his right arm and strangely, it functioned normally with only slight discomfort. He tried to use his talent to sense if there was anybody around, a deep frown immediately creasing up his already wrinkled forehead.

It wasn't that he couldn't sense anyone; he simply couldn't use his talent. It was gone.

He suddenly knew what it was like to live without the cursed gift.

He sat up and inspected his shoulder. Last night he was certain that his shoulder was crushed.

'Perhaps I was wrong,' he muttered to himself.

'Wrong about what?' Brighton asked entering the room holding a tray.

'Morning, Brighton,' Thomas said cheerfully.

'Morning, Thomas. Wrong about what?' Brighton repeated.

'My shoulder. I thought it was shattered but it seems it isn't,' Thomas replied.

'It was,' Brighton said. 'Here, I brought you some lemon juice and biscuits.'

Brighton put the tray on the bed and sat down on a chair he brought from the kitchen earlier.

'I found the biscuits….' Brighton started but the old man had no interest in food.

'What do you mean, "It was",' he interrupted.

'Your shoulder was broken but it healed,' Brighton replied.

'Overnight?' Thomas asked.

'Uh…looks that way,' Brighton said.

'That's impossible. Nothing can heal that fast,' Thomas exclaimed.

'I'm just telling you what I saw,' Brighton defended. 'You're a Dark One. Maybe you got some energy from someone and it helped heal your shoulder,' Brighton offered.

'From whom? You were the only one here and we both know I cannot steal energy from you,' Thomas countered. His eyes narrowed a little as a though struck him.

'Did you do something?' he asked looking into Brighton's eyes.

'No,' Brighton answered looking down.

'You're a very bad liar,' Thomas observed, 'You did something but you don't want to tell me what,' he accused.

Brighton did not answer.

Alarm rose in Thomas' mind.

'You know that my instincts will take over and try to steal energy from anywhere when my life is in danger. Did you bring people here and force them to touch me so that I could steal their energy?' Thomas asked.

'No,' Brighton replied looking straight at Thomas.

'That looks like the truth,' Thomas said.

Brighton remained silent. Thomas could see that Brighton wasn't going to share any more information. He decided to leave it for now; maybe later Brighton will be more forthcoming.

'Where did you learn to hit that hard?' he joked.

'I'm so sorry,' Brighton apologized. 'I was angry

and…..'

'Relax, young man, I was joking with you,' Thomas soothed.

Brighton hung his head in shame not knowing what to reply.

'Come to think of it, it's not a bad question. I've never seen anybody with that much strength,' Thomas said.

Brighton smiled slightly and said, 'Maybe Lily was right. She said I'm as big and strong as an oak tree.'

'Stronger,' Thomas laughed. 'You snapped my oak walking stick and crushed my shoulder with one blow.'

'I'm sorry about that and about the walking stick. I'll make you another,' Brighton apologized again.

'Stop apologizing. It's over and the damage has been repaired,' Thomas said flexing his shoulder, adding, 'As for the walking stick, I have three more just like it.'

Brighton got up.

'Will you be all right?' he asked.

'Yes, of course,' Thomas replied. 'Where are you going?'

'To see Lily,' Brighton replied.

'Yes, that's a good idea. Go be with someone you love,' Thomas said.

Brighton nodded but did not move. Thomas instantly recognized the look of despair in the young man's eyes.

'Come back here when you've seen Lilian. I will help you bury Clarissa,' Thomas offered carefully.

'The house burned down,' came the soft reply.

Before Thomas could ask Brighton added, 'I set it alight.'

Thomas decided it was best to leave the subject for later.

Instead, he said, 'You're welcome to stay here for as long as you like. I'll even share my lemon juice with you.'

That brought a wry smile to Brighton's lips.

'Thank you, I might just do that,' he replied gratefully.

*****

Martha opened the door almost immediately after Brighton knocked.

'What?' she snapped at Brighton.

'Is Lilian here please?' he asked politely.

'No,' Martha barked and slammed the door shut.

Brighton knocked again.

'What do you want?' Martha screamed as she flung the door open again.

'Could you tell me where she is please?' Brighton asked still trying to be polite.

'Gone!' Martha yelled.

Before she could slam the door again, Brighton stepped inside pushing Martha back into the house.

'Where?' he growled.

He was getting tired of her rudeness.

'I don't know. A man came last night and took her,' Martha said.

'Took her where?' Brighton asked.

'I don't know,' Martha barked.

Panic started to fill Brighton's mind.

'What did this man look like?' he asked, fearful of the answer he might get.

'It does not matter! She is gone!' Martha screamed.

'What did he look like?' Brighton growled.

Martha sighed heavily as she dropped her gaze. It suddenly seemed that she had lost the will to live.

'It was Seth,' she whispered fearfully.

'Seth, the Supreme?' Brighton frowned.

Martha nodded silently.

'What does he look like?' the young man demanded.

'Almost as tall as you, thin, white long hair, eyes deep in his head,' Martha said.

'What did he wear?' Brighton asked, the panic rising

even more.

'A black robe with a hole on the chest,' Martha replied.

'Oh no!' Brighton exclaimed.

He turned to leave but thought of something else.

'Which way did they go?' he asked Martha.

'There is only one way out of Four Mountains,' she said. 'That's the way they went.'

Brighton's mind was overcome with grief. His mother murdered, his only friend gone. The only two people he loved gone in one day. He slowly turned again and walked out.

He was almost at Thomas' house when four figures approached him.

'Look, it's one of the lovebirds,' Garth mocked.

Brighton ignored him. Garth mistook the grief on Brighton's face for fear. This gave him courage and he stepped right in front of Brighton blocking his path.

William and Brent flanked Garth on his right with John on the left.

'Time to teach you a lesson,' Garth said.

He slapped Brighton with an open hand across the face.

'Come on coward, aren't you going to do something?' Garth mocked.

'Leave me alone,' Brighton said softly.

His mind was filled with grief and this was the last thing he needed.

Garth tried to get a reaction from Brighton, 'I like it when little girls beg. I'm going to find that girlfriend of yours and make her beg right before I....'

He got more reaction than he bargained for.

Blind rage exploded through Brighton's mind. His left fist flashed, crushing Garth's nose in an instant. Before the others could move, Brighton's right fist found Brent's jaw. It snapped with a sickening sound.

Brighton turned to his right to face John but

immediately knew that was a mistake. William was still behind him.

John put up his hands and stepped back.

'Please don't hurt me,' he whimpered.

He turned and fled.

Brighton spun around uncertain why William had not attacked him from behind yet. William was lying on the ground clutching the back of his head. Old Thomas stood right behind him leaning on a walking stick.

'Nothing a stiff knock to the head can't fix,' he winked at Brighton.

'Thank you,' Brighton muttered.

'Come, let's get going. John is probably already telling his father what happened. Violence is not well received in this town. You might just have an angry mob chasing after you soon,' he urged.

Without a word, Brighton followed Thomas to his house.

Inside Thomas asked, 'What happened out there?'

Brighton seemed not to hear.

'Wasn't Lilian home?' Thomas tried again.

Again, Brighton didn't respond.

Thomas gently touched Brighton's arm.

'Where is Lilian?' he asked.

'Gone,' Brighton said past the lump in his throat.

'Gone where?' Thomas pressed.

'I don't know. Martha said Seth came and took her away,' Brighton whispered.

Trying to keep his voice calm, Thomas asked, 'Seth? Are you sure? What did he look like?'

Brighton gave a brief description and then told Thomas about their encounter with Seth the previous day. When he finished Thomas looked gravely concerned.

'A white light shot from you and knocked him backwards?' Thomas asked.

'Lilian seems to think it came from me. I'm not sure

where it came from,' Brighton replied.

'This is very disturbing,' Thomas said.

Brighton walked to the door.

'I have to go,' he said.

'Go where?' Thomas asked.

'I'm going to find Seth, knock his head off his shoulders, and bring Lilian back,' Brighton declared.

'And how do you propose to do that?' Thomas asked.

'I don't know yet but I'll work it out as I go along,' Brighton said defiantly. 'Don't try to talk me out of it, it won't work.'

'I wasn't going to,' Thomas said. 'I just think you need to have a better plan than simply knocking his head off his shoulders.'

'Any suggestions?' Brighton asked.

'For starters, you should stay here until tonight. No use getting into another fight with some of the town folk. I can guarantee you they will be looking for you before long,' Thomas argued.

'Makes sense,' Brighton conceded. 'Anything else?'

'Plan your moves. If you simply rush headlong into a fight like before you don't stand a chance,' he advised.

'You already think I'm going to get killed, don't you?' Brighton accused.

'Not at all,' Thomas replied. 'In fact, I think you're the only one with a chance of actually doing a Supreme some damage.'

'Why? I'm nobody special,' Brighton said.

'Ah, but you are,' Thomas said. 'I can't feel your energy, remember. Hopefully other Dark Ones can't either.'

'Hopefully?' Brighton exclaimed. 'That's not very comforting. And besides, what does this help me?'

'If I'm correct you could get close to a Dark One without them knowing. Even if they see you their biggest weapon is useless against you,' Thomas theorized.

He could see the gears of thought had started turning in Brighton's mind. The young man was starting to think clearly.

'Dark Ones might have this cursed talent but we are human, flesh, blood and bone. A stiff knock to the head works on anybody. Your plan of knocking Seth's head off his shoulders might just work. You just need to get close to him first. That will be the challenge. Remember that you are human too. You're as strong as an ox and definitely have some form of the talent but a stiff knock to your head will do the same damage. Even you cannot face five or ten men intent on harming you,' Thomas offered his thoughts.

'You think I have the talent. Why?' Brighton asked.

'Well, there is that white light you shot at Seth....'

'I told you, Lilian thinks it came from me but I'm not sure,' Brighton interrupted.

'There is something else,' Thomas said slowly. 'How much has Clarissa told you about your birth?'

'Nothing,' Brighton said. 'I asked her once who my father was. She said she didn't know and that I should not worry about such things. Do you know something?'

'I don't know about your father but I do know about your birth,' Thomas said.

'My birth? I thought I was born in the house we lived in, nothing special about it,' Brighton said with a confused look on his face.

'That is not true. Your birth was very special,' Thomas countered.

'How do you know?' Brighton asked.

'Clarissa shared the details with me once,' Thomas shrugged.

'Then tell me please,' Brighton asked.

'Clarissa was not your real mother. She kind of adopted you and raised you as her own,' the old man said slowly.

'That's ....' Brighton started but slammed his mouth

shut when Thomas raised his hand.

'You were born in the woods near a town called Avarya,' he continued.

'Where is that?' Brighton asked.

'About halfway between here and Zedonia, a good two weeks travel. Actually, Avarya and Zedonia are about the same distance from here but you can't travel straight towards Zedonia because of an impassable swamp. You need to travel east to Avarya and then turn north to Zedonia, but that is beside the point. Clarissa's family was travelling to Avarya when they came upon a pregnant woman lying in the road. The woman was in labour so they stopped to help. When the baby, you, were born there was a white light shining all around you. It was as if the light was coming from inside you. Everybody was scared; they did not know what to do. Your birth mother knew she was dying so she begged the travellers to take the baby but everyone refused. Instead they carried your mother and you off into the woods and left you there.'

'Why? That's horrible!' Brighton exclaimed.

'You must understand that people are very superstitious and scared. What if you were some sort of demon? What if the Dark Ones found a glowing baby with them? They were scared that all of them will be killed simply for helping you and your mother,' Thomas said.

He paused for a sip of lemon juice and then continued.

'The travellers continued on to Avarya. Everyone put the incident out of his or her minds except Clarissa. She wanted to go back but her father forbade it when she asked him. After travelling another five days and almost at Avarya, Clarissa decided to defy her father. She snuck out of camp and went back to the spot where they left you. She knew that you and your mother were probably dead but she felt compelled to check anyway.

It took her only three days to make the distance. She found you alive next to your mother's dead body.'

'I survived for eight days out in the woods?' Brighton asked doubtfully.

'That's not the most amazing thing. Clarissa said that for about ten paces all around you the trees, bushes and grass were dead. There were also two dead wolves,' Thomas continued.

Brighton was speechless.

'Clarissa could not leave you again. She picked you up and started walking. Somehow, she found the path leading to the pass on the eastern mountain and made it over. That's when I found her,' Thomas finished the tale.

'Are you sure this is all true?' Brighton asked.

'Yes, it's the truth. I got Clarissa and her baby settled in this house and travelled to the spot where she said she found you. I needed to see for myself. It was as she described, all the plants were dead. I've been back there a few times and still nothing grows there. It's like all the life was sucked out of the plants and the soil,' the old man replied.

'How is that possible?' Brighton asked.

'I have no answer for that. What I can tell you is this: The Supremes and their children can steal energy from all living things, even plants. Nobody else is able to do this, only their talent is strong enough,' Thomas explained patiently.

'Steal energy from plants? That's ridiculous!' Brighton snorted.

'Is it? Plants are living things too. They also have energy. I've heard that the Supremes don't do it often though. Because plant energy is different from human or animal it's apparently very difficult to do,' Thomas countered.

'Who killed all the plants around me?' Brighton asked.

'You did,' Thomas said flatly.

'Me! That's ridiculous! How can I do that? I'm not a Supreme!' Brighton scoffed.

Calmly Thomas said, 'Think about it. A new-born baby survives without any food for eight days in the woods. What does that tell you?'

Brighton knew the answer but didn't want to voice it.

'What about the wolves? Obviously they came to see if there was an easy meal on offer but they too were dead. It's logical. You must have used the energy around you to stay alive,' Thomas pressed.

Brighton thought about it for a long time. This was too much for one day.

Eventually he spoke, 'If everything you said is true then I am also a Dark One.'

Thomas nodded waiting for Brighton to finish the thought.

'But why can't you sense me?' he asked eventually.

'Your energy is hidden from me somehow. I really don't know why,' Thomas answered.

'So, what am I?' Brighton asked.

'I cannot even venture a guess. I don't think the world has ever seen someone like you,' Thomas said.

'Will the Supremes know? They are the oldest people in the world,' Brighton said hopefully.

'The Supremes are highly suspicious of anything or anyone that could challenge their dominance. They would sooner kill you than give you an answer,' Thomas said sternly.

'But you said I'm the only one that can do the Supremes harm,' Brighton defended.

'That's my theory,' Thomas replied. 'If I'm wrong, you're dead. Do you want to take that chance?'

'I have to. Seth has Lilian and I have to rescue her,' Brighton said. 'I simply have to find them and bring Lilian home!' he added heatedly.

'You might not have to,' Thomas said.

'Why?' Brighton frowned.

'Seth knows now that you exist. That is probably why he went to your house. If you were there he would have killed you, or tried anyway,' came the reply.

'What are you saying?' Brighton asked.

'Sooner or later Seth will come for you and you had better be ready,' Thomas warned.

Brighton shook his head.

'I have a better idea, I will find him and keep the element of surprise,' he said.

'I'm still wondering why Seth came here in the first place,' Thomas muttered. 'I thought he was after me but if that were the case I'd be dead. Why then come to such a far-off place if not to kill me?'

Brighton wanted to go after Seth and Lilian immediately but he knew Thomas had a point, no use getting into more fights with town folk so he made himself comfortable and waited for night to fall. Thomas suggested trying to sleep so that he could be fresh when darkness came. That way he might even be able to travel all night and make up some time. Brighton curled up on Thomas' bed and soon he was asleep.

The emotional trauma of the last two days had drained him.

*****

Brighton woke up to complete darkness. He got up and felt his way to the kitchen.

'Thomas!' he called.

No answer.

'Thomas!' he called again.

Still no answer.

Brighton was anxious to get going. He wanted to say goodbye to Thomas but also did not want to waste anymore time. He stepped outside.

'Thomas!' he tried one last time.

When no answer came, he decided to start his journey. Thomas would understand. Brighton took the road that led east.

He suddenly remembered the goats. With all that had happened, he completely forgot about them. When he passed the clearing, he saw the dead bodies. A deep sadness filled his already stressed mind.

He did not stop, he knew he was far behind Seth and Lilian and didn't want to waste time. The sky was clear so travelling was easy. For the next few days, he covered a lot of distance. He travelled mostly at night when it was cool and rested during the hottest time of day. Berries and fruit were plentiful this time of the season so he didn't have to hunt for food, a blessing as he had never hunted before.

Thomas explained to him how to find the spot where he was born. Brighton found it and saw that Thomas was telling the truth, all the plants for at least ten paces from the middle were dead. He also saw three skeletons, two animals and one human. He assumed that the first two must be the wolves Thomas spoke about and the human skeleton his birth mother. Brighton didn't stay long as there was nothing to see.

He encountered some travellers along the way. Most people kept to themselves with only a few offering a greeting. Brighton tried asking if they had seen a man with a little girl come past, but he only got suspicious looks.

He lost track of the days but estimated he must be close to Avarya from what Thomas told him when he noticed a woman sitting on a rock next to the road.

'Hello traveller,' the woman greeted when he came past.

Brighton stopped and greeted her back.

'Thirsty?' she asked holding out a water skin.

Brighton accepted gratefully.

He didn't think to bring anything on his journey. Food wasn't a problem as long as he was satisfied with a constant fruit diet but fresh water was hard to come by. He had only crossed one large river and a handful of smaller streams.

After a few gulps from the water skin, he felt refreshed.

'Thank you,' he said to the woman handing her back the water skin.

She looked to be about seventy winters, had short brown hair and a pleasant smile. Slight of frame, she was more than a head shorter than he was.

'I'm Carmen,' she introduced herself.

'Brighton,' he said as he reached for the outstretched hand.

Just before he took it, he remembered what Thomas told him about shaking hands and pulled his back.

'Sorry, my hands are dirty,' he mumbled.

'Quite all right, young Brighton,' Carmen smiled and then added 'May I walk with you please?'

Suspicion rose in the young man's mind.

Every other traveller he encountered hardly spoke to him and now this woman wanted to join him.

When he didn't answer, she added, 'I would love the company.'

'Sure,' he said. 'I travel mostly at night though.'

'Me too,' Carmen said. 'A lot cooler that way, don't you think?'

Brighton nodded his agreement.

'How far to Avarya?' he asked.

'Less than half a day,' she replied as she got up from the rock.

He was worried that such an old woman will slow him down but instead Carmen set a brisk pace towards Avarya.

'Are you going to Avarya, young Brighton?' she asked.

'Yes. Well, no, not really,' Brighton said.

'Unsure of where you're going then?' she smiled.

'I'm looking for two people,' Brighton explained.

'Oh, well, what do they look like? I may have seen them,' Carmen asked.

'A tall man wearing a black robe and a young girl,' Brighton replied.

Carmen stopped dead.

'Seth?' she asked fearfully.

'Uh....no.....who is that?' he tried.

Carmen looked at him the way Clarissa used to when he was trying to tell her a lie.

'Ok, yes, I'm looking for Seth. He kidnapped my friend,' Brighton admitted.

'Was she a pretty girl with blue eyes and long blond curls?' Carmen asked.

'Yes, yes,' Brighton said excitedly. 'Have you seen them?'

'I did,' Carmen confirmed.

'Where?' Brighton asked, anxious to get some information.

He still didn't know what he was going to do when he caught up with Seth and Lilian but that wasn't important. What mattered was that he was catching up to them.

'In Avarya, the day before yesterday. Maybe you should sit down. I have bad news,' Carmen said gently.

'What do you mean?' Brighton asked.

'Two days ago Seth walked into town carrying the little one. She had a deep cut on her head. Seth said she slipped and hit her head on a rock. He demanded the best healers be brought to tend to her but it was in vain,' Carmen said softly.

Brighton heard the words but somehow they didn't make sense.

'You mean she's......'

He couldn't say it.

'I'm afraid your friend died,' Carmen said softly.

Brighton was dumbfounded, a myriad of confusing thoughts rushing through his mind all at once.

'Where is her body? Has she been buried yet? Show me where,' he demanded.

'Seth burnt the body and left,' Carmen said sympathetically.

'Are you sure it was her? Maybe it was another girl,' Brighton tried.

Carmen held out her hand.

'About this tall, fair skin, gorgeous blue eyes, long blond curly hair with little pink ribbons in,' she described the girl.

Brighton sank to the ground. His legs couldn't hold him up anymore.

A single tear rolled down his cheek.

'You loved her?' Carmen asked softly.

Brighton could only nod.

Carmen softly touched his shoulder.

'Where will you go now?' she asked.

'I don't know,' he whispered. 'Everything I know is gone.'

'Why don't you come with me? My house is not far and I have an empty room. A proper meal and nice bath will do you the world of good,' Carmen offered.

Brighton got up and wordlessly followed Carmen, all the sadness and anger in him suddenly making way for numbing depression.

Chapter 6

BRIGHTON DIDN'T KNOW for how long they walked, he didn't care. They reached Carmen's house before it was fully dark. The house was on the outskirts of Avarya.

'Come in, make yourself at home,' Carmen invited.

Brighton sat down on a chair.

Carmen poured lemon juice into two mugs and offered Brighton one. He took a sip and noticed that it was diluted.

Thomas wouldn't like this he thought.

'Would you like something to eat?' Carmen asked.

Brighton simply shook his head.

'I'll warm up some water for a bath,' Carmen offered.

'No thank you, I prefer it cold,' Brighton said softly.

'The bath is in the other room, take as long as you need. There is also a bed there for you to sleep on,' she smiled.

'Thank you, you're very kind,' Brighton managed, his voice barely above a whisper.

He remembered how Lilian always told him how kind he was. The memory threatened to close up his throat, so he quickly banished it from his mind. He got up and walked to the other room. After a quick bath, he flopped down on the bed.

He was asleep in moments.

*****

For the next few days the routine stayed the same. Brighton didn't eat, he just sat in front of the house staring out over the field all day. Carmen never tried to force him to eat, she simply put the food down and left. Later she would collect the full plate again without a word. At night Brighton would have a cold bath and immediately afterwards go to bed.

Six days went by like this and Carmen was getting worried. She wondered how to get Brighton to eat. On the seventh morning, Carmen put a plate of food next to Brighton and sat down with her own.

'Beautiful day,' she said. 'I am going down to the river later. Do you want to join me?'

Brighton looked down at the plate. He took a small piece of meat and put it in his mouth. Silently he ate and soon the plate was clean.

Carmen silently watched, hope rising in her.

'When were you going to the river?' Brighton asked.

'As soon as you've finished washing the dishes,' Carmen replied.

Brighton picked up the plates and disappeared into the kitchen. A while later he reappeared.

'Done,' he said.

'Good. Now let me show you the river,' Carmen said.

They walked in silence until they reached the river. It wasn't far from the house. Carmen found a smooth rock and sat down.

'I like sitting by the river,' she said. 'The sound of the water is calming.'

Brighton also sat down. Carmen was right, the sound did have a calming effect on him.

'Do you know anything about goats?' she asked.

'Yes, I used to have a few of my own,' Brighton answered.

'And vegetable gardens?' she inquired.

'We had a garden back home,' Brighton told her. 'We had so many vegetables we had to give most away.'

'Good. I'll make you a deal,' Carmen said. 'You look after my goats and vegetable garden and I will provide you with food and a place to live.'

Brighton did not answer. He just sat staring at the water.

'Please Brighton?' Carmen pleaded. 'I'm getting too old to look after the goats and the garden. You would really be helping me a lot.'

Brighton looked at her and managed a small smile.

'I'll help you,' he said softly.

*****

Thomas waited on the rock where Carmen and Brighton first met. He was staring at the ground, deep in thought. When he looked up Carmen was standing in front of him.

'Hello Thomas,' she greeted.

'I wish you wouldn't do that,' he complained.

He got up and gave Carmen a tight hug.

'Hello Carmen,' he greeted back.

'If you used your sense you would have known I was coming,' she observed.

'The pot calling the kettle black now?' Thomas asked.

Carmen chuckled. 'Yes, I suppose so.'

Thomas said, 'You're the one that convinced me that

this talent is a curse. Are you suggesting we go back to the old ways?'

'No,' she sighed. 'It is a curse but perhaps we could use it to help young Brighton. That would make it all worth it, wouldn't it?'

'I think so. How is he?' Thomas asked.

'Sad. But he will get through this,' Carmen said.

'I know he will. That young boy is a fighter,' Thomas agreed.

Carmen pointed at the longbow that was standing against a tree.

'Where did you get that?' she asked.

Thomas gave her a look that said, "You don't want to know".

'You didn't kill anyone for it?' she asked carefully.

'Of course not,' Thomas said indignantly. 'But the poor fellow will probably have a headache until next summer.'

'I see. The old "walking stick against the head" trick,' Carmen smiled.

'We agreed, Carmen. You won't ask me about the things I bring and I won't ask how you got those people to move out of their house in a day,' Thomas said.

'As long as no one gets harmed,' Carmen added.

'Yes,' Thomas agreed.

'Where did you get those goats?' Carmen asked casually.

'Carmen!' Thomas snapped.

She smiled an apology.

'I don't know how to use a bow,' she said changing the subject.

'Just give it to Brighton, he will work it out,' Thomas replied.

Carmen pulled two lemons from the front pocket of her dress. She tossed one to Thomas and sat down on the rock. Thomas sat down next to her. They ate in silence for a while.

With the last slice of lemon in his mouth, Thomas started talking, 'How is......'

'Thomas! Don't speak with food in your mouth,' Carmen scolded.

'Sorry,' he mumbled.

He swallowed and tried again.

'How is the vegetable garden doing?' he asked.

'It's only been a few days since Brighton started working in it, but he is working from sunrise to sunset everyday. He has already made it four times bigger than what it was.'

'And the goats?' Thomas asked.

'They graze nearby where Brighton can watch them,' Carmen answered.

'I mean don't they try to eat the vegetables?' Thomas asked.

'They tried but Brighton built a fence around the garden yesterday,' Carmen answered.

'In one day?' Thomas gasped.

'Yes. That boy is exceptionally strong,' Carmen smiled.

'I know,' Thomas said touching his right shoulder.

Carmen noticed and asked, 'How is the shoulder?'

'Healed,' was all Thomas said.

'How is it possible that Brighton punched through a walking stick, broke your shoulder and his hand did not have a scratch on it?' Carmen asked.

'That's a mystery,' Thomas said.

'No bones broken in his hand?' Carmen asked.

'He was using his hand like nothing happened. I'm assuming there was no damage whatsoever,' Thomas answered.

'Amazing!' Carmen exclaimed, 'And how did your shoulder heal so quickly. You're an old man, you know,' she teased.

'Not as old as you,' he teased back.

'Oh please. At our age two winters is nothing. Another mystery is why your talent disappeared for a day,' Carmen pondered.

'Yes, something else I can't answer,' Thomas sighed.

Carmen got up.

She retrieved the bow and quiver, and leaned over to give Thomas a hug.

'Goodbye Thomas,' she smiled

'Goodbye Carmen. We'll meet here again in seven days,' he smiled back.

Brighton was working in the vegetable garden when he sensed Carmen approaching.

Without looking up he said, 'I hope you brought me some juice.'

'Good morning Brighton,' she said.

'I'm sorry. Good morning Carmen,' he replied.

'Would you like some juice?' Carmen offered.

'Yes, that would be nice, thank you,' Brighton replied with a smile.

Carmen insisted that everybody should have good manners. Brighton was sure she took it upon herself to teach the entire Avarya the "proper way" as she called it. He took the offered cup and drained it in one gulp. He held out the cup hoping for a refill but Carmen ignored him.

'Please may I have some more?' he finally asked.

'Of course,' she replied cheerfully and filled the cup again.

This time he sipped slower.

Looking out towards the grazing goats he remarked, 'The spotted one is pregnant.'

Carmen looked at the goat.

'How do you know?' she asked.

'I just know,' Brighton replied.

'How far is she?' Carmen enquired.

'Only about three or four days,' he replied.

'You're teasing me!' Carmen accused.

Brighton shrugged his shoulders. Carmen looked at his face and saw that he was serious.

'It's not possible to know a goat is four days pregnant!' Carmen said in disbelief.

'She's pregnant,' he repeated.

Changing the subject Carmen said, 'I brought you a present.'

She held out the longbow and quiver to him. Brighton took the bow and inspected it.

'It's beautiful,' he remarked.

Next, he took the quiver and pulled an arrow from it.

'Well made,' he observed.

'Where did you get it?' he asked, still inspecting the arrows.

'Um….it was Matthew's,' she replied.

'Your late husband?' Brighton asked.

Carmen nodded.

'What did he do with it?' Brighton asked curiously.

'You hunt with a bow. What else could you do with it?' Carmen replied. 'You can have it if you promise to hunt for us.'

'Why?' Brighton asked, 'We already have more than enough vegetables and the goats provide all the meat we need,' Brighton objected.

'I don't like goat meat,' Carmen said.

Brighton thought that was silly. Everybody likes goat meat. He decided not to argue.

'Have you ever shot with a bow before?' Carmen asked.

'No,' Brighton replied.

'Then you will need to practice first before you go hunting,' Carmen instructed.

'Ok, as soon as I finish here, I'll go to the river and practice. It's probably best I don't shoot anywhere near you or the goats,' he said.

'Yes, that's a good idea,' Carmen agreed.

Brighton put the bow down and continued working in the garden.

'Why are you making the garden bigger if we already have enough food,' Carmen asked.

'It keeps me busy,' he replied.

And keeps the painful memories out of your mind Carmen thought.

*****

Brighton finished his work in the garden fairly late in the afternoon. He saw Carmen sitting in front of the house on the grass. Although she averted her eyes as soon as he looked up he knew she was watching him. He didn't mind, she was simply worried about him.

The house was a simple square wooden building.

Perhaps I should build Carmen a porch to sit on, Brighton thought.

'Carmen, I'm going to the river, do you want to join me?' he shouted.

Carmen didn't move or look up. Brighton picked up the bow and quiver and walked closer.

'Did you hear me?' he asked.

'Yes,' she replied.

'So why didn't you answer?' he frowned.

'It's rude to shout at someone, especially an old lady. Walk up to the person and speak in a civilized manner,' she admonished him.

'Sorry,' he muttered.

'Was there something you wanted to ask me?' Carmen said.

'I'm going to the river. Do you want to join me?' he repeated.

'That would be nice. Help me up, please,' she said holding out a hand to him.

Brighton took her hand and easily pulled her to her

feet.

Carmen slipped her hand inside his arm and they walked down to the river. When they reached the river, Carmen sat down on a smooth rock.

Brighton nocked an arrow and asked Carmen, 'What should I shoot at?'

She looked around and spotted a big tree about fifty paces away.

'Do you see the white mark on that tree?' she said pointing. 'Aim for that'

Brighton pulled the string back until it touched his cheek, took aim, and let the arrow go.

It slammed straight into the mark Carmen pointed out.

Carmen's eyes went wide. It was the luckiest shot she had ever seen.

'Marvellous,' she cheered, clapping her hands.

'It's too close. I'm going to aim for that one,' he said pointing at a tree more than ninety paces away.

He retrieved the arrow, nocked it again and took aim. The arrow flew straight towards the tree and hit it square in the middle.

'Are you sure you've never shot a bow before?' Carmen asked casually, careful to hide the surprised look on her face.

'Never,' Brighton replied.

'Then you must be a natural,' she remarked.

Brighton got another arrow from the quiver and took aim again.

Just before he let the arrow fly, he saw a rabbit running behind the tree. Without thinking, he aimed for the rabbit and released the arrow.

It found the mark.

'Brighton, that's incredible! How did you do that?' she asked in amazement.

'I aimed, I shot. Do you like rabbit stew?' he grinned.

'Yes, I do,' she stammered.

Carmen had seen some expert archers in her life and she was sure not one of them could make that shot. A running target almost a hundred paces away, it was not possible and yet she just saw it happen.

Brighton retrieved the rabbit.

'Let's go home,' he suggested.

'Aren't you going to shoot more?' Carmen asked.

'No, I'm more interested in that rabbit stew you're going to cook for us,' Brighton said with a smile.

It was the first genuine smile she saw from Brighton since they met. Carmen smiled back at him and got up.

'Ok young man, since you shot the rabbit I'll cook it. Next time I shoot and you cook,' she joked with him.

The next seven days went by quickly. Brighton never questioned Carmen when she disappeared for a while.

She was grateful for that. She didn't want to lie to him and Thomas made it very clear he didn't want Brighton to know he was close.

Carmen disagreed. She believed Thomas should visit Brighton but the old man stubbornly refused. Carmen felt that Brighton should have something familiar in his life and that's why she recreated his living conditions from Four Mountains.

With this, Thomas agreed.

Tending a vegetable garden and looking after goats was all Brighton ever knew. They agreed that this would keep the young man's mind occupied and away from painful memories. Time would eventually dull the pain.

Carmen arrived at the meeting place early. She sat down on the rock to wait for Thomas. When he arrived, he looked ragged.

Carmen jumped up and rushed over. His shirt was torn and he had scratches all over his body. It looked like he was running through some thick undergrowth.

'What happened to you?' she asked concernedly.

Thomas didn't answer immediately. He took the water skin from Carmen and almost drained it.

'Thank you,' he said handing it back.

Carmen made him sit down on the rock. She tore a small piece of cloth from her dress. Using the cloth and the last of the water, she cleaned the scratches on his face and hands. She was relieved to see they were all just skin-deep.

'So?' she prodded while she continued cleaning the blood.

'Just a little argument. Nothing to worry about,' he answered.

'Take off your shirt, I want to clean the wounds on your arms,' she said.

'It's just scratches, leave it,' Thomas replied.

'Don't argue Thomas!' Carmen said sternly.

Slowly Thomas removed his shirt. Carmen immediately saw why he was so reluctant. There was a black mark high up on his left arm.

'They found you,' Carmen whispered, her voice trembling.

'Only one,' Thomas replied.

'Stronger or weaker?' Carmen asked, tears welling up in her eyes.

'Stronger,' Thomas said.

'How did you get away?' she asked.

Thomas waved his walking stick in front of her.

'I see,' Carmen said, eyeing the thick piece of oak.

She wet the cloth again and started cleaning the blood off his arms.

'Tell me,' she demanded.

'Not much to tell,' Thomas tried.

'Tell me,' Carmen said slowly.

Thomas knew it was futile to argue with Carmen when she was in this mood.

'I was on my way here when she found me,' he

started.

'She?' Carmen asked.

'Yes, a woman. I ran into the woods to get away. That's where I got all these little scratches. She caught up with me and grabbed my arm. Luckily they all think they are invincible and she decided not to kill me quickly but rather to make me suffer.'

Carmen understood. 'Nothing a stiff knock to the head can't fix,' she said in a deep voice mimicking Thomas.

Thomas laughed.

Carmen almost shouted, 'It's no laughing matter! You've always been fast enough with that cane but now one actually touched you. You were lucky.'

'I guess so,' Thomas shrugged.

'Will they ever stop hunting you?' Carmen asked.

'Seth never forgets. He has all the time in the world. No, he will not stop. But I've got a plan,' Thomas said with a wink.

'Really?' Carmen asked hopefully.

'Yes. I'll simply die of old age before his minions can kill me,' Thomas joked.

'Thomas! That's not funny,' Carmen complained but he saw a slight smile on her lips.

'Enough of that. Tell me about the boy,' Thomas said as he pulled his shirt back on.

'He's doing well. Working hard, keeping busy. It sometimes looks like he still thinks about her but he tries to hide it,' Carmen said.

'That's to be expected. It hasn't been very long,' Thomas said thoughtfully.

'You were right, he is very special,' Carmen said.

'I know this but tell me why you say so?' Thomas asked.

'Well, it is as you said. I can't sense him but he seems to always be aware of everyone around him,' Carmen said slowly.

'I thought you noticed something I didn't,' Thomas said disappointedly.

'I did,' Carmen replied. 'I gave him the bow.'

Thomas sat up and asked, 'How did he do?'

'You won't believe me,' Carmen said.

'Try me. I will believe almost anything when it comes to Brighton,' Thomas assured her.

'We were at the river. Brighton took aim at a tree about fifty paces away. He hit his target on the first try.'

'Not spectacular,' Thomas grumbled.

'On his second try he hit a tree ninety paces away,' Carmen continued.

'Better, but still not amazing,' Thomas muttered to himself.

Ignoring him Carmen continued, 'And on his third attempt he hit a running rabbit at almost a hundred paces.'

'Now you're just teasing me,' Thomas accused.

'I couldn't believe it myself at first. I thought it must be blind luck but he hit a smaller rabbit yesterday at almost a hundred and thirty paces.'

She paused for a moment and then added 'And the rabbit was running.'

Thomas was speechless.

'Incredible, isn't it,' Carmen said.

'How is that possible?' Thomas gasped.

'I don't know either, I'm just telling you what I saw. It's like he can control the flight of the arrow,' she said.

'Energy,' Thomas muttered to himself.

'Pardon?' Carmen said.

'Nothing. It's a wild thought that just popped into my head. I need to think it through,' Thomas replied.

'I have to go,' Carmen said. 'Brighton does not ask where I go but I don't want to stay away too long. He might get curious.'

She gave Thomas a tight hug.

'I love you, old man,' she whispered.

'And I love you, old woman,' Thomas whispered back.

*****

The days seemed to fly past. Brighton kept working hard. The vegetable garden flourished and the goats just kept having babies. The little spotted goat was pregnant just as Brighton had said. It gave birth to twins a hundred and forty five days after Brighton had told Carmen that it was pregnant.

Carmen asked Brighton about it a few times. He always shrugged his shoulders and said, 'I just know.'

His estimate of when the goats would give birth was always spot on.

Brighton and Carmen started trading milk, cheese, goats and vegetables for other goods.

At first Brighton did not understand the concept of trading goods for other goods.

'If you want something, you make it,' he told Carmen.

'And if you can't make it?' she countered.

'Then you don't really need it,' he said confidently.

'What if you have too much vegetables or milk?' she asked.

'Then you give it to people who don't have any,' he replied.

It always worked this way in Four Mountains. Everyone shared their goods. Carmen was unsure of how to explain it to him when she noticed her worn sandals. She asked him to make her a new pair. He thought about it for a moment and said that he couldn't but that they should ask someone in town. The next day she sent him to town to ask for sandals.

He returned very angry.

'I saw a lot of sandal makers but nobody would give me a pair for you,' he shouted.

Carmen picked up a bushel of vegetables and told

him she would be back soon.

She returned wearing a new pair of sandals.

'How did you do that?' he asked in amazement.

'I traded the vegetables for the shoes,' she explained.

She could see the concept started to make sense to him.

Brighton started trading their surplus goods for things they needed. He even started keeping an inventory of what they needed and what was surplus. He always knew exactly how much food they needed to keep and how much they could use for trading purposes.

One of the first things Brighton traded for was a new dress for Carmen. When he gave it to her, she buried her face in the material and cried softly.

Seeing her cry made him worry that there was something wrong with the dress or the colour, so he offered to take it back. Carmen cried and laughed at the same time, hugged him tightly and told him the dress was perfect.

Brighton decided that women were very strange creatures.

He also got some wood and tools. This was used to build a porch and new chairs so Carmen would have somewhere comfortable to sit.

'You're the kindest person I know,' she once told him.

Instead of happiness, she saw a flash of pain cross his face.

She never asked about it, she knew it would be related to his past.

*****

It was a day much like any other. Three winters had passed. Brighton walked around the vegetable garden. There was nothing for him to do except wait for the plants to grow but he still checked every morning for weeds.

Seeing none, he decided to check on the goats. None of them showed any signs of illness or injury.

Brighton went to the house, picked up his bow and said to Carmen, 'I'm going to see if there are any deer around.'

He shot one three days ago and there was still plenty of salted meat but Carmen didn't say anything. She knew he wouldn't kill anything unless it was to provide them with food.

Brighton walked out the door and headed for the river. He never went to the place where all the town folk got their water and washed their clothes. Upriver there was a much better place only he knew about.

It was a small clearing right next to the river surrounded by big oak trees. There was no path leading to it, if you didn't know where it was you would never find it.

Brighton strolled leisurely, there was nothing rushing him.

As he was about to enter the woods a strong sense of extreme danger washed over him. Something was in the woods.

The feeling of danger intensified, whatever was in the woods was moving towards him.

There was also a strange familiarity about the feeling.

Brighton waited anxiously.

A big black panther emerged from the trees followed by a slightly smaller one. The panther spotted Brighton, froze for a moment, and then charged. As fast and strong as Brighton was, he was no match for the speed and strength of the cat.

The panther knocked him over with ease. The bow and quiver went flying. Brighton was flat on his back expecting the panther to go for his throat.

White-eyes looked down at him. The cat started licking him in the face.

'Mischief! Stop it!' Brighton shouted.

He wriggled free from under the cat and stepped back.

'Dear angels, you have grown,' he said to Mischief.

It was easily the biggest panther Brighton had ever seen.

He looked over to the other cat.

'Velvet!' he called to her.

She just stood looking at him.

'Come here, girl,' he encouraged.

Slowly she limped closer.

'What's wrong?' he frowned as Velvet sank to the ground.

Brighton had a good look at the cat. A deep gash ran from her left shoulder blade halfway down her leg.

'I'll carry you home and clean this up,' Brighton said to her.

As he picked her up Mischief started growling in a low menacing way.

'I feel it too boy,' Brighton said.

He sensed several people approaching so he put Velvet back on the ground. Mischief took up a protective position in front of his mother. Brighton retrieved the bow and nocked an arrow.

A man burst out of the treeline two hundred paces away. Another followed, then two more all carrying hunting spears.

'There it is,' shouted the leader pointing to the cats.

'Don't come closer!' Brighton shouted at them.

Mischief's muscles were tense, his tail flicking through the air. A low growl came from deep within his throat.

'Easy boy,' Brighton soothed.

'I don't know what your involvement is with those beasts but it's best you run home now!' the leader shouted. 'They stole our deer. I was about to take it down when that thing jumped out of the bushes and killed the deer right in front of our eyes.'

'But at least you wounded it!' one of the others shouted.

All of them laughed and hooted.

'You wounded the panther?' Brighton shouted at them, rage building in him.

'I sure did and if that big one didn't distract me we would be eating panther meat now. We've been tracking them for three days,' came the reply.

Brighton could see that these men would not back down. Violence was the only language they understood. He pulled the bowstring to his cheek.

'Leave now. Last chance!' he shouted.

The leader dropped his spear and held up his hands.

'Please don't shoot. We are all very scared of you!' he shouted mockingly.

The others laughed and hooted some more.

'That bow cannot reach here. Come on, take your best shot!' the man shouted still holding up his hands.

He glanced at his companions, but his head snapped forward again as an arrow slammed straight through his right hand. Brighton already had another nocked. Instantly the men were silent. The leader looked at his hand in shock.

'Please leave!' Brighton shouted, 'I do not want to kill you!'

'Get him!' the leader shouted as he yanked the arrow free of his hand.

The men charged forward. The distance was too great for their throwing spears so they had to get closer.

An arrow went through the first man's upper right arm. Another found the exact same spot in the second man's arm.

Both of them dropped their spears and howled in pain. The third stopped dead in his tracks when he saw another arrow was already nocked. For a moment, the men stood staring at Brighton and then they slowly retreated into the woods.

Brighton sensed them moving further away. He slung the bow over his shoulder. Gently he picked Velvet up and carried her towards the house, Mischief following close behind them.

When they reached the vegetable garden Brighton shouted, 'Carmen! Carmen!'

'What did I tell you about shouting?' she said as she came outside.

She instantly went as stiff as a board. Brighton saw the fear in her eyes.

'I know these panthers. We're friends. They won't harm you,' he assured her.

'If you say so,' Carmen said in a trembling voice.

'Please get some cloth and clean water,' Brighton asked as he put Velvet down on the porch.

Mischief lay down just in front of the porch on the grass.

Carmen retreated into the house.

She came out almost immediately with a cloth and a bowl of water.

'This is Velvet,' Brighton said, 'and the big one is Mischief.'

Carmen was speechless. She knew Brighton was a very special person but this was far beyond her wildest dreams.

'Go say hello to Mischief. He won't do you any harm,' Brighton said.

Carmen trusted Brighton but she was not about to touch the most dangerous animal known to man and most certainly not one as big as that.

She had seen panthers before but none even close to Mischief's size.

As if the big cat understood what Brighton had said, he got up and walked over to Carmen. He rubbed against her arm, purring softly.

'Go ahead, scratch his belly,' Brighton said as he continued cleaning Velvet's wound.

'And if he bites my arm off?' Carmen asked slowly.

Brighton laughed.

'I never thought you would be scared of anything,' he said.

'Have you seen how big this panther is?' Carmen asked sarcastically.

She looked down.

'Brighton, have you seen his eyes?' she asked, her fear forgotten.

'Yes,' Brighton said absently, his mind focused on Velvet.

'This wound is not that bad. It's deep but I can't see damage to the bone or muscles.'

He scratched Velvet behind the ears.

'You'll be fine girl. Just rest here for a few days and this will heal nicely.'

'What?' Carmen gasped, 'No no no! We are not having panthers live on our front porch,' she said wagging her finger.

'Inside the house then?' Brighton asked.

'No!' Carmen shouted wide eyed.

She thought for a moment. It was no use arguing with Brighton about it.

'Ok, on the porch is fine,' she agreed.

Brighton got up and gave Carmen a light kiss on the cheek.

'Thank you,' he said.

*****

Over the next few days, Velvet's wound healed quickly.

Within four days, she was walking without a limp. The next morning the cats were gone. Brighton was a little sad but knew that they were wild animals and could not stay with him.

They belonged in the wild.

Chapter 7

―◦◦◦◦◦―

MORE DAYS WENT by and soon it was six winters that Carmen and Brighton were living near Avarya.

Carmen stood on the porch and shielded her eyes from the bright sun with her hand. Brighton was working on the far side of the vegetable garden next to the road.

He had grown another half a head in the last six winters and his shoulders were also broader than before. His muscles were well defined and there was not a hint of fat anywhere on his body.

Even though Carmen had lived with him for six winters, she never quite got used to the sheer size of the young man. He still looked like a giant to her.

'Brighton, lunch is ready!' she shouted.

Brighton seemed not to hear.

'And he calls me old. It's his hearing that's not good anymore,' she muttered irritably to herself.

She hiked up her long purple skirt and walked down to where Brighton was working.

'Didn't you hear me?' she snapped at him.

'I did,' he replied.

'So why do you ignore me?' she demanded.

'It's rude to shout at someone. You should walk over to them and speak in a civilized manner,' Brighton replied.

Carmen burst out laughing. Her irritation was instantly forgotten.

'Yes, you're quite right,' she agreed. 'I'm glad you remember the things I teach you.'

'What is it that you wanted to say to me?' Brighton asked innocently.

Carmen punched his rock hard shoulder and said, 'You already know. Now come, I don't like eating cold food.'

He took a deep bow.

'Yes, my queen,' he teased.

Carmen started walking back to the house but turned around again.

'Where is Velvet?' she asked.

'She left this morning. I think Mischief was close so she went to him.'

He didn't tell Carmen that he sensed Mischief in the woods earlier. Although the cats visited often, Carmen was still slightly scared of Mischief. Carmen turned and started walking towards the house again.

'I'm just going to wash up,' he called after her.

She wagged her finger in the air.

'Don't shout at your queen, young man,' she joked.

A water barrel was standing not far away. Brighton was glad he filled the barrel earlier. If he had to go to the river to wash up he would certainly be late for lunch and that would not please Carmen.

As he walked to the barrel, he took his shirt off and tossed it on the ground. Immediately he scooped it up again and glanced towards the house to see if Carmen had noticed.

'Almost made a lot of trouble for myself,' he chuckled.

He hung up the shirt on a tree branch nearby and walked to the water barrel.

People were constantly travelling to and from the river for water. Previously it bothered him always feeling their energy but, over time, he got used to it. Now he just ignored it.

He felt the presence of another person passing but did not take any notice. Bracing himself for the cold water, he was just about to dunk his head when a small voice behind him spoke.

'Bri?'

Brighton froze. Only one person ever called him that.

She died six winters ago.

Memories of Lilian flooded back.

'Bri, is that you?' the soft voice asked.

Slowly Brighton turned around.

She was the most beautiful woman he had ever seen. Her long blond curls, decorated with small pink ribbons, reached all the way down to her bottom. Her blue eyes seemed to shine in contrast with her fair, perfect skin.

She wore a white dress with pink trim around the edges.

His mind could not form a proper thought. He staggered back knocking the water barrel over.

'Lilian?' he whispered.

Perhaps he was in the sun too long and was seeing ghosts, flashed through his mind.

Lilian stared back at him with those deep blue eyes. She too had trouble forming an intelligent thought. Tears started streaming down her cheeks.

'Please tell me it's you, Bri?' she pleaded.

'Lily?' was all he could get out.

Suddenly his mind started working. Lily was standing

right in front of him! He believed her to be dead but here she was.

'Lily!' he screamed and scooped her up in his strong arms.

She flung her arms around him and buried her face in his neck.

'Oh Lily, I thought you were dead!' Brighton exclaimed.

'I...thought...the...same...of...you,' she stammered through her tears.

They hugged fiercely for a long time before Brighton put Lilian down. He stepped back and looked at her.

'You've grown since I last saw you,' he observed.

'So have you,' she replied, her eyes travelling over his muscular body.

Although she grew a lot she was still very petite and far shorter than Brighton. If he put his arm out straight, she would fit under it.

'I see you're still as short as ever,' he teased.

'I'm not short, it just seems that way to giants,' she teased back.

Brighton looked at her dress.

'And still wearing dirty dresses,' he said.

Lilian looked down at her dress and pulled a face.

'It was clean this morning. That's what a girl gets for hugging dirty giants,' she teased.

'So it's my fault?' he played along. 'I'm so sorry princess. How can I ever make this right?' he teased.

'Wash my dress,' she commanded playfully.

Brighton got a sly smile on his face.

'As you wish,' he said.

'Oh no, I know that look,' Lilian said as she turned to run away.

Brighton caught her easily, picked her up, and flung her over his shoulder.

'Bri! No!' she shouted, pounding her small fists on his back.

'You don't even know what I'm going to do,' he said as he headed towards his private little spot next to the river.

He grabbed his shirt as he walked past the tree.

'I know exactly what you're planning,' Lilian screamed.

'And what might that be?' Brighton asked innocently.

'You're going to throw me in the river,' she replied.

'Clever girl,' Brighton smiled.

She continued to protest all the way down to the river.

Brighton acted as if he was deaf saying 'What?' every so often.

They reached Brighton's spot and he put Lilian down.

'I won't do it if you don't want me to,' he said. 'I was just teasing.'

Lilian looked at him for a moment. She turned and ran for the river.

'Last one in is a stinky old goat,' she shouted.

'Wait!' Brighton shouted but it was too late, Lilian was already almost waist deep in the river.

'Not fair,' he said.

'I smell a stinky old goat,' she teased.

Brighton tossed his shirt away and charged into the water. Lilian let out a yelp and tried to get away but his big arm circled her waist. He picked her up and fell backwards into the waist deep water. Both their heads disappeared under the water. They came up spluttering and laughing.

'Is this old goat still stinky?' Brighton asked.

She stepped closer, put her head on his chest and her arms around his waist.

'No, not at all,' she said softly.

Brighton's arms snaked around her and he held her close. They stood hugging in the water for a while. Brighton became aware of her firm smallish breasts against his body.

This caused an unfamiliar stirring in him. He released

Lilian and stepped back.

'What's wrong?' she asked.

'Nothing. I…uh….I'd better wash your dress before you break my arm off and give me a hiding with it,' he stuttered.

Lilian giggled and without hesitation started unbuttoning the dress. He had seen her in her undergarments more times than she could remember.

'I'm not a little girl anymore. I can wash my own dress,' she said.

She moved to the shallow water and slipped out of the dress, her back towards Brighton. He could not help but stare. She was wearing undergarments but not the bulky ones he remembered.

White, thin, delicate material hugged her bottom like a second skin.

His eyes travelled up her back. No more thick woollen vests either but instead the same delicate material with only thin straps going over her shoulders covered her upper body.

She turned around and caught him staring.

'All the girls in Zedonia are wearing this now. Do you like it?' she asked in a slightly husky voice.

The wet, almost completely see-through material was clinging to her skin.

'Just like that? In the streets?' he asked flabbergasted.

'No silly. Under their clothes,' Lilian laughed.

Brighton's face went red.

That was a stupid question, he berated himself.

Lilian dunked the dress and proceeded to wash it.

'Give me your shirt, I'll wash it for you,' she said without looking up.

Brighton walked out of the water, picked up his shirt and held it out to her.

She took the shirt and said, 'Trousers too.'

'They're clean,' Brighton said quickly and retreated.

He found a comfortable rock to sit on. Pulling his legs

up to his chest, he sat silently watching Lilian, old memories battling with reality in his mind.

The pretty child he knew had grown into an impossibly beautiful young woman.

Lilian looked up and smiled at him.

She finished with the dress and hung it up on a branch. Back in the water, she started working on Brighton's shirt.

He could not stop staring at her.

'There, all clean,' she finally declared.

She hung the shirt next to her dress and came over to where Brighton was sitting.

The way that wet, see-through undergarments clung to her body made Brighton's mind spin.

'Do you still carry a hairbrush with you?' she asked.

Brighton didn't trust his voice so he just shook his head. His heart was pounding, his breathing fast.

Lilian couldn't hide her disappointment. She was hoping he would brush her hair like he always used to do.

'You'll never get dry sitting like that. Lie down,' she said as she lay down on the warm rock next to him.

She got comfortable and closed her eyes. Brighton leaned back on his elbows, keeping an eye on Lilian.

Slowly he let his gaze travel up and down her petite form, savouring every moment as if it was the last time he would ever see such beauty again.

A thought popped into his head. He imagined slowly running his hand over her stomach up to her breas…

'Brighton!' Lilian gasped as her eyes shot open.

'What?' he said, eyes snapping to meet hers.

It looked like she was about to admonish him as if she knew what he was day-dreaming about but then thought better of it.

'Nothing,' she said covering herself with her arms.

She got up still holding her arms in front of her chest.

'I have to go,' she said and headed for the dress.

Brighton jumped up and followed her.

'Why?' he asked, very confused.

'I just have to,' she said.

Brighton caught up with her, his arms snaking around her waist.

'Please don't,' he pleaded softly.

Lilian leaned back against him. His touch made her legs go weak.

Brighton leaned down and whispered in her ear, 'Please stay a while.'

Lilian could not resist. Her breathing was fast and shallow. She put her hand over his and slowly guided him up her stomach exactly as he had imagined just a moment ago. Their hands reached the rounding of her breast.

She hesitated.

Brighton slowly, gently slid his hand over her breast. He could feel her chest rising and falling rapidly. She turned in the circle of his arms. Brighton started to apologize but she put a finger over his lips.

Stepping back, she pulled the vest over her head. Only one word stood out in the jumble that was Brighton's mind.

Perfect.

For a moment, he stared at her naked body and then stepped closer. His lips pressed softly against hers for just a moment. When he pulled back, she followed him.

Her lips parted and found his. With his left hand on her naked back, he pulled her tight against him. His right hand slid down and found her firm small bottom.

Passionately their lips crushed together, Lilian's naked breasts pressing hard against his chest.

'Brighton!' a familiar voice shouted from the woods.

Lilian jumped back.

'Who is that?' she gasped, reaching for her clothes.

'It's Carmen,' Brighton replied, alarm and disappointment battling in his mind.

For a moment he wondered if Carmen would find them if they remained quiet but banished the thought almost instantly.

'Get dressed, I'll go stall her,' he suggested.

He stole another quick glance at Lilian's almost naked body just before she pulled the dress over her head.

How can anyone be that perfect? he thought.

She smiled at him as if she could hear his thoughts.

Brighton dashed into the woods. He ran into Carmen almost knocking her over.

'Carmen,' he said breathlessly. 'What are you doing here?'

'What are you doing here?' she replied irritably.

For a moment, Brighton thought that Carmen must have seen him and Lilian.

'The food has gone cold long ago. I waited and waited but you never came,' she accused angrily.

Brighton couldn't think of an answer.

Lilian's voice came from behind him.

'I'm afraid that's my fault. I'm sorry,' she said.

Brighton spun around. When he saw that Lilian was fully dressed he breathed a sigh of relief.

'Introduce us,' Carmen instructed Brighton.

He pointed to Carmen and stuttered, 'This...um....this is...'

Politely Carmen said, 'Hello, I'm Carmen.'

'Pleased to meet you, I'm Lilian,' came the reply.

'Lilian, you must be quite a girl. Brighton can't even remember my name,' Carmen smiled.

She managed to hide the alarm that shot into in her mind.

Brighton stammered, 'We were just...'

He took a breath and tried again, 'Lilian needed to wash her dress.'

'Oh? Where were you while she had no dress on? And where is your shirt?' Carmen asked with a slight smile.

Brighton didn't know what to say. It felt like his

whole body was on fire.

'Keeping a lookout,' Lilian lied. 'I also washed his shirt,' she added holding it up.

Carmen saw the lie but decided not to press the issue. She was also young once.

Lilian handed Brighton his shirt. When he took it, their hands touched. They both lingered a moment before pulling away.

'Thank you,' Brighton said sheepishly.

Carmen caught the touch. She smiled inwardly.

Oh to be young and in love. Such a beautiful thing she thought.

'I would love to stay here and talk but since Brighton just disappeared into the woods with his girlfriend I had to go look for him and haven't had lunch yet,' Carmen said to them.

Lilian and Brighton started speaking together trying to explain that they were not a couple but Carmen just smiled and walked off.

She called over her shoulder, 'Come, there is enough food for everybody.'

'I'd much rather go back to the river,' Brighton mumbled.

Lilian blushed and said, 'Yes, me too.'

They followed Carmen just out of earshot.

'You were getting quite excited back there,' Lilian said with a sly smile.

'Why do you say that?' Brighton asked carefully.

Lilian just winked at him with a devilish look in her eyes.

Brighton went bright red. He opened his mouth but no words would come out.

His discomfort made Lilian giggle.

'Don't be embarrassed. I know what boys think about,' she said.

'How do you know? Have you been with…uh…others?' he blurted out.

As soon as he said it, he was sorry. He thought Lilian would get angry and shout at him.

Instead, she answered honestly, 'No, but where I live there are many girls who have been with men. They like to talk about it.'

Brighton stammered an apology for the direct question.

'I'll forgive you if you tell me whether you've been with a girl,' Lilian said seriously.

'Never,' Brighton replied. 'Today was the first time I've even kissed a girl,' he confessed.

'Me too,' Lilian said. 'I mean kissed a boy,' she quickly added.

Brighton looked at Carmen. She wasn't looking back so he gave Lilian's bottom a quick squeeze.

'I can't wait to do it again,' he whispered in Lilian's ear.

'Me neither,' she smiled. 'But next time I'm not the only one getting out of my clothes.'

The memory of Lilian's perfect naked body ran through Brighton's mind.

*****

Brighton, Lilian and Carmen sat on the porch after lunch. There were only two chairs so Lilian sat on Brighton's lap. Neither of them minded.

Carmen asked a few carefully selected questions to make sure that Lilian was in fact the girl from Brighton's childhood. They told Carmen of their games of hide and find, playing in the river and chasing goats.

Carmen brought lemon juice out but Lilian didn't like it. Brighton got used to drinking it undiluted far quicker than he thought possible. He chuckled remembering the first time he tasted it. It felt like a lifetime ago.

'Lilian, did you ever see Velvet and Mischief?'

Carmen asked.

'Only once the day after Mischief was born,' Lilian replied.

She assumed Brighton had told Carmen about the cats.

'Mischief is the biggest black panther I've ever seen. He still scares me half to death,' Carmen remarked.

Confused Lilian turned to Brighton.

'Oh, I haven't told you. Velvet and Mischief found some time ago. Velvet was injured but I fixed it for her. Mischief is enormous now!' Brighton said excitedly.

Lilian clapped her hands with delight and planted a kiss right on Brighton's lips. Embarrassed she glanced at Carmen who pretended not to notice.

'I can't believe they found you,' Lilian said, still smiling.

'Mischief will always be drawn to you,' Carmen said to Brighton.

'Why do you say that?' Brighton asked, frowning.

'Well, you helped bring him into this world. Animals don't forget that sort of thing. You've also helped Velvet twice. She will also trust you always.'

'I know they trust me but you said, "drawn" to me,' Brighton pressed.

'I meant to say trust,' Carmen replied.

Brighton suddenly thought of something else.

'Why did you think I was dead?' he asked Lilian.

Carmen tensed. This was dangerous territory.

'About five winters ago I went back to Four Mountains and my mother told me your house burnt down with you in it. And you? Why did you think I was dead?' she asked.

'Carmen told me when we first met,' Brighton said, looking straight at Carmen.

'I'm sorry Brighton; I heard it from someone else. I never saw it for myself,' she lied.

'Who told you?' Brighton pressed.

'I can't remember,' she replied.

Brighton started speaking again but Lilian cut him off.

'It was long ago. Forget about it now,' she said softly.

Changing the subject Carmen said, 'It's getting late. Where are you staying Lilian?'

'Here with us,' Brighton replied before Lilian could speak.

Both women shifted uncomfortably.

'I'll sleep in the kitchen and Lily can have my room,' Brighton said.

Lilian didn't know what to say. She knew she couldn't stay but didn't want to disappoint Brighton either.

Carmen spoke first.

'That won't work. Lilian obviously already has accommodation. Whomever she is staying with will worry if she doesn't come home.'

Lilian looked at Carmen gratefully.

'But we could go tell them she is staying here,' Brighton argued.

'I'm travelling with my father. He will not allow it,' Lilian said.

'I'll go ask him,' Brighton said defiantly.

'No!' Lilian said quickly. 'Carmen is correct. It will not work.'

Brighton nodded disappointedly.

'Will you come back tomorrow?' he asked hopefully.

'Yes, definitely,' Lilian replied.

Carmen could see it was a lie but said nothing.

'What is your father doing in Avarya?' Carmen asked instead.

'He just came to visit some people,' Lilian said carefully. 'I got bored and decided to go to the river. That's when I saw Bri.'

Another lie Carmen thought.

'Will you stay for supper?' Brighton asked.

'That would be lovely,' Lilian smiled. 'If the lady of the house agrees,' she added turning to Carmen.

'We'll be more than happy to have you,' Carmen said honestly.

She got up and said, 'Brighton, go check on the goats and fetch some fresh water please. Lilian, would you like to help me prepare the vegetables? The secret to good stew is starting early.'

Uncertain Lilian said, 'Ok, I'll try.'

Brighton blew Lilian a little kiss and walked off to do his chores.

*****

In the kitchen, Carmen gave Lilian a knife and told her to peel potatoes. Lilian clumsily tried but didn't really know how.

Carmen showed her and asked, 'Have you never cooked?'

'No,' Lilian said a little embarrassed.

'Where do you get food from?' Carmen asked.

'The servants bring it,' Lilian replied.

Carefully Carmen asked, 'Where do you live?'

'The palace in Zedonia,' Lilian replied.

'How come you live in the palace?' Carmen pressed on.

'My father insists. I only ever get out when I'm travelling with him.'

Carmen feared asking the next question but she had to.

'Who is your father?'

'Seth,' Lilian replied flatly.

'So you're a Dark One, child of a Supreme,' Carmen stated.

'Yes,' Lilian said in a small voice. 'Please don't tell Bri,' she begged.

'It is not my place to tell him, that is your duty,' Carmen said sternly.

'I'm not. When I leave he will know where I'm going

and come after me,' Lilian said.

'So why are you here now?' the old woman asked.

'I love Bri like I've never loved anyone. My heart hurts just thinking I have to leave him again, but I don't have a choice. When I saw him today I couldn't help myself, I had to make sure it was him. Then we went to the river. Just before you came I had decided to....um...' Lilian shifted uncomfortably.

'Give yourself to him?' Carmen asked.

Lilian nodded.

'So you were going to make love to him and then just disappear again? That's cruel!' Carmen said heatedly.

'I didn't think of it like that,' Lilian said in a small voice.

'Seems to me like you didn't think at all,' Carmen corrected.

'When Brighton touches me, my knees go weak. When he kisses me it's like the world stands still and it's only the two of us in it,' Lilian tried to explain.

Carmen looked at Lilian closely.

'You really love him,' she said.

'And that is why I have to go,' Lilian said. 'I don't want my father to see Brighton. Seth might hurt him.'

'Not likely,' Carmen muttered to herself.

'What do you mean?' Lilian asked.

'Nothing. Continue please,' Carmen said quickly.

Lilian carried on, 'Lately Seth has been in a very bad mood. He kills people for no reason when he gets angry. He has been looking for someone for a very long time but that person keeps evading him.'

'Who is he looking for?' Carmen asked.

'An old man, that's all I know,' Lilian said.

Thomas, Carmen thought immediately. *Will Seth never stop hunting him?*

Lilian spoke again, 'Today he was questioning people in town. Apparently, the man has been seen in these parts. I hate it when Seth questions people so I asked if

I could go to the river. Seth hardly lets me out of his sight but luckily he was very busy and just waved me off.'

'Do me a favour, please? Use your talent and tell me where Brighton is,' Carmen asked.

Lilian concentrated for a moment and said, 'He's with the goats, coming this way.'

Carmen stiffened.

How was that possible? How could she sense Brighton?

'You're gifted too, why didn't you look for him?' Lilian asked.

'I'm old and tired. Besides, I don't like using the gift,' Carmen said honestly.

'Me neither,' Lilian said.

Carmen was slightly surprised by this. Lilian was the child of a Supreme. Normally they are bloodthirsty and power hungry.

'Why not?' Carmen asked.

'It's wrong to steal energy from other people,' Lilian said. 'I don't mind sensing where people are but I never take their energy.'

'What does your father say about this?' Carmen asked.

'It's the reason he keeps me so close to him. He's trying to teach me that other people are here purely to serve us. He is wrong!' Lilian said angrily.

'Why don't you run away?' Carmen asked already knowing the answer.

'I tried. He finds me every time,' Lilian answered.

She dropped her eyes in shame.

'I've also tried killing him a few times. It is not possible, he is very powerful.'

'I'm sorry,' Carmen said. 'It must be hard for you.'

Lilian just nodded.

'Please go tell Brighton to hurry up with the water,' Carmen asked.

Lilian nodded. She left without another word. Carmen went to the door and watched Lilian go. She waited until Lilian reached Brighton before she used her talent. Both Brighton and Lilian immediately looked towards the house.

As always, she could not sense Brighton.

'Why can you sense him, young girl?' Carmen said to no one in particular.

*****

Shortly after supper they were sitting outside on the porch. Carmen didn't join them for which they were both glad. They enjoyed the privacy.

Lilian sat on Brighton's lap. He slipped his hand under her dress and stroked her leg. He loved the feeling of her perfect skin.

When Lilian said it was time for her to go, Brighton resisted the urge to argue and instead gave her a long, tender kiss. Lilian melted into the kiss, she wanted it to last forever.

Brighton ran his hand further up Lilian's leg but she gently stopped him and whispered in his ear, 'Next time.'

Although he was sad that she had to go, he smiled at her and gave her bottom a squeeze.

'Are you coming to visit tomorrow?' he asked.

She nodded and smiled, struggling not to cry.

As she walked into the night, the tears were streaming down her cheeks.

*****

Lilian walked into town. She didn't know where Seth was and didn't use her sense to locate him. He would find her shortly, he always did.

'A kiss for your father,' the soft, rumbling voice said

behind her.

'I'd rather drown myself,' she said.

'Careful, Lilian,' Seth said raising his hand.

She stood her ground.

'Kill me or not, I don't care! Your little hand trick doesn't scare me anymore!' she screamed.

'You're testing my patience child,' he warned.

'Oh, really?' she mocked. 'And still you won't do anything about it. Well, here is the excuse you need!' Lilian screamed as her energy link slammed into Seth's head.

Seth allowed her to take some energy and then reversed the link. He did not take any from her; he simply stopped her stealing his.

'Feels good, doesn't it,' he said softly.

'No. But one day when I kill you it will,' Lilian said.

She broke the link. If he wanted to retaliate, he would have done so already. He was very quick to measure out punishment. Strangely, he never hurt her.

The last time was six winters ago, back in Four Mountains.

Chapter 8

THOMAS RAN FOR his life.

How did they find me again? he wondered as he dodged branches and undergrowth.

He jumped over a fallen tree and stopped as an idea formed in his head. He went down on his haunches behind the big tree and waited. Sensing the assailant coming he braced himself. He knew the Dark One could sense him too; he was counting on that.

The Dark One was running at breakneck speed.

Good Thomas thought.

Just don't stop before you reach the tree.

He didn't. Instead, the young man jumped clean over the fallen tree hoping to turn around and corner Thomas. As he flew over the tree Thomas brought his trusted walking stick up with all the force he could muster.

The stick caught the man between the legs. He

crashed into the ground holding his groin, screaming in pain. Thomas got up making sure he stayed outside of arms reach.

'When will you lot learn? You are human too,' Thomas said slowly.

Before the man could speak, Thomas swung the walking stick. The Dark One's head exploded like a melon.

Slowly Thomas walked back to a stream he saw while he was running. He sat down next to the water. First, he washed his face and had some big gulps of water. Next, he rinsed off his arms and then cleaned the blood off his walking stick.

He rested a while, continuously scanning the area with his talent. He knew the Dark Ones could find him easier this way but at least he also knew when they were coming.

Night was approaching. Slowly he got up feeling very old.

'I am very old,' he chuckled to himself as a shiver ran down his spine.

Winter was almost over and never very harsh in these parts but the cool air still settled deep in an old man's bones.

He hadn't seen Carmen in a long time, not since the start of the previous winter.

At first, they spoke often, every few days, but as Brighton settled into his new life, the meetings between Thomas and Carmen became less and less. This gave Thomas the time to travel and gather information. He needed to know what Brighton's talent was and how it worked if he was going to help the young man. So far, he had found nothing of value, just a few theories.

Thomas missed Carmen terribly but he knew it would be better if they didn't have much contact. He always returned to this area after one of his travels. Carmen would leave a signal at the rock where they used to meet if she needed him.

Thomas got up and started walking towards the meeting place.

Somehow, the Dark Ones kept finding him. There was never any small talk; they simply tried to kill him. So far, he had not run into a Supreme or one of their children. He knew that day would come and then he had no chance of survival. His walking stick would be useless against an energy link.

When he reached the rock, he sat down on it. Looking straight into the woods, he checked the branches of the third tree. Nothing. No red cloth.

Thomas sat for a while. He was hoping to see the signal but also glad it wasn't there. The red cloth would mean trouble but at least he would see Carmen again.

He got up and started walking into the woods. Suddenly he changed his mind and took the road towards Avarya.

*****

Lilian walked behind Seth. Her mind was racing. They were travelling back to Avarya from Farrendale where Seth had questioned more people. He killed them all when he didn't like their answers. Normally this bothered Lilian for days afterwards but today she had something else on her mind.

Her half-sister Paige had joined them in Farrendale for the questioning. She seemed to enjoy it as much as Seth did.

Afterwards Seth sent Paige to convince Lilian to start using her talent but instead they ended up speaking about the family. Lilian could not remember anything Paige said except the part about Evangeline's bracelet.

Evangeline was their grandmother, Seth's mother.

Paige told her it was a bracelet Evangeline wore until the day she died. Somehow, a part of Evangeline's talent stayed behind in the bracelet after she passed on.

When it was time to leave, Paige elected to stay in the small town.

Lilian walked faster and caught up to Seth.

'Seth, tell me about your mother's bracelet please?' Lilian asked.

'No.'

'Please?' she begged.

'No.'

'Why not? It's just a bracelet,' Lilian said irritably.

'It's not just a bracelet. It's very powerful,' Seth retorted.

'What does it do?' Lilian asked.

'It drains the power of anyone who wears it,' Seth answered.

'How?' she asked.

Seth ignored her.

'How?' she repeated the question.

'Stop asking. I will not talk about it anymore,' Seth said slowly.

He never raised his voice at her. In fact, he never raised his voice at anyone.

A thought formed in Lilian's head.

*****

Brighton walked into the house. He was in a terrible mood. Lilian last visited four days ago. She had promised to come back, but so far, she hadn't shown up.

Carmen was busy preparing supper.

'Did you manage to find berries?' she asked.

Brighton wordlessly put a basket half full of berries on the table.

He sat down heavily on a chair and muttered, 'Thomas was right.'

Carmen looked at him quizzically.

'I knew this old man back in Four Mountains called Thomas. He once said that a man will never know if a woman truly loves him, he will just have to guess. Thomas was right.'

Sounds like Thomas, Carmen thought with a smile.

'You know that I love you,' she said.

'That's different. You're like my grandmother or something,' Brighton replied.

Carmen laughed.

'I prefer "Mother" if you don't mind. Grandmother makes me sound so old,' she said.

Brighton often teased Carmen about her age. She didn't mind, it was all in good spirit. This time, however, he did not say anything. Carmen went back to preparing supper.

Brighton looked at the door moments before the knock came. Instinctively Carmen used her sense.

She smiled.

She recognized the energy. Brighton got up and opened the door.

'Thomas!' he gasped.

Before the old man could speak, Brighton grabbed him and gave him a big hug, lifting the old man clear off the ground.

'Thomas, I'm so glad to see you! Where have you been? How did you find me?' Brighton fired off the questions as he put Thomas down.

Thomas ignored the questions and looked past Brighton.

Carmen was facing them, hands clasped tightly in front of her, tears welling up in her eyes.

'Thomas,' she said softly.

'Hello Carmen,' Thomas croaked past the lump in his throat.

Excitedly Brighton said, 'Carmen, this is Thomas, he's the …'

Thomas walked over to Carmen.

He put his arms around her and they hugged for a long time.

'It's been too long,' Thomas managed.

Tears were streaming freely down Carmen's face. She couldn't speak.

'Wait, you two know each other?' Brighton asked with a frown.

Still the two old people ignored him.

'I missed you,' Carmen said through her tears.

'And I missed you,' Thomas croaked.

Finally, they separated.

Carmen looked more closely at Thomas.

'Another run in with the Dark Ones?' she asked.

'Several,' Thomas replied.

Brighton couldn't stand it anymore.

'What's going on here?' he asked impatiently.

Carmen spoke.

'Brighton, I would like for you to meet....'

'I know who Thom...'

One look from Carmen made him slam his mouth shut.

'I would like for you to meet Thomas, my brother,' Carmen finished.

'Your brother?' Brighton gasped.

'Yes, my younger brother,' Carmen replied.

Brighton's mouth was hanging wide open.

'I can't believe it,' he said excitedly, 'what are the odds of that?'

He gestured towards Thomas. 'I leave Four Mountains, run into your sister and I end up living with her.'

He shook his head in amazement.

'Wait for it,' Carmen whispered to Thomas.

Brighton frowned.

'Wait....what are the odds of that happening?' he frowned, looking at Thomas.

'It never takes very long,' Carmen whispered.

'Stop whispering and tell me what's going on,' Brighton demanded.

'Do you want to?' Thomas asked Carmen.

'Not really,' she replied, 'I'll cook supper and you tell Brighton what you've done.'

'Me?' Thomas replied indignantly. 'You were a part of it,' he accused heatedly.

'But you were the mastermind behind it all,' Carmen countered, her voice rising.

Brighton couldn't believe it. Here were two people of more than five hundred and sixty winters and they were arguing like children.

'Stop it!' he shouted. 'Tell me what's going on here,' he demanded and quickly added 'Please?' when he saw the expression on Carmen's face.

Thomas sat down and gestured for Brighton to do the same.

Carmen continued with supper.

'Carmen is my sister…' Thomas began.

'Yes, that part I already know,' Brighton interjected.

'Brighton,' Carmen said without looking up.

The young man mumbled an apology.

'I see she has taught you some manners,' Thomas laughed.

Brighton decided not to say anything. He waited patiently for Thomas to speak.

'Like I said, Carmen is my sister. Much older sister I might add,' Thomas teased Carmen.

One look from Carmen and Thomas quickly mumbled, 'Sorry'.

'I see she taught you some manners too,' Brighton whispered to him.

They shared a knowing look.

'When you said you wanted to leave Four Mountains, I was worried. If you did manage to catch up to Seth and Lilian, who knows what might have happened. You could have been killed, Lilian could have been killed. I decided to try and avoid that so I left before you. Carmen lived in the woods just outside Avarya. I came to her and asked for her help. Together we devised a plan to try and protect you.

'To make a long story short, we set up the entire thing hoping that you would abandon your quest to save Lilian. Obviously it worked.'

Brighton frowned, 'You mean all of this was a setup? Where did the house come from? And the goats, the vegetable garden?'

Thomas replied, 'I found the goats and Carmen convinced the people who lived here to give her this house. The vegetable garden was here already.'

Brighton turned to Carmen, 'You convinced the people to give you their house? In one day?'

'I asked nicely,' Carmen replied.

'Wait,' Brighton said. 'You're Thomas' sister. That means you're a Dark.....'

Thomas shook his head urgently.

'.....uh... also talented like him. Did you use your talent on the people that lived here?'

The question brought a very dark look from Carmen.

'I guess not,' Brighton said quickly.

'What was the idea behind all of this?' Brighton asked.

'To make you forget about Lilian, Clarissa, Seth and everything that happened,' Thomas said.

Carmen spoke, 'Tell him the truth.'

'It is the truth,' Thomas defended.

'All of it,' Carmen instructed.

'Fine. It was also to hide you,' Thomas said with a sigh.

'Hide me? Why would you want to hide me?' he asked. 'And besides, this is a terrible hiding place! It's right in the open next to a road. Wouldn't somewhere deep in the forest have worked better?'

'It's a brilliant hiding place,' Thomas said heatedly.

He continued more calmly, 'Very few people stay

deep in the forests. If Seth passed anywhere nearby, he would have sensed Carmen's energy and investigated. That means he would have found you. If you lived in town there is the risk of a chance encounter with him. The road next to this house leads only to the river, nowhere else, so the likelihood of Seth travelling past here is slim. He won't go fetch his own water; he has servants to do that. If he happened to cast his sense this far he would only pick up a single old woman living just outside of town; nothing suspicious about that.'

Brighton had to agree, it was brilliant.

Thomas carried on, 'You have to understand, these are all guesses I had to make in a day. Perhaps living deep in the forest would have worked, or even in town. As it turned out this hiding place has been good for six winters. Besides, it gave you the chance to do something you know and love,' Thomas said, referring to the garden and goats.

'Why hide me in the first place?' Brighton asked.

'Now that is a good question. I didn't understand at first but now I do,' Carmen commented.

'Understand what?' Brighton asked her.

She kept quiet and let Thomas continue.

'You're a very special person,' he started.

'Well, thank you. You're pretty special too but what does that have to do with hiding me?' Brighton interrupted sarcastically.

Thomas smiled.

'You still don't know when to keep quiet and just listen,' he said.

Brighton opened his mouth but another black look from Carmen made him change his mind.

He sat back and listened to Thomas.

'There are a number of things in your life that does not make sense. Think about your birth. Did you go to the place?'

Brighton nodded.

'How is it possible for a new-born to survive like that?' Thomas continued. 'Why were all the plants dead? And what about those wolves? These would be the first questions that need answers if we are going to understand you.'

'I have travelled far and wide in the last few winters. I spoke to everyone I know, and I know a lot of people, to try and get some answers. Nobody knows anything useful. I've thought about the story of your birth for a long time and there is only one explanation. You're talented like us. Actually, more like a Supreme.'

Thomas paused to read Brighton's reaction.

The younger man sat stone faced.

Thomas continued, 'There is no way you could have survived the way you did, unless you have the talent. This theory presents a few other questions though. Why can't you use it like other Dark Ones? You've never stolen energy from anyone or anything, apart from the time of your birth.'

Again, Thomas paused.

When Brighton stayed quiet Thomas asked, 'What is a human's most basic instinct?'

This time Brighton spoke, 'Survival?'

'Yes!' Thomas said smiling. 'Survival! You wanted to survive and your instinct took over. You took energy from the only available source. Two animals and the plants around you. It's also possible that the wolves were threatening you and your instinct was to kill them before they killed you. Whichever way that happened doesn't matter. What does matter is that you did it, you took their energy and made it your own.'

Thomas was expecting an argument from Brighton but instead he nodded and said, 'Yes, that makes sense.'

Thomas carried on.

'The next question is why haven't you used the talent since then? Perhaps you were simply not aware that you have it. From a very young age most Dark Ones are aware of the talent. This was not the case with you.'

Brighton held up his hand.

'Wait,' he said, 'There is something you don't know.'

Thomas leaned forward expectantly.

Slowly Brighton spoke, 'I have always been aware of things around me.'

'You mean you can see them?' Thomas asked.

'No, I can feel them,' Brighton answered.

It was Thomas' turn to stay quiet. This was interesting.

'What do you mean feel them?' came the question from Carmen.

'I mean I can sense people and animals around me, just like Thomas said he could sense people. And you I suppose,' Brighton said to Carmen.

'Incredible,' Carmen gasped. 'I never knew you could do that!'

'That confirms my theory, you have the talent,' Thomas said.

He suddenly frowned. He just thought of something else.

'Strange that I've never felt it when you use your sense. Have you, Carmen?' he asked.

'No, I've never felt it,' she replied.

Brighton was looking from face to face, highly confused.

'I sense both of you right now. And the goats outside,' he said.

Thomas thought for a moment.

'Perhaps we can't feel it because our sense is blind to you. That would mean we are also blind to your talent. Yes, that must be it.'

'Do you use it often?' Carmen asked.

'What do you mean?' Brighton said with a frown.

Thomas also frowned.

'It's a simple question. Do you use it often?' he

repeated Carmen's question.

'I don't intentionally use it. It's just always there,' Brighton replied.

'Constantly?' Carmen asked carefully.

'Yes, all the time,' Brighton answered.

'Right now?' Thomas asked.

'Yes!' Brighton answered irritably.

'This is interesting,' Thomas remarked, thinking deeply about the new information.

Carmen smiled and said, 'I know of one time when you were not aware of anybody except one very beautiful young woman.'

Brighton instantly went red.

Thomas glanced at Brighton. He saw the opportunity to lighten the mood a bit.

'Now this is something I want to hear about. Brighton and a pretty girl. Tell me more,' he said to Carmen, rubbing his hands together.

Carmen smiled slyly.

'Well, I didn't really see them together but I'm sure they were...'

'We didn't do anything,' Brighton quickly interjected.

'Oh really? You lost your shirt and I happen to know she wasn't wearing her dress,' Carmen teased. 'I think...' she started but quickly stopped when she saw the sadness on Brighton's face.

She touched his shoulder and softly said, 'I'm sorry.'

Brighton got up and walked out mumbling something about checking on the goats.

'What just happened?' Thomas asked, very confused. 'Brighton found a girlfriend, what could be better?'

'Lilian,' was all Carmen said.

'No...not Lilian from Four Mountains,' Thomas stammered.

'Yes,' Carmen said flatly.

'That's not good, not good at all,' Thomas said slowly.

'I was hoping he would forget about her. Now he

might just try to go after her again like six winters ago. That's a distraction he doesn't need.'

'There's more. Seth is in Avarya. Or he was four days ago at least.'

'Seth is here! Dear angels, that is really bad!' Thomas gasped. 'Wait, how do you know? Did he come here?' Thomas asked, panic rising in his mind.

'Lilian told me,' Carmen answered.

'How does Lilian know Seth? Come on woman, tell me everything, don't make me beg!' Thomas prodded.

'Lilian is Seth's daughter. He was here questioning people about someone he has been hunting for a very long time,' Carmen said softly.

Thomas' eyes went wide.

'Me,' he whispered. 'That explains why there are so many Dark Ones around lately.'

'How many?' Carmen asked softly.

Thomas knew she wanted to know how many he had killed.

'Three in the last five days or so.'

Carmen didn't want to ask but she had to know.

'And before that?'

'Eight this winter. Seven since the start of last winter,' Thomas said honestly.

He saw how much this disturbed Carmen so he tried to joke, 'If it goes on like this I will have them all dead in a few winters and we can live in peace.'

'That's not funny Thomas!' Carmen berated him.

She turned around so he wouldn't see her tears.

Thomas got up and put his arms around her.

'When will it end?' Carmen sobbed.

When I'm dead Thomas thought but didn't say anything, Carmen was upset enough already.

*****

Brighton was sitting on a rock next to the river. He

was at the private little spot only he and Lilian knew about. Memories of her ran through his mind. Her soft skin, her blue eyes, those long blond curls. The way she moved, how she felt in his arms. He could still see her there, pulling her vest over her head. He could feel her firm breasts against his chest, her lips on his. Over and over he relived those moments.

As dawn broke he finally got up and slowly walked home. He didn't notice the goats or look at the vegetables.

Thomas and Carmen were sitting on the porch. They had been up all night talking.

'Morning Brighton!' Thomas shouted when he saw the young man approaching.

Brighton walked up to the porch before he answered.

'Morning Carmen, morning Thomas,' he said softly.

'That's something you never learned,' Carmen accused Thomas.

'I remember what you said about shouting, I just choose to ignore you,' Thomas teased.

Turning to Brighton he said, 'Carmen tells me you're rather good with a bow. Would you like to show me?'

Brighton smiled, the memories of Lilian pushed to the back of his mind for the moment.

'Yes, let me fetch it quickly,' he said and ran into the house.

He loved shooting with a bow. Moments later he was back carrying three bows and a quiver full of arrows.

'I've been experimenting with different types of wood and string.'

He held up the longest one.

'This one is the best. I made it from Yew wood. The willow bow is also pretty good. Oak does not make good bows. Do you want me to teach you how to shoot? Carmen says I'm a good teacher. She uses the oak bow because it's the easiest one for her to handle, the string is not that tight.'

Brighton babbled on for a while longer about arrows, feathers, tips and a few other things Thomas did not understand.

Carmen smiled at Thomas. It was good to see Brighton this excited.

'...so you have to aim higher. You also have to compensate for any wind there might be.'

Thomas nodded his head as if he understood everything Brighton just said. He gestured towards the corner post of the garden fence.

'Do you think you could hit that from here?'

It was only sixty paces away. Brighton looked at Carmen and rolled his eyes. It was she that answered Thomas.

'He never misses.'

'Never?' Thomas asked in disbelief.

'Never,' Brighton said proudly. 'I hit a fowl at over two hundred paces last week.'

'You're teasing me,' Thomas accused.

'It's true,' Carmen said. 'I was there.'

Brighton decided to show Thomas. He grabbed a lemon from the table and ran down past the garden.

While he was gone, Thomas said to Carmen, 'You must be playing a joke on me. What you're saying is impossible! A bow cannot even shoot that far, never mind killing a fowl at that range.'

'Watch,' was all Carmen said.

Brighton returned.

'Do you see the lemon?' he asked Thomas.

Thomas squinted his eyes; he could just make out the lemon about two hundred and fifty paces away.

'Yes, I see it,' Thomas answered.

Brighton took the Yew bow and nocked an arrow. He pulled the string to his cheek, aimed for just a moment, and let the arrow fly. It whistled through the air and moments later split the lemon in half.

Thomas was speechless.

'I told you he never misses,' Carmen said smugly.

Brighton had a wide smile on his face.

'If I could build a bow with more power I would be able to hit the lemon from even further away,' he boasted. 'This bow is very accurate.'

A thought formed in Thomas' mind.

'It's not the bow,' he said slowly.

Before Carmen or Brighton could speak, Thomas was up. He took another lemon and tossed it about twenty paces away.

'Shoot that,' he said to Brighton.

'But it's only....'

'With your eyes closed,' Thomas cut him short.

'What? If I close my eyes, I can't see it. If I can't see it, how am I supposed to shoot at it?'

'Just try,' was all Thomas said.

Brighton closed his eyes, pulled the string back, and let the arrow go in the general direction of the lemon. It missed by an arms length.

'I told you,' Brighton said irritably.

'Patience, you will understand soon,' Thomas said.

Scanning the big tree next to the house, he spotted a dove.

He pointed to it and said, 'Shoot that dove with your eyes closed.'

Brighton looked at Carmen. She shrugged her shoulders.

Brighton nocked an arrow and closed his eyes. He took aim at where he thought the dove might be and let the arrow fly. The arrow passed through the dove's body and slammed into the tree stump beyond.

'How...' Brighton stammered. 'How can that be?' he finally managed.

'One more test, then I will tell you what I think,' Thomas said.

He looked in the tree and spotted another dove high up in the branches.

'Shoot that one,' he said pointing.

'Should I close my eyes again,' Brighton asked as he nocked an arrow.

'No need. Just try your best to hit it,' Thomas replied.

Brighton pulled the string to his cheek. As he let it go, Thomas screamed and clapped his hands loudly, scaring the bird.

The dove quickly abandoned its perch and launched itself into the air. Just before the arrow reached the spot where the dove was a moment before, it changed course and found its target mid-air.

Thomas danced around and shouted, 'I knew it. I knew it. I knew it!'

Both Carmen and Brighton were too shocked to speak.

'I knew you could do it!' Thomas shouted.

Brighton found his voice.

'How did that happen? How can an arrow change direction in the sky like that?' he asked, staggered at what he just saw.

'You made it change direction,' Thomas said confidently.

'I did what? That's ridiculous!' Brighton scoffed.

Thomas stopped dancing and poked a finger at Brighton's face.

'And I know how you did it,' he declared.

'This should be good,' Carmen quipped. 'Please, enlighten us.'

Thomas was too excited to sit down. Instead, he paced up and down the porch while talking.

'Brighton has the talent, this we are all agreed on,' he stated.

Carmen and Brighton nodded.

'I believe his talent is more than just taking energy. He can also manipulate it,' the old man said.

He looked at them to see if they understood.

Carmen said slowly, 'You've been in the sun too long. Your brain has melted.'

Brighton laughed and agreed with her.

'Think about it,' Thomas said without taking notice. 'How did Brighton make that arrow change course?'

Brighton stopped laughing and said, 'I'm not convinced that I did that. Perhaps a gust of wind blew it in the right direction.'

Ignoring the statement Thomas asked, 'Have you ever missed when shooting with your bow?'

'Well, no. But that's because I'm a good archer,' Brighton said proudly.

'Even when your prey is a small rabbit, two hundred paces away and running?' Thomas asked.

'Any good archer could do that,' Brighton said.

Carmen touched his arm.

'Brighton, I've seen many archers. Nobody can make the shots you do. Thomas has a point. Let's listen to him.'

To Thomas she said, 'Let's assume for a moment that you are correct about Brighton's ability. There is still one flaw. An arrow is made from dead wood. There is no energy in it.'

'Ahhhh, that's where you're wrong,' Thomas countered wagging his finger.

'How does an arrow fly?' he asked Brighton.

'The string pushes it away. The stronger the pushing force, the further it will fly,' Brighton answered.

'Yes! The string imparts energy onto the arrow. Although the arrow has no energy of its own, it receives enough from the string to fly towards the target. Brighton manipulates that temporary energy in the arrow to make small adjustments in its flight. That's why he never misses. He guides the energy of the arrow towards the energy he feels from his target. This is also why he could hit the first bird with his eyes closed. He does not need to see it, he feels it and guides the arrow towards it.'

Carmen was speechless. What Thomas said made

sense, she could not think of any valid argument against it.

Brighton, however, did argue.

'But I missed the lemon with my eyes closed.'

'True, but I can also explain that. When you pick a lemon off the tree, it's separated from its life force. It receives no more energy from the tree.'

Brighton finished the sentence, 'And that's why I can't sense it. It's essentially dead. In a few days it will rot and soon there will be nothing left of it.'

'Correct,' Thomas said with a wide smile.

Brighton picked up the bow and nocked an arrow.

'Let see if you're correct.'

He let the arrow fly into the field concentrating hard on trying to change its path. It flew straight.

He tried again. Again, the arrow flew straight.

He turned to Thomas.

'It seems your theory is wrong. I tried my best but could not manipulate the arrow at all.'

'What did you aim at?' Thomas asked.

'Nothing, I just shot into the field,' Brighton replied.

'And that's why you didn't make the arrow change course,' Thomas said.

Brighton nodded his head in understanding.

'I see. I wasn't trying to hit anything so there was no need to change the arrow's path.'

'Correct,' Thomas replied.

'But how come I didn't even know I was doing this,' Brighton asked.

'Instinct,' was all Thomas said.

'Like breathing,' Brighton said slowly. 'It just happens, you don't have to think about it.'

Carmen finally spoke.

'I still have doubts about this, but let's assume Brighton is in fact talented and his talent is somehow different from ours....'

Thomas interrupted, 'And much stronger.'

Carmen gave him a dark look and said, 'Don't interrupt, it's rude'.

She continued, 'So his talent is stronger than ours, why can't we sense him but he can sense us?'

Thomas answered quickly, 'It must be something to do with his birth.'

Both Carmen and Brighton started speaking but Thomas held up his hand.

'Think about it. When Brighton was born the very people who offered their help shunned him. Even Clarissa left him and only went back eight days later. This is his first impression of the world and its people. I think he instinctively hides his talent for fear of being shunned again. Clarissa raised him as her own. In time, I think, if she had the talent she would have been able to sense Brighton because there was a bond of love. He trusted her.'

Brighton's head snapped up.

'Lily,' he said.

Carmen nodded, 'Yes, it makes sense…'

Brighton wasn't listening to her. He jumped up and looked towards town.

'Lily is coming,' he said and ran for the road.

Thomas asked Carmen, 'What were you going to say?'

'Lilian can sense Brighton and now I understand why. He loves her very deeply. He would give his life to her if she asked. He does not hide from her who he is.'

'I see your point,' Thomas answered.

'That would mean Lilian knows he is talented,' he continued. 'This is not good.'

'Why not?' Carmen asked. 'He loves her, she loves him. She is a very sweet girl and exceptionally beautiful. What could be better for Brighton?'

Thomas looked at her as if she had lost her mind.

'She is Seth's daughter!' he said heatedly.

'So?' Carmen shrugged.

'Seth will use her to get close to Brighton. Brighton's

love for her makes him vulnerable,' Thomas said gesturing wildly with his arms.

'Lilian loves Brighton. She would never do anything to harm him. Besides, she hates Seth. There is no way she will help Seth get close to Brighton. She would give up her own life for Brighton, the same as he would for her,' Carmen stated.

'She will betray him,' Thomas said flatly. 'That's what women do.'

'Thomas!' Carmen snapped. 'Because of one incident almost seventy winters ago you distrust all women?' she asked angrily.

Thomas started to speak but Carmen noticed Brighton and Lilian coming down the road. They were walking close together, arms around each other.

Carmen wagged her finger in front of Thomas' nose.

'Not a word of this to either of them,' she said in a stern voice.

'But Brighton needs….' the old man tried.

'Thomas!' Carmen cut him off.

He kept quiet instantly. They waited in silence until the young couple reached the house. It seemed that nothing could wipe the smiles off those young faces.

'Lily, do you remember old Thomas from Four Mountains?' Brighton asked.

'Yes, I do,' she replied.

'Hello Thomas, hello Carmen,' she said politely.

Carmen echoed her greeting, Thomas stayed quiet.

'Lilian and her father had to travel to Farrendale, that's why she didn't come back here until now,' Brighton said happily.

'I'm so glad you came to visit again,' Carmen said to Lilian.

'Come, help me with lunch,' she added.

Addressing Thomas and Brighton, she said. 'Go see if there are any rabbits around. Bring at least six if you can.'

Brighton started saying he would rather stay with Lilian but an urgent tug on his arm from Thomas made him shut his mouth.

Instead, he asked, 'Don't we have enough food?'

'Yes we do,' Carmen answered. 'But have you seen the state of Thomas' clothes? I want you to go to town and trade the rabbits for new clothes for him later this afternoon. Now go, lunch will be ready when you get back.'

Brighton picked up the Yew bow and followed Thomas towards the woods.

Carmen gestured for Lilian to follow her into the house.

*****

Seth watched the two men disappear into the woods. He was hiding in the trees on the other side of the road. This was so much better than what he had hoped for. He'd been searching for six winters and finally he found the young man whose energy he can't feel, the young man who gave him this round black mark on his chest. Better still, the older man fits the description of the man he had been hunting for much, much longer.

He touched the scar on his face.

I'll repay you for this he thought.

His intention when he followed Lilian was simply to kill this boy she was so infatuated with but now he changed his mind. Seth was not prone to hasty action; time was never a factor for him.

Lilian told him about the boy that morning. At first, he was not interested. He had seen many girls swoon over handsome young men. When she told him that she believed the boy had the gift he reminded her about the law forbidding two gifted people from being together.

Lilian reminded him about Evangeline's bracelet. Seth

instantly understood what Lilian's plan was. She wanted to use the bracelet to drain both her and the boy's talent so that they could be together. He agreed simply to stop her nagging.

Slowly he made his way through the trees to a more comfortable spot. He knew they would come back this way so he didn't follow them. The man he hunted had the talent. If this was that man and he used his sense, he might realize Seth was close by. Patience was the answer for now.

Both these men would die soon enough.

Chapter 9

CARMEN LOOKED LILIAN in the eyes. They were in the kitchen preparing lunch.

'What are you doing here?' she asked.

'I came to see Bri,' Lilian responded.

'You're just as bad a liar as Brighton,' Carmen remarked. 'The truth please?'

'I want Brighton to go with me and Seth to Zedonia,' Lilian answered honestly.

Carmen had to take a moment to control her voice.

'Why?' she asked softly.

'We can be together there,' Lilian said unwilling to reveal her plan to the older woman.

'Why not here?' Carmen asked.

'It won't work here,' Lilian said, avoiding Carmen's eyes.

'You know he will go if you ask him,' Carmen said.

'I hope so,' Lilian answered.

'He will. What's the harm in telling me why it can only work in Zedonia? I love Brighton too. I only want the best for him.'

Lilian thought for a moment. Carmen was right, what would be the harm in telling her the plan?

'In the palace there is a bracelet that belonged to my grandmother, Evangeline. This bracelet can drain a gifted one's power. Both Brighton and I could use this and become normal people, that way we could be together,' Lilian explained.

'So you know Brighton has the talent?' she asked.

Lilian nodded.

'I felt his sense for the first time when we were at the river the other day. Can you feel it?'

'Yes,' Carmen lied.

'He seems to be using the sense constantly,' Lilian said, looking quizzically at Carmen.

Carmen had to think quickly. This business of lying and keeping secrets was starting to irritate her.

'He doesn't. Perhaps he just uses it when you're with him,' she lied again.

'Why would he do that?' Lilian asked, still confused.

'To make sure you're safe, I think. He can feel danger approaching and wants to keep you out of harm's way.'

'He didn't sense you coming,' Lilian remembered.

'Do I look dangerous to you?' Carmen asked with a smile.

'No,' Lilian laughed. 'You're a sweet old...I mean a sweet lady.'

'I'm old?' Carmen asked with mock surprise. 'Give me a mirror so I can see! When did this happen?'

Lilian played along and pulled a small round piece of highly polished steel out of her pocket.

'Here's a mirror, see for yourself. You're older than the mountains!' she giggled.

'Oh dear, that's bad. I suppose Brighton would never look at such an old woman when a beautiful young girl like you is around,' Carmen joked.

Lilian was laughing so hard now she had to sit down.

When she was able to speak again she said, 'What about Thomas? He's handsome.'

'Yes, he is but he is my brother. Don't worry, I've known love. I was married once,' Carmen said, sadness creeping into her voice.

She could see the question in Lilian's eyes.

'Matthew was killed when we were young,' Carmen explained, 'I never loved another in that way.'

Lilian's face turned serious.

'Do you think that a person can only ever love once?' she asked.

'Yes,' Carmen said without hesitation.

'Then you understand why I have to take Brighton to Zedonia? He is my one true love.'

'Do you know where this bracelet is?' Carmen asked.

'In the palace. Seth keeps it in his room,' Lilian answered.

'And you will just walk in and take it?'

'No, Seth agreed to let us use it,' Lilian explained.

Carmen spoke carefully, 'Seth is a bad man. Are you sure he will let you use the bracelet? You can't trust him.'

'I know he can't be trusted but this will suit him. I think he's getting tired of my refusal to steal energy and my constant nagging,' Lilian said confidently.

'Why doesn't he just let you go,' Carmen asked.

'I'm the daughter of a Supreme. It would be bad for them if I were allowed to roam free without them controlling me. My talent is very strong. If, however, I did not have the talent anymore they have nothing to worry about.'

'That makes sense. You're a clever young woman,' Carmen complimented her.

Brighton let out a loud whoop.

'That was the furthest yet!' he shouted.

'I understand why you never miss but how does that bow shoot so far?' Thomas mused.

Brighton ran over to the dead rabbit.

'That makes six!' he shouted as he picked it up.

He walked back to Thomas.

'Now we can get you new clothes,' he said.

Thomas didn't hear him. He was deep in thought.

'No bow can shoot that far. There is something else here that we're not seeing yet,' he muttered.

'What are you on about old man,' Brighton asked with a smile. 'We already know why I never miss.'

'Yes, we do, but how can that bow shoot so far?' Thomas asked.

'Strong wood,' Brighton offered.

'No, that's not it,' Thomas mumbled.

He looked at the river.

'Do you think you can hit a tree on the other side of the river?'

Brighton's mouth dropped open.

'That's too far. It's easily twice the distance of the furthest shot I've ever made.'

'Try,' was all Thomas said.

'Here we go again,' Brighton said under his breath as he nocked an arrow.

'Aim for something specific, don't just shoot.'

Brighton took aim at a tree on the far side of the river. He let the arrow fly. It dropped into the water only twenty paces short of the tree. Brighton looked at the bow and then at Thomas.

'How....' he stammered.

'It's not the bow. It's you,' Thomas supplied.

'Yes, we know I can make the arrow change course but it still only has the energy from the string that pushed it. There is a limit to that energy.'

'You're right, but the arrow is also getting energy

from somewhere else. You,' Thomas said.

Brighton frowned.

'You are adding some of your own energy to the arrow, that's how it can go that far,' Thomas said excitedly.

Brighton thought about it for a moment.

'I understand what you're suggesting but if that were true how come the arrow did not reach the tree,' he said pointing across the river.

'You already have the answer to that,' Thomas said cryptically.

Brighton starred across the river.

Slowly he said, 'There is a limit.'

'Yes!' Thomas shouted excitedly, 'There is a limit to the amount of energy you can put onto the arrow.'

Brighton looked across the river again.

'I guess we've established the limit of my skills with a bow,' he said.

He picked up all the rabbits.

'I'm hungry, let's go see what's for lunch,' he said to Thomas.

They started walking back to the house.

'Do you remember when you broke my shoulder,' Thomas asked.

'Yes,' Brighton said uncomfortably.

'I've often wondered how it healed that fast. I know the bones were completely crushed but the next morning there was only a dull pain left.'

Thomas saw the guilty look on Brighton's face.

'Don't worry, I'm not trying to make you feel bad. I'm just wondering about something else,' he said quickly.

'It never stops with you, does it?' Brighton sighed.

Ignoring the comment Thomas went on, 'I did not steal energy from anyone to heal my shoulder. What if you gave me some of yours? Your talent seems to work purely on instinct. You hurt me and wanted to fix it.'

Brighton just nodded. He was tired of all this talk

about his talent and what he could do. Thomas also had a valid point so he decided not to argue.

Thomas went on, 'This is probably why your vegetables and goats do so well. You're helping them with your energy. There is an abundance available to you, just look at all the trees, plants and animals around. I think you…'

Brighton turned to the old man and softly said, 'Thomas, please. Let's stop talking about this for a while.'

Thomas was about to tell Brighton that his talent did not work for almost two days afterwards. He looked at the pleading expression on the young man's face and decided it could wait for some other time.

Instead, he asked, 'So what clothes do you think I should get?'

'Best we ask Carmen first,' Brighton replied. 'If we get the wrong things she will chase us back to town with that walking stick of yours.'

'Yes, you're right,' Thomas laughed.

*****

When Thomas and Brighton got back to the house, lunch was ready.

'Let's eat on the porch, it's such a lovely day,' Carmen suggested.

Brighton and Lilian sat close together, whispering and giggling.

As soon as lunch was finished, Carmen said to Thomas, 'Come, let's go fetch water to do the dishes.'

For once, Thomas didn't argue, he realized that the young people would like some privacy.

Carmen gave Thomas the bucket to carry and they set off for the river.

As soon as they were out of earshot Carmen said, 'Brighton is leaving.'

'How do you know?' Thomas asked.

'Lilian will ask him and he will say yes,' Carmen said matter-of-factly.

'Why?' Thomas asked, a bit confused.

'Seth has a bracelet that can extract the talent from someone. Brighton and Lilian both want to use it so that they can be together,' Carmen answered.

Trying hard to stay calm Thomas said, 'Will you stop him?'

'No. why should I?' she replied.

'Then I will!' Thomas said heatedly.

'Yes, I know you will try. Good luck with that,' Carmen said calmly.

'How can you be so calm about this?' Thomas shouted.

'Brighton has his own life, it's not ours to control. We've done enough of that already,' Carmen replied, still staying calm.

'First we need to understand his talent!' Thomas said, not willing to let it go.

He continued heatedly, 'I think Brighton can take and give energy as well as manipulate it. This has to be explored!'

'No, Brighton has to explore and understand his talent, that's not for us to do. We've helped him enough. It's time he goes on his own path. If he chooses to give up the talent there is nothing we can do about it,' Carmen said slowly.

She had to concentrate to keep calm. All she wanted to do was run back and try to stop Brighton from going. She knew he would go, he would never miss an opportunity to be with Lilian. It broke her heart but she knew he had to make his own choices.

When she was sure she could control her voice she said, 'Please don't turn this into another argument. Brighton will go, no matter what we do. Do you really want to send him off with anger in his heart?'

Thomas was beside himself, 'He is a boy! He does not know what's best for him.'

He waved his walking stick around aggressively.

'I'll use this if I have to but Brighton is staying,' he declared angrily.

Despite her sadness, Carmen smiled.

'I would give up my best dress to see you try that,' she said.

'I'll…he won't…uh…' Thomas stuttered.

He took a deep breath.

'Yes, perhaps using the stick on Brighton is not my best idea ever,' he said more calmly.

'That's a shame, it probably would have been the funniest thing ever to see you try. Seriously though, Brighton will break more than your shoulder if you were really that stupid. He will leave and we will never be quite ready. We will make excuses to try and keep him here just a little while longer. That is not fair on him,' Carmen said gently.

*****

Lilian sat down on Brighton's lap.

'I'm sorry it took so long for me to come back. You must have thought I disappeared again,' she said looking into his eyes.

'No, I knew you would come,' he lied.

'Carmen is right, you're a bad liar!' Lilian giggled.

'I should keep the two of you apart,' he said teasingly.

'We had a really good talk about you. I know all your secrets and bad habits now,' she teased.

'Well, it can't be that bad. You're sitting on my lap right now. If my logic is correct that means you still like me a little,' he teased back.

Lilian's face got serious as she said, 'No, I love you!'

He pulled her closer. Their lips met tenderly. Lilian's arm snaked around his neck. She pressed her lips more firmly onto his, parting them slightly.

He responded. Her heart was racing, she could feel his did the same. Finally, when they both needed to breathe, the kiss ended. They sat in silence for a while just enjoying being close to each other.

'Bri, can I ask you something?' Lilian broke the silence.

'Anything,' he said.

'If I wanted you to come to Zedonia with me, what would you say?'

Brighton thought for a moment.

'I would go but why can't we stay here?' he replied.

'You know it's the law that two gifted people can't be together?' she asked.

Without waiting for an answer she went on, 'That's a problem for us.'

'Why?' Brighton asked.

'Isn't it obvious?' Lilian asked, a little confused.

'No, not to me. That law does not apply to us,' Brighton replied.

I have the talent and you have the talent. It applies,' Lilian countered.

'No I don't,' Brighton said.

'Bri, I can feel it when you use your sense, like right now. You have the talent,' Lilian said.

Brighton stiffened.

'You can feel it?' he asked carefully.

'Yes, all Dark Ones can feel each other's sense when they use it. Didn't you know that?' she asked.

'No, I didn't,' he lied.

'Besides, I only have the sense, nothing else,' he lied again.

This time Lilian did not see the deception.

'So you see; the law does not apply,' Brighton concluded.

Lilian decided to try a different approach.

'What if we could both get rid of this talent then we

wouldn't have to worry about the law. We could be together without worrying that we were breaking some obscure and ancient law?'

'Now that's an interesting concept,' Brighton said. 'It would certainly be better than trying to argue with the Dark Ones that we're not breaking their stupid laws.'

'Then let's do it!' Lilian said excitedly.

'How?' Brighton asked. 'You can't just walk into town and trade your talent for a dress and some shoes.'

Lilian was getting more and more excited.

'I know a way,' she said breathlessly, 'My father has a bracelet that can remove the talent from us.'

'Markus? Back in Four Mountains?' Brighton asked.

'No, my real father,' Lilian said carefully.

'Markus is not your father? Then who is?' Brighton asked with a frown.

'Do you remember the man that attacked us in Four Mountains?' she asked.

'Yes. Thomas thought it might have been Seth, the Supreme,' Brighton recalled.

'It was,' she said softly.

Brighton waited for her to continue but she just sat watching his face.

Suddenly his body went rigid and his eyes wide.

'No!' he shouted.

Lilian jumped off his lap and stood back very quickly. She wrung her hands together.

Brighton got up. He towered over Lilian.

'No. Tell me Seth is not your father,' he pleaded.

Lilian stared at him. Her big blue eyes were filling with tears.

'Bri, please…' she tried.

'That monster took you away from me!' Brighton shouted, 'If I ever see him again I will rip him to pieces!'

'I hate him too, but he can make it possible for us to be together without fear,' Lilian said softly.

Brighton was so angry he almost didn't hear Lilian.

He was pacing up and down the porch.

'I'm going to rip his…'

He stopped.

'What did you say?' he frowned.

'Seth can help us,' Lilian repeated.

Brighton's frown deepened as he asked, 'He has this…this…this thing?'

'Bracelet,' Lilian helped him.

'Yes, that!' Brighton said a bit more harshly than he wanted.

He saw the fear on Lilian's face. Tears were streaming down her cheeks. Brighton stepped closer and gently put his arms around her. She felt so small in his big arms.

'I'm sorry,' he said, pressing his lips into her blond hair.

He hugged her tight and whispered, 'I didn't mean to scare you. None of this is your fault.'

They stood like that for a long time.

*****

Carmen and Thomas approached the house.

'Behave,' she whispered urgently to him.

He grunted something that vaguely resembled agreement. Brighton and Lilian were standing on the porch, hugging. Carmen feigned a cough to let them know they were back. Reluctantly the young people separated. Carmen noticed Lilian's eyes were red. She couldn't help but wonder what had transpired while she and Thomas were away.

Ever diplomatic, she didn't ask. If the young couple wanted them to know, they would tell them. With relief she saw that Thomas hadn't noticed. She knew he would simply demand to know what happened.

'Anyone for some lemon juice?' she offered.

Everybody accepted. Lilian mostly because she didn't want to be rude. She still could not understand how anybody could drink it undiluted. Carmen disappeared into the house to fetch the juice.

Thomas sat down quietly. He knew if he started talking, he would try to persuade Brighton not to go with Lilian. That would bring Carmen's wrath down on him. Deep down he also knew that she was right, Brighton had to make his own decisions. Thomas just wished they had a little bit more time to explore what Brighton could do with his talent.

Carmen reappeared with a makeshift tray.

'Brighton, take the tray,' she instructed.

Brighton jumped up and did instructed.

'Now hold it for the ladies first,' she said.

She was expecting some sarcastic remark or light-hearted comment but Brighton simply did as she told him. He waited for Carmen to sit and held the tray for her. She took a cup and thanked him. Next, he went to Lilian.

'The one to your left my dear,' Carmen said to Lilian.

Lilian took the indicated cup and sipped. It was lemon juice but heavily diluted.

'Thank you,' she mouthed to Carmen.

The old woman smiled at her.

Thomas took his cup off the tray, still determined to remain silent.

Brighton put the tray down and took the last cup. He sat down next to Lilian.

'I'm going to Zedonia with Lily,' he said flatly.

Typical Brighton, Carmen thought.

No time for small talk, just come out and say what's on your mind. A lot like Thomas.

She smiled to herself. She looked at Lilian and for a moment thought the young woman looked surprised.

'When are you leaving?' Carmen asked calmly.

Brighton was taken aback momentarily. He expected

an argument from Carmen. He looked at Thomas. Surely the old man would argue.

Thomas remained stone faced.

'Um…tomorrow,' Brighton said.

He actually didn't know what Lilian's plans were but was not about to admit that.

He didn't want Thomas and Carmen to know that the discussion between him and Lilian never finished.

'Good, that gives me time to bake fresh bread for the road,' Carmen said.

'Brighton…' Thomas started.

Carmen's eyes snapped to him.

Please don't start a fight she silently begged.

Thomas looked at Carmen sideways and back at Brighton.

'Good luck on your travels. Perhaps you can visit sometime. Lilian, look after him, sometimes he is still just a big baby,' the old man said softly.

Brighton was speechless. He had tons of arguments ready but neither of the old people even wanted to discuss his decision. They seemed to support it fully.

Makes it easier for me he thought.

'Actually, we have to check with Lily's father. I don't really know when we're leaving,' Brighton admitted.

Lilian found her voice.

'I will go later and ask my father.'

'I'll go with you,' Brighton said. 'In fact, why, don't we go now?'

Carmen softly said, 'Finish your juice first.'

Brighton drained the cup in one gulp.

'There, it's empty,' he said holding the cup for Carmen to see.

Lilian was less enthusiastic about going immediately. She was very nervous about Brighton meeting her father.

Brighton sat watching her impatiently, wondering why she sipped so slowly. He felt the presence of someone on the road but didn't take notice, lots of people passed by on their way to the river.

Lilian looked up and her body went rigid. Fear was clearly visible in her blue eyes. Seth was approaching the house. Thomas also noticed but his eyes did not show fear. His whole face was a mask of intense hate.

'Good afternoon,' Seth said pleasantly as he reached the house.

Everybody got up.

'And a good afternoon to you, sir,' Carmen said politely. 'Would you like to join us for some lemon juice?'

'It is very kind of you. Yes, thank you, I will,' Seth replied with a smile.

Turning to Lilian, he said, 'A kiss for your father?'

Lilian did not move, she felt like her feet were stuck to the ground.

Brighton's eyes went wide. This was the man who kidnapped Lilian six winters ago. The urge to rip his head clean off his shoulders was almost too much for Brighton.

He struggled to keep his composure as he said, 'Good afternoon sir, I'm Brighton.'

'Ah, yes, I'm assuming you're the young man who stole my daughter's heart. I'm very pleased to meet you. I'm Seth.'

Carmen spoke up, 'I'm Carmen and this is Thomas,' she said gesturing to her brother.

'I'm pleased to meet you both,' Seth said politely.

Thomas was gripping his walking stick so tight his knuckles went white.

Carmen noticed and quickly said, 'Please excuse Thomas, he doesn't meet strange people very often. He lives in the woods.'

'No offense taken,' Seth replied pleasantly.

Brighton stepped aside and offered Seth his chair.

That brought an approving nod from Carmen.

She said to Lilian, 'My dear, please pour your father some juice.'

'Water will be perfect,' Seth said quickly.

Just for an instant Thomas thought he felt Seth using his sense. It was so fleeting that he was uncertain but the way Brighton looked at Seth confirmed his suspicion.

Now he knows what my energy feels like. No doubt he will kill me at the first opportunity.

Worse, he probably realized that he couldn't sense Brighton.

Seth turned to Brighton.

'So, young man, has Lilian asked you to accompany us to Zedonia?'

Still keeping his composure Brighton nodded and said, 'We were just on our way to discuss the travel arrangements with you when you arrived, sir.'

Seth smiled and said, 'Carmen taught you well but please, call me Seth.'

Lilian handed Seth a cup of water.

'Thank you,' he said to her. 'What do you think, Lilian? Should we leave tomorrow morning?'

Lilian stood rooted. She didn't know what to answer. Seth had never asked her opinion on anything.

Carmen spoke instead, 'Perhaps that's a good idea. I will have time to bake some bread for the trip.'

'Thank you Carmen, that would be wonderful,' Seth said with a smile, 'Brighton, Lilian, are you in agreement with this?'

Both nodded their heads. Lilian had never seen Seth this friendly or talkative. She wondered if he found the man he was looking for. Maybe it's just that he would be rid of her finally. Whatever the reason, she was happy that he wasn't his moody, brooding self.

Seth drained the cup and handed it back to Lilian.

'I'd better be off then. I'm glad we sorted out our arrangements,' he said.

As he stepped off the porch Lilian followed but he

stopped and turned back.

'Why don't you stay here tonight?' he said to Lilian.

Turning to Carmen, he added, 'If the lady of the house approves, of course.'

'It would be our pleasure,' Carmen replied.

Seth looked at Lilian for an answer.

'Um...yes...yes, thank you, father,' she stammered.

'Meet me on the road to Zedonia where that big tree has fallen over. Do you know the place?' he said.

'I remember,' Lilian answered quickly.

'Be there at sunrise,' Seth said as he turned and walked away.

Chapter 10

―⁂―

NOBODY SPOKE UNTIL Seth was almost out of sight.

Brighton found his voice first.

'That was slightly awkward,' he said.

'Slightly awkward?' Lilian echoed. 'No, that was downright strange!'

Carmen asked, 'Why do you say that?'

'I've been with Seth for six winters now. I've never seen him that friendly to anyone, not even the other Supremes!' Lilian said.

'Perhaps he was just being polite,' Carmen suggested.

'Seth? Polite?' Lilian exclaimed with surprise, 'No, Seth is never polite. Rude, obnoxious, arrogant, demanding, but never polite. That was very, very strange. I wonder if he finally found the man he's been looking for all this time.'

Thomas spoke softly, 'He has.'

Brighton looked at him quizzically and asked, 'What do you mean?'

Thomas just sat staring into the blue sky.

'Thomas is the one Seth has been hunting,' Carmen explained softly.

Brighton and Lilian were both speechless.

'It's been over sixty winters that Thomas has been able to evade Seth.' Carmen said softly, paused and then added, 'I started believing Thomas could stay hidden forever.'

Brighton found his voice.

'Why is he after you?' he asked breathlessly.

'Did you see the scar on his face? Thomas gave that to him,' Carmen answered.

Hundreds of questions ran through Brighton's mind but before he could speak, Carmen said softly to Thomas, 'You should tell them.'

Thomas didn't speak; he just sat still, staring into the sky.

Brighton opened his mouth but a quick shake of the head from Carmen made him decide to stay quiet and wait for Thomas.

Eventually Thomas looked at the young people.

'Do you remember the story I told you about the uprising in Zedonia?' he asked Brighton.

'Yes,' Brighton answered.

Turning to Lilian he asked, 'Do you know about it?'

'Everyone in Zedonia knows about it,' she replied.

'How much do you know?' Thomas asked.

'Only that there was talk of a rebellion against the Supremes. Seth squashed it and it's never happened again,' Lilian answered.

Thomas nodded.

'Yes, few people know what really happened that day.'

'So the story you told me was a lie,' Brighton asked.

'No, all of it is true but I left out certain parts,' Thomas replied.

He thought for a moment and then continued.

'The leader of the rebels was a Dark One called Andreas. This is the real reason seven of the eight Supremes made an appearance that day. They could not allow one of their own to rebel against them. It was as much a display of power for the people as it was for other Dark Ones. The Supremes made sure that no talented person would ever doubt the superiority of the Supremes again.'

Brighton asked, 'This Andreas, he was the one Seth killed?'

'Yes,' came the reply.

'Did you know him?' Brighton asked.

Thomas whispered, 'He was our brother.'

'And that's why you hate Seth,' Brighton surmised and then asked, 'But why does he hunt you? Did you have something to do with the rebellion?'

It was Carmen that answered, 'No, but Matthew did.'

'Matthew? Your late husband?' Brighton frowned.

'Yes,' Carmen answered.

'Was he the second man Seth killed?' Brighton pressed.

'Tried to kill,' Thomas corrected.

Lilian frowned.

'Tried to kill? Seth doesn't try to kill someone. He does or he doesn't, it's that simple for him,' she said.

Thomas explained, 'After Seth instantly killed Andreas he must have decided to take his time with Matthew. Perhaps as a display of power, I don't really know why. Carmen and I were in the crowd watching. When I saw Andreas drop dead and the energy link slam into Matthew's head I couldn't help myself. I picked up a rock and flung it at Seth. It was purely a reaction on my part so I didn't even aim properly but the rock struck Seth on the side of his face. It had a sharp edge that cut him deeply. That's the scar you see today.'

'Didn't he see you?' Brighton asked, very surprised at what he was hearing.

'No, I disappeared into the crowd immediately. Only two people saw who it was that threw the rock,' Thomas answered.

Brighton waited for Thomas to say who saw him but he just remained silent. Carmen saw the question in Brighton's eyes.

'I was the one person. Louisa was the other,' she supplied.

'Don't mention that witch's name in front of me,' Thomas snarled.

Brighton and Lilian were both taken aback by the hatred in Thomas' voice. Neither of them wanted to ask who Louisa was.

Carmen answered the unspoken question.

'Thomas and Louisa fell in love and got married about five winters before the rebellion. They had a beautiful little girl. Thomas loved them both very much.'

'I loved Mandy very much, not that witch that was her mother,' Thomas whispered, remembering his daughter.

Lilian asked softly, 'Loved? What happened to her?'

Again, it was Carmen that answered.

'Only Louisa and I knew who threw the rock. The Supremes immediately put a reward out on Thomas' head. Anyone that could point him out would receive the gift. It was like a free pass into the royal family and immortality. Louisa went to the Supremes the next day and gave them a description of Thomas. She betrayed him.'

Lilian frowned. 'As far as I know you have to be born with the talent, it can't be given to you.'

'Correct,' Thomas answered. 'The Supremes lied.'

'What happened to Louisa?' Brighton asked.

'She got what she deserved! The Supremes killed her,'

Thomas spat.

Almost choking he added, 'Mandy was with her.'

Lilian put her hand over her mouth, tears welling up in her eyes.

Brighton looked confused.

Softly Carmen said to him, 'The Supremes killed her too.'

Thomas was openly crying now. It was so long ago but every time he thought about it, he still cried for his little girl.

Lilian went to him and tenderly put her arms around him.

'I'm so sorry Thomas,' she whispered.

Thomas tried to smile at her through his tears.

Brighton whispered to Carmen, 'What happened to Matthew?'

Carmen shook her head but Thomas heard the question and answered.

'I killed him,' he said flatly.

Brighton and Lilian were shocked.

Lilian, still hugging Thomas said, 'You must have had a reason?'

'Seth had taken a lot of Matthew's energy by the time the rock hit him,' Thomas said.

He took a deep breath and added, 'He was in excruciating pain. We tried to help him but by that evening, I knew he would die. I decided to end his suffering.'

'We decided,' Carmen corrected.

When Thomas did not react she continued.

'We made that decision together but I wasn't strong enough to do it. You did both Matthew and me a great service that day,' she said tenderly.

Brighton slowly said, 'So Seth has been hunting you all these winters with only a description of you. He has never seen you or felt your energy. He basically does not know who you are. Why do you think he recognized you today?'

'That witch gave a very detailed description of me. My hair did not go this white because I'm aging; it's always been this way,' Thomas answered.

'I see,' Brighton said slowly. 'Seth knows exactly what you look like so he would have recognized you anywhere.'

'He used his sense for just a moment so now he knows what your energy feels like. He could basically kill you at any time he wishes,' Brighton continued.

'How far do you think his sense can reach?' he asked.

Lilian, releasing Thomas from the hug, answered, 'From here halfway to Farrendale, maybe a bit further. But he won't use the link. He is sadistic, he likes the feeling of skin on skin.'

'That is a day's walk! How come his talent can reach that far?' Brighton asked, astonished.

Thomas answered, 'He has had a long time to hone his skills.'

Brighton had another thought.

'Maybe he's just decided to let it go,' he offered hopefully.

This time Lilian answered, 'No, not Seth. He never forgets or forgives.'

Brighton thought for a moment.

'So the only answer is for you to get as far away as possible. Maybe you can go back to Four Mountains.'

Thomas nodded.

'Seth will be busy for a while now. Zedonia is two weeks travel from here. That means it will be at least four weeks before he could get back here,' Lilian worked out.

'If you start tomorrow you can be in Four Mountains long before Seth returns,' she concluded.

Carmen got up.

'Well, that means I'll have to bake two breads, one for Thomas and one for you two,' she said gesturing towards the young people.

'You have to leave too. Go with Thomas,' Lilian said quickly.

'I'm too old...' Carmen argued but got interrupted.

'Seth will torture you to find out where Thomas went,' Lilian said. 'I've seen it. You have to go.'

'But my house...' she tried again.

'...was never yours,' Thomas finished. 'This is one argument you won't win. I'll throw you over my shoulder and carry you if need be,' he said sternly.

Carmen opened her mouth but Thomas did not give a her a chance to talk.

'You will be safer with me, I have this,' he added waving his walking stick in the air.

Lilian was confused.

'What can that walking stick do to a Dark One?' she asked.

'That's the attitude I'd like to see in all Dark Ones,' Thomas said, smiling and added, 'I learnt one thing from throwing that rock at Seth. Dark Ones, even Supremes, are humans first and foremost.'

Lilian still looked confused.

Carmen saw and said, 'Nothing a stiff knock against the head can't fix,' imitating Thomas.

Lilian giggled behind her hand, not at what Carmen said but rather the way she said it.

'I understand,' she said. 'You knock them unconscious with your stick before they can touch you. That tactic might just work with Seth.'

Thomas didn't correct her.

There had been enough talk about death already.

*****

Carmen spent the afternoon teaching Lilian how to bake bread and biscuits.

'Carmen, could I ask you something?' Lilian said

carefully.

'Anything my dear,' Carmen replied without looking up.

She was busy mixing the ingredients for the bread.

'Something strange happened the last time I was here. When Brighton and I were down by the river, we swam. Afterwards I lay on a rock to get dry and warm. I suddenly started feeling warmer and then it was like Bri's thoughts came into my head.'

Carmen's hands went still.

'How do you know it was his thoughts?' she asked.

Lilian shifted uncomfortably. These were private moments between her and Brighton.

'Well, I got an image in my head of Bri's hand...um...on me,' she said.

Carmen looked at Lilian, alarm rising in her mind.

'Did you use the energy link on him?' she asked sternly.

'No! I would never do that!' Lilian replied quickly. 'I know that thoughts can travel with the energy through the link but this was different. These thoughts were...sort of...pushed into my mind.'

'And you're sure this image in your head was not your own?' Carmen asked, her hands busy again. 'I remember being in love. Your mind can play tricks on you.'

Lilian replied confidently, 'I'm sure it wasn't my thoughts. The peculiar thing is that I did not feel Bri's sense before then. As soon as I became aware of it, the image came into my head. It was like he suddenly opened up to me.'

Carmen remained silent for a while. She remembered what Thomas said earlier about Brighton taking and giving energy. If that theory was true then perhaps Brighton saw that Lilian was cold and gave her some energy to warm up.

Of course, Brighton would not have realized he was

doing it, his instinct would have taken over to help the woman he loves. It could explain why his thoughts ended up in her head. He probably established an energy link without either of them knowing.

'Carmen? Any ideas?' Lilian said softly.

'No, I don't know,' she lied.

*****

The men sat on the porch. Brighton was making new arrows and Thomas was carving another walking stick. Thomas knew Brighton didn't want to talk anymore about his talent. He was going to give it up anyway to be with Lilian. This disturbed Thomas.

Brighton's talent was unique. Thomas believed there was much more to be learnt about it. The old man needed to tell Brighton about his own talent disappearing temporarily after Brighton healed his shoulder.

It was the younger man that spoke first.

'Don't get scared, just stay calm,' he said without looking up.

Thomas looked at Brighton, very confused.

'What are you talking about?' he asked.

'Just stay calm,' Brighton repeated.

Out of the corner of his eye, Thomas saw some movement just off the porch. It was the biggest black panther he had ever seen, walking straight for the porch. Thomas immediately brought the half-finished walking stick up with one hand, knife in the other.

'Thomas! Stay calm,' Brighton repeated.

The big panther walked past Thomas seemingly without noticing him.

'Hello Mischief,' Brighton said to the cat.

He put the arrows on the floor next to him. Mischief reached him and put his big black head in Brighton's lap. Brighton scratched Mischief behind the ears bringing soft purrs from deep within the cat's belly. Brighton ran his hand over Mischief's back and sides, checking for injury.

As usual, there was none. Mischief lay down almost on top of Brighton's feet. Moments later he was asleep.

Thomas' fear had turned into amazement.

'You're friends with a black panther?' he whispered to Brighton, fearful of waking the cat up.

'Yes. You don't have to whisper, Mischief will sleep through a thunderstorm,' he smiled.

'Mischief,' Thomas repeated the name.

His eyes went wide in recognition.

'This is the panther you helped when she was giving birth!' he exclaimed.

'No, that's Velvet. This one is her son,' Brighton corrected.

With a smile he added, 'I don't think Mischief would appreciate you calling him a girl.'

'So, this is the one with the white eyes,' Thomas said, remembering the conversation they had all those winters ago.

'Yes. If he were not sleeping, I'd show you. Nothing can wake him up so we'll have to wait,' Brighton said.

'Carmen!' he called. 'Mischief is here.'

Lilian came running out the door but stopped dead in her tracks when she saw the cat. Her eyes went wide.

'Carmen said he was big but this is ridiculous!' she said breathlessly.

'Come closer, he won't do anything,' Brighton said.

Lilian shook her head.

'He's sleeping anyway,' Brighton said. 'I promise it will be fine.'

Lilian slowly stepped closer and put her hand on his side. Mischief's eyes snapped open, a menacing growl escaped his throat. Lilian shrieked and jumped back. Mischief got up and faced her, softly growling, teeth bared.

'I thought you said nothing can wake him,' Thomas quipped.

Brighton shot the old man a concerned look and then turned his attention back to Mischief.

'Don't you remember Lilian?' Brighton asked the cat. 'You slept in her lap when you were only one day old.'

Incredibly, the cat seemed to understand. He stopped growling.

'Come scratch his ears,' Brighton said to her.

Lilian stood frozen with her back against the wall.

Brighton spoke to the big cat.

'Go say hello but be gentle, she is afraid of you,' he instructed.

Again, he seemed to understand Brighton. Slowly, with his white eyes cast downward, he approached Lilian. Gently he nudged her hand with his wet nose. When she didn't respond, he pushed his head under her hand, softly purring.

'He wants a scratch. It's his way of telling you he won't do you any harm,' Brighton explained.

Still Lilian stood frozen. Carmen came out and held two pieces of dried meat towards Lilian.

'Feed him this. He will be your friend for life!' she said.

Slowly Lilian took the meat from Carmen and held one out for Mischief. He gently took it from her in those powerful jaws. Flopping down at her feet, he started chewing.

Carefully Lilian stepped around him and stood behind Brighton, her hand on his shoulder. Brighton was working on the arrows again.

'Thomas, please pass the knife,' he asked.

Thomas held out the knife towards Brighton. Mischief moved like lightning. In a flash, his big powerful jaws closed around Thomas' forearm.

Brighton swatted him on the nose.

'Relax boy, I asked Thomas for the knife,' he scolded.

Mischief let go of Thomas' arm and stepped back. Facing Thomas, he held his head low and shuffled closer. It was almost as if the cat was trying to apologize to Thomas.

Thomas looked at his arm.

Not a scratch.

'Incredible!' he gasped. 'Mischief thought I was threatening you. He wants to protect you. I've never seen anything move that fast!'

Brighton took the knife.

Mischief was still standing next to Thomas, head low.

'He's apologizing,' Brighton said.

Thomas looked at the cat and formally said, 'I accept.'

'He can't understand you. Scratch his ears or tummy,' Brighton laughed.

Thomas gave Mischief a quick scratch behind the ears. The cat lifted his head and looked at Thomas briefly with those white eyes before returning to the treat Lilian had given him.

Without taking his eyes off the cat, Thomas said to Brighton, 'He seems to understand you.'

Carmen spoke from the door. 'He does understand when Brighton speaks. There is a bond between them.'

Brighton ignored the comments and said worriedly, 'I wonder where Velvet is?'

He answered his own question, 'Probably hunting somewhere. If she was hurt she would have come to me.'

Lilian, still standing behind him, said, 'Mischief doesn't look hurt. Why is he here?'

Brighton cocked his head back to look at her.

'They don't only come here when they are hurt. Sometimes they come just to visit,' he explained.

'I think it's for those tasty treats,' Carmen quipped.

Mischief ears perked up. The first piece of dried meat was finished. He got up and approached Lilian. She held out the other piece of meat to him. He took the meat and rubbed his head against Lilian's leg.

'That means thank you,' Carmen said.

Thomas laughed.

'Carmen will teach everybody manners, even the animals,' he teased her.

Brighton got an idea.

'Mischief, come here boy,' he said.

Mischief immediately dropped the meat and came to stand in front of Brighton.

Brighton held the cat's head in his hands.

'Thomas and Carmen will be travelling to Four Mountains tomorrow. I want you to go with and protect them,' he said to Mischief.

He turned to Carmen.

'Pack lots of those meat treats; it will get Mischief to follow you,' he said with a smile.

Brighton let Mischief's head go. The big cat returned to chewing on the piece of meat Lilian gave him.

Lilian stroked Brighton's neck.

'Do you really think he can understand you?' she asked.

'I don't know but sometimes it looks like it,' Brighton replied.

A thought popped into his head.

'Lily, do me a favour. See if you can sense Mischief,' he asked.

Lilian concentrated for a moment.

Slowly she said, 'No, I can't. I wonder why?'

'Carmen and Thomas can't either. I don't know why,' Brighton replied.

Thomas stared at Mischief for a moment and then turned his gaze toward Lilian.

'I can offer a theory. Brighton said nothing can wake Mischief but he reacted to your touch, Lilian. He felt your dark abilities. I think he has some form of sense or gift similar to Brighton's,' he stated.

'That seems a bit far fetch,' Brighton smiled.

'Not at all. There is more evidence to support my theory. I looked into his eyes and have no doubt he is completely blind,' Thomas argued.

'Blind? That's not poss...uh...well...if he...' Brighton frowned.

'...possesses a supernatural sense he does not need eyes,' Thomas finished.

'I've never thought of that,' Brighton mused.

*****

The evening was spent preparing for the upcoming travel.

Carmen added straps to all the knapsacks so they could be carried on the shoulder or back. Lilian baked more bread and biscuits while Brighton finished the arrows. He now had a full quiver again and Thomas finished his new walking stick.

When it was time to go to bed Brighton insisted that the older people take the beds. He and Lilian had already decided that they would sleep out on the porch since it was a very warm evening.

'No real privacy there,' Thomas teased making both young people blush.

*****

Lilian's head was on Brighton's bare chest. She slept cradled in his strong arms all night. Slowly she woke up.

The sun was just rising. It took only a moment for her to realize where she was. She kept very still, so as not to wake Brighton.

His chest rose and fell slowly. A thin blanket half covered them. Lilian was thankful for this as she was sleeping only in her underwear. Things may have been a bit awkward if Thomas or Carmen came out and saw her sleeping half-naked with Brighton. She carefully adjusted the blanket so that it covered her bare shoulders.

'Are you awake?' Brighton asked sleepily.

'Only just,' she replied softly.

'Perhaps we should get dressed quickly,' he said.

Lilian got up and reached for her clothes. Brighton could still not believe how beautiful she was.

Her long blond curls falling over her back made his heart race.

She looked over her shoulder at him and smiled.

'You're staring at me again,' she said in a husky voice.

He didn't look away.

'You're gorgeous,' he said softly.

Lilian smiled at him as she got dressed.

Brighton also got up and reached for his shirt.

Before he could put it on Lilian stepped closer, her arms snaking around him.

She put her head against his bare chest.

'I wished we could have been alone last night,' she breathed.

Brighton's heart was racing.

'Me too,' he stuttered.

'Oh really? And what would you have done if we were alone?' Lilian asked innocently.

'I...uh...nothing....I mean....' he stammered.

Desperate to change the subject he looked around the porch and said, 'Have you seen Mischief?'

Lilian looked around as well and said, 'No. Can't you sense him?'

Brighton shook his head.

'When I'm with you I can't sense anybody or anything around me. Let's go see if Carmen made some breakfast,' he suggested, pulling his shirt on.

They walked into an empty kitchen.

Breakfast was laid out on the table and the travel food all neatly wrapped up next to it.

'Carmen!' Brighton called.

He checked both rooms.

'Nobody,' he said to Lilian.

'Looks like they're gone,' she said. 'How far can your sense go?'

'As far as the river. I don't feel them. How about yours?' Brighton answered.

'To the other side of town, but I don't feel them either,' Lilian answered.

'That far?' Brighton said, astonished. 'It's ten times further than mine'.

'I'm the daughter of a Supreme. My talent is strong,' she said trying to sound like a princess.

Remembering Seth, she suddenly went stiff.

'Oh no! The travel! We're supposed to meet Seth at sunrise,' she said, panic rising.

They grabbed the food and stuffed it into the two rucksacks.

Brighton grabbed his bow and quiver.

'I would have liked to say goodbye,' he said as they rushed out the door.

'We'd better hurry, Seth is not a patient man,' Lilian urged him along.

Chapter 11

WHEN THEY REACHED the meeting place, Seth was already waiting. Lilian nervously started apologizing.

Seth waved it off casually.

'I just got here,' he said.

Lilian, a little surprised, breathed a sigh of relief.

'Shall we get going?' Seth asked, smiling.

Without waiting for an answer, he took to the road.

Brighton and Lilian walked a few paces behind him.

'I didn't expect that,' Brighton whispered.

'Me neither,' Lilian replied. 'I hope his mood stays this good.'

Over his shoulder Seth said, 'I see you brought a bow young man. Good, you can hunt for us. I hate killing animals with the talent. It makes the meat taste funny.'

'Not a problem sir,' Brighton answered.

'I told you yesterday, please call me Seth,' the Supreme said.

'Not a problem, Seth,' Brighton repeated.

*****

Carmen walked right behind Thomas. They were on a narrow trail deep in the woods. Thomas insisted on taking the lead. He claimed to know this trail.

Carmen knew he wanted to be in front of her in case they walked into danger. So far, they hadn't seen anyone.

'That's the third time,' Thomas said nervously.

'Yes, I can feel it too. It does not mean anybody is looking for us,' Carmen replied.

'Who else could they be looking for?' Thomas asked over his shoulder.

'Perhaps they are hunting. It's easier when you know where the animals are,' Carmen said sarcastically.

'They are hunting, but not animals,' Thomas replied.

'Thomas, stop it,' Carmen said exasperated. 'You're imagining the worst as always.'

They had been travelling for hours. As soon as they were sure the young people were asleep, they set off. Carmen hated leaving without saying goodbye. She wanted to wake them but Thomas stopped her.

Thomas set a blistering pace. He knew Carmen was tired, so was he, but didn't slow down. They needed to get away, far away, as soon as possible. Thomas had his walking stick in one hand and Brighton's willow bow slung over his shoulder. Carmen thought it was silly but Thomas took the bow anyway.

They came across a large clearing.

'The trail continues on the other side. Stay behind me,' Thomas said. 'Let's cross this open field quickly, I feel safer in the woods.'

Carmen rolled her eyes but did as Thomas said.

As they were just about across, six people stepped out of the bushes in front of them. Thomas stopped so abruptly that Carmen bumped into him. He changed course to the right but two of the six people moved to cut them off.

Turning around Thomas saw another six people emerging from the woods. They were surrounded.

Thomas dropped the walking stick. The bow was instantly in his hand. He nocked an arrow and let it fly towards the nearest man in a single motion.

*****

Seth used his sense to scan for life.

'I'd like to make sure we're not being followed,' he explained, knowing that Lilian and possibly Brighton would notice this.

He smiled when he picked up Thomas and Carmen's energy. It was on the edge of the range for his sense.

It didn't matter though; Thomas cannot fight off twelve Dark Ones.

Today is the day Thomas will die Seth thought.

'Someone is following us,' Seth said.

'I can't feel anything,' Lilian said, using her sense to scan the area.

'It's a bit too far for you,' Seth replied. 'Don't worry, I know the person. Perhaps they just wanted to tell me something. You two carry on, I'll wait here for them and catch up later,' Seth instructed.

Brighton and Lilian kept walking.

Seth sat down on a rock. He could clearly feel Thomas, Carmen and a dozen Dark Ones closing in around them. He wanted to kill Thomas personally but this will have to do. Brighton is much more important.

There was another energy present.

Probably some sort of animal he thought.

The arrow found the man's shoulder. He howled in

pain. Thomas nocked another arrow and aimed again. This time the arrow found its mark. The Dark One dropped, an arrow sticking out of his eye. The other Dark Ones rushed forward.

Thomas let one more arrow fly wounding the woman closest to them in the arm. He dropped the bow and picked up the walking stick. Carmen and Thomas were standing back-to-back waiting for the onslaught.

A black form raced out of the woods. Mischief leapt onto an assailant's back. Big jaws closed around an exposed neck.

With a growl, Mischief ripped halfway through the Dark One's neck.

Another black form raced through the line of attackers, focused on one man.

Velvet leapt, attacking from the man's side. He lifted his arm trying to fend off the cat but this was a fatal mistake.

Velvet's jaws ripped through his exposed ribcage just under the arm. She raced forward and took up position in front of Carmen.

Mischief ripped flesh and bone from the chest of another attacker. The man tried using his gift on the animal but it was too late. The cat had already moved on to the next target. With incredible speed, he leapt forward going for the throat. The Dark One had his arm up. Big jaws closed around the forearm.

Jaw muscles flexed and the arm came off just below the elbow. Before the man could scream, the jaws closed around his face. With a powerful rip, his head was separated from his body.

'Retreat!' came the shout.

The remaining seven Dark Ones ran in all directions. Mischief started to follow but Thomas shouted for him. The big cat stopped and turned around. Blood was dripping from his jaws. He slowly walked towards Thomas, Carmen and Velvet.

Carmen sank to the ground. Her legs couldn't hold her up anymore.

The Dark Ones ran to the edge of the clearing where they regrouped. After a quick, heated conversation, they approached again, very slowly.

The leader spoke.

'Remember, kill those panthers first.'

Velvet was still in front of Carmen and Mischief stood next to Thomas. A deep growl came from his throat.

The Dark Ones charged. Velvet and Mischief leapt forward again, the bigger cat reaching the attackers first. His jaws ripped through flesh and bone again and two more attackers went down almost instantly. Velvet crashed into a woman, claws ripping at the face in front of her.

Thomas saw someone else's hand press into Velvet's side.

'No!' he shouted and charged forward but he was too late. The Dark One had used his talent on Velvet. The panther was dead before she hit the ground.

Mischief's jaws and nails ripped through the attackers and then a hand found his side.

The Dark One tried to use his talent but nothing happened. Mischief turned and ripped the man's hand clean off. A big claw hit the side of the man's face. His neck snapped like a twig. Thomas reached the fight, swinging his trusty oak cane.

Bones crushed under the thick wood. Mischief moved like black death between the Dark Ones.

Moments later, it was all over. Thomas and Mischief stood amongst the mangled bodies of the Dark Ones.

'Velvet!' Carmen screamed.

She rushed over and kneeled next to Velvet's lifeless body.

'Oh no, Velvet,' Carmen sobbed.

She looked at Thomas through her tears.

'She gave her life to protect us,' Thomas said softly.

Seth was confused. He was so sure that Thomas could not escape again. How could twelve people fail to kill one old man? Something else much more urgent crept into his mind. He knew the animal that was close by attacked the Dark Ones, he could feel their energies colliding, but something else was also there. That something killed eight or nine of his minions. He felt their energy just flicker out.

He could only feel Carmen and Thomas now.

'If you want something done right, do it yourself,' he muttered as his hand came up.

He didn't want to do it this way but he was tired of chasing Thomas.

*****

Mischief stood over Velvet, licking her head. Carmen sat with her hand on his back.

'I'm so sorry Mischief. She was very brave. We will never forget her,' Carmen said softly to the big panther.

Thomas, who was standing behind her, suddenly just dropped to the ground.

'Thomas!' Carmen shouted.

She just caught a glimpse of the black smoke attached to Thomas' head before it disappeared. She knew Seth had done this.

She waited for the energy link to slam into her head.

*****

It took Seth the rest of the day to catch up with Brighton and Lilian. They were resting next to a stream.

Seth didn't stop. He walked past and said, 'Come.'

He was clearly in a bad mood.

Brighton looked at Lilian. She quickly got up and

gestured for Brighton to do the same. Brighton got up and started walking with Lilian.

'I wonder if he got bad news,' he said.

'No, this is the Seth I know,' Lilian answered.

They travelled until late into the night. Lilian knew better than to complain, Seth would just ignore her. Brighton noticed how tired she was and took her bag from her. When they finally stopped to make camp Lilian was exhausted.

Still she said nothing. She was used to travelling with Seth.

He always set a murderous pace.

*****

The next morning Seth woke them before sunrise. He barely waited for them to pack their things before he started walking. Just like the day before he walked in front with the young people following a few paces behind. For most of the day Seth was quiet.

Late in the afternoon he spoke.

'Brighton, I understand you want to give up your talent to be with my daughter,' he said.

'Yes, that is the plan.' Brighton answered. 'Lilian says you have a way of extracting the talent from us.'

'True,' Seth replied.

'And that you agreed to help us,' Brighton pressed.

'True again,' Seth replied.

When it was clear Seth wasn't going to elaborate, Brighton asked, 'Would you mind telling me how this will be done?'

'Not at all, I just assumed Lilian told you already,' Seth said.

'Lily mentioned a bracelet, that's all,' Brighton said.

Seth walked a little slower.

When Brighton and Lilian were next to him, he started speaking again.

'My mother, Evangeline wore a bracelet almost all her life. It's nothing fancy, just a very simple silver bracelet with a hinge on the one side and a clasp on the other. When she died some part of her or her talent stayed behind in the bracelet. We found that putting this bracelet on someone drains their talent. This is how we will do it for you and Lilian.'

Concerned for Lilian, Brighton asked, 'Does it hurt?'

'No, you'll feel nothing,' Seth replied.

Brighton pressed on, 'How long does it take?'

'Depends on how strong your talent is. Lilian is my daughter, her talent is very strong. For her it shouldn't be more than half a day. I'm unsure how strong your talent is.'

'Not very,' Brighton lied. 'I can only sense people around me, nothing else.'

Seth looked at him.

'Well, then it will be faster for you,' he said.

'How do you know the talent is really gone?' Brighton asked.

'You will feel it. When you cannot sense people around you anymore, it's gone. The same goes for Lilian,' Seth replied.

He casually touched Brighton's arm and said, 'This is a serious decision. Are you sure you want to give up the talent?'

Brighton answered immediately, 'Yes, I want to. I love Lily, I will always choose her.'

Seth asked the same of Lilian.

'I am certain this is what I want,' she said, looking into Brighton's eyes.

Seth smiled at them both.

'I can see you love each other. I will be happy to help you be together,' he said.

*****

Carmen didn't continue on to Four Mountains. Instead, she turned around and went back to the house she and Brighton called home for six winters. She still could not understand why Seth killed Thomas and not her. He could have easily done it. She reasoned that if he didn't kill her when he had the chance, he probably never would.

Mischief stayed close by. Carmen was glad for this. Not just for the company but also for the protection the big black panther offered. They got home around mid morning.

As they approached the house, Carmen saw that a pack of wolves had found the goats. Mischief took off like a flash.

The wolves did not retreat, they probably felt there was strength in numbers. Mischief tore into them with a vengeance. It took only moments for the wolves to turn tail and run for the woods. Four of them would never run again.

Carmen reached the porch and sat down on one of the chairs. The last time she was this sad was when Matthew died. Thomas was gone, Brighton was gone, Velvet was gone.

Mischief came to lie down at her feet.

'Do you want to go to Brighton?' she asked softly, stroking his back.

At the mention of Brighton's name, the cat's ears perked up.

'I'll be all right now, go if you want to,' Carmen urged him.

She got up and went inside. She did not bother to eat something or have a bath. She went straight to bed. Carmen was dead tired. She slept until late afternoon. After making something small to eat, she went outside.

Mischief was gone.

Good, she thought, *Brighton and Lilian will need you*

more than I will.

She walked back into the house. An intense feeling of loneliness came over her. She picked up her rucksack, went outside, and took the road towards Zedonia.

The days went by quickly. They spent at least one day in every town they passed.

'Business,' was all he said, when Brighton asked Seth about it.

Brighton hunted while Seth was on his "business".

He would go off by himself and always brought back a rabbit or a fowl. Lilian gathered fruit and berries while he was gone. They covered the distance from Avarya to Zedonia in twenty days; normally it was a fourteen-day travel.

Zedonia was a huge city. The surroundings were almost completely flat apart from a large hill, almost a mountain, in the middle of the city.

Lilian pointed at it.

'That's the palace,' she said.

'Looks like a hill to me,' Brighton replied.

Lilian laughed.

'The first time I saw it I also said that,' she told him. 'It's enormous inside. There are caves that run everywhere under it.'

'I've heard it's very luxurious,' Brighton said.

'Yes it is,' Lilian replied.

'Do only the Supremes live there?' Brighton asked.

'No, a lot of their children and grandchildren live there too,' Lilian said.

'I have my own room. You can share it with me,' she added with a sly smile.

Seth looked around.

'There are guest quarters. Young Brighton will stay there,' he said.

'But...' Lilian started.

'Until your talents have been removed; after that you may live where you please. Of course, as you are my daughter, you will always have a room in the palace. Have you thought about marriage?' Seth asked.

Brighton didn't know how to respond to that.

Lilian glanced at him and said with a smile, 'Well, he hasn't asked me yet but I'm sure he will.'

Brighton regained his wits.

'I'm waiting for the right time,' he said mysteriously.

Seth smiled at that.

Brighton gawked at everything as they walked through the streets. He had never seen such a big city. Everything was new to him. There were a lot of hawkers trading all kinds of goods. Brighton noticed that the hawkers approached almost everyone in the streets except them.

He asked Lilian about that.

'Nobody will approach a Supreme. They are simply too scared,' she replied.

Brighton remembered the story Thomas told about the rebellion. He understood why everyone would be scared after that.

The travellers reached the outer city at midday but it took them until late afternoon to get to the palace. There were no houses near the palace. Woods surrounded the hill for at least two hundred paces.

'Nobody wants to stay this close to the Supremes,' Lilian whispered when Brighton enquired about that.

The two massive doors were made of wood decorated with gold. They swung open as soon as Seth approached. As they entered, Brighton looked back. It took five strong men to open each door.

'How did they know we were here?' he whispered to Lilian.

'There are lookouts everywhere. These people knew we were coming since yesterday,' she replied.

A servant approached, head down, and offered them

refreshments. She was wearing a very short black skirt. The top was little more than a black piece of material around her neck draped over her breasts.

Seth ignored the tray of fruit and juices and said to the servant, 'Show Master Brighton to the guest quarters.'

Brighton looked at Lilian.

'Master Brighton?' he said, almost laughing at the sound of that.

Before Lilian could answer another servant came up to her.

'May I take your bag, Miss Lilian,' she asked, eyes cast downward.

'No thank you Marian,' Lilian answered, smiling at the young girl.

Seth turned around.

'Join us for supper,' he said.

It was more like an instruction than an invitation.

'Yes father,' Lilian replied quickly.

Brighton just nodded.

Seth walked into one of the hallways pulling the young girl with the tray along. He had a brief, quiet conversation with her then let her go.

Brighton finally had time to look around. They were standing inside an entrance hall. There were four corridors. One lead back to the entrance, one left, one right and one leading seemingly straight into the hill. Looking down the left and right corridors, he noticed that both of them also turned in the direction of the hill after only a few paces.

This did not look like the inside of a cave at all. The floors and walls looked like polished granite. Tapestries and golden chandeliers adorned the walls. All the candles in the chandeliers were lit. Satin sheets covered the ceilings.

'This place is amazing,' Brighton whispered, head going from side to side.

Thomas had some of the details wrong he thought.

'I would prefer to live in your house,' Lilian said. 'If you were going to ask me to be your wife, that is,' she quickly added.

Brighton smiled.

'Patience my love,' he said smiling at her.

'We'd better get cleaned up and dressed for supper,' Lilian said.

'How will we know when it's time?' he asked.

'A servant will come get you,' she replied.

Brighton noticed two servants hovering close by. He approached the one who had the tray earlier. Strangely, the tray had disappeared.

'Excuse me, could you please show me where the guests' rooms are?' he asked politely.

The girl looked bewildered for a moment.

She regained her composure and said, 'Certainly Master Brighton, please follow me.'

Brighton gave Lilian a hug.

'Don't go looking at other pretty girls now,' Lilian teased.

'What? There are other girls here? I didn't even notice,' Brighton said with mock surprise.

Lilian pulled his head down to hers.

'Just to remind you who you belong to,' she said and gave him a long passionate kiss.

Brighton swayed on his feet as Lilian walked away, shadowed by a servant girl.

'Stay close to Adri, you don't want to get lost in this maze,' she called over her shoulder.

'Isn't she absolutely gorgeous?' Brighton said to the remaining servant girl.

'If you say so Master Brighton,' the girl answered.

'Oh yes, I do say so,' Brighton said with a smile.

He looked at the young girl next to him. She had probably seen fifteen or sixteen winters and reminded Brighton a lot of Lilian.

'The guest rooms please?' he asked.

The girl walked down a corridor without another word. It was a short walk to the guest rooms. At the third door, Adri stopped and opened it.

'Your room, Master Brighton,' she said.

'What's with calling me Master Brighton,' he asked her.

She just stood looking at the floor not answering.

'Call me Brighton,' he said as he walked into the room.

'Dear angels,' he whispered. 'It's bigger than my whole house.'

Adri remained just outside the door.

'I'll be right here should you need anything,' she said and closed the door.

'Thank you, but I'll be fine,' he replied, but the door was already closed.

Brighton put his backpack down and looked around the room. A large bed was in the middle of the enormous space. Numerous sets of fresh clothes were laid out on it. The ceiling was high and also had satin covering it. There were chandeliers everywhere, all the candles lit. The floor and walls looked the same as in the corridor.

'Cave walls and floors aren't this smooth, someone made it this way,' Brighton said to himself.

A bath was standing close to the left wall.

'Well, I guess I will bathe and get dressed for dinner,' he said to the empty room.

He walked over to the steaming bath and put his hand in. It was far too hot. Brighton preferred the cold running water of rivers, not hot standing water in a bath. He walked to the door and cracked it open.

'Yes, Master Brighton?' Adri said immediately.

He opened the door fully.

'I want to bathe...' he started

'Do you require help?' Adri said quickly.

'No, I...' the young man stammered.

'Perhaps I can call one or two more girls to satisfy your needs,' Adri offered.

'What? No!' Brighton gasped.

Adri cast her eyes downward and said in a small voice.

'How many girls does Master Brighton require? I am here to...'

Brighton grabbed her arm and yanked her into the room.

'I am here to serve all your needs,' Adri said as she started removing the material covering her chest.

Brighton saw tears in her eyes. He caught her hands preventing her from getting undressed.

'Stop and listen to me,' he said gently.

He let her hands go. Her arms flopped to her sides, her head dropped.

'Please let me be of service to you,' she pleaded. 'If you tell Supreme Seth I was not good he will punish me.'

Her whole body was shaking.

Brighton slowly said, 'I'm not going to tell Seth anything of the sort.'

Confused, the girl looked up.

'Then why did you pull me into your room?' she asked.

'The water in the bath is too hot,' he said sheepishly.

'I will fix it immediately,' Adri said, eager to please him.

She ran off to fetch some cold water, returning quickly carrying a full bucket. Brighton saw that it was heavy and tried to take it from her but she didn't want to let it go.

'I must do it,' she protested, trying to pull the bucket away from him causing a small spill. Adri let go of the bucket and jumped back.

'I'm so sorry Master Brighton. I will clean it up,' she said, almost crying.

'Adri, relax a little!' Brighton said exasperated. 'What have these people done to you?'

She just stood with her head down.

'I'm going to bathe now. I will call you if I need you,' Brighton said as calmly as he could.

'I will help you,' she declared and reached for his trousers.

'Adri! Stop it,' he shouted.

The young girl burst into tears.

'If I don't serve I will be punished,' she sobbed.

Brighton tried to speak in a soothing tone.

'Look, only one person has ever seen me naked and she was my mother. I'm shy so I would like some privacy,' he said.

'I'm not a person, I'm a servant,' Adri said softly.

Brighton took her face in his hands. He tilted her head upwards so that he could look her in the eyes.

'You are a person, not just a servant,' he said gently.

She looked at him with big brown eyes, confusion on her face.

'You're different from the others,' she said.

'Yes, I've been told that before,' he replied. 'Now please, wait outside so that I can bathe.'

Adri turned around and walked out closing the door behind her.

Brighton emptied the bucket into the bath muttering, 'It will have to do.'

After he finished bathing he looked at the clothes on the bed. He selected a simple shirt and trousers and got dressed.

'Time for supper I guess,' he muttered.

When he opened the door, Adri was still standing there.

'Yes, Master Brighton?' she asked.

'Call me Master one more time and I'll spank you,' he tried to joke.

Adri's face was a mask of fear.

'It's a joke,' Brighton quickly said. 'A silly little joke.'
'Yes Mast...um...' Adri stammered.
'Brighton, just Brighton,' he helped her.
'Yes Brighton,' she said uncomfortably.
'When and where is supper? he asked.
'Follow me,' she replied.
'I hope Lily is there,' Brighton muttered.
When Adri looked at him quizzically he said, 'Lilian.'
'Oh, Miss Lilian,' Adri said.
Adri led him through a maze of passageways.

Finally they reached the dining hall. It was a dome shaped room and like everything else in the palace, it was enormous. Passageways led into it from all directions. A large, half circle table followed the curve of the wall on the far side. Some people were huddled in small groups, deep in conversation while others were seated already.

Brighton estimated the table had fifty or sixty seating places.

Brighton looked in the crowd for Lilian. Small arms circled his waist from behind.

'Hello my love,' she said pressing up against his back.
'Ah, the lady of my heart,' he said and turned around.
'Come, let's go sit,' Lilian said.

They interlocked fingers and she led him towards the large table. Her usual place was next to Seth's.

Lilian pointed out the Supremes.

'That's Amber, Lauryn, Raina, Michael, Richard and Theresa,' she said.

'And who are all the other people?' Brighton asked.

'Their children mostly and a few grandchildren,' Lilian replied.

'Who is the little girl with Seth?' was Brighton's next question.

'Hannah, my half sister. She is Seth's youngest child, born nine winters ago. I'm second youngest. I think she is the reason Seth agreed to help us,' Lilian replied.

Brighton looked puzzled.

'Why?' he asked.

'Seth wants to teach Hannah the Dark One's ways. My presence is hampering that. If I don't have the gift anymore he can focus on Hannah. He can't let me run around with the gift if I haven't been properly trained,' Lilian replied.

Brighton nodded. It made sense now why Seth was so eager for them to give up the talent.

'I thought there were eight Supremes. I only see seven,' Brighton remarked.

Lilian spoke softly.

'Nobody talks about it. All I know is that Danika died. Raina named her second daughter Danika in honour of their sister.'

Seth moved to his chair. Just before he sat down Adri approached him, head down. He listened briefly to what she was saying then slapped her hard across the face. She stumbled backwards, fell, and quickly crawled away.

Silence fell and everyone else quickly found a seat. In moments, Seth was the only one left standing. Without a word he sat down.

Servants started bringing food out. There was far too much for the number of people present but servants with trays just kept coming. As soon as Seth had helped himself, everyone else started.

Brighton didn't recognize half the food on the table. He decided to play it safe and took some meat and bread.

Seth leaned over so he could see Lilian and Brighton.

'As soon as supper is finished we will use the bracelet. Brighton will go first. Agreed?' he said to them.

Both nodded.

Seth did not speak to them again throughout supper. He only spoke when people spoke to him first and then it was mostly monosyllable answers.

Supper was a long, drawn out affair. Brighton couldn't wait for it to finish. He already had plans to have Adri show him where Lilian's room was after their talents had been drained.

Finally, the servants started clearing the table. Most of the people left, only the Supremes and a few of their children stayed behind.

Seth spoke to Brighton.

'It's time,' he said softly.

'What do I do?' Brighton asked.

'Stand in the middle of the room, I will join you soon,' Seth replied.

He disappeared into one of the hallways.

Moments later he came back carrying a small wooden box. Standing right in front of Brighton, he opened the box. Lilian came to stand beside him.

Carefully he removed a thin silver bracelet from it.

'I'm going to put this on your arm. When the talent is successfully extracted, you will feel it. It won't hurt. Are you ready?' Seth said slowly.

Brighton looked at Lilian and smiled.

'Yes,' he said.

Seth put the bracelet around Brighton's arm. He tried to close the clasp but it refused to stay closed. Every time it just popped open again.

'Strange,' Seth said softly.

'Why is that happening?' Lilian asked.

'The bracelet won't close if the person is not willing to give up their talent,' Seth answered.

'But I am willing!' Brighton protested.

'The only other reason is that sometimes it has to be put on by someone you trust. You don't trust me so your instinct is to protect yourself, This is not going to work,' he said, disappointment showing in his face.

Lilian spoke, 'Can I try?'

Turning to Brighton she said, 'You trust me, don't you?'

'Yes, I do,' he answered.

Seth thought for a moment.

'It's worth trying,' he said, handing the bracelet to Lilian.

She put it around his arm. The clasp closed on the first try.

Brighton was not prepared for the shock that followed.

*****

White eyes watched the palace entrance from behind a thick bush. At night, Mischief was seldom seen. He easily slipped through the city. A familiar hand touched his back.

'What do you see boy?' Carmen asked.

She was less than a day's travel from Avarya when Mischief joined her. They travelled together to Zedonia. He mostly stayed close by in the woods. Mischief had to slip through the city but Carmen simply walked. It was not a strange thing to see people going to the palace.

She wanted to see Brighton to make sure he was alright. She also wondered if they had used the bracelet yet.

'I can go in there because I'm a Dark One,' Carmen told Mischief.

A thought formed in her head. She didn't really want to leave the big cat behind. He could take care of himself but she'd gotten used to the protection he gave her. On the way to Zedonia two bands of robbers approached her. As soon as Mischief came out of the woods they turned tail very quickly.

'We can go to the gate and say you're a gift for the Supremes. People bring them gifts sometimes. Once we've seen Brighton and Lilian you can slip out again.'

She suddenly felt silly for talking to a black panther.

'I wish you could understand me,' she said to the cat.

Carmen decided to come back the next day, it was late and Brighton might be asleep already.

*****

Brighton's arm jerked away from Lilian. He looked at her strangely as he sank to his knees.

'What's happening?' Lilian screamed.

Seth grabbed her by the arm and pulled her back.

'Now we watch,' he snarled.

'Watch what?' Lilian screamed at him. 'You said it would not hurt him!'

'Oh, it's going to hurt a lot,' Seth replied with a smile. 'Right up to the point when he dies.'

The other Supremes were all laughing.

'Dies? No!' Lilian screamed as she tried to get to Brighton.

Seth held on to her arm tightly.

'There is nothing you can do now. The bracelet won't come off until he is dead,' Seth said calmly.

Lilian yanked free from him and raced to Brighton. Furiously she tried to get the bracelet off but it wouldn't budge. Seth pulled her away again.

Brighton's body was twisting in painful spasms.

'You lied to me!' Lilian screamed as she pounded her tiny fists against Seth's chest.

'Yes,' he said.

'Why?' Lilian screamed, close to tears.

'Your boyfriend has a very special talent. I don't know exactly what it is but he could possibly threaten us. We have to get rid of him,' Seth replied in that evil voice.

'How do you know he has a special talent?' Lilian sobbed.

'Nobody can sense him. It's as if he is protecting himself with his talent. It's the first time I've ever come across this,' Seth explained.

'But...but...' Lilian sobbed. 'How could you do this to me, to us?'

Seth just smiled.

'Where did you get this cursed bracelet?' she asked through her tears.

'I took it off my mother's arm right after I killed her,' Seth said matter-of-factly. 'Danika wanted it so I put it on her wrist. She died a painful death. That's how we know of its power. It can only be put onto someone by a trusted or loved one.'

'And I played right into your hands,' Lilian said softly.

'Yes, you did,' Seth laughed.

He sat down on his chair.

Lilian sank to the floor.

Brighton's body was still jerking violently.

Chapter 12

BRIGHTON OPENED HIS eyes. He was lying flat on his back looking up at a blue sky. There was just a hint of clouds. He lifted his head. He was in the clearing close to Four Mountains where he used to take the goats.

Slowly he looked around. Everything was as he remembered; even the little white goat was there.

Did I dream everything?

Someone was approaching.

Brighton got up. He walked closer and saw that it was Thomas.

'Thomas!' he shouted, waving his arms.

Thomas waved back. Brighton ran to meet him.

'Young Brighton, so good to see you again,' Thomas greeted when he got close.

Someone else approached. He didn't know the woman.

'Who is that?' he asked Thomas.

'Evangeline,' Thomas replied.

'Seth's mother?' Brighton asked.

Thomas nodded.

Maybe I'm dreaming now, Brighton thought.

Nothing made sense.

'How come she is here? She died a long time ago,' Brighton said.

'True,' Thomas replied.

Evangeline was close now.

'Good day, young man,' she greeted pleasantly.

'Good day, ma'am,' Brighton replied.

Evangeline held out her hand to him.

'I'm Evangeline,' she said.

Brighton looked at the offered hand.

'I'm Brighton,' he said. 'Sorry but I prefer not to shake hands.'

Evangeline laughed.

'I see Thomas has been teaching you some things,' she said.

'What's going on?' Brighton asked. 'Didn't you die a long time ago?'

'Yes, I did,' she smiled.

'Then how come...' Brighton started.

Understanding crashed into his mind like a falling tree.

'Oh no! Oh no! I'm dead too,' he gasped wide eyed.

'Yes,' Thomas replied quickly.

'No,' Evangeline countered.

'Yes, he is,' Thomas said heatedly. 'He is here, isn't he?'

Before Evangeline could answer Brighton said, 'Here? Where exactly is here?'

Evangeline answered, 'Heaven, the afterlife, the spirit world, a different dimension, a higher existence. People call it by different names.'

'That helps,' Brighton said sarcastically. 'How do I get

back to Lilian?' he asked.

'You don't,' Thomas jumped in.

'Enough, Thomas,' Evangeline said seriously. 'Give Brighton and I some privacy.'

Thomas fell silent but did not move.

'Now!' Evangeline said sternly.

He turned and started walking away.

'I knew she would betray you,' he muttered as he walked.

'What do you mean?' Brighton called after Thomas.

When the old man did not answer, Brighton started going after him. Evangeline stepped in front of him.

'We need to talk, time is precious,' she said.

'Talk about what? Thomas said I'm dead. I can't go back to Lily,' Brighton said despondently.

'Not quite,' Evangeline said. 'Concentrate. Do you feel a link to somewhere else? A different place?'

Brighton concentrated for a moment.

Slowly he said, 'Yes. It's as if I'm here but also somewhere else.'

'That's because your spirit is here and your body is somewhere else. It's still in the world of the living,' Evangeline answered.

'How can that be?' Brighton asked with a frown.

'The talent is very strong in you. The strongest I've ever seen. You're using it right now to keep your body alive,' Evangeline replied.

Before Brighton could speak she shook her head and said, 'No, that's not accurate. Your body is technically dead but your spirit is still keeping a link to it.'

Brighton didn't really understand this explanation but decided not to ask questions.

'Have you seen many talented people?' Brighton asked.

'Yes, every person that dies comes here,' she replied.

'And I'm the strongest?' Brighton asked.

'Yes, by far,' Evangeline confirmed.

'If my body is elsewhere, what is this?' Brighton said gesturing to himself.

'Your soul, your essence, your life force. Again, different people call it by different names.'

Brighton looked around.

'Why does it look like the place where I grew up?' he asked next.

'That's a function of your mind. There is in fact nothing here, but to me it looks like the caves where I was born,' she answered.

'What did Thomas mean when he said she would betray you? Was he talking about Lily?' he asked carefully.

'That is for you to decide,' Evangeline answered.

'She put the bracelet on me. She must have known of its real power. It certainly looks like she betrayed me,' Brighton frowned.

Before Brighton could ask another question, she spoke again.

'We have little time. Your talent is strong, but there is also a limit to how long you can keep the link to your body. Do you wish to know how your talent works?' she asked.

'Well, I think I can give, take and manipulate energy and it only works on instinct. I have no control,' Brighton answered.

'Not entirely correct. You're right about giving, taking and manipulating energy but wrong on the instinct part. You can control it,' Evangeline answered.

'How?' Brighton asked.

Without warning Evangeline touched his head. Understanding flooded into his mind. Brighton instantly knew exactly what his talent was capable of and how to control it. He also understood the limits and boundaries.

'I understand now,' he said. 'How did you do that?' he asked in amazement.

'In this place I am very powerful. This is just one of the things I can do,' she replied.

'How do I get back to my body?' Brighton asked.

'Do you remember that little black panther cub you helped more than six winters ago?' Evangeline asked.

Brighton nodded.

'When animals die they also come here. That little cub was with me already but you pulled him back. It has never happened before. It's the reason I know it's possible to re-join the living. Think of how you did that,' she replied.

Brighton thought of that day so many winters ago.

Understanding came to him again.

'I know how to do it,' he said.

Evangeline just smiled.

'Do you know where Mischief is now?' Brighton asked, suddenly concerned for his friend.

'Closer than you think. That is one very special animal. When you pulled him back to the living, a part of your talent stayed in him. The talent protects him as it protects you. A Dark One cannot harm him or you unless you let them. You are vulnerable only to my children, the Supremes.'

Brighton's eyes went wide.

'Seth couldn't get the bracelet on me. That's why Lily put it on. They knew that it would take someone I trusted to do that. Lily did betray me!' he said with great sadness.

'Don't be too hasty in your decisions. Perhaps it was all planned but it's also possible that she didn't know and Seth deceived you both,' Evangeline warned.

'I will go and find out,' Brighton said heatedly.

'Before you go, may I ask a favour of you please?' Evangeline asked.

'Yes, anything,' Brighton replied.

'Send Seth and his siblings to me. It's time their mother had a serious talk with them,' Evangeline said, struggling to keep the disgust out of her voice.

'I think it will be more than just a talk. I promise you will have all your children with you soon,' Brighton said.

Evangeline nodded her thanks.

'Will you be alright?' Brighton asked, 'Seth and the other Supremes are strong.'

'I told you, in this place I'm very powerful. No need to worry about me,' she replied with a smile.

Brighton concentrated. He could feel himself slipping back into his body. Evangeline said something as he was almost gone.

Something about her husband.

*****

Brighton opened his eyes. He didn't have to look where he was; he knew he was back in the palace dining hall.

Slowly he got up. People were sitting at the table eating what looked like breakfast.

How long was I gone? he wondered.

The room went silent. The only sound came from the little silver bracelet hitting the floor. Everybody was staring at him just standing there.

Seth got up slowly, confusion on his face.

'How is this possible? Why aren't you dead?' he screamed.

Lilian was seated next to Seth. Her eyes were red and swollen. Brighton noticed that her plate of food was untouched. She tried to get up but Seth put a hand on her shoulder pushing her back into her seat.

He lifted his other hand.

The energy link raced towards Brighton. As it touched his head, it recoiled. Seth howled in pain.

'How?' he said softly.

Lilian struggled to get out from under his grip but he

held firm.

'Brighton, run!' she shouted.

Brighton stood looking from face to face. He wasn't going to run. He was going to destroy them all.

Everybody was suddenly talking at the same time. Seth was in urgent conversation with Amber standing next to him. Lauryn joined the conversation.

Brighton caught a few words.

'...work together...can't resist us all...must be killed...'

He watched the hand on Lily's shoulder carefully. Seth gestured wildly with his free hand. He kept his other hand firmly on Lilian's shoulder.

Still Brighton watched.

Finally, Seth got too distracted and lifted his hand. Brighton snapped an energy link to Lilian. It was a thin white line between his head and hers.

Nobody noticed.

*****

Lilian could not believe it. Brighton was standing in the middle of the room. He was not dead. Seth's hand lifted from her shoulder

She didn't move. If he wanted to, he could kill her instantly. She needed to stay calm and wait for the right opportunity.

Lilian.

She looked around. Her head was spinning. Who was calling her name?

Lily.

It was a voice in her head. Her eyes snapped to Brighton. He was looking straight at her.

Lily, don't react, the voice said.

Bri? she thought.

Yes, it is me.

Bri, I'm so sorry...

Shh, I know you didn't betray me. I know you love me.
Lilian started to stand up.
No, don't!
Seth noticed. He looked at Lilian and then at Brighton. He saw the white energy link. In a flash his hand was back on Lilian's shoulder.
'Now you die,' he snarled at her.
He used his talent but nothing happened.
Bri, what's happening? Lilian's panicked thought reached Brighton.
He's trying to kill you but I'm preventing it with my talent. I'm protecting you, Brighton's voice came into her head.
His face was a mask of concentration. It was draining his energy to protect himself and Lilian. Seth realized his talent wasn't working on Lilian. He grabbed a knife. Cutting her throat would have the same result.
A bolt of pure white light slammed into his head knocking him all the way to the wall.
The room fell silent, everyone's eyes fixed on Brighton's raised hand.
Lily, come to me, quickly!
Lilian jumped over the table and ran to Brighton. She grabbed on to his arm. The energy link disappeared.
'As long as you touch me it's easier for me to protect you,' Brighton whispered.
Seth got up slowly. There was a round burn mark on his forehead.
'A neat little trick,' he said to Brighton. 'But it won't save you.'
He lifted his hand again. All the other Supremes did the same. Seven energy links raced towards Brighton's head.
Brighton blocked all of them.
Confused, the Supremes looked at each other.
'Again!' Seth shouted.
The seven links shot towards Brighton again and as before, they could not enter his head. Over and over

they kept trying. It was all Brighton could do to keep blocking them.

His strength was fading fast. There were no other life forms around that he could get energy from. He was worried about letting in one of the links and then reversing it. It might just be more than he could handle right now.

'Wait,' Seth shouted. 'Kill the girl first!'

The seven energy links went for Lilian's head. She shrieked and closed her eyes.

'Don't be afraid, they can't touch you,' Brighton whispered.

Some of the Supremes' children joined in.

They were eager to please their parents. Six more energy links tried to get through Brighton's defences. For just a moment, he faltered. Seth's link touched Lilian and a moment later her lifeless body dropped to the ground.

'No!' Brighton shouted.

He was searching desperately for some form of energy to steal. The mountain itself answered his call. Brighton felt the power flowing through him. He dropped his defences.

Thirteen energy links slammed into his head.

The power that flowed through him was incredible. The more energy the Dark Ones took from him, the more he got from the mountain. They could not kill him.

Suddenly he sent a huge burst of power down Amber's link. The amount of energy flowing into her body was so much she burst into flames.

He attacked Theresa in the same way. She too burst into flames. Six white bolts of lightning shot from Brighton's body. It passed straight through the six Dark Ones that were trying to help the Supremes. They all dropped instantly to the floor, neat round holes where their hearts used to be.

'Stop!' Seth shouted.

Brighton sank down next to Lilian's body.

He put his face on her head.

'No, no, no, no,' he whispered into her blond curls.

Seth stepped closer.

'Impressive. Nobody has ever been able to kill even one of us.'

Brighton looked up.

'Stay back or you're next,' he snarled.

Seth smiled.

'We both know you have nothing left. You're done. I'm going to kill you slowly.'

Brighton knew his limits. He had done everything he could. The link to the mountain was gone, he had nowhere else to get energy from, and even if he could, it would kill him. Too much energy had already passed through him.

Slowly he got up.

'Then do it,' he said slowly.

Seth lifted his hand. The energy link slammed into Brighton's head.

A big black form raced over the smooth floor. Mischief's jaw closed around Seth arm instantly ripping it clean off. Mischief did not stop the attack. Claws ripped chunks of flesh from the Supreme's other arm, chest and then found his throat.

Slowly Seth sank to the ground, confusion on his face as he tried to stop the blood gushing from his throat with his remaining hand.

People were running everywhere trying to get out of the dining hall.

Brighton was lying next to Lilian. He looked at her one last time. His eyes closed. Mischief stood over Brighton and Lilian growling at the remaining people in the room.

Lauryn came forward, hand raised.

Her energy link shot across the room to Mischief.

*****

Seth opened his eyes. He was in a cave. Evangeline was standing over him.

'Time to pay for your sins,' she told him.

Seth jumped up and raised his hand.

Nothing happened.

'That cursed talent won't work here,' Evangeline said slowly.

She reached out and touched his head. Excruciating pain shot through his head. When it stopped, he was on his knees in front of his mother.

'Come, your sisters are waiting,' she commanded.

When Seth didn't come immediately, Evangeline touched his head again. The pain was unbearable and it lasted longer this time. When it eventually stopped, he was on the ground.

He couldn't remember how he got there.

'Come,' she ordered again.

He scrambled to his feet. Amber and Theresa were standing behind Evangeline.

'Kill her!' he shouted at his sisters.

They both looked at him with fear in their eyes. Evangeline touched his head again. The last thing he heard was 'slow learner' before he passed out.

He woke up hoping it was all a dream.

Evangeline stood over him.

'Come,' she said.

Seth obeyed immediately. They walked out of the cave. A multitude of people was standing in the clearing in front of the cave.

Evangeline addressed her three children.

'These are the people you killed; now they can do with the three of you as they please.'

Amber and Theresa started protesting that they didn't have anything to do with it.

Evangeline held up her hand for silence.

'You knew it was happening and did nothing to stop it. You're as guilty as Seth,' she declared.

She turned around and strolled back into the cave.

Frightened, Amber and Theresa clung to each other.

Seth shouted at Evangeline, 'At least I killed Brighton!'

Softly she said, 'Don't be so sure.'

Thousands of people stormed the three Supremes with sticks and stones in their hands.

*****

'Brighton,' a soft voice said.

Evangeline? Brighton thought.

He slowly opened his eyes.

White satin sheets.

Funny, he thought. *Last time I was back in Four Mountains.*

'Brighton,' the soft voice came again.

It didn't sound like Evangeline. He turned his head slightly.

'Lily?' he whispered. 'Are you dead too?'

Lilian started crying. She tried to speak but the words wouldn't come. She was sitting next to him clinging on to his hand. A rough tongue licked Brighton's other hand.

He tried to sit up but couldn't. His body wouldn't respond.

'Is that Mischief?' he asked.

Lilian nodded, tears streaming down her face. Brighton tried sitting up again. He managed to press himself up on one elbow.

'Why are we still in the palace? If we're dead we should be in Four Mountains,' he said.

Lilian was still crying so much she couldn't speak.

'What happened?' Brighton asked.

'I saw,' a small voice said.

Brighton turned his head and saw Adri standing not far off. There were bodies all over the floor. It seemed that he, Lilian and Adri were the only living people left.

'Would you like some water?' she asked.

'Yes, please,' Brighton nodded.

He sat up, his body protesting. Adri scurried to the table and returned with a glass of water for Brighton.

After a few gulps he felt slightly better.

'So, what happened?' he asked again.

Adri spoke in a trembling voice, 'That black demon killed almost everyone.'

Mischief pushed his wet nose into Brighton's hand.

'Hello boy. Where did you come from?' he asked.

'He came in with an old lady,' Adri answered.

'Carmen,' Lilian sobbed.

'Carmen is here?' Brighton asked excitedly.

'Was here,' Adri corrected.

'Where did she go?' Brighton asked.

'She's also dead,' Adri responded.

'No! Mischief would never harm her,' Brighton tried to shout.

It came out more like a croak. He had some more water. Adri stood with her hands clasped together in front her.

'He didn't,' she whispered.

'Who did?' Brighton prodded.

'I don't know,' Adri replied fearfully.

'Just tell me what happened, please?' he asked softly.

'The black demon came charging in here with the old lady right behind him. He started ripping through everybody. They all ran for their lives. I hid behind the table over there.'

She pointed to the far end of the half moon table.

'When there was nobody left but you and Miss Lilian the demon went to sit next to you. The old lady ran to you. She screamed and pounded on your chest but it looked like you were dead. She put her hands on your chest and said something about taking her energy. A white light started shining from your body. The light touched Miss Lilian and she started breathing again. You also started breathing again after a while. The old lady fell over your chest. I crept closer to look. Luckily, that demon just ignored me. I pulled the old lady off you. There she is.'

Brighton looked where Adri was pointing.

'Carmen,' he said past the lump in his throat.

He took a moment to gain control of his voice and then asked, 'What happened then?'

'Miss Lilian woke up. She's been sitting with you since then,' Adri replied.

'How long has it been?' Brighton asked.

'Two days. I brought Miss Lilian food and water. She didn't want to leave your side and you were too big for us to move. Besides, that demon got angry when I touched you,' the young girl replied.

Brighton looked at Lilian.

She threw her arms around him. He barely had the strength to hold himself up but he didn't say anything. He hugged her back passionately.

'Are you alright my love?' he asked.

She nodded and buried her face in his neck.

Brighton looked at Carmen again.

'She gave her life for us,' he said.

Adri came a little closer, keeping an eye on Mischief.

'Is there anything you need Mast...uh...Brighton,' she asked.

'Help us up please,' he said.

Adri helped Lilian up and then Brighton.

'Where is the nearest bed?' he asked.

'Master Seth's room,' Adri replied.

'Take us there.'

Brighton had to lean a little on Lilian as they followed Adri.

When they got to the room, they sat down on the bed. Brighton didn't even notice the size or exquisite decorations.

'Adri, would you mind bringing us some food and water?'

Adri ran out without a word. She was back in a flash, a tray with all kinds of food and drink in her hands.

'Thank you,' Lilian managed.

Her throat was raw from crying. She offered Brighton some bread and meat. He eagerly took it and began eating. With every bite he felt better.

Lilian also ate a little. Adri hovered close by in case they needed something else. Mischief sat next to the bed.

'Perhaps we should sleep for a while, regain some strength,' Lilian suggested.

Brighton smiled at her.

'You're just trying to get me out of my pants,' he teased tiredly.

Lilian playfully punched him on the arm.

'I thought I lost you again,' she said seriously.

'And I thought the same of you,' he replied.

They lay down on the bed, Lilian cradled in Brighton's strong arms.

They were both instantly asleep.

Chapter 13

BRIGHTON SLOWLY WOKE up. He didn't know if it was day or night. It took a few moments for him to realize where he was. His eyes snapped fully open.

'Lily?' he said, looking next to him.

'Yes my love,' her voice came from the other side of the room.

She was standing at a table pouring juice into cups, her back towards him.

'I thought you might like some breakfast in bed,' she said.

Brighton watched her back. She was wearing a long white nightgown. It had thin straps going over the shoulders; the back was open almost down to her bottom. Her long hair was neatly tied up with a pink ribbon.

She came towards the bed carrying a cup and a plate. The front of the nightgown was in a V-shape and cut very low, well below her breasts. With the light behind her, he could clearly see the shape of her body through the gown.

She reached the bed holding out the cup and plate.

'Lemon juice, fruit and bread,' she said with a smile.

Brighton sat up and put his feet on the ground. Instead of taking the plate or cup his arm snaked around her. He pulled her close to him. Softly he stroked her naked back.

She held the cup and plate high, out of the way. Brighton laid his head between her breasts. He could hear her shallow breathing and the quick beating of her heart.

'Someone is coming,' he said pulling away from Lilian.

'Probably Adri, she is preparing a bath for you,' Lilian said. 'Did you sense her?'

'No, I can hear footsteps. I'm not using my sense at the moment,' Brighton replied.

Lilian cocked her head and listened. She also heard footsteps but very faintly.

'You're right, I can't feel you using your sense. Is it gone?' she asked.

'No, I can control it now,' Brighton replied as he took the plate and juice from her.

'Thank you,' he said smiling at her.

'Tomorrow morning I want breakfast in bed,' she teased as she sat down on the bed next to him.

'Yes, my queen,' he said between mouthfuls of bread and fruit.

Adri knocked and entered the room. She was carrying a bucket of water.

'Mas…I mean Brighton, it's good to see you awake. I'll have your bath ready in a moment. It's not too hot. I hope it will be to your satisfaction. I can get more water if…'

'ADRI!' Lilian and Brighton said together.

'It will be fine,' Brighton said. 'Now please give us some privacy.'

Adri nodded and walked to the bath in the far corner of the room. She emptied the bucket and left without another word.

'She is very eager to please,' Brighton observed.

'All the serving girls are. They were punished for even the smallest transgression. Sometimes the Supremes would hurt them just for fun,' Lilian said bitterly.

'That's wrong!' Brighton said heatedly.

'Yes, I know,' Lilian said. 'That's why I always tried to be kind to them. I think I'm the only one in this place that knows the serving girls' names.'

Brighton got up and walked over to the bath. He looked back at Lilian.

'Would you mind if I bathed quickly?' he asked.

'Not at all,' she said, folding her legs.

She put her elbow on her knee and rested her chin in her palm.

Brighton looked uncomfortable.

'Don't you have something to do?' he asked her.

'No,' she said with a smile.

'Can you at least turn around then please?' he pleaded.

'No,' she said again, her smile widening.

Brighton sighed and turned his back towards her. He started taking off his clothes.

Looking over his shoulder, he said to her, 'You're staring at me. It's making me uncomfortable.'

Not taking her eyes off him she said, 'I told you before, don't be embarrassed. Besides, I've seen you almost naked and I've been naked in front of you.'

Brighton quickly climbed in the bath.

'That's not entirely true,' he said. 'You kept that tight undergarment on last time.'

Lilian thought about it for a moment.

'Yes, I suppose that's true,' she agreed.

She got up and walked towards the bath. As she walked, she slipped the thin straps of her nightgown off her shoulders and let it fall to the ground. She stood next to the bath and slowly removed her underwear.

'There, now we're both naked,' she said.

She swung her legs over the edge of the bath and climbed in.

Brighton was speechless.

Lilian reached for the soap.

'Let me help you,' she said.

They both stood up and Lilian started soaping his muscular body.

'Sit down and rinse off,' she said softly, struggling to control her breathing.

Brighton rinsed the soap off and said, 'Your turn.'

He imitated what she had done a moment earlier. His hands were gliding over her soft skin. Her legs were so lame they could hardly hold her up. His touch was exquisite.

Brighton finished the soaping. She turned around and sat with her back towards him.

'Wash my hair please,' she asked breathlessly.

He sat down and started washing her long blond curls. His hands were trembling. Although her hair was long, he finished very quickly.

Brighton climbed out of the bath, turned around and picked Lilian up. He carried her to the bed. They were messing water everywhere but didn't care, they were only aware of each other.

Gently Brighton put Lilian down on the bed. He straightened up and looked at her wet, naked body on the white sheets.

'You're beautiful,' he whispered.

Lilian reached over and grabbed his arm.

'Tell me later,' she breathed and pulled him onto the bed with her.

*****

Late in the afternoon when they were both exhausted, Lilian covered them with a sheet and called for Adri.

She entered immediately.

Brighton frowned.

'Were you standing there the whole day?' he asked.

'Ye…um…No, I just got here,' Adri answered trying to hide her smile.

Lilian sat up clutching the sheet to her chest.

'Would you mind getting us something to eat and drink,' she asked Adri.

'Certainly Miss Lilian,' Adri answered.

She turned and with a big grin on her face muttered, 'Sounds like you need it.'

'Adri!' Brighton called her back.

'Yes, Brighton?'

'Could you do me another favour please? Bring my things from the guest room,' he asked.

'I will do that right after I fetch you some food and drink,' she replied and rushed off.

Lilian turned to face Brighton.

'Do you think Adri knows?' he asked.

'I think all of Zedonia knows. I can't stay quiet when you do that to me,' she said giggling a little.

Brighton replied by snaking his hand under the blanket onto her leg. Lilian's breathing quickened again when Brighton's hand moved higher.

'Let's see if you can stay quiet,' he said teasingly.

Adri pushed the door open with her back and entered carrying a tray full of food and juice. Brighton did not remove his hand from Lilian's leg, he slid it even higher.

'Brighton,' Lilian whispered urgently.

'Yes?' he whispered back innocently.

Adri approached the bed but Lilian stopped her.

'Just put it on the table, thank you. We will get it there,' she said trying hard to control her voice.

It didn't quite work. Adri grinned from ear to ear and nodded. She put the tray down and walked to the door.

As she was about to leave she turned and said, 'I will bring Brighton's things later, much, much later.'

Lilian just nodded not trusting her voice. As soon as the door closed, she let the sheet drop and flopped back. Brighton pulled the sheet off her completely and gently stroked her body.

'Enough teasing,' Lilian breathed and pulled him down to her.

*****

They fell asleep in each other's arms late that night.

When they woke up, there was fresh food and juice on the table. Brighton's things were also on the table. He got up and brought the tray to the bed. They ate giggling and teasing each other. As soon as breakfast was done, they got dressed. Brighton thought they should get some fresh air for a change.

Lilian opened the door. Another serving girl, Michaela, was standing with her back towards them. She was also about sixteen winters old like Adri but a bit taller. She jumped around and dropped her head.

'Good morning Miss Lilian, Master Brighton. Is there anything I can do for you?' she said, her voice trembling.

Brighton sighed.

'Not the *Master* thing again,' he said.

He put his hand under Michaela's chin and lifted her head so that he could look into her eyes.

'My name is Brighton, please call me that,' he said with a smile.

'Yes, Master Brighton,' she replied through trembling lips.

The young girl was close to tears.

'No. Brighton, not Master, just Brighton,' he said to her in a soft voice.

She just stood staring at him, eyes wide. Lilian touched her shoulder.

'Michaela, it's alright, he won't hurt you,' she soothed the frightened girl.

Michaela looked at Lilian with big eyes.

'But he killed Supreme Amber, Supreme Theresa and a lot of Dark Ones,' she said, tears welling up in her eyes.

'Some people say he is going to kill all of us,' she sobbed. 'They call him "The White Demon".'

Brighton put his hands on his hips.

'Ridiculous,' he whispered.

Lilian spoke to the girl again.

'Michaela, how many people are left here? I thought everybody ran away?' she asked.

Michaela answered through her tears.

'Only some of the servants are left. And two cooks. All the Dark Ones and Supremes fled. There is also a black demon roaming the halls.'

'Supremes?' Brighton asked, alarmed.

He thought they were all dead.

'Weren't they all killed?' he asked Michaela.

She shook her head, too afraid to speak to him.

'Well, who is left? I killed Amber and Theresa. Mischief got Seth. That leaves Raina, Michael, Lauryn and Richard. Did all four of them escape?'

Michaela shook her head again.

'The black demon ripped Supreme Lauryn's head off and tore Supreme Michael apart. The demon also killed another eight Dark Ones. There was nothing they could do to stop it. Supreme Raina and Supreme Richard fled. Nobody has seen them since.'

Brighton headed towards the dining room. Lilian followed and gestured for Michaela to do the same.

They found an empty hall. There were no bodies on the floor, everything was clean. Brighton was confused but Lilian understood instantly what happened.

'Everything always had to be spotless. That was one of the rules the Supremes made. The servants must have cleaned this up.'

She looked at Michaela who nodded a confirmation.

Brighton paced up and down, thinking hard.

Lilian sat down on a chair. She told Michaela to do the same but the girl refused.

'Servants are not allowed to sit,' the girl said.

'You're not a servant anymore,' Lilian told her but still Michaela refused to sit down.

'I promised Evangeline,' Brighton muttered to himself as he continued pacing.

'Did you say something?' Lilian asked.

He didn't hear her.

'I have to do it, I promised,' he muttered again.

He stopped and faced Michaela.

'Gather everyone. Bring them here please.' he said.

He concentrated for a moment.

'They are that way,' he said pointing down the passageway leading to the servants' quarters. 'Twenty-two people in total'.

Michaela rushed off instantly. Lilian got up and walked to Brighton.

'What are you planning?' she asked.

'I made Evangeline a promise and I intend to keep it,' he answered.

'The Supremes' mother? Did you speak to her?' Lilian asked carefully.

'Yes. You were dead for a while, didn't you meet her?' Brighton replied.

'Briefly, we didn't speak,' Lilian lied.

She didn't want to tell Brighton what Evangeline said to her, it was far too disturbing.

Slowly people started entering the dining hall, mostly

young girls. Fear showed on every face.

When it looked like everybody was there Brighton climbed up on the table. He spread his arms and started talking to them. Cries of panic came from the small crowd, some falling down on their knees crying.

Brighton shot a confused look at Lilian. She gestured he should drop his arms. Brighton realized that's how the Supremes used to establish an energy link. He quickly dropped his arms and started talking again. The crowd instantly went silent.

'Listen to me. I am not here to harm any of you. I am sorry for the events that took place in this hall. It was unavoidable. The reign of the Supremes is over. Most of them are dead, only two survived.'

Silence greeted him. Lilian realized that the servants would not dare ask questions. She asked instead.

'Who will rule in their place?'

Brighton thought for a moment.

'We will form a council with representatives from every city and town. This council will not rule but rather serve the people. The people will choose the members of the council.'

He looked at Lilian to see what she thought of the idea. She nodded her agreement.

'What about the remaining two Supremes and the Dark Ones?' a small voice came from the crowd.

It was Adri.

'I will track them down. They will agree to this,' Brighton answered.

Adri spoke again.

'And if they don't?'

Shouts came from the small crowd.

'He's a demon, he's going to kill us all,' one voice rose up.

Brighton quickly lifted a hand. Silence fell immediately.

'I am not a demon. I am a person just like you. I am

not going to harm any of you. If the Dark Ones do not agree with my idea I will persuade them.'

He thought it better to say this than to share his real plan with them. The two remaining Supremes were going to die, he promised Evangeline. If the Dark Ones agree with the idea of a council elected by the people he will let them live.

'Go and spread the news that the Supremes' rule has ended. Tell everybody you come across that I will address the people of Zedonia tomorrow at noon in the centre of town. This is your task now; nobody is to stay behind in these caves. Nobody will ever live here again,' Brighton finished.

Brighton got off the table. Wondering if Mischief was still around, he used his sense. He recognized the cat's energy just outside the caves. He also picked up something else. There was still one more person in the servant's quarters.

'Michaela,' he called.

The young girl rushed to his side.

'Yes, Master Brighton?'

'There is someone in the servant's quarters. Why didn't you bring everyone?' he asked, trying not to scare her.

Michaela looked confused.

'Everyone came. The only person left there is Robert,' she answered.

'Who is that and why did he not come here?' Brighton asked.

Lilian answered.

'I clean forgot about him. Robert is the Supremes' father. They kept him locked up in a room just past the servant's quarters.'

'Why?' Brighton asked.

'Seth is...was a very cruel man. He killed Evangeline in front of Robert and then locked him up. They forced him to steal energy from the servants to stay alive,'

Lilian answered.

'How do they force him? Why doesn't he just refuse? Eventually he will die,' Brighton asked.

Michaela answered. She was growing more confident around Brighton.

'They take one of us to Robert. If he refuses to steal our energy, they kill the girl. They bring another; if he still refuses, they kill her too. Robert doesn't take all our energy, only a little. As long as he keeps doing that, we stay alive. We sometimes sit outside his door and beg him not to refuse the Supremes.'

Brighton was horrified.

'By taking your energy he saves your life? That's cruel beyond comprehension,' he spat.

Suddenly he knew what Evangeline said to him just as he left her to return to his body.

'Take me to him, please,' he said softly.

Michaela led the way, Brighton and Lilian followed.

When they got to the door, Michaela took a key from a hook on the wall and opened the door. The man inside didn't look up. He was sitting on a small bed.

He softly said, 'I'm sorry to do this to you, child. If I don't they will kill you.'

He stuck out his hand.

'Come closer I need to touch you,' he said without looking up.

Brighton stepped in and took Robert's hand. Seeing a big male hand when he expected a small female one made him look up. He had the face of a man at least ninety winters old.

'Who are you?' he asked.

'I am Brighton, this is Lilian and Michaela,' Brighton said.

Robert looked from face to face. He pointed to Michaela.

'Is this the young girl I am to torture next?' he asked.

'No, that will never happen again,' Brighton said

softly.

'Then what are you doing here?' Robert said with a frown.

'I've come to help you,' Brighton replied.

'Nobody can help me,' the old man sighed.

'I've spoken to Evangeline. She wants you to go to her,' Brighton replied.

'Evangeline, my love,' the old man said to himself.

'Do you want to go to her?' Brighton asked.

'I saw her die many winters ago, I can't remember how many. How can I be with my love again?' Robert asked.

'I can help you. Do you want to go to her?' Brighton asked again.

'I would give anything just to spend a few moments with her again,' the old man said, tears streaming freely down his face.

'Lie down and close your eyes,' Brighton said gently.

Robert did as Brighton said. Brighton turned to Lilian and Michaela.

'Please wait outside,' he said.

Wordlessly they left, Lilian closing the door behind her. She understood what Brighton was going to do. There was no cruelty in it but rather an act of mercy.

Brighton put his hand on Robert's forehead. He felt the old man's frail energy. He knew Robert only took tiny amounts from the servants. Perhaps he was hoping to die of old age soon. Brighton closed his eyes and summoned his talent.

Robert's breathing stopped immediately. He was dead.

'Now you can be with your love again,' he said softly to the corpse.

He thought he heard Evangeline and Robert's voices say 'Thank you.'

Brighton exited the room and closed the door behind him.

Lilian hugged him tenderly. She knew that must have been a very hard thing to do. Brighton looked around the hallway. He needed some fresh air and to feel the sun on his skin again.

'Michaela, please go get my things. Meet us outside. Be quick about it,' he said to the young girl.

'Show me the way out please,' he said softly to Lilian.

Lilian took his hand and led him to the entrance of the caves.

Chapter 14

Once outside, he used his sense to make sure nobody was in the caves anymore.

'Nobody will ever live here again,' he said as he gathered energy from the trees and bushes around him.

He sent a huge bolt of white light through the massive doors. It destroyed everything in its path until it reached the middle of the hill where it exploded. All the passageways collapsed.

Brighton looked around. Everybody was gone except for three young girls still standing there. Adri, Michaela and little Hannah.

Hannah's hands were balled into tiny fists, her eyes glaring at Brighton.

'You monster! You killed my father and destroyed my home,' she shouted at Brighton.

She picked up a rock and threw it at him. Brighton easily dodged the flying rock.

'Hannah, wait,' he tried to calm her down. 'I didn't kill your father!' was all he could think to say.

'Your pet demon did. It's the same,' she shouted picking up another rock.

Lilian tried to talk to the little girl.

'Hannah, please calm down,' she pleaded.

'And you're a witch!' Hannah turned her anger towards Lilian.

'If you just did as Father told you he could have spent more time with me! I'll make sure you're all sorry for this,' she said and lifted her hand. Brighton snapped a link to Lilian. Hannah's energy link could not penetrate the protective barrier Brighton had put around them. Again and again she tried. Brighton and Lilian kept trying to calm her down but nothing worked.

'Fine, if I can't kill you, I'll kill them,' she screamed turning towards the other two girls clinging on to each other.

Her hand lifted towards the scared girls.

'Hannah. No!' Brighton shouted.

He shot a bolt of white light. The bolt entered Hannah's head on the side just above her ear and went straight through. It hit a tree, setting it alight. Brighton felt the energy of the fire. He concentrated on it and slowly it died.

'How did you do that?' Lilian asked in amazement.

Before he could answer, Adri and Michaela rushed towards him. They grabbed him around the waist and hugged him so tight he thought they would never let go again. Adri mumbled something while crying uncontrollably.

Brighton thought it sounded like 'Thank you,' but couldn't be sure. He put an arm around each of them and gave them a soft squeeze.

'You're safe now,' he said to them.

He wriggled out of their vice-like hugs and went over to Hannah's lifeless body.

Squatting next to the corpse he said, 'Any Dark One who opposes me will get the same treatment. There will be no more senseless killing, the days of the Dark Ones are over.'

Lilian spoke softly behind him.

'I'm a Dark One.'

'No, you're not. You have the talent; this does not make you a Dark One. It's how a person uses the talent that counts, not simply that they have it,' he replied.

Lilian nodded. She looked at the slightly blackened tree again.

'Bri, how did you put out that fire?' she asked.

Brighton got up and faced her.

'When I was with Evangeline in the spirit world she showed me how to use my talent properly. I am in complete control of it now; it does not work purely on instinct anymore. Fire has energy. I simply removed the energy from the fire and channelled it into the ground. Soil doesn't burn so the energy simply dissipated. If you feel the ground I was standing on it should still be warm.'

Adri and Michaela reached down and put their hands on the ground. Excited shouts of confirmation came from them both.

'I can control and manipulate all forms of energy, even temporary energy like a fire or an arrow in flight,' Brighton continued.

Lilian's eyes were wide as she said, 'That means you're stronger than the Supremes. You're the most powerful man that ever lived.'

'True,' Brighton answered. 'But I also have my limits. Seven Supremes and six Dark Ones were too much for me. Mischief showed up just at the right time.'

Brighton looked into Lilian's eyes.

'Do you still love me, now that you know all of this?' he asked carefully.

Lilian stepped closer and gave him a tender kiss.

'I loved you before we even knew about this talent business and I will continue to love you forever,' she said softly, looking into his eyes.

Brighton smiled with relief.

'In that case I will have to ask you soon to marry me,' he said.

Lilian frowned.

'We can't.' she said.

'The Supremes' rule is over, their laws don't apply anymore,' Brighton argued.

'Yes, I know that, but the Supremes appointed Dark Ones to oversee the marriage ceremony. Only the chosen ones or a Supreme can marry two people. That's how they made sure two talented people never got married. All of that is gone now. Who is going to perform the ceremony for us?' Lilian pointed out.

Brighton thought for a moment and said, 'It will have to be one of the duties of the new People's Council. Their representatives will perform the ceremony of marriage.'

Lilian clapped her hands.

'Yes, that's a good idea,' she said excitedly.

'Well, I guess we better get started with this People's Council thing so that we can get married,' Brighton said as he picked up his bow, quiver and rucksack where Michaela had dropped it.

'Or find one of the two remaining Supremes to do it for us. Somehow I don't think either of them will be very helpful.'

Lilian turned around and with her back to Brighton, she winked at the two girls.

'But you haven't asked me yet. How do you know I will say yes?' she teased.

'I just assumed…' Brighton started.

Still smiling and winking at Adri and Michaela she continued, 'I saw the way you hugged these two young girls.'

Adri decided to play along.

'Yes, he hugged me real tight, it was so nice,' she said putting her arms around herself imitating the hug, while elbowing Michaela in the ribs.

'Uh...yes, yes, me too,' Michaela managed to squeak out. She was less comfortable with this line of conversation.

Brighton couldn't find words fast enough.

'I was just...they were...had to comfort...'

He stepped in front of Lilian.

She had her hand over her mouth to keep from laughing.

'You're teasing me,' Brighton said with relief.

Lilian and Adri doubled over with laughter, Michaela was still nervous but couldn't help laughing a little.

'...have to... sit... down,' Lilian managed breathlessly between laughing fits.

Brighton put his hands on his hips and looking from face to face he said, 'You three are horrible, I'm going to spank all of you.'

It immediately looked like Michaela was about to cry.

Lilian noticed and said to her, 'He's joking.'

Brighton gave her a little tap on the bottom and said, 'Really?'

'Yes, really' Lilian assured Michaela.

Brighton looked at the sun. It was past midday.

'You three find a place to make camp for the night. I'm going to find us some food,' he said.

Walking past Michaela and Adri, he swatted their bottoms lightly with the bow.

'And when I get back I'm spanking all three of you,' he said watching Michaela carefully.

She stiffened a little but relaxed when Lilian smiled at her.

*****

Brighton used his sense to track down a deer. He slowly crept forward. As soon as he saw the deer, he nocked an arrow and took aim. The arrow flew true and found its target. Brighton could have used his talent to kill the deer but he loved shooting the bow so he used that instead.

He got a knife from the rucksack and cut four chunks of meat.

'Mischief!' he called.

The cat came out of the bushes.

'You can have the rest; it's too much for us. But don't get used to this, next time you do the hunting,' he told the big cat.

Brighton quickly returned to the women using his sense to pick up where they were. When he got to the camp he saw that they had already built a lean-to and made a bed from leaves and grass. They were desperately trying to get a fire going.

'Stand back,' he said.

A small bolt of light jumped from his finger setting the dry wood alight.

Lilian smiled at him.

'Now that's the best use of your talent I've seen so far,' she said.

Michaela and Adri came over to take the meat from Brighton but he held on to it.

'Tonight we will make you supper', he said.

Both girls looked very uncomfortable with this but didn't say anything.

Brighton waited a while for the fire to turn to embers before he started cooking the meat.

The women fashioned chairs from rocks and wood.

Brighton cut small pieces of meat and gave some to Michaela and Adri first. He and Lilian then got some meat and they all sat down to eat.

'Some beans or bread would have been good with this,' Brighton commented.

Lilian giggled a little and said, 'We could have found some wild beans to cook but when you destroyed the palace you also buried all the pots. We have no way of cooking anything.'

'Sorry,' Brighton mumbled. 'Maybe we can get a pot in town tomorrow.'

After supper they were all rather tired. The events of the day drained them physically and emotionally.

Brighton looked around but saw only one grass bed.

'We won't all fit on there,' he said.

'Michaela and Adri made that for us. They made two more behind those bushes,' Lilian said, pointing.

'You might need some privacy,' Adri said with a naughty smile.

'Yes…um…no, that's not necessary,' Brighton stammered, his ears going red.

Lilian laughed.

'The most powerful man that ever lived and he still gets embarrassed! That's funny.'

Brighton shifted uncomfortably.

'I saw a river earlier. I'm going there for a bath,' he said quickly.

Lilian slipped her arms around him and asked seductively, 'Do you mind if I join you?'

Brighton felt uncomfortable with this display of affection in front of the two younger girls.

'Let's go,' he said quickly to Lilian.

They walked hand in hand to the river.

'Bri, don't be shy in front of other people. We love each other and I want the whole world to know,' Lilian said gently.

'I don't mind people knowing either but what if Adri and Michaela thought we were…you know…' Brighton replied.

'They already know,' Lilian replied.

Brighton didn't reply.

Lilian made sense; maybe it was silly that he was

embarrassed about it.

They reached the river.

'So, are you going to help me again,' Lilian said with a sly smile.

'Of course, my lady,' Brighton replied with a smile.

He started unbuttoning her dress.

*****

They returned much later to the camp. Adri and Michaela were sitting by the fire talking softly. They jumped up as soon as they saw the couple coming.

'Sit, relax,' Brighton said casually.

He and Lilian sat down on some makeshift chairs.

Brighton looked at the two young girls.

'Things might get a bit rough tomorrow in town. Don't be scared, just stay close to me,' he instructed them.

'You too,' he said to Lilian.

'If there is a Dark One or Supreme there, I will take care of them.'

Michaela spoke in a tiny voice, 'How close should we be to you?'

'Close enough to touch me. If a fight breaks out I can protect you as long as you touch me. Doing it over a distance is much harder,' Brighton said.

'Why?' Adri asked.

'I put a kind of barrier around the person I'm protecting. It takes a lot of my energy to maintain that barrier and a link to that person. If you touch me I don't have to use a link,' he explained.

Lilian asked the next question.

'Do you use your own energy or get it from somewhere else?'

'I can draw power from all living things around me but there is a limit to what my body can take. If too much energy flows through me I will die,' Brighton said to her.

'Don't be alarmed, it will not happen, I can feel it when I'm close to my limit. I should be able to protect all three of you and myself without too much trouble.'

'Remember, I'm telling you this just as a precaution. In all likelihood there will not be trouble. Michaela, Adri, I should show you how I use a link to protect you, just in case. I don't want you to panic if it does become necessary.'

The girls both looked panicky but Lilian said, 'It does not hurt, it feels kind of warm. Don't be frightened.'

Michaela wasn't happy with this at all.

'But you said we must touch you,' she protested.

'It feels the same,' Lilian said.

'And it might be necessary to use the link,' Brighton added.

He studied their young faces.

'Are you ready?' he asked.

Although frightened they both nodded.

'And you?' he asked Lilian.

She also nodded.

Brighton snapped a link to Adri and then to Michaela. He wove a protective barrier around them both. Next, he established a link to Lilian and placed a barrier around her. Finally, he put a barrier around himself. He drew energy from the surroundings.

It felt comfortable.

Without dropping the links he said, 'This is good, I can easily maintain all four barriers and the three links for a long time. It might get difficult if I have to fight someone though.'

He dropped the barriers and broke the links.

Adri was the first to speak.

'It felt kind of nice. Warm, like Lilian said.'

'That's because the energy first has to enter your body before I can manipulate it into a barrier,' Brighton explained.

Michaela asked in a small voice, 'Can you take energy from us?'

'Yes, but I prefer not to,' Brighton replied looking her in the eyes.

She lifted her chin slightly and said, 'If you need to take some of mine, you may.'

'Me too,' Adri added.

Brighton smiled. He had won their trust; that was important.

'Thank you, but it will probably never be necessary. There are numerous energy sources around us.'

Lilian put her head next to his.

'You already take my energy, but not in that way,' she whispered and nibbled seductively on his ear.

'Lily!' he whispered back urgently.

Adri looked at Michaela and said, 'Let's go to bed.'

They both got up.

Adri spoke to Brighton and Lilian, 'Is there anything we can do for you before we go?'

'No, thank you,' Lilian said. 'Remember, you are not servants any more.'

'I know,' Adri said. 'But I don't mind.'

Michaela echoed the sentiment.

As they walked away Michaela asked Adri, 'Do you think they will...you know...make noise again?'

Adri responded quickly, 'No, they already did that down by the river. Didn't you see the smiles on their faces when they got back?'

Brighton wished the earth would open up and swallow him.

Lilian giggled.

'I told you they know these things. They were both servants in the palace from a very young age. They saw and heard a lot of things in that place,' she said.

'Do you think...' Brighton started but stopped quickly.

He tried again, 'I heard that Seth had a taste for young

girls. As young as them?'

'No,' Lilian replied. 'Luckily for them they were just a little too young, even for Seth. Another winter or two and they would have both caught his attention.'

Even though Seth was dead, Brighton couldn't help getting angry.

'He was a monster. What about the other men in the palace?'

'No, the girls were Seth's property. He didn't allow anyone to touch the serving girls unless he said so,' Lilian said.

Brighton spoke slowly.

'When Adri took me to the guest quarters she was eager, almost insistent to please me. She even offered to fetch more girls if that's what I wanted. Seth briefly spoke to her just before that. I wonder if he instructed her to do that.'

Lilian nodded, 'Most definitely. Did you see him slap her in the dining hall? His plan was obviously to make me angry at you so that I will put the bracelet on your arm. As it turned out I was a fool and did it anyway,' she said sadly.

Brighton put his arm around her.

'It wasn't your fault. Seth deceived us both.'

Lilian leaned against him.

'You could have died,' she whispered.

'But I didn't and now I know how to use my talent properly. So you see, it all worked out well,' he assured her.

'Tomorrow is going to be an interesting day,' he said trying to change the subject.

Concerned Lilian asked, 'Do you expect trouble? Is that why you tested the barrier on all four of us?'

'I don't know what to expect. I just want to be prepared,' he replied.

'Raina and Richard are not close, I can't sense them, but there are a lot of Dark Ones around. They might not be too excited about the idea of a People's Council,' Brighton said thoughtfully.

'You can sense Dark Ones?' Lilian asked.

'Yes,' Brighton replied. 'Their energy feels slightly different from normal people.'

Lilian nodded. She was afraid of what might happen tomorrow, but had also decided to use her talent if need be.

After all, she is the daughter of a Supreme. Only two people, except Brighton, remained alive whose talent is stronger than hers.

If she had to kill all the Dark Ones in Zedonia to protect Brighton, she would.

*****

Brighton woke up just after sunrise. Lilian was not next to him. He looked around and saw her and the two younger girls coming from the direction of the river. They had been collecting fruit for breakfast and went to the river to wash it.

'Good morning, my love,' Lilian said cheerfully.

Brighton got up and gave Lilian a kiss. Adri came closer and gave Brighton a quick hug. Michaela saw this and nervously also came for a little hug. Brighton saw that her eyes were red from crying and she had a shallow cut on her forehead. He put his hands on her shoulders and held her at arms length to inspect the wound.

'What happened to you?' he asked her.

'I fell,' she squeaked out.

'Just like that? You were on your feet and just fell over. Perhaps I should teach you how to stand,' he joked with her.

Lilian was quite cheerful so Brighton wasn't too worried; this was probably just a small mishap. Michaela's lips turned upward in a small smile.

'No, I was running,' she replied.

'Then I should teach you how to run. It's the left foot, then the right, then the left again, then the right again. Go on, try it. Don't try to run with just one leg, that's when you will fall and hit your head,' Brighton said trying to look serious.

Michaela couldn't stop herself giggling.

'I know how to run, silly!' she said and punched him in the stomach.

He doubled over and fell backwards, acting as if he was in extreme pain.

'I'm sorry!' Michaela said immediately, concern showing on her face.

She kneeled next to Brighton and put a hand on his shoulder.

'I'm sorry,' she repeated.

Brighton grabbed and pinned her down.

'No you're not, but you will be,' he said as he started tickling her.

Michaela was laughing so hard she couldn't speak properly.

'...sorry...really...' was all Brighton heard.

He stopped tickling her.

'Mmm, yes, now I think you're really sorry,' he said as he let her go.

Lilian stood watching the spectacle with a wide smile on her face. She was so glad Brighton managed to win their trust. They have been mistreated all their lives. To have someone who will protect them and be kind to them was like heaven for these young ones.

Michaela got up and sat down next to Adri who whispered to her, 'Did you really think you could hurt him? He is as hard as a rock!'

Michaela just smiled, a little embarrassed.

Brighton got up and stood close to Lilian.

'What happened?' he asked softly.

'Mischief,' Lilian answered.

Brighton understood instantly. Mischief probably came to greet them, Michaela tried to run away and fell with her head on a rock.

'They will have to get used to him. I think he will be staying close to us for a long time. He thinks he needs to protect us,' Brighton said.

'Well, I'm glad. Having that panther close is comforting,' Lilian commented.

'Did he apologize?' Brighton asked.

'Yes, he stood next to her with his head down until she scratched his ears. It took a lot of convincing to make her do that!' Lilian replied.

Brighton sat down and called Michaela over. He pulled her down to sit on his knee.

'Let's see if we can fix your head,' he said putting his hand over the wound.

Slowly he let a small amount of his energy flow into the wound. When he took his hand away, the cut was closed. Only a small scar remained on her forehead.

'There, that's better. The scar will fade quickly and you will be as pretty as ever,' Brighton said.

Michaela blushed and mumbled a thank you as she returned to Adri's side. Lilian came to sit on his lap.

'You're so good with them,' she whispered in his ear and gave him a long kiss.

They all sat down to have some breakfast. Brighton was deep in thought. When breakfast was finished he told Lilian and the girls it was time to go. He wanted to get to the town centre early.

*****

Town centre was a busy place. It looked like an ant's nest to Brighton. Looking around he decided to borrow a table from one of the shops to use as a stage. The four of them approached a shop owner to ask for a table. As soon as the man saw Lilian he cast his eyes downward and said, 'Take anything you want.'

Brighton was flabbergasted.

Lilian whispered to him, 'I used to come here with Seth.'

Brighton nodded his understanding.

Addressing the man, he said, 'Sir, may we borrow a table from you, please? I will return it as soon as possible.'

The man looked up, clearly confused. He stuttered his agreement.

Lilian quickly added, 'And a small pot, please?'

She looked at Brighton and said, 'I want beans tonight.'

Brighton put the table right in front of the shop. This way he had the shop at his back and could address everybody where he could see them.

As midday approached, the town centre filled up with people. Brighton had never seen so many people in one place. When it looked like the town centre was packed full, Brighton decided to address the people. He reasoned that anybody that wasn't present or couldn't hear him would soon be informed about the news anyway. He climbed up on the table and spread his arms.

This brought almost instant silence.

Lilian and the girls were behind the table within reaching distance of him.

'People of Zedonia, I stand before you with great news today. The rule of the Supremes and the Dark Ones has ended.'

Pandemonium broke out. Brighton lifted his arms again but this time it took long for order to be restored.

'A People's Council will be formed. Representatives of every town will serve on this Council. The purpose of this Council will be to serve the people's best interest.'

People started shouting again. The questions Brighton could hear revolved mostly around whom he was and how he knew the Supremes' rule has ended. Again, he lifted his arms for silence.

'My name is Brighton. I am the one who ended the rule of the Supremes,' he announced.

A single voice shouted from the crowd.

'How?'

Brighton answered, 'I killed some of them; two fled and are still missing.'

Silence fell. The crowd was stunned. Brighton thought that nobody believed him. A former palace servant came forward.

In a small voice the girl said, 'It's true. I saw some of it.'

She pointed to Brighton.

'He is the White Light that killed the Supremes.'

Only a few people in front heard her but the words were repeated and spread everywhere in the crowd.

Shouts of "impossible" rose from the people.

One man shouted, 'I was at the palace this morning. It's collapsed, there is nothing left of it.'

Another shouted, 'I saw that too.'

More people confirmed this. Slowly the crowd started to believe what Brighton was telling them. A few cheers came from the crowd, then a few more. Soon everybody was cheering and clapping. Brighton let this go on for a while before he lifted his hands again. Slowly silence came to the gathering.

'Who is considered the leader of your city?' he asked.

Nobody spoke.

Lilian tugged on his pants.

'The Dark Ones were the leaders and they've all fled.'

Brighton bent down and said quietly to her.

'No, there are a few in the crowd, I can sense them. They must be afraid to come forward or maybe they want to see first how this all pans out.'

Brighton straightened up again.

'I need to know who is considered to be a community

leader. This person cannot be a Dark One. Please step forward!' he shouted.

Shouts of 'Graham the baker' rose from the crowd.

An older man got pushed forward.

'I'm Graham, the baker,' he said. 'Most people know me; I guess they consider me a leader here.'

Before Brighton could speak again another man stepped forward.

'The Dark Ones will always rule,' he shouted and lifted his hand towards Graham the baker.

Brighton snapped an energy link to the Dark One and drained him instantly. The man's lifeless body dropped to the ground.

'Are there more Dark Ones here that wish to challenge me?' Brighton shouted, the anger in his voice clearly evident.

He didn't expect anyone to speak but five people stepped forward.

One of them spoke.

'We are in control of this city. You cannot stand against us all.'

A thin line of black smoke slammed into the man's head. It came from behind Brighton. Lilian killed the man without a second thought. She got up on the table.

'I am Lilian, daughter of Seth. I stand with Brighton. The rule of the Dark Ones is over!' she shouted, more at the remaining four Dark Ones in front of them, than at the crowd.

One of the talented ones stepped in front of the other three and spoke to Lilian.

'I am also the child of a Supreme, our powers are equal. You and this man cannot battle all four of us. Stand down and we may let you live.'

Graham the baker slowly stepped back into the crowd. He didn't want to be caught in the middle of this.

Brighton didn't want another fight but it looked like

there was no choice.

'Any Dark One who opposes me will die. Make your choice,' he snarled at the man in front of the table.

The man replied angrily, 'Enough! This little gathering is over.'

The black smoke from his hand raced towards Brighton's head. Brighton blocked it easily. He jumped off the table and stood in front of the confused man. The Dark One tried again and again but could not establish an energy link.

Brighton pulled a knife from his belt and slammed it up to the hilt into the man's chest. The Dark One slid to the ground, knife still protruding from his chest.

Brighton turned to the other Dark Ones, two men and one woman.

'Make your choice,' he said to them.

All three rushed forward at the same time. Brighton sidestepped the attack, his fist flying through the air connecting with the woman's face. Her head jerked back so violently that her neck snapped instantly. Brighton spun around, his big arm closing around the one man's neck breaking it with a powerful twist.

The third Dark One was against the table.

'No, please,' he begged, hands in front of him.

'Why should I spare you?' Brighton asked. 'You made your choice when you attacked me.'

'I'm sorry, I won't do it again,' the man pleaded.

When Brighton didn't answer he added, 'I will not oppose you or this People's Council.'

Brighton turned around to retrieve his knife. He heard the man behind him flop to the ground. Brighton turned back, not at all surprised.

Lilian dropped her hand.

'He was going to leap for you,' she said.

'I know, I was ready,' Brighton said. 'But thank you for watching my back.'

Brighton got back on the table.

Before he could speak a cheer rose up from the crowd. The people in the back didn't know what happened but seeing Brighton on the table told them all they needed to know. He gestured for Graham to come forward again.

'This is Graham the baker. Most of you know him. If any of you are willing to serve on the People's Council, tell him. In two days all the candidates must be back here. The people will then decide who will be Zedonia's representative by means of voting. We will travel to other towns where the same process will take place.'

Graham carefully asked, 'And what then?'

'The chosen ones from every town will come to Zedonia and the People's Council will be formed.' Brighton explained to the crowd.

To Graham he said, 'We will travel to Avarya and deal with the towns along the way. Use the former palace staff as messengers to other towns and spread the word. All the representatives must come to you. Give them shelter and food. The messengers work for the people, that means the people must look after them.'

Graham nodded his agreement.

Brighton got off the table and a buzz started in the crowd. He turned to the shop owner whose table he had borrowed.

'Thank you, sir' he said.

'It's my pleasure,' the man said with a smile. 'Is there anything you need for your journey?'

Lilian said she would take care of that if Brighton wanted to talk to the people some more. She noticed a few standing around unsure of how to approach him. Brighton answered a few questions on how he thought the voting should be done. Graham waited until everyone had left before he spoke.

'What do we do if the Dark Ones return?' he asked

with a worried look on his face.

Brighton pointed to the corpses on the ground.

'If they oppose the People's Council, do that,' he said flatly.

'But how?' Graham asked. 'They have powers that we don't.'

'They are human too. I could have killed them with my talent; or power as you call it, but I didn't. I killed them with a knife and my bare hands to show everyone here it can be done,' Brighton explained.

Graham thanked Brighton and left. Lilian had all the things they needed for the travel and was patiently waiting for Brighton.

He came over to her and said, 'There is a lot of daylight left. We should get going.'

Michaela and Adri each picked up a rucksack.

Brighton frowned at them and said, 'Where do you think you're going?'

Lilian answered, 'Don't bother, I've already tried. They are determined to go along.'

Adri added, 'You will need someone to cook proper food. Eating just meat isn't good for you.'

Michaela also chipped in, 'And someone to protect you.'

Brighton smiled.

'Oh really? You're going to protect me?' he asked.

'And Lilian,' Michaela said. 'You look very big and strong but I punched you down with one shot, remember?'

Brighton laughed as he said, 'Very well.'

He and Lilian also picked up a rucksack each and headed for the road towards Avarya.

Chapter 15

THE FOUR TRAVELLERS stopped at every village they passed. There were no Dark Ones in the small towns; they seemed to keep to the bigger cities. The news of the fall of the Supremes was well received everywhere. Brighton explained the process of choosing a representative that will serve on the People's Council. Mostly a person was chosen immediately and sent to Zedonia.

The first big town they got to was Brasten. It had taken them seven days to get there. Brighton decided to make camp just outside town since it was almost dark.

'This is a bigger town, there might be Dark Ones here,' he said to Lilian and the girls. 'I'm going to use my sense to see if I can find out.'

He concentrated for a moment.

'Lily!' he exclaimed.

Lilian looked up from where she was busy cooking

beans.

'Yes, my love?' she answered.

Brighton rushed over to her, picked her up, and spun around.

'Lily, you're pregnant,' he shouted happily.

'Pregnant? How did that happen?' Lilian asked, frowning.

Adri looked at Michaela and said, 'I hope we won't have to explain that to them!'

Michaela giggled behind her hand.

'Actually I know exactly how it happened so don't start explaining. What do you know about these things anyway, young lady?' she asked Adri.

'Oh nothing,' Adri replied innocently.

Brighton put Lilian down.

'Well, aren't you happy?' he asked excitedly.

'Yes, of course I'm happy but how do you know this?' she replied.

'I felt it when I used my sense,' he explained.

Lilian's eyes widened, her jaw dropped.

'You can feel a baby growing inside me?' she asked softly.

With a wide smile Brighton nodded and held up two fingers.

Lilian frowned at the two fingers.

'Did you feel it twice?' she asked with a confused look on her face.

Adri jumped in, 'No silly, he means two babies.'

Brighton's smile widened as he nodded.

'Really?' Lilian whispered.

Brighton was still nodding. Lilian jumped into his arms screaming.

'Bri! We're going to be parents!'

She kissed him all over his face.

Brighton hugged and kissed her back, swirling around.

Adri said to Michaela, 'Come, let's go get water and

look for wild beans. They're going to be doing that until the sun comes up!'

The two young girls walked into the forest but Brighton called them back.

'Lilian and I want to bathe in that stream we saw earlier. Why don't you stay here and we'll bring back a rabbit or fowl for dinner,' he said to them.

Michaela pulled a face and said sarcastically, 'Oh yes, I'm sure you two are going to bathe.'

Brighton quickly defended, 'That's all we're going to do! Nothing else.'

Michaela nodded and said, 'Yes, I'm sure that's all. I believe you.'

Brighton's ears were burning.

'No, really...'

Lilian put her finger over his lips.

'The more you argue, the more they're going to believe they are right,' she said with a smile.

She hugged him tightly and added, 'I'm actually hoping they are right.'

Brighton looked around uncomfortably. The younger girls always seemed to know when Lilian and he made love and teased him endlessly about it.

'Mischief!' he called.

The black panther materialized out of the shadows.

'Look after Michaela and Adri,' he instructed the cat.

Mischief flopped down next to the girls and promptly fell asleep.

Brighton and Lilian walked off into the forest reaching the stream quickly. Lilian started unbuttoning her dress.

'You bathe while I'm going to get us dinner,' Brighton said.

Lilian seductively let the dress fall to the ground, her back towards Brighton.

'If that's what you want,' she said in a husky voice and slowly pulled the vest over her head.

Brighton stood rooted looking at her naked back. She removed her underwear very slowly and looked over her shoulder at him.

'Well, off you go then. Go find us dinner,' she said as she walked into the water.

The bow and arrows fell to the ground.

Lilian walked into the water waist deep, went down all the way to her neck, and turned around. Brighton came forward but Lilian shook her head.

'You can't bathe with clothes on,' she said.

Brighton quickly removed his shirt and then his trousers.

'May I join you now?' he asked with a sly grin.

'Yes, please do,' Lillian replied breathlessly.

Lilian stood up as he approached her. His arms circled her waist, their lips pressing together. She thrust her hips towards him.

'I want you now,' she breathed.

Brighton picked her up and carried her to the shore. They lay down on a grassy patch. Lilian pushed him down flat on his back. She swung her leg over him.

Brighton's hands glided over her wet skin down her back to her small bottom.

'I love you,' he said softly.

'I love you more,' she breathed.

*****

Mischief stood in front of Michaela and Adri growling at the men facing them. The girls each had a small bow in their hands, arrows nocked. Brighton made the bows for them and had been teaching them how to use it. There were at least twenty men armed with knives and hunting spears. The leader spoke.

'Where is the one called "The White Light"?' he asked the girls in a menacing voice.

Mischief didn't like that at all and stepped closer to

the men, muscles tense. He was ready to leap at any moment.

Adri spoke in a soothing voice to the cat.

'Mischief, don't do it.'

The leader spoke again.

'Best you keep that pet under control. I would hate to kill such a beautiful animal.'

Michaela pointed a finger at him and said, 'Best you stay back. Mischief can kill all of you in a heartbeat.'

The leader chuckled a little.

'He certainly is a magnificent panther but he does not stand a chance against twenty hunters. Now tell me where "The White Light" is before I lose my patience.'

Michaela started talking again but Adri interrupted her, 'He will be here any moment. Why don't you and your men stand back a little? That will calm our cat down and we can avoid bloodshed.'

'A good suggestion,' Brighton said as he and Lilian emerged from the forest behind the girls.

The bow was in his hand, arrow nocked. The leader spoke to Brighton.

'Are you the one called "The White Light"?'

'I suppose I am,' Brighton answered. 'What do you want with me?'

'I am under orders to kill you on sight,' the leader answered.

'And whose orders would that be?' Brighton asked calmly.

He had already used his sense and knew none of these men were talented.

'Supreme Raina!' the man answered.

Brighton nodded slowly.

'And are you going to try?' he asked the man.

All the hunters laughed at that.

'Try?' one of them shouted. 'Brac is the best hunter and fighter in Brasten. If he wanted you dead you would be already.'

Brighton dropped the bow and stepped in front of Mischief.

He gestured for Lilian and the girls to stay back.

'Ok then, you may keep your weapons, I'll fight barehanded,' he said to Brac.

Brac stepped forward but Brighton quickly said, 'Wait.'

The men howled with laughter.

'He's scared of you, Brac,' someone shouted.

Brighton smiled and said, 'Actually, I was going to suggest you and five of your best men come forward.'

Brac looked confused.

'Do you want to die? You're built like an oak tree but you cannot fight six men,' he said with a frown.

'I like a fair fight. Pick your men, I'm waiting,' Brighton answered.

Brac studied Brighton's face. He could see that the young man was deadly serious.

'First I would like to know why Supreme Raina wants you dead so badly. She told us not to return unless we have your head in a bag. We heard rumours of someone killing the Supremes and ending their reign. Is that true?' he said.

'Yes, that is true,' Brighton answered.

'And you did that, I have to assume,' Brac said.

'Yes,' Brighton answered again.

Brac dropped his hunting spear and held out his hand to Brighton.

'I will not kill the man who ended the Dark Ones' rule. I'm Brac,' he introduced himself.

Brighton stepped forward and shook the outstretched hand.

'Brighton,' he replied.

Although he didn't like shaking hands he knew Brac was not a Dark One so it was safe.

He pointed to Lilian and the girls.

'This is Lilian, Michaela and Adri.'

Touching Mischief's head he said, 'And Mischief.'

Before Brac could say anything one of the hunters leapt forward with a cry, spear raised. He went straight for Brighton.

Before anybody could react, Mischief leapt. His jaws closed around the man's neck and instantly the man's life ended.

Brac turned around and shouted at the men.

'I will personally kill anyone that even thinks of harming these people. We are joining Brighton and his party. Anyone who disagrees had better leave now.'

A murmur spread through the men.

'But what about Supreme Raina and the Dark Ones?' one man asked.

Brighton spoke, 'I will take care of them.'

The man that spoke stepped out of the group.

'I don't believe you can. I am going back to Brasten to tell Supreme Raina about this treachery.'

He turned and started walking towards town. A throwing-knife appeared in Brac's hand as if by magic. His arm flashed.

The man dropped, knife sticking out of the back of his neck.

'Anyone else?' Brac shouted.

The men remained silent until one voice shouted, 'We're with you Brac!'

Everybody in the group yelled their agreement.

Brac turned to Brighton and said, 'Well, there you go. You now have Brasten's best hunters on your side. How can we help?'

Brighton looked at the group of men.

'Well, for a start you can tell your men to retreat a little. I would hate for Mischief to misinterpret something and kill all of them.'

Brac laughed and gestured for the men to give them some space. They disappeared into the forest soundlessly.

He turned back to Brighton.

'That cat is big but do you really think he could take all my men?' he asked.

Brighton answered seriously, 'Last time Mischief got angry there were corpses everywhere within moments, all of them Dark Ones.'

Brac's eyes went wide when he saw that Brighton was not joking.

'And he doesn't harm any of you?' he asked.

'No, he protects us,' Brighton replied.

'We were about to make dinner, would you like to join us,' he invited Brac.

'No, thank you, I've eaten. Would you mind if I stay and talk a little though?' Brac replied.

'Not at all, I need to talk to you too,' Brighton said.

The girls had already gathered wood for a fire.

They made a small pile and Michaela said to Brighton, 'Light that for us please.'

Brighton pointed at the wood and sent a small white bolt of energy into it. Instantly the wood was burning.

Brac's mouth dropped open.

'How...what...' he stammered.

Brighton put his hand on the man's shoulder. Brac pulled away quickly.

'You're a Dark One or something,' he accused, a throwing-knife in his hand.

'No, I'm not,' Brighton replied calmly. 'I do have a form of the talent but it's not at all like the Dark Ones have. I don't steal energy from people unless it's for protection.'

Brac relaxed a little but did not put the knife away.

Brighton pretended not to notice. He sat down next to Lilian.

Michaela and Adri were preparing the rabbit he shot earlier. No matter how much Lilian and Brighton insisted that they could also cook, the younger girls refused to let them.

'Sit down, relax a little,' Lilian said to Brac.

Brac put the knife away and found a seat.

'You were not joking earlier when you were going to fight six of us,' he stated.

'No, I wasn't,' Brighton replied.

'But what if the rest of my men joined the fight? You would have been killed,' Brac pressed.

'Mischief would have ripped through your men. Alone he could take at least ten. Lilian is talented and the girls over there are pretty good with those bows. So, although it looked like you outnumbered us, we would have killed all of you,' Brighton said honestly.

'I can see that,' Brac said. 'I'm glad things didn't go that way.'

Brighton looked Brac square in the eyes.

'Can your men be trusted?' he asked flatly.

'Most of them,' Brac answered. 'There were five new hunters in the group, now it's four. I don't know them well enough to vouch for them, but the rest of the guys I trust with my life.'

Brighton nodded. It was better than he expected.

'Be sure to tell them Lilian is my partner and the young girls are under my protection.'

Brac understood Brighton's warning and nodded.

'Tell me about Raina,' Brighton asked.

'She came into town with Richard a few days ago. They gathered all the best hunters and told us to patrol the woods around town. As I said, we were ordered to kill you on sight. Richard left almost immediately; he told Raina he was going to Avarya to gather more Dark Ones and hunters there,' Brac told them.

'And why did you decide not to follow their orders?' Brighton asked.

'Before Raina and Richard arrived, some other people came into town. Mostly young girls like these two,' he said gesturing towards Michaela and Adri. 'They told us of "The White Light" that ended the rule of the

Supremes. It's time for a change; they've ruled for long enough. I will support anyone who can oppose them.'

'Thank you. We will need that support to free Brasten from the Dark Ones,' Brighton said.

He told Brac about the People's Council and how things would work in future.

Brac whistled and his men all came out of the woods. Two of the new men were missing.

Brac briefly told them what Brighton had said and then turned to one of the men.

'Joshua, take five men and hunt down the two that fled. They must not reach Brasten.'

Joshua nodded, picked five hunters, and jogged into the woods.

'He is very young,' Brighton commented.

'Seventeen next winter. One of the best hunters and trackers I've ever seen,' Brac replied.

Brighton and Brac spoke for a while longer until Adri told them dinner was ready.

Brac got up and said, 'Enjoy your dinner. We will set up a perimeter around the campsite so you can have a good night's sleep. Sounds like you have a big day tomorrow.'

Brighton thanked him and sat down for dinner.

'Do you trust him?' Lilian asked as soon as Brac was gone.

'I don't know,' Brighton answered. 'He seems honest. I'll tell Mischief to stay close and I'll stand watch just to be sure.'

All three women quickly volunteered for guard duty. Brighton suggested that Lilian should not have to since she is pregnant. Lilian protested but Brighton, Adri and Michaela quickly took a vote and the matter was settled.

Michaela and Adri stood watch until midnight when Brighton relieved them. Mischief stayed in the camp all night.

Just before sunrise Brighton heard some shouts. He used his sense to find out what was happening. Some distance towards Brasten there was some fighting going on. Mischief was staring intently in that direction. Lilian got up and came to stand next to Brighton, her hand stroking Mischief's head.

'Sounds like there are some people who want us dead,' she commented.

'Yes. Also sounds like Brac was as good as his word,' Brighton answered.

He turned to Lilian and said, 'Remember not to use your sense, the Dark Ones will pick that up. I'll keep scouting the area with mine since they can't feel it.'

Lilian nodded.

The sounds of fighting died down. A short time later Brac jogged into the camp breathing heavily. Lilian quickly fetched a water skin and handed it to him. He took a few big gulps and then washed some blood off his arms.

Brighton couldn't wait any longer.

'So, what happened?' he asked impatiently.

Brac caught his breath and said, 'It seems one of those two traitors made it back and told Raina where you were. She sent more men to come kill you.'

'How many?' Brighton asked.

'I stopped counting at thirty,' Brac answered. 'Possibly fifty or more in total. They were bakers and farmers, no match for my men.'

'How many did you lose?' Brighton asked.

'Two,' Brac replied.

'I'm sorry,' Brighton said.

'I made it clear that we could all lose our lives protecting you. They knew the risk and stayed,' Brac replied.

Lilian touched his arm lightly.

'Thank you,' she said softly.

The sun was just starting to show itself.

Joshua jogged into the camp and spoke briefly to Brac.

'It seems we got all the attackers,' Brac announced.

Adri and Michaela woke up and told Brighton they were going to the river to clean up.

'Take Mischief,' Brighton said to them.

Michaela called Mischief and the three headed for the river.

'Also take your bows. See if you can get a deer or a few rabbits,' Brighton called after them.

Lilian understood immediately that Brighton wanted to make the men some breakfast to thank them for their service. She packed some wood together and asked Brighton to light it. Joshua's eyes went wide when he saw how Brighton did it but kept quiet. Brac shared some of the details of what happened earlier with Brighton and Lilian while Joshua went off to bring the men back to the camp.

Brighton was just getting worried about the girls when Michaela rushed into the camp.

'I did it!' she screamed as she danced around.

Brighton looked quizzically at Adri who was following close behind Michaela.

'She got a deer,' Adri explained.

Brighton got up and hugged Michaela.

'Well done!' he congratulated her. 'But where is it?'

'It's too big for us to carry back,' Michaela said excitedly. 'Please come help us'.

Joshua immediately got up.

'I'll do it if the young lady will show me where it is,' he offered.

Michaela smiled shyly and bumped Adri with her elbow but didn't move.

'Miss Michaela, you will need to show me where it is please,' Joshua said hesitantly.

Michaela giggled at being called "Miss Michaela" and gestured for Joshua to follow her. The two disappeared into the woods.

'Where is Mischief?' Brighton asked.

'I told him to protect the kill,' Adri responded.

'Won't he eat it?' Brac asked.

Brighton shook his head.

'Tell me more about the battle,' he said.

'Not much of a battle,' Brac answered. 'Like I said, they were no match for my men.'

Brighton asked a few more questions which Brac answered as best he could. What he didn't know, some of the men filled in the details.

Michaela emerged from the woods followed closely by Joshua. He was carrying the deer across his shoulders. Although he was a strong young man it looked like the deer was slightly too heavy for him. He tried to hide this by smiling and casually dropped the deer on the ground. Michaela and Adri immediately got to work. Joshua offered to help and Adri handed him her knife.

'I'll make the beans,' she said.

Joshua sat down close to Michaela and helped her with the deer. Every time their hands or legs touched a small giggle escaped Michaela's lips. Lilian noticed that Joshua was stealing quick glances at her whenever he could. She smiled, remembering what it felt like when she first fell in love with Brighton.

Looking over to where Brighton was talking to the men, she whispered to herself, 'And I am still very much in love with you.'

Brighton looked at her as if he heard and gave her a smile. She could see the worry in his eyes even though he tried to hide it.

He and Brac came over to her.

'As soon as the men have eaten we will go to Brasten,' Brighton told Lilian.

'Do you have a plan?' Lilian asked.

'A pretty simple one,' Brighton replied. 'I will take care of Raina and the Dark Ones and Brac's men will protect us from untalented people.'

'Then why are you worried? You are far more powerful than Raina and all the Dark Ones in town. I can also help, only Raina is stronger than me,' Lilian said.

'I can only protect you and the girls. These are all good men. I would hate for more of them to lose their lives protecting us,' Brighton replied.

Brac quickly said, 'We have a part to play if this world will ever be free from the Dark Ones. We are ready.'

Looking at Lilian he asked, 'What did you mean when you said only Raina is stronger than you?'

'I am Seth's Daughter,' Lilian answered honestly.

'You're a Dark One?' Brac asked wide-eyed.

'No. Having the talent does not make you a Dark One, it's what you do with it,' she answered.

'That makes sense,' Brac said thoughtfully. 'You're Brighton's wife and I trust him which means I trust you.'

Lilian was about to correct him but Brighton took her hand and gave it a squeeze.

She assumed he didn't want her to mention that they weren't married so instead she said, 'Looks like the food is just about ready. Would you like to go help yourself?'

Brac called Joshua over from where he was helping Michaela cook the meat.

'Tell the men they can come eat. Five at a time, maintain the perimeter.'

Joshua nodded and jogged off.

Brac walked over to the fire.

'The food looks really good, thank you,' he said to Michaela and Adri.

Adri smiled at him and Michaela asked, 'Is Joshua coming back?'

'When it's his turn to eat, why?' Brac answered.

'I was just curious,' Michaela said quickly.

Five men appeared from the woods.

Lilian said to Brac, 'I'm sorry but we don't have enough plates.'

'We spend a lot of time in the bush, we are always prepared,' he said as he produced a plate from his knapsack.

The other men did the same and stood in a single line.

'Thank you ma'am,' every man said as they received their portions.

They ate quickly and disappeared into the woods again.

The next group of five men came. All of them were very polite to the young girls.

Joshua was with the last group. Michaela smiled at him and cut him a slightly bigger piece of meat.

'Thank you, Michaela,' he said and gave her a shy smile.

Lilian said to Brac, 'All your men got food, your turn to eat.'

Brac thanked her and went to get some food.

Lilian took Brighton's hand and led him away from where the men were eating.

When they were out of earshot she asked Brighton with a smile, 'Did you see how Michaela and Joshua were looking at each other?'

'No,' Brighton said, a little confused.

'I think they like each other,' Lilian said.

'I'll have a talk with Brac about that,' Brighton said quickly.

'No Bri, leave it,' Lilian pleaded. 'Don't you remember what it felt like the first time you knew you were in love with me?'

Brighton thought for a moment and smiled.

'Yes, I remember.'

Lilian also smiled as she remembered.

'I had butterflies in my stomach when we used to play together back in Four Mountains.'

'Me too,' he replied.

Lilian was surprised.

'Really? I never knew that,' she said softly.

'Yes really. Unfortunately I only realized after you were gone that I was hopelessly in love with you.'

Lilian had a sly smile on her face.

'Are you sure it had nothing to do with seeing me in my underwear after we met again in Avarya?'

Brighton saw that she was teasing him.

'When was that? I don't even remember,' he teased back.

She smacked him on the chest.

'Of course you do. You had very naughty thoughts about me that day.'

Brighton laughed and gave her bottom a squeeze.

'And you did not have those same thoughts?' he asked.

'I'm pregnant, remember? That should tell you all you need to know,' she said.

Brighton pulled her close and gave her a tender kiss.

'I liked it when Brac called you my wife,' he said.

'Me too,' Lilian replied.

Brighton shifted uncomfortably.

'I don't really know how this is done, so I'm just going to ask. Lily, will you be my wife?'

Lilian's eyes welled up with tears.

She hugged Brighton tightly, unable to speak.

'Well?' he asked. 'Is that yes or no?'

'Yes,' she choked out. 'Yes, of course I'll be your wife. Nothing would make me happier.'

They kissed long and passionately, forgetting about everybody around them.

Brac feigned a cough. He was standing close by looking at his shoes.

'Yes Brac?' Brighton said.

'All the men have eaten. We are ready to go when you are,' Brac reported.

'Thank you, we'll leave immediately,' Brighton told him.

To Lilian he said, 'We'd better get this People's Council organized soon so that we can be married.'

They walked back to the camp. Only Brac, Michaela and Adri were there. Brighton knew that the men were probably close but used his sense anyway to make sure there was nobody else in the woods.

'Stay close to me and keep your bows ready,' he told the girls.

He picked up his bow and quiver and headed for Brasten with Lilian and the girls by his side.

Mischief disappeared into the woods but Brighton knew he would stay close.

*****

Brighton cast his sense wide. They were approaching Brasten and he wanted to know where Raina and the Dark Ones were.

Lilian spoke softly, 'I wonder why Raina and the Dark Ones haven't used their senses?'

Brighton knew why.

'They want to surprise us. We're being watched by untalented people who carry messages to them regarding our progress. Brac's men already killed at least four such messengers,' he replied.

'What do you think they're planning?' Lilian asked fearfully.

'Raina saw what I did to the other Supremes. She won't try to use her talent. A spear through my heart will do the job,' Brighton answered.

'But why hasn't she tried to kill me?' Lilian wondered.

'Because she knows I will protect you with my life.'

They walked into town, Brighton's bow ready with an arrow nocked. The streets were strangely quiet.

Brighton knew Brac's men were fanned out around

them and it gave him a measure of comfort.

It took a while to reach the town centre. Brasten was half as big as Zedonia.

When they rounded the last corner, they saw why the streets were deserted.

Everybody was in the town centre. Raina was standing on a chair right in the middle of everybody. She raised her arms which brought a cry from the people close to her.

'Ah, young Brighton,' she called to him. 'So good of you to join us. As you can see, the town's people are standing with me. You are not welcome here so please turn around and go back to that hole you crawled out of.'

Brighton looked at the people's faces. They all showed fear.

He whispered to Lilian, 'She is using them as human shields. Her idea is probably that I will not attack her with so many innocent people around.'

'What are you going to do?' Lilian whispered back.

'This,' he said and raised the bow.

The arrow flew straight and true. Raina had no chance; the arrow entered her left eye and went straight through her brain, half of the shaft sticking out the back of her skull as she tumbled off the chair.

The crowd was stunned.

Brighton climbed on top of a low wall.

'Are there any more Dark Ones who wish to oppose me?' he shouted.

His sense told him that there were twenty-seven and exactly where they were in the crowd but he wanted to give them a chance to surrender. He promised Evangeline he would send her children to her, not all the Dark Ones. Most of the Dark Ones fled but five came to stand before him. One of them stepped forward and spoke to Brighton.

'We do not oppose you or the people,' he said.

'You know this means you will never be allowed to use your talent again,' Brighton told the five Dark Ones.

All of them nodded and voiced their agreement. Brighton addressed the crowd.

'These five people are no longer Dark Ones. They have given their word not to use their talent any longer. They must not be harmed.'

To the five in front of him he said, 'Please don't make me regret this.'

Brighton explained the concept of the People's Council to the crowd and how a representative should be chosen. A farmer called Garth was chosen immediately. Brighton spoke with him for a while explaining that he should go to Zedonia and seek out Graham the baker.

Brac was standing a few paces away. As soon as Brighton was finished with Garth, he came closer.

'We managed to kill twelve of the Dark Ones that fled and that demon cat got three more,' he reported.

'That leaves seven that got away,' Brighton worked out. 'Any losses on our side?'

Brac shook his head.

'None. My men knew not to get too close but rather use the hunting spears. If I didn't see that demon cat with my own eyes rip three Dark Ones apart I would never have believed it. He saved Joshua's life. How come the Dark Ones cannot harm him with their touch?'

'He's like me. We are almost completely immune to their talent,' Brighton replied.

He thanked Brac and asked him to keep hunting for the remaining seven Dark Ones.

Turning to Lilian and the girls he said, 'Let's find the road to Avarya. We can make camp at the first river we come across.'

They picked up their things and headed out of town.

'Did you manage to get more supplies?' Brighton asked Lilian.

'Yes, while you were talking to Garth. I got you some more string for the bows and a few blades,' she answered.

Chapter 16

BRIGHTON SHOT A deer not far from the camping spot. Michaela and Adri quickly prepared the meat and some rice for everybody. As before, Brighton decided to give Brac's men a good meal as thanks for their assistance.

Brac came to Brighton with a serious look on his face.

'We've taken a vote and all the men want to accompany you on your travels,' he said.

Brighton shook his head.

'No, your task now is to protect Brasten and its people. The Dark Ones could return and you understand now how to fight them. Besides, we are not entirely defenceless.'

Brac laughed.

'No, I guess you're not, especially with that cat always staying so close to you. Very well, I will tell the men that we're staying. Joshua is not going to like that very much though. You may have noticed he is quite taken with young Michaela,' Brac replied.

He vanished into the woods.

A short while later he was back with Joshua in tow.

'All the men, except Joshua, are glad we're staying since they have families here. This young man is insisting on going with you though,' he said jabbing a finger at Joshua.

'Please sir, I can be of great service on your journey,' Joshua pleaded.

Brighton looked at him for a while before answering.

'What about your family?'

'I have none, the Dark Ones killed them a long time ago,' the young man replied.

Brighton thought for a moment more and said, 'If you promise to treat Michaela with respect you can come along.'

'That's not why...uh...I mean I want to come with to protect you and the ladies,' Joshua stammered.

Brac laughed and slapped him on the back.

'One young lady in particular, I think,' he said.

Brighton joined in with the teasing.

'Yes, looks to me like when young Michaela is around, Joshua's brain can't function properly. She might have to protect him.'

Joshua looked from Brac to Brighton and back again, his face as red as the sun. He didn't know what to say.

Lilian saved him.

'Enough you two! Joshua, welcome to the group. I'm sure you will do your best to protect all of us. Can you hunt?'

'Yes Ma'am,' he replied proudly.

'Good, then you can also help with that,' Lilian said. 'And my name is Lilian, not ma'am,' she added.

'Call me "sir" again and you're in trouble,' Brighton chipped in.

Joshua thanked them and went over to Michaela to

tell her. She clapped her hands and gave him an awkward hug. When they saw everybody looking at them, they quickly separated.

Lilian turned to Brighton and Brac.

'You two are horrible,' she accused.

*****

Brac and his men guarded the campsite for the rest of the night. The next morning he reported no signs of trouble. They said farewell and Brighton's little group went on their way to Avarya. Joshua was a welcome addition to the group. He knew exactly where to look for wild potatoes, tomatoes and many other things to make meal times more interesting.

Lilian was glad. Meat and beans every day was getting a bit much for her. Joshua also taught the girls how to make a very nice sweet sauce from berries to go with the meat.

Two days out of Brasten the group came across a pack of wolves. Joshua immediately put himself between the hungry animals and the girls, spear in one hand and throwing-knife in the other. His skills with those knives were almost equal to Brac's. The wolves were discouraged very quickly when Mischief made an appearance. Brighton noticed how protective Joshua was of the girls. He said a quiet word of appreciation to the young man.

Shortly after that they reached a small village. The people welcomed them with open arms. Rumours of the travelling group had reached them already. A representative was quickly selected and sent on his way to Zedonia.

The same happened in the next village. The Dark Ones were nowhere to be found. Even using his sense to its limit Brighton could not pick up any. Travelling was easy in these parts.

The road ran past a long mountain range. At places there were sheer cliffs hundreds of paces high. A wide river separated the road from the mountain.

As they neared Avarya though, he sensed Richard and a great number of Dark Ones.

'I wonder what their plans are?' he said, mostly to himself.

'The Dark Ones?' Lilian asked.

'Yes, and Richard. He is the last Supreme left. Surely news of Raina's death, and how it happened, reached his ears by now,' he replied.

'He will try to fight you, that is how the Supremes have done things for centuries,' Lilian guessed.

'Perhaps. If he's clever, he won't. He saw what happened in the palace. He must know he can't win,' Brighton said thoughtfully.

'Not alone but what about all the Dark Ones with him?' Lilian asked.

Brighton shrugged his shoulders. He didn't tell Lilian that he sensed over a hundred Dark Ones in Avarya. She was still not using her sense for fear that Richard might feel it and lash out at her. Brighton couldn't keep an energy link and protective barrier around all of them permanently.

'Let's retreat a little and set up camp. We'll go into town tomorrow,' Brighton suggested.

They walked back until Brighton guessed Richard wouldn't be able to sense them if he tried. There was no way of knowing this, Seth had an enormous range with his talent, but he also practiced it often. According to Lilian, the other Supremes never used their sense; they simply ordered people from Zedonia to the palace when they wanted to steal energy. Brighton also guessed that because of this, Richard wouldn't know what Lilian or the two young girl's energy felt like, so even if he used his sense, he wouldn't recognize them.

Since Richard couldn't sense him the group would

simply seem like four unknown travellers if he did use his sense. Camp was set up in a small clearing in the forest. They could see the mountain and the river was not too far away.

'Do you think you can sneak into town tonight and have a look around?' he asked quietly.

Joshua nodded and asked, 'What am I looking for?'

'Any form of defences or large numbers of people gathering. I would go but the people know my description. You will be able to get around without being noticed,' Brighton answered.

'I'll go right now,' Joshua said.

Brighton nodded his thanks and watched the young man jog off into the woods.

When he returned to camp Michaela asked, 'Where is Joshua?'

'I asked him to do me a small favour. He'll be back soon,' Brighton replied.

Michaela nodded with a worried look on her face. Lilian gave her a quick hug.

'Brighton would never deliberately put any of us in danger, don't worry,' she comforted the girl.

Michaela relaxed a little and went with Adri to cut some grass to make soft beds. Lilian looked at Brighton with questioning eyes. He understood that she wanted him to confirm what she had just told Michaela.

'I'm sure nothing will happen. He will look like just another hunter. There is no reason anybody should take any notice of him,' Brighton said to her.

'I hope you're right. Michaela is very fond of him and he feels the same about her,' Lilian replied.

'I'll keep tracking him with my sense if that will make you feel better,' Brighton suggested.

Lilian nodded her thanks.

Just after the younger girls went to bed, Brighton said quietly to Lilian, 'Joshua is on his way back.'

Lilian was relieved.

'Michaela will be happy,' she replied.

'No, he is running hard. There are at least thirty Dark Ones not far behind him. Wake the girls,' Brighton replied.

Just as Joshua got to camp Brighton felt an energy link race towards the young man. He snapped a link to Joshua.

Brighton barely had time to place an energy barrier around Joshua before the black smoke reached him. The black smoke tried numerous times to enter Joshua's head but without success.

'Everybody get over here, make sure you touch me!' Brighton urged them.

Joshua raced to Brighton and put a hand on his shoulder. Adri and Michaela both put their tiny hands in Brighton's big right hand and Lilian took hold of his left. The black smoke hovered above them. It tried to enter everybody except Brighton.

Brighton had enough of this; it was time to do something. He gathered energy from the forest around him. Sending his own energy link into the air he connected with the black smoke. For a moment the black smoke and white light battled for supremacy. Brighton sent a huge amount of energy down the link. The white energy raced along the line of black smoke, destroying it as it went along.

Brighton felt the owner of the black energy link simply disappear. He slowly sat down. Having that much energy flowing through his body is exhausting. Everybody hovered nervously around him.

'Get ready, the Dark Ones are almost here,' he said as he cast his sense out again.

The Dark Ones were getting close. Suddenly the energy from one of the Dark Ones simply disappeared, then another. More disappeared as the Dark Ones got closer.

'Mischief is ripping into them,' Brighton said as he got

up.

They all moved to the middle of the camp, a bit further away from the trees. He didn't know how many Dark Ones he could battle but it wasn't a lot. Sending that much energy through the link had pushed his body almost to the limit.

Joshua took up position in front of the girls. Mischief burst through the trees and crouched in front of Lilian and Brighton. The girls and Brighton had their bows ready, Joshua his spear and throwing knives.

Brighton quickly formulated a plan.

'Adri, you shoot first, Michaela you second. I'll go last. Joshua, keep your spear for hand-to-hand defence if it comes to that but let them have it with those knives after I've shot my first arrow. Lilian, only use your talent on the ones you know are weaker than you.'

The first Dark One burst through the trees. Adri's arrow took him in the chest. Michaela took down the second Dark One, Brighton the third. Joshua's knife flashed taking the next man in the throat. Mischief was off like a flash. He disappeared into the trees. Brighton felt the temporary energy from an arrow coming towards them. He barely had time to manipulate it and deflect the arrow away. More arrows came through the trees. In desperation, Brighton threw up a white wall of pure energy just in front of the defenders. Most of the arrows hit the defensive wall and fell to the ground but one got through.

Joshua groaned as the arrow pierced his upper leg.

More Dark Ones rushed out of the trees, more arrows flew towards them. Brighton gathered more energy from the forest and threw up another energy wall. More arrows got through this time.

Lilian dropped to the ground, an arrow protruding from her shoulder. Brighton had one arrow in his chest and one in his arm.

Adri and Michaela kept firing with deadly accuracy.

As soon as a Dark One showed himself he was greeted by a well-aimed arrow. One woman slowly snuck through the undergrowth until she was almost behind the defenders. From where Lilian was lying on the ground she spotted the attacker. Her hand lifted and a black energy link slammed into the woman's head. Lilian killed her instantly.

Adri missed with her next shot but Mischief surprised the man from behind. His head was separated from his body in an instant.

Two more arrows flew out of the woods towards them. Brighton knew if he let more energy from the forest flow through his body it would kill him. Instead, he used what energy he had left in his body and threw up a defensive barrier again. He saw the two arrows drop out of the sky just before his world went black.

*****

Brighton slowly came to. He opened his eyes. The sun was at its highest in the blue sky. He turned his head slightly. Lilian was on a bed of grass next to him, her eyes closed. He tried to sit up but gentle hands kept him on his back.

'Lie still,' a voice said softly.

'Lilian?' he asked.

'We're all fine. Lilian too. She is just sleeping,' Adri replied.

Joshua's head came into his field of vision.

'I'm glad to see you're still with us,' he said cheerfully.

'Nice to see you too,' Brighton replied.

Michaela brought a water skin.

'Sit up, drink some water,' she instructed.

Brighton sat up but didn't take the water. He leaned over and put his hand on Lilian's chest. She was breathing evenly.

Adri said, 'Her injury was only slight. She stayed up all night to watch you but finally succumbed to exhaustion a while ago. I'm glad she's sleeping now so don't wake her please.'

Brighton nodded and took the water skin.

He drank slowly; everything in his body seemed to hurt.

'What happened after I blacked out?' he asked.

Michaela answered.

'Somehow the arrows slowed down a lot before they got to us. The wounds are all rather shallow except the one in your arm. Joshua fought off another four Dark Ones with his spear, Adri and I kept shooting, Lilian killed two more and Mischief must have gotten the rest.'

Brighton nodded.

'I threw up an energy barrier in the air, that's what slowed the arrows down.'

Michaela threw her arms in the air.

'I told you it was him!' she said to Joshua. 'You owe me a kiss.'

The young man awkwardly bent towards her and gave her a little peck on the cheek. Michaela put her hands on her hips and frowned at him.

'A proper kiss,' she said and pouted her lips.

Joshua looked at Brighton for assistance but instead the slightly older man said, 'If you lost a bet you have to pay up.'

Joshua leaned over and lightly pressed his lips onto Michaela's.

He quickly stepped away, face reddening fast.

'If I won the bet you would have owed me a kiss,' he said.

'I know,' Michaela beamed. 'There was no way I could lose!'

'Looks to me like you both won,' Lilian said from behind Brighton.

'Lily, you're awake!' Brighton said as he turned to her. She sat up and hugged him fiercely.

'I was just tired; you were the one that was injured,' she said without letting him go.

The small wound in her shoulder hurt a lot but she tried not to show it.

'Let's see your wounds,' she said as she opened his shirt and removed the bandages.

There was only a slight red mark on his shoulder and nothing on his chest. Joshua's eyes went wide.

'I pulled two arrows from you and dressed the wounds! How is this possible?' he exclaimed.

'It's my instinct,' Brighton replied. 'As soon as my body was ready to get more energy from the forest my instinct took over. My body automatically got enough energy to heal the wounds.'

Joshua didn't understand fully, but decided not to ask any more questions.

Brighton pulled Lilian's blood soaked dress open slightly to look at her shoulder. The wound was not deep. He put his hand over it and let some energy flow into her shoulder. When he took his hand away the wound was gone.

'Come, your turn,' Brighton said to Joshua.

'No thank you,' the young man said. 'I'll heal the normal way. Besides, it's only a scratch.'

'Big baby,' Michaela teased him.

'Tease me again and I'll tickle you,' he threatened.

'Promise?' Michaela said slowly, trying to hide a smile.

Joshua answered by trying to grab her but she was already running. He chased after her into the bushes. A lot of giggling and laughing came from the woods.

Lilian watched the youngsters with a smile but Brighton's mind had already turned to other thoughts.

'What are you thinking my love?' she asked.

'I was wondering who attacked us with the energy

link,' Brighton answered.

'Not Richard?' she frowned

'No, I didn't recognize the energy. It had to be one of the Supremes' children. Richard is still alive and he knows how to attack us. He almost succeeded. I think this was a test to see if his tactic would work.'

'That's bad news,' Lilian said worriedly.

Brighton nodded and said, 'We have to strengthen our defences and I have an idea how.'

Lilian started asking what he had in mind but Joshua and Michaela returned to the camp, their clothes and hair full of grass.

'I don't think I'm going to ask them what they were doing,' Brighton whispered to Lilian.

He called Joshua over and asked, 'Why did the Dark Ones follow you back here? They don't know you.'

Joshua didn't take any offense at the question; he knew he should have been more careful and observant.

'Richard apparently made a rule that everybody had to be with at least two other people known to them. That way there are always two people that can vouch for a person. I didn't notice this until it was too late. They spotted me alone in the streets and I ran. I'm sorry; I will do better next time.'

Brighton waved off the apology.

'Not your fault. I should have expected Richard to take precautions. He knows I'm coming for him. We have to be ready for the next attack.'

He called Adri over.

'I have an idea but you might not like it,' he said to all of them, mostly to Lilian.

'Well, let's hear it and then we can decide,' Joshua suggested.

'I can transfer energy into any object; this is how my arrows can travel so much further than others. If I can transfer an energy shield into your spear and bows, you could use that to block further attacks from

Richard or other Dark Ones who can use the energy link. That way I will be free to attack and destroy them.'

'It sounds like a good idea, which is the part we won't like?' Lilian frowned.

'We need to test it,' Brighton said flatly.

Only Lilian realized what he was suggesting.

'NO! I can't do that!' she protested.

'Do what?' Joshua asked.

Brighton answered.

'I will create the shield, Lilian will try and break through it with her talent. She won't be taking any energy from you, simply trying to establish a link.'

Lilian put her hand on his shoulder.

'Bri, please don't ask me to do this. You know I hate using the talent,' she begged him.

'My love, if I had another idea I would try that first but I don't. This could work and we need to strengthen our defences. We barely escaped with our lives last night.'

Lilian nodded slowly. She knew he was right.

Brighton turned to Joshua.

'Are you willing to try?' he asked.

Joshua nodded and fetched his spear.

Brighton took the spear in both hands and concentrated on it. Energy flowed from him into the wood. He handed the spear back to Joshua.

'It's warm,' Joshua said.

'It's the energy you're feeling. If I put any more into it, the spear will go up in flames. It's a good way to know when the temporary energy is spent, the spear will be cold,' Brighton explained.

'Hold the spear in front of you,' he instructed Joshua and nodded to Lilian.

She slowly lifted her hand. Nothing happened.

'Bri, I can't do it,' she said.

'Please my love, we need to test this,' he said softly.

'No, you're misunderstanding. I am unable to call my talent forth. It's like I don't have it anymore,' she explained dropping her arm.

Brighton was confused.

'Your talent is gone? How can that be?' he asked.

'I don't know,' she replied.

She lifted her hand again. Still nothing happened.

Joshua put the spear against a tree.

'What does this mean?' he asked.

Brighton scratched his chin.

'I think I know. It might have something to do with me healing your wound,' he said to Lilian. 'Maybe when I used my talent on you, it removed yours.'

Brighton's eyes narrowed a little as another thought occurred to him.

'Mischief. When he was born I healed him. In fact, I brought him back to life with my talent. It seems to have had a permanent effect on him. Dark Ones can't sense him, just like me,' he said slowly.

'And you think I am now like you and Mischief?' Lilian asked.

'No, your wound was small, Mischief was dead. I think the effect will be temporary in you. For the time being Dark Ones can't sense you,' Brighton explained his theory.

'This could be a big advantage. Keep trying to use your sense and tell me when it's back,' he said to Lilian.

Lilian nodded. She still could not use her talent no matter how hard she tried.

Brighton lay down on the grass again.

'I need to rest a while. It still feels like a tree fell on me,' he said.

Lilian lay next to him, her head on his chest.

Chapter 17

Adri gently shook Brighton to wake him up.

'Michaela and I need to go fetch some water but Joshua won't let us go alone. He won't leave you unguarded either so I decided to wake you. I hope you don't mind.'

'Not at all. Go, I will wake Lilian,' he said, looking up at the darkening sky.

Adri nodded her thanks and quickly left with Michaela and Joshua in tow.

Brighton leaned over and gave Lilian a tender kiss on her forehead.

Slowly her eyes opened and a smile spread across her face.

'From now on I always want to wake up to that,' she muttered.

Brighton gave her another kiss and said, 'I'm sorry to wake you but it's getting late. We need…'

'It's back!' Lilian exclaimed.

'What's back?' Brighton asked, quickly scanning the area with his sense and eyes.

'My talent,' she said. 'I can use it again.'

Brighton breathed a silent sigh of relief.

He used his sense again to make sure no Dark Ones were around. 'Use your sense, see if you can pick up where the others are,' he encouraged.

She closed her eyes, concentrated for a moment and then pointed.

'There,' she said.

A few moments later Joshua and the girls entered the campsite exactly where Lilian was pointing.

Brighton got up and said to Joshua, 'We are going to try something else to improve our defences. Please remove the bandage on your arm.'

Silently the young man complied.

'Sorry, but I have to heal this. It's part of a small test,' Brighton said as he placed his hand over the wound.

When he took his hand away the wound was gone.

'Try now,' he said to Lilian.

She concentrated for a moment then got a confused look on her face. She tried again but her confusion remained.

'I can't sense him,' she said slowly.

'Michaela, Adri, come over here please,' Brighton called.

He touched each of the girls with some healing energy.

'Try now,' he said to Lilian.

She used her sense again.

'I can't feel any of them,' she said, flabbergasted.

'Great!' Brighton grinned, 'We have a way of hiding from the Dark Ones,' he added.

'But how does that work?' Lilian asked, amazed at this new development.

'My talent must somehow counteract yours,' Brighton

said. 'Some of my energy is in Joshua and the girls, that's why you can't sense them. Eventually it will be expended and you will then be able to sense them again. I brought Mischief back from the dead and that's why it had a permanent effect on him. When I used my energy to heal you, it rendered your talent unusable for half a day. My energy counteracts the talent of the Dark Ones,' Brighton explained.

'That's brilliant!' Joshua exclaimed. 'The perfect defence against that energy link you keep talking about.'

'Yes!' Brighton said excitedly.

Lilian was still frowning.

'So how come I can sense you when other Dark Ones can't?' she asked Brighton.

Brighton smiled at her.

'Love and trust. I have willingly given myself to you because I love you. My life is yours,' he answered.

'Ah, I see,' Lilian smiled.

'This is not just a defence; it's a means of attack. I can render the Dark Ones' biggest weapon useless with this little trick,' Brighton added.

'But you will need to touch them,' Adri offered her opinion.

'No, anything I can do by touch, I can also do via the energy link. It just takes a little more energy and is therefore more difficult.'

'Bri, my love, you're not just handsome, you are also clever,' Lilian said as she slid her arms around him.

Brighton smiled from ear to ear. This was an amazing discovery. Although he was in complete control of his talent and knew his limits, he never knew how it would interact with other forms of talent or energy. He planted a kiss right on Lilian's lips.

He rose, stretching his arms.

'I am so stiff from sleeping, a walk in the forest will do me good. Join me?' he said to Lilian, holding out his hand.

'Not a bad idea,' Lilian said as she took his hand and pulled herself up.

'See you children later,' Brighton said as they walked off into the forest.

'Who is he calling a child?' Michaela asked indignantly.

'Us,' Adri answered.

'I'm not that much younger than him. I'm not a child anymore,' Michaela complained.

'Yes, but he has lived through some terrible tragedies. Did you know he believed for six winters that Lilian was dead and that he found his mother murdered by the Dark Ones in their home? In winters he might only be five or six our senior but in experience he is much, much older than us. We can learn a lot from him,' Adri answered.

Michaela suddenly felt ashamed about her outburst.

'I guess that's why he is so protective. He's already lost so much, he doesn't want to lose any more people in his life,' she said softly.

'How do you know all of this?' Joshua asked.

'Lilian told me some time ago,' Adri replied.

She didn't say that it was the night after the massacre in the palace. There was no need to remind Michaela of that terrible event.

*****

Brighton and Lilian returned to camp much later. The girls were asleep and Joshua stood watch. He had just added wood to the fire; the flames were high and bright. Mischief had joined them again and was asleep next to the girls. Adri had her arm draped over his body.

'I can't believe that panther can sometimes be so docile and in the blink of an eye become death itself to anyone who would dare to threaten us,' Brighton said.

He gave Joshua a slap on the back.

'Go to bed. Lilian and I will stand watch; we slept all day so we're still wide awake,' he said to the younger man.

Joshua nodded his thanks and went to lie down. Brighton and Lilian sat down on a big rock.

The night air was cool. Joshua noticed that Michaela and Adri were curled up trying to stay warm under just one blanket. He put his own blanket over them and lay down.

'Why don't you shift a little closer, that way we can all share the blankets,' Michaela said in a sleepy voice.

Joshua looked over at Brighton. Brighton pretended not to notice or hear anything. Joshua shifted closer to Michaela and covered himself with the blanket. He slipped his arm around Michaela. Soon they were all fast asleep.

Lilian whispered to Brighton, 'Thank you for ignoring that.'

He whispered back, 'Like you said, they can make their own decisions. Now shift closer and keep me warm.'

'How am I supposed to keep you warm? You're built like an oak tree and I am tiny,' she giggled.

'Ok, shift closer so I can keep you warm,' Brighton offered.

She shifted as close as possible to him. He put his big arm around her shoulders and pulled her close. She thought that this must be the safest she could possibly feel in her whole life. Brighton looked at the fire and then back into the woods.

He muttered something.

'Did you speak to me?' Lilian asked.

'No, I was just thinking aloud,' he answered.

'About?' Lilian prodded.

'Look at the fire and then into the dark,' he said.

She did as he told her.

'I can't see anything now,' she complained.

'Exactly,' he said excitedly.

'You make it sound like it's a good thing,' Lilian said, a little confused.

'We can use this. If we make fires all around the campsite any intruder will be blinded when they get here,' Brighton explained.

'And we'll be able to see them coming while they can't see us,' Lilian added.

Brighton nodded, 'Yes, that's true. Now we just have to hope Richard attacks at night.'

He looked around the camp.

'We need to find a better place tomorrow, somewhere that is easier to set up defences,' he said.

'What are you planning?' Lilian asked.

'Richard will send more people to attack us, I'm sure of it. He will not wait for us to go to him. He has more than seventy Dark Ones with him. He will probably threaten other people into joining his troops. We are horribly outnumbered so we can't take them head on like we have been doing. It's time to get clever,' he said.

Lilian stayed quiet for a long time.

Eventually she said, 'Bri, could I ask you something?'

Brighton nodded.

'Why is it that you have a limit on the amount of energy you can use but the Dark Ones don't?'

Brighton thought for a moment before he answered.

'There are two reasons I can think of. First, I've only been doing this for a short while. The more you do it, the more energy you can handle. Most of the Dark Ones have been using their talent for many winters; their bodies are used to the energy. Second, they only let energy flow into their bodies. I let energy flow through my body, in and out. It's a lot harder to do.

The Dark Ones also have their limits. They just very seldom get close to it with the amount of energy they steal. It's actually how I managed to kill Amber, Theresa and the last Dark One that attacked us. I simply sent more energy than they could handle down the link,' he explained.

'What will happen to you if more energy than your body can handle flows through you?' Lilian asked wide-eyed.

'If it happens fast, I will probably burst into flames like Amber and Theresa. If it happens slowly, I think my body will simply fail and I will die,' Brighton answered honestly.

Lilian was suddenly very afraid of losing him.

'Please be very careful,' she said softly.

*****

Lilian fell asleep sitting against him just after midnight. He gently picked her up, put her on the grass bed and made sure she was warm enough. Feeding the fire a little bit of wood every once in a while gave him enough heat and light to work at. He modified his own bow first and then that of the girls. When the sun was just about to rise he woke everybody up.

'Lily, Michaela, Adri, please see to breakfast. Joshua come with me,' he instructed.

Brighton disappeared into the woods followed closely by Joshua.

They returned just as breakfast was ready. Everybody sat down to eat and Brighton laid out his plan for them.

'Not far from here is a place that is easier to defend, just where the river breaks away from the mountain.'

Joshua nodded.

'Yes, I've seen the spot. The mountain goes straight up on the one side and the river looks like a snake on the other. It looks like an island between the mountain and the river.'

Brighton nodded.

'Yes, that's the place. The river curves away from the mountain and then almost all the way back again. If we set up our defence there we will have the river at our back and left side while the mountain is on the right. There will be only one approach. We should go there now and prepare.'

'Prepare for what?' Adri asked.

'Tonight we're going to lure the enemy into a trap,' Brighton replied with a smile.

Everybody gathered their things. Adri held up her bow and looked quizzically at Brighton. A blade was fitted on one end in line with the bowstring. Brighton picked up his bow, which had a similar modification done.

'Hold the bow with the blade at the bottom. When the enemy comes too close for arrows you side step and then bring the bow up quickly like this.'

Brighton demonstrated how to bring the bow up in a slashing motion while dodging a make-believe attacker.

Michaela tried it and smiled.

'Yes, that will work well,' she commented.

Adri wasn't convinced.

'I like the idea but why don't we hold the blade at the top and cut downwards?' she asked.

'Act like you're attacking me with a knife,' Brighton told her.

She put her bow down and lifted her arms.

'Hold it there,' Brighton stopped her.

'Your arms are up. If I try to cut you from above you will easily fend off my knife with your arms. I will cut you but it will be a superficial wound. Coming from the bottom with the knife gives me a clear path to your exposed stomach,' he explained.

Adri saw the logic and agreed Brighton's way was better.

'Let's get going, we can talk more on the way,' Brighton said.

They quickly gathered their things and set off. Brighton and Lilian led while the others followed a few paces behind. Mischief disappeared into the bushes as usual but Brighton knew the big panther would stay close.

Lilian looked back to make sure they were far enough ahead to have a private conversation.

'What did you and Joshua do in the woods before breakfast?' she asked.

'Not much, we just had a little talk,' Brighton replied, avoiding Lilian's eyes.

'Was it about Michaela?' she pressed.

'Yes,' Brighton quickly replied.

'You're still a bad liar,' Lilian accused with a slight smile. 'Tell me please?' she asked seriously.

Brighton sighed.

'You won't like it,' he said looking into her eyes.

'Let me be the judge of that,' Lilian replied.

'Ok, I asked him to lead the Dark Ones to us once we've got our defences set up,' Brighton replied honestly.

'You're right, I don't like it,' Lilian complained. 'But I trust your judgment,' she quickly added.

Brighton had a worried look on his face.

'I'm not convinced it's the right tactic. It might be best if I go with Joshua and kill as many of them as we can before they reach our defensive position,' he said mostly to himself.

Lilian didn't like that idea either but also knew they had to have a plan if they were going to survive.

Brighton continuously scanned the area with his sense to make sure they were alone. There were no Dark Ones nearby and nobody had used their sense to track them. They reached the spot Brighton and Joshua spoke about. Lilian looked up at the mountain. It went straight up for hundreds of paces; there was no chance of an attack from that side. She looked around at where Brighton was standing next to the river. It was less than a hundred paces from the mountain to the river. Joshua was right. It looked like an island between the river and the mountain. The river curved back towards the mountain leaving a narrow gap as the only approach to the spot.

Brighton called everyone together.

'Lilian, you and the girls cut some thick branches, about eight will do. They need to be slightly longer than what I am tall and stripped of all twigs and leaves. Also, gather enough firewood for at least four fires. Joshua, you and I are going to set some traps.'

Brighton got some bowstring out of his bag and the two men walked back the way they came.

The men returned long after the firewood was gathered and the branches were cut.

In a serious tone Brighton said to the women, 'If you need to leave this area, be very careful. A safe passage has been marked on the trees like this.'

He went to one tree and cut an X into the bark as high as he could reach.

'Look out for the marked trees and always pass to the right of them,' he instructed.

The girls all nodded their understanding.

Lilian held up the branches.

'What are these for?' she asked.

Brighton explained his plan to everybody. For the rest of the afternoon they all worked furiously to get all the preparations done. Just before sunset everything was ready.

Brighton took Lilian in his arms.

'If everything goes well we should be back shortly. Be ready,' he said as he hugged her.

She nodded and gave him a long kiss.

'Please be careful,' she whispered in his ear.

The men gathered their weapons and set off towards Avarya.

*****

Joshua's throwing-knife took the Dark One in the throat at the same time as Brighton's arrow pierced another's heart. The third Dark One, a woman, barely had time to look up before Brighton's white energy link slammed into her head. The woman dropped to the ground without a sound.

Brighton whispered, 'Good, it went better than expected. Let's hide the bodies and find more Dark Ones.'

They dragged the three bodies into a small side street and covered them with hay.

The two men continued sneaking through the almost deserted streets of Avarya. Brighton guessed that Richard's rule of three people together at all times was still in effect. So far he sensed only Dark Ones in the streets; everybody else seemed to be indoors. He was thankful that it was dark moon; it made hiding in the shadows easier.

Brighton sensed three more Dark Ones not far from where they were. He peaked around the corner of a building. The three people were slowly walking down the road in their direction. He gestured for Joshua to stay still, he wanted to wait for the Dark Ones to pass them and then surprise them from behind. The two silent attackers crept deep into the shadows and waited.

Brighton whispered to Joshua, 'Remember to go for the throat. If they can't breathe, they can't scream.'

Joshua nodded, knife ready.

The three unsuspecting Dark Ones slowly passed by. Brighton was glad he touched Joshua with his healing energy earlier. The Dark Ones use their talent often to scan the city, but the two assassins have remained invisible to the eye and the talent.

Carefully Brighton and Joshua approached them from behind, knives ready.

Joshua's knife flashed once, Brighton's twice and the three Dark Ones' lives ended without a sound. Quickly they hid the bodies in the same alley as the other three.

'I hope this continues,' Joshua whispered.

'The more we can kill now the better,' Brighton answered. 'Sooner or later someone will start noticing the Dark Ones disappearing. It looks like they are patrolling specific routes.'

Brighton was glad he didn't have to use his power too much now, the less energy flowing through his body the better. When the time came to start using the full force of his talent, he wanted to be fresh and ready.

The two men continued creeping through the city killing Dark Ones whenever they could. Close to sunrise they snuck out of the city and jogged back to camp. As they got closer Brighton used his sense to scan the area for life. He knew Lilian would feel it, that's how they agreed he would let her know they were returning.

She would signal the other girls not to start shooting.

The two men jogged into camp. There was a huge pile of wood in the middle and six figures made from the branches the women cut earlier. All of the stick figures were dressed in woman's clothing stuffed with grass. Mischief was lying under a big tree looking at them with those white eyes.

'You can come down now,' Brighton called looking up into the tree.

He spotted the three girls easily between the branches.

Joshua also looked up and spotted Michaela climbing down.

'If you stare too long you will go blind,' Brighton joked with him.

Joshua almost didn't hear. He was spellbound by the young woman dressed only in her underwear. The camisole was a bit small for her so it stretched very tightly over her body.

Brighton's eyes were fixed on Lilian as she dropped to the ground followed by the two younger girls. They were all dressed only in their underwear as they had to use their dresses to make the stick figures look real.

Joshua still couldn't take his eyes off Michaela.

Lilian made a face at Brighton and said, 'You're also staring, why aren't you blind yet?'

Brighton just grinned and picked up three blankets.

He gave Adri and Michaela each one to cover themselves and put the third over Lilian's shoulders. She wrapped it tightly around her body.

'It's cold sitting in a tree all night with almost no clothes on! Next time we're using yours,' she complained.

Brighton put his one arm around her to share some of his warmth. Joshua did the same with Michaela leaving Adri standing alone. Brighton stretched out his other arm and beckoned her over. She gratefully shuffled closer until she was right next to him. He put his arm around her and hugged her close.

'Let's make a small fire to cook some food and get warm,' Brighton suggested. 'And get dressed otherwise young Joshua won't be able to concentrate on anything for the rest of the day.'

Joshua's face went red but he remained quiet.

'How did it go in Avarya?' Lilian asked, hoping to change the subject.

'We got twenty seven Dark Ones without being detected. That leaves Richard and about fifty others. This tactic won't work again, we hid the bodies but they probably already found them,' came the reply.

'That's a lot! I thought you might kill six or seven!' Lilian exclaimed.

'They're still relying on their talent to detect us. It's working in our favour for now but I don't know how long it will be before they realize their mistake,' Brighton commented.

Lilian replied but Brighton's mind was already elsewhere.

'Yes, it will do,' he muttered.

'Huh?' Lilian grunted.

'May I have the blanket please?' Brighton asked.

Wordlessly she handed it over, knowing he had just formulated another plan to aid in their fight.

He produced a knife and cut two holes in the blanket. Lilian watched him but did not say a word.

He came to stand behind her and holding up the blanket said, 'Put your arms through the holes please.'

She did as he asked.

'Now wrap it around you,' he instructed.

The blanket was long enough to go almost all the way down to her ankles and also cover her head.

'I see,' Lilian said. 'We can keep warm and use our arms at the same time.'

'And you're harder to spot in the trees,' Brighton said. 'When we came back I saw you easily in that white underwear.'

Brighton quickly cut the other two blankets and handed them back to the girls.

'Tonight you must climb three different trees. Those ones look good,' he said as he pointed, 'It will be even harder to see you,' he added.

Addressing Joshua and the girls he said, 'You three sleep now, we will stand watch.'

The three gratefully accepted the offer and were quickly asleep on the grass beds they made.

Brighton and Lilian chose a rock to sit on.

'You can also sleep, I will stay awake,' Brighton said to Lilian.

'I'll stay awake with you,' she smiled as she shifted

closer to him.

He softly stroked her legs.

Dreamily she said, 'I wish this was over. You could build us a little house near Four Mountains and we will raise our children there.'

'That sounds good,' Brighton agreed. 'We will have goats and a vegetable garden. I can hunt and you bake bread and biscuits.'

He was still telling her what the house would look like when he noticed her breathing had gone slow. She was fast asleep with her head against his chest.

Brighton didn't move. He liked it when Lilian slept against him like this.

From time to time he used his sense to scan the area. Only once did he pick up a single person heading in their direction. Well before the unknown person reached the camp he turned around and headed back to Avarya. It wasn't a Dark One so Brighton decided it was probably just a hunter.

He wasn't concerned.

*****

'Did you track them?' a deep voice asked the old hunter.

'Yes, Supreme Richard, I know where they are hiding,' the hunter answered.

'Good,' Richard said mostly to himself.

They were in a dimly lit bedroom inside the hunter's house. The hunter, Elric, shifted his weight from one leg to the other and back again. He was not comfortable in the presence of a Supreme but his curious mind wanted to know what was going on.

Curiosity won.

'If I may ask, Supreme Richard, what are you planning?' he asked respectfully.

Richard seemed to look through Elric.

'Last night that boy killed a lot of my people. He thinks I will only use Dark Ones to defend this city. We are going to do what he doesn't expect. Did you gather four more hunters?' Richard replied.

'Yes, I did as you commanded. I can get another twenty if that is what you require,' Elric answered.

'No, Brighton expects us to attack with force. Instead, we will do to them what they did to us last night. We will sneak into their camp and kill them before they know what's happening,' Richard snarled.

'But what if they return to Avarya tonight?' Elric asked.

'The Dark Ones that escaped Brasten reported three women in the group. We know there were two men in the city last night so we can assume there are only five of them. If the men come into the city again, that will work well for us. If they return to their campsite to find their women's corpses it will anger them greatly,' Richard said with a wicked smile.

Looking straight at Elric he answered the question in the man's eyes, 'Angry men make mistakes and men who make mistakes are easier to kill.'

Elric nodded and quickly left the room to gather his men.

Chapter 18

Well past midday life returned to the camp. Joshua woke up first and then the girls. Brighton tried to signal to them to be quiet but Lilian woke up from the sound of their voices.

'Time for you to have a nap,' she said sleepily.

'I'll sleep later. We need to get close to Avarya before nightfall. I want to see if Richard has changed the patrolling routines or perhaps made other defensive plans,' he replied.

Joshua gathered his spear and knives and said a quick good bye to Michaela. Brighton got his bow and arrows and gave Lilian a long kiss before the two men disappeared into the bushes. The two men jogged along the safe route away from the camp.

Brighton sensed five people nearby so he changed course to intercept them. They were probably hunters but he wanted to make sure. Brighton slowed to a walk when they were close to the five people.

'Don't make threatening moves but be ready,' he told Joshua.

He spotted a man through the trees.

'Hello there!' he called, waving at the man.

The man looked startled for a moment before he raised his hand in a greeting.

'Hello,' he called.

Brighton and Joshua walked closer to the man.

'I'm Brighton and this is Joshua,' he introduced themselves.

'Elric,' the man replied, looking uncomfortable.

Four more men approached them.

'Are you hunting?' Brighton asked.

'Yes, we're tracking a deer,' Elric replied.

'We just came from that direction,' Brighton said pointing back to their camp. 'We didn't see any deer.'

Elric nodded, 'Thank you, we must have lost it then. We'll go back and pick up the tracks again. What are you doing in the forest?'

'Also hunting, but we're looking for rabbits since it's only the two of us,' Brighton lied.

'Well, good luck. If you will excuse us we need to get that deer before dark,' Elric said.

Brighton and Joshua said good-bye and headed for Avarya.

They jogged for a while until Brighton suddenly stopped so quickly Joshua bumped into him.

'What's wrong?' Joshua whispered.

Brighton spoke in a normal voice, 'Elric didn't introduce us to his men. It was as if they already knew who we were. All of them looked very hostile towards us. Did you notice?'

Joshua thought for a moment and said, 'Maybe they thought we scared their prey away or took it for ourselves.'

'No, you're a hunter. You know that hunters don't

think of prey as theirs until the kill has been made. Even then they are always willing to share. Besides, there are no deer around,' Brighton answered as he used his sense to find out where Elric and his men were.

He broke into a dead run back to camp.

'Come, they're heading straight for the camp!' he shouted.

The two men ran as hard as they could back to the camp. They went past the first set of traps. One of the hunters was lying dead on the ground. The traps they set were very basic but effective. They picked trees with branches growing at about chest height. Another branch with a knife fitted to the end was tied to it. The branch was then pulled back and a trip wire set. They used trees with lots of leaves to conceal all of this. When someone, like the dead hunter, set off the trip wire, they got a knife to the chest in a flash.

Brighton didn't stop to look, he ran as hard as he could along the safe route. They burst through the trees into the camp. One of the hunters was holding Michaela from behind around her waist, his other hand groping her breasts. She tried to fight him off but was no match for his strength.

Joshua stormed forward without thinking, knife raised. He screamed at the man to leave Michaela alone.

Brighton stopped and took the situation in.

Lilian and Adri were nowhere to be seen. Apart from the man holding Michaela there was only one more hunter. Joshua raced across the small clearing but before he got halfway the other hunter let his spear fly. They were used to taking down running prey, the throw was perfect. At the same time the man holding Michaela pulled his knife across her throat.

Joshua crashed to the ground with the spear sticking out of his chest. Michaela also dropped to the ground, blood pouring from her throat. Brighton knew instantly they were both dead.

Both hunters produced throwing-knives and faced Brighton.

He didn't hesitate again. Two bolts of pure white light shot from his body. Two lifeless bodies fell to the ground, their heads missing.

Elric stepped into the clearing, hands held high. Lilian, Adri and Mischief were a few steps behind him. All of them saw the dead bodies immediately. Adri's hand shot to her mouth trying to stifle a cry.

Brighton spoke to Lilian, 'What happened?'

'Adri and I went to the river for water when two men tried to attack us. Mischief killed the first one. I stopped him from killing this one; we might get some answers out of him.'

Brighton stepped closer to Elric. The old hunter opened his mouth to speak but Brighton's fist connected hard with his nose.

Elric fell hard on his back. Mischief leapt onto him, his big jaws closing around the man's throat.

'No Mischief!' Brighton shouted.

The cat released his grip on Elric immediately but remained standing over him growling menacingly.

Brighton squatted next to Elric and put his hand on Mischief's back.

'I ask, you answer. Lie to me and I will let the panther rip your head off,' he said without any emotion.

Elric nodded, the fear dancing in his eyes.

'Who are you?' Brighton asked.

'Elric, a hunter from Avarya,' the answer came quickly.

'Why did you attack my people?'

'Supreme Richard sent us,' Elric answered.

Brighton looked at Lilian. It was as he thought.

'Mischief, get off him,' Brighton commanded the cat.

Mischief reluctantly stepped away.

'Get up,' Brighton said to Elric.

To Lilian and Adri he said, 'Go wait by the river. Take Mischief along.'

Lilian took Adri's hand and called Mischief. They walked off without argument. The old hunter slowly got up, fingers pinching his nose to stop the bleeding. He looked at the two headless corpses.

'What happened to them?' he asked quietly.

Brighton didn't answer, instead he asked Elric one last question, 'Why do you follow Richard's orders?'

'Because the Supremes are the true leaders of the world. All of Avarya follows Supreme Richard, he is our leader,' Elric answered.

Brighton's white energy link slammed into Elric's head. He did not drain the man's energy immediately. Instead, he just took enough to cause pain. Elric screamed and dropped to his knees.

'I am far more powerful than Richard and yet I don't force my will down on the people,' Brighton said calmly.

He stopped the energy drain for a moment but did not sever the link.

'Please, don't,' Elric begged.

Brighton pointed to Michaela's corpse.

'Did you give her a chance?' he asked as he drained more energy from Elric.

The hunter's body twisted in pain again. Brighton concentrated on his left arm. The bones inside snapped with a sickening pop.

'Please!' Elric begged.

'What about him?' Brighton asked softly, pointing to Joshua.

Elric's right arm snapped back, the bones also shattering.

Brighton severed the link.

Elric knew he would never use his arms again.

'Please kill me,' he begged.

'Oh no,' Brighton said. 'You are going to take a message back to your master.'

He walked to the pile of wood and picked up a piece slightly thicker than his arm.

'Get up,' he commanded.

The hunter struggled to get to his feet. As soon as he was standing Brighton swung the stick in a large arc and brought it down on the man's right ankle. The bones crushed instantly under the heavy blow. Elric fell to the ground again screaming in pain.

'Get up,' Brighton commanded again.

'I can't,' Elric screamed.

Brighton brought the stick down on Elric's right knee, also crushing it.

'Get up,' he said again.

Elric didn't move.

Brighton brought the wood up and aimed for Elric's left ankle.

'No wait! I'll get up,' Elric cried.

He struggled to his feet putting all his weight on the good leg only.

Brighton tossed the wood away.

'This is my challenge to Richard: I will fight him anywhere, anytime. He can pick the weapons or we can simply pit our powers against one another, I don't care. Should he not accept the challenge I will hunt him down like the coward he is. Now repeat this back to me word for word.'

Elric repeated the words.

'Good, now go,' Brighton said softly.

'But I can't walk,' Elric complained.

Brighton picked up the piece of wood again.

'If you don't go now I will make sure you can only crawl for the rest of your miserable life,' he threatened, tapping the stick against Elric's good leg.

Elric quickly hopped out of the campsite, wincing in pain.

Brighton looked at the two headless bodies. In a fit of anger, he unleashed two white bolts of energy onto them. Both were ashes in an instant.

He walked off to go find Lilian and Adri. They were waiting for him at the river.

He put an arm around each of them and whispered, 'I'm so sorry.'

Adri was crying uncontrollably against his chest. Lilian's face was also wet from the tears but she wasn't crying anymore.

'It's not your fault,' she said to him.

They stood like that until Adri calmed down.

'Wait here, I'll go bury Joshua and Michaela,' Brighton told them.

'May I help please?' Adri asked in a small voice.

'Me too?' Lilian added.

Brighton nodded and they set off back to camp.

The burial was quick and simple. As soon as they were finished Brighton picked up his bow and quiver.

'Are you going somewhere?' Lilian asked.

'Yes,' Brighton said.

'Are you going to share some more information,' Lilian prodded.

'Elric will take about a day and a half to reach Richard. Add another day and a half to that for Richard to make up his mind and send someone back here. That gives me only three days,' Brighton answered.

Lilian and Adri looked at each other.

Neither knew what Brighton was going on about.

'You will need to explain a bit better,' Lilian said to him.

'I need to go get Brac and his men. Richard will undoubtedly try to lure me into Avarya where he has lots of protection. I need someone to handle the untalented people so I can concentrate on Richard and the Dark Ones,' Brighton explained.

Lilian's mouth hung open.

'It took us five days to get here. How are you going to make it to Brasten and back here in three days?' she asked. 'And why will it take Elric so long to get back to Avarya?'

'First, you don't want to know about Elric. Second, we stopped a lot along the way travelling from Brasten. I will get energy from the surroundings so I can run all the way there and back. I plan on bringing Brac and five men here so I should be able to feed them energy through a link so they can keep up with me,' Brighton answered.

'This is insane!' Lilian exclaimed.

'Perhaps, but I don't have any other ideas. Wish me luck,' Brighton said as he scooped Lilian up in his arms and gave her a long kiss.

He gave Adri a tight hug and whispered, 'Look after her for me.'

Walking past Mischief he gave the cat a quick scratch on the head and said, 'Keep them safe.'

Brighton set off towards Brasten almost at a dead run.

*****

Elric collapsed. He was exhausted. Travelling through the woods in his state was extremely difficult. It had taken him all night and most of the morning to reach the road. He knew he couldn't stop, he needed to deliver Brighton's message to Richard.

Richard will not take it lightly; he will probably go after Brighton himself.

Elric tried to get up but nearly passed out. He tried again, gritting his teeth against the pain. Finally, he was standing on his good leg. Just before he resumed hopping towards Avarya, he looked around.

Two travellers were coming his way. He shouted as loud as he could. The travellers, two women, spotted him and picked up their pace. When they reached him both started talking immediately.

'Wait!' he shouted.

Both women clamped their mouths shut instantly.

Elric spoke as calmly as he could, 'I need to get to Avarya urgently but both my arms, my left knee and left ankle is broken. Will you help me please?'

The women quickly agreed. Without hesitation they started cutting branches to make a litter for Elric. In no time it was complete.

'You two certainly know what you're doing,' Elric commented.

'We are healers. We travel between towns and help people,' the one woman replied.

The other produced a small vial from her rucksack.

'Here, drink this. It will dull the pain,' she said.

When Elric made no move to take the vial, she realized that his arms were useless.

'Sorry,' she apologized and held the vial to his lips.

He swallowed the bitter tasting fluid in one gulp.

The women helped him onto the litter. They picked it up, one at the front and one at the back.

'You two are stronger that you look,' Elric commented, his mind starting to spin a bit from the pain medicine.

'Lots of practice,' one woman replied.

'I'm Bertha,' she said.

'And I'm Katryn,' the other introduced herself.

Elric introduced himself.

'We will take it slow, that way there will be less pain,' Bertha said to him.

'No, I need to get to Avarya in a hurry. It's a matter of life and death,' Elric urged them.

'In that case we will hurry. Tell us when the pain is too much,' Bertha replied.

They set off at a brisk pace. Elric floated in and out of consciousness. He didn't know whether it was from the pain or the bitter fluid they gave him. Along the way, the two women peppered him with questions about what had happened to him and why he was in such a hurry.

'A band of robbers attacked me,' he lied and didn't say anything after that.

Eventually the women gave up and started talking to each other.

They reached Avarya just after midday. Elric directed them to his house. A number of Dark Ones were standing guard at the front door.

'We'll take him now,' a Dark One told the two healers.

Two Dark Ones picked Elric up from the litter and carried him inside.

Richard was sitting in the kitchen having lunch. They put Elric down on the floor in front of Richard and left.

'Supreme Richard, I have a message from Brighton,' Elric began.

'Did you kill the women?' Richard asked slowly.

'We killed one girl and the younger boy. Brighton and the other two girls are still alive,' Elric replied.

'The five best hunters in Avarya cannot kill three girls. How pathetic,' Richard snarled.

Elric didn't like where this conversation was going.

'Brighton is clever. He set traps that killed one of my men and killed two more himself. There was also a big black panther that killed the last hunter and very nearly got me. I barely escaped with my life but not before Brighton tortured me. He is very powerful.'

Richard's black energy link slammed into Elric's head but he didn't drain the hunter's energy immediately.

'He is nothing but a boy! I am the most powerful human alive! I have no need to prove this to him!' he shouted at Elric.

Slowly he started stealing Elric's energy.

'You have a message for me?' he asked.

Elric repeated Brighton's message through gritted teeth. Richard's anger reached boiling point. He instantly drained the last of Elric's energy.

*****

Brighton slowed to a jog. He had been running all night and most of the morning. Earlier he sensed four people in the woods. He left the road and headed in that direction. It was still a fair way to Brasten but perhaps Brac's men patrolled this far. He slowed to a walk.

'That's far enough,' a voice called to him.

Brighton stopped. He suddenly realized that he did not know what Brac's energy felt like. Although he had used his sense when Brac was around he never put the face to the energy signature.

He knew the man was slightly to his left but didn't look.

'I'm looking for Brac,' Brighton shouted back.

'Brighton?' a familiar voice called from his right.

'Brac? Is that you?' he called back.

Brac came out of the bushes.

'What are you doing here? Shouldn't you be in Avarya?' the hunter asked.

'Well, yes, but we have some trouble there,' Brighton replied.

'Come sit, have something to eat and tell me about it,' Brac invited.

'Thank you but I have no time. I've come to ask for your help,' Brighton replied.

'Anything. You know we stand with you,' Brac replied.

'Yes, I know. I need you and about five men to come with me to Avarya,' Brighton said.

'There are only four of us here. I will send word for one more,' Brac said as he made a gesture with his hand.

A man materialized out of the bush but before Brac could talk to him Brighton said, 'No, that will take too long. We need to leave immediately. We'll just have to make do with four.'

'Three. And why are you in such a hurry?' Brac said.

'There are four people here, you said so and I can sense them,' he said to Brac.

'True, but if we're going to join you, I need to send one man back to my troops in Brasten. If we're not back by sunset they will send out a search party.'

Brighton nodded his understanding.

'Very well, three it is. I hope these guys are as good as you at being invisible.'

Brac just smiled at Brighton.

He had a quick word with the young man still standing close by. The hunter disappeared into the woods.

'Now tell me why you're in such a hurry,' Brac repeated his question from earlier.

'We need to get back to Avarya in two days,' Brighton replied.

Brac started laughing but then saw that Brighton was serious.

'That's impossible,' he declared flatly. 'We can run hard but not for that long.'

'I just made it in less than a day and a half,' Brighton countered.

'Surely you're joking,' Brac exclaimed. 'Nobody can run that fast for that long.'

'I can and if you guys stay close to me you can too,' Brighton said.

Brac shrugged his shoulders.

'I don't understand but I trust you,' he said.

Another hand gesture from him brought the other two men out of the undergrowth.

'Listen carefully,' Brighton said to the three hunters. 'We're going to run fast and for a long time. You will feel a warm sensation in your body from time to time, just ignore it and keep running. If you get tired don't stop, just let me know.'

The three men nodded.

'Last thing, stay close to me,' Brighton said as he turned and set off.

Chapter 19

THEY RAN UNTIL Brighton was getting tired. He slowed slightly and gathered some energy from the surroundings. One by one he established a link to each of the men and let some energy flow into them. He picked up the pace again. The three hunters kept up easily. They reached the campsite just after sunrise.

Lilian flew into Brighton's arms and buried her face in his neck. He gave her a tight hug.

'I was so worried. Are you alright?' she said softly.

'Yes, I'm fine. Any disturbances here?' he replied.

She shook her head.

'You came back faster than I thought. It hasn't been three full days yet,' she commented.

'I was lucky. I found them at least half a day's run this side of Brasten. It saved us a full day,' Brighton explained.

Brac stepped closer.

'Miss Lilian, Miss Adri, so nice to see you again. This is Liam and Nelson,' he introduced the other hunters.

Lilian and Adri exchanged greetings with the men.

Brac stepped closer to Brighton and spoke softly, 'Would you mind telling me how we just ran for that long without getting tired?'

'I gathered energy from the forest and shared it with you through a link,' Brighton replied as if it was the most natural thing in the world.

Brac didn't quite understand but nodded anyway.

Lilian touched Brighton's arm.

'How is your body holding up having all that energy passing through it?' she asked with concern in her eyes.

'I'm learning exactly how much energy to let through my body. I feel fine,' Brighton answered.

'But I thought Evangeline showed you everything you needed to know about your talent?' Lilian asked.

'Yes she did, but knowing what I can do and doing it effectively are two different things. I used far too much energy to kill the Supremes back in Zedonia and when the Dark Ones attacked us a few days ago. Smaller amounts would have been sufficient to get the job done. I'm starting to understand exactly how much energy is needed to perform a certain task,' Brighton explained.

'That's good news,' Lilian replied.

She struggled to imagine Brighton becoming more powerful but she knew he would since he now started honing his skill.

Brighton explained the situation they faced in Avarya.

'We can't simply walk into Avarya like we did in Brasten. There are far too many Dark Ones here, and Richard also has many loyal untalented followers. I need to find a way into the city without harming innocent people. I don't believe that all of Avarya follows Richard like Elric suggested.'

'We can help,' Brac immediately replied. 'These two

men are like ghosts. They can disable any defences Richard might have set up along the route. My only concern is the Dark Ones and Richard. As I understand it they can sense us coming. There is no way of hiding from them.'

'I can do something about that,' Brighton said with a wide smile.

He explained the use of healing energy and how it hides a person temporarily from the Dark Ones' sense.

Brac was happy with this solution, but Liam cleared his throat.

'What about Richard? Isn't he a Supreme?' came the question.

Brighton answered, 'He is the last Supreme. I will deal with him. Time to rest, soon we will have plenty to do.'

Brac suggested that they rotate guard duty but Brighton told him it was unnecessary.

'I'm using my sense constantly. I will know if anyone approaches long before they get here,' he explained.

The three hunters found themselves each a comfortable spot and were asleep quickly.

Just after midday Brighton sensed someone approaching. When he told Lilian she wanted to wake Brac.

'No need. It's a young girl, maybe thirteen or so. She is not talented. We should go meet her, so Brac and his men can sleep a bit longer,' Brighton replied.

'You're jesting,' Lilian accused.

Brighton looked at her quizzically.

'Why do you say that?' he asked.

'How do you know it's a young girl?' she replied.

'I can feel it,' he said shrugging his shoulders.

Lilian's mouth hung open.

'Really?' she stammered.

'Yes. You know I can feel whether a person is talented or not. Lately I've also been able to distinguish between male and female and make an accurate guess as to the person's age,' Brighton answered.

'Incredible!' Lilian gasped.

Brighton took Lilian's hand and started walking.

'Why do you want to go meet this girl? Maybe she is just travelling to Brasten or Zedonia?' Lilian asked.

'She's too young to travel alone. I'm guessing Richard sent her to us with a message,' Brighton answered.

They reached the road and Brighton decided to wait there for the girl.

'Have you ever wondered why there are roads here?' he asked Lilian as they sat down.

'That's an odd question. Roads are used to travel between cities and towns,' she smiled.

Brighton got up and paced from one side of the road to the other.

'I know that but why are the roads wide enough for at least eight people to walk side by side? And why does the road follow the contour of the country side?' Brighton asked pointing at a section where the road curved around a small hill.

'I don't know,' Lilian answered.

Brighton scratched his chin.

'It doesn't make sense. Someone built these roads for a purpose. If everybody travelled on foot, the roads would be much narrower and straighter. If we had to travel to Avarya from this spot, we would go over that hill, not around it. It seems that the roads were built for something larger,' he muttered.

'Like what?' Lilian asked.

She still didn't understand why Brighton would be so interested in the roads. Brighton didn't answer. He looked towards Avarya.

'She is close, let's go meet her,' he said.

Lilian got up and put her hand in Brighton's.

They were almost at the curve in the road just as the young girl came around it.

'Hello traveller,' Brighton greeted as they stopped.

He didn't see any weapons but was ready to defend himself and Lilian if need be. The girl stopped about ten paces from them.

'Um...hello,' she stammered.

'Where are you travelling to?' Brighton asked.

'Nowhere,' she replied. 'I'm looking for someone.'

It was as Brighton thought; Richard had sent this young girl to him with a message.

'Who? Maybe we've seen them?' Brighton prodded.

'His name is "Brighton, the White Demon",' the girl answered in a small voice.

She looked to be very close to tears.

Lilian stifled a giggle.

'The White Demon?' she asked.

The girl nodded fearfully.

'Are you him?' she asked Brighton.

'Well, my name is Brighton but I'm not a demon,' he replied with a smile.

The girl relaxed a little.

'Then it's not you I'm supposed to find,' she answered. 'Please excuse me, I have to find the White Demon.'

She started walking again.

'Who sent you to find this demon?' Brighton asked.

She stopped and answered, 'Supreme Richard. Do you know where the White Demon is?'

'There is no demon. I'm the one you're looking for,' Brighton answered in a calm soothing voice.

For a moment it looked like the young girl would turn and run but then she fell to her knees and started pleading, 'Please don't kill me.'

Brighton stepped closer and put a hand on her shoulder. Before he could speak she jumped up and tried to run. Brighton reacted without thinking and caught her arm. She fought as if her life depended on getting out of his grip, screaming, kicking and hitting Brighton everywhere. Fortunately, she was not very strong and couldn't do much damage.

'Wait, I won't hurt you,' Brighton tried but she didn't hear him above her screams.

He let her go realizing that she would never calm down while he had her in his grip. She ran almost ten paces down the road but Brac stepped out from the woods in front of her. Trying to stop she lost her footing and fell face first onto the hard ground. She didn't move, she just lay in the dirt, whimpering. Brighton started walking towards her but Lilian put a hand on his arm.

'You scare the wits out of her. Let me go,' she said softly.

She walked closer and squatted next to the girl.

'We won't hurt you,' she said softly.

'Please don't kill me,' the girl replied through her tears.

'We would never do that,' Lilian assured her.

'But you're a witch and he is a demon,' the girl squeaked out.

Brighton couldn't hide a chuckle. Lilian shot him a dark look but he just kept on grinning.

Holding out her water skin she asked, 'Are you thirsty?'

The girl sat up and nodded but did not take the water. Lilian took a few sips from it.

'See, there is nothing wrong with the water,' she said.

Gratefully the girl grabbed the water skin and gulped down a good quantity of water.

Her nose, hands and knees were bloody from the fall she took. Lilian tore a small piece of cloth from the bottom of her dress and held it out to the girl.

'Wet it and clean your wounds,' she suggested.

The girl carefully took the cloth and started cleaning the blood off her hands.

'What is your name?' Lilian asked gently.

'Claire,' came the soft reply.

'Why do you think I'm a witch?' Lilian asked.

That brought some more giggles from Brighton and Brac and another dark look from Lilian.

'Supreme Richard said so,' Claire replied.

'Don't witches have dark hair?' Lilian asked.

'Yes, I suppose so,' Claire muttered.

Lilian pulled her long blond curls over her shoulder.

'Look, I don't have black hair. I cannot be a witch,' she told Claire.

She felt one of the tiny pink bows in her hair and got an idea.

'Would you like a pink bow for your hair?' she asked Claire.

Claire nodded eagerly. The little pink bows in the blond curls were the most beautiful thing she had seen in her life.

Lilian took one out of her hair and asked, 'Can I put it in your hair for you?'

'Yes please,' Claire said excitedly.

She was relaxing more and more.

Lilian certainly didn't look like the witch Richard described her to be.

When the ribbon was secure in Claire's hair Lilian pulled out a small piece of polished steel from her pocket. She held it up so Claire could see herself. The young girl didn't even notice her bloody nose. All she could see was the pink bow in her short brown hair.

'Thank you,' she squeaked and gave Lilian a tight hug.

'It's my pleasure,' Lilian said gently hugging her back.

'Now, tell me, why are you looking for Brighton?' she pressed on.

'Supreme Richard sent me with a message,' Claire squeaked out.

'I see. Would you like to deliver your message?' Lilian asked still using a soft soothing voice.

Claire looked at Brighton with intense fear in her eyes.

'I'm only supposed to give it to him,' she answered.

Brighton knew Claire would run again if he moved towards her. Instead, he sat down on a rock next to the road.

'I'll sit here and you can deliver your message from there,' he suggested with a smile.

Claire nodded and got up still clutching the bloody cloth in her hands.

'Supreme Richard said he will meet you at the centre of the town market at midday tomorrow. He only wants to talk so no weapons are allowed.'

She seemed relieved that the message was finally delivered.

'Well done, you're very brave,' Lilian praised her.

Claire smiled a little although she didn't feel brave.

'Can I go now?' she asked looking into Lilian's blue eyes.

'You may go at anytime you wish, we will not stop you,' Lilian replied. 'But wouldn't you like something to eat first? Maybe we can also clean those wounds better at the river.'

Claire nodded, she was starving. Lilian took her hand and gestured for Brighton to keep back. She led Claire to the river with Brighton and Brac following a few paces behind. Claire looked over her shoulder often to make sure the men didn't come closer.

Brac spoke softly to Brighton, 'Why didn't you wake us?'

'There was no need,' Brighton replied. 'But I'm glad you showed up when you did. I really didn't feel like running after her.'

'What do you make of the message?' Brac asked.

'It's a trap. Richard would not be interested in talking. He knows I'm coming to kill him and his only way out is to kill me first,' Brighton replied.

'What are we going to do now?' Brac asked.

'First we try to get more information out of young

Claire and then you and your men will get me into the city unnoticed,' Brighton said.

'Do you think she has any more useful information?' Brac asked.

'I don't know but it's worth a try,' Brighton sighed.

*****

They reached the river and sat down next to it in a small clearing. The men still kept a good distance away from Lilian and Claire. Brighton asked Brac to fetch Adri from the campsite. He knew Liam and Nelson were in the bushes not far from them.

'Tell her to pack up the camp please, we won't be going back there.' he told Brac.

Brac disappeared into the bushes. Brighton was anxious to talk to Claire, but he also didn't want to scare her away. He decided to let Lilian continue what she was doing and hopefully they will get some more information from the young girl that way.

Lilian was sitting next to the water helping Claire clean all the blood off her arms, legs and face.

'Would you mind if Brighton comes closer? He may be able to help with these wounds,' Lilian tried.

Claire looked at him fearfully.

'Won't he hurt me?' she asked in a small voice.

'No, he is the kindest person I know,' Lilian reassured her.

Claire nodded. She held on to Lilian's hand while Brighton slowly stepped closer.

'Hello Claire. I'm sorry I scared you earlier,' he said softly.

Claire nodded again. She bit down on her fist to keep from crying. Brighton sat down next to Lilian keeping her between him and Claire.

'May I look at your hands please?' he asked.

Claire held out her one hand for him to see. The

scrapes were minor but Brighton made a show of looking horrified.

'That looks very sore,' he said pulling a face. 'I can help you with that if I may touch your hand.'

Claire looked at Lilian who smiled and said, 'He can really make it better.'

The young girl nodded at Brighton.

He took her small hand gently in his and let some healing energy flow. When he opened his hand the scrapes were all gone. Claire looked at her hand in amazement.

'How did you do that?' she asked, her fear forgotten.

'I can heal other people's wounds. It's a gift I have,' he replied. 'Would you like me to heal your other wounds? I don't think a pretty girl like you should have all those cuts on her nose.'

Claire blushed and answered, 'Yes please.'

He shifted closer to her and started healing all the scrapes.

Claire sat very still until he finished.

'There, all done,' Brighton said as he moved away a little.

Claire felt her nose and looked at her hands and knees.

'Thank you,' she whispered.

'It's my pleasure,' Brighton replied.

'You're not really a demon, are you?' Claire asked feeling a lot more confident.

'No, I'm not. But Lilian is a witch,' he said with a wink.

Lilian slapped him on the shoulder.

'No I'm not!' she snapped, worried that Claire might get scared again.

The young girl didn't, instead she was laughing so much she could hardly breathe.

When she caught her breath she said, 'Lilian is the prettiest woman I've ever seen. She can't be a witch.'

'You're right about that! She is the prettiest woman in the whole wide world,' Brighton agreed.

Lilian smiled and gave Brighton a quick kiss. Claire looked at them with understanding in her eyes.

'You love each other,' she stated.

'Yes, very much,' Lilian confirmed.

'Claire, would you mind if I ask you about Richard?' Brighton asked carefully.

Fear returned to the young girl's eyes but she bravely nodded.

'Thank you for delivering the message to me. Did Richard say anything else to you?' he started gently.

'Not to me but he spoke to a few other people while I was in the room,' Claire answered.

'Did you hear any of it?' Brighton continued.

'Yes. Richard said to the other people they must let everyone know the White Demon is coming to town tomorrow. He also said that they must make sure you're killed before you get to town.'

'So it is a trap,' Brighton mused to himself. 'Going to Avarya tomorrow is not an option.'

Claire spoke again, 'He said to one man he didn't think you would come and that will be perfect for him. That way they can tell everybody that you're not interested in talking but instead just want to kill people.'

Lilian frowned.

'What could be the purpose in that?' she asked.

'He's trying to convince the people of Avarya that I'm evil. If I go tomorrow the archers will kill me and claim that I attacked them first. If I don't go he will do as Claire said, spread rumours that I don't want to talk and that I'm only interested in killing.'

'So what are we going to do?' Lilian asked

Brighton got up and walked away a few paces.

He turned and said, 'There is something we're not seeing here. Claire, are you or your parents loyal to

Richard?'

Claire quickly snapped, 'No! He killed my parents and made me watch. He said that I would get the same treatment if I don't deliver the message.'

'Why did he do that?' Brighton asked.

'My parents were part of a group that wants Richard out of Avarya. He found out and killed them. My punishment was to come here,' Claire said with tears in her eyes.

Lilian put her arm around the young girl's shoulders.

Brighton didn't want to upset Claire further but he thought he knew what Richard had planned.

'Claire, how come you overheard what Richard said to the others? Why didn't you leave after he gave you the message?' he asked.

'I tried but two men were blocking the door. I stood in a corner until they moved, then I ran out and came here,' she replied.

'I see,' Brighton said in understanding.

He knew exactly what Richard was planning.

Lilian looked at him with questioning eyes.

'Richard wanted Claire to hear the plans. He was hoping that she would share the information with me,' Brighton explained.

'But why?' Lilian asked.

'I thought his archers would kill me if I try to enter the city but that's not true. He knows I will sneak in and try to make contact with the resistance. If his people can follow me they can then root out the rest of the people who oppose Richard. He will gain a stronghold in the city,' Brighton said.

'But what if Claire only delivered the message and did not give you the rest of the information?' Lilian asked.

'It still puts me in a bad situation. Richard knows I will not let him live and he's not coming out, that means I will have to go to him. Even if I don't make contact with the resistance he will have me trapped. If, for some reason I don't try to get into the city his following will still increase as people will believe his lies.'

'This really is a bad situation,' Lilian said worriedly. 'What do we do now?'

'There are two options. I can simply get close to Avarya and kill Richard with my talent or we can play his game and do exactly what he wants,' Brighton replied.

'Neither of those options seems good to me,' Lilian complained.

Brighton smiled.

'Killing Richard is the first priority. If he is out of the equation, things will get easier for us. However, if I kill him myself it might have the opposite effect, the Dark Ones will gain more followers. It would be best to let the people decide his fate,' he said thoughtfully.

'And how are you going to orchestrate this?' Lilian asked.

'I will do exactly what Richard wants. I will go into the city and make contact with the resistance,' Brighton answered.

'That will get you and a lot of innocent people killed. It's not really a good solution,' Lilian argued.

'Not necessarily. We have someone Richard is not aware of,' Brighton smiled.

'I see,' Lilian said in understanding.

Claire looked from face to face.

She didn't understand what they were talking about.

'What do you have that Richard doesn't know about?' she asked.

'Me,' a voice came from a bush less than two paces behind her.

Claire screamed and grabbed onto Lilian burying her face in the white dress.

'Brac!' Lilian shouted. 'That was not funny!'

Brac stepped out from behind the bush.

'I'm sorry,' he said. 'But it was a little funny.'

Brighton also thought so but the look on Lilian's face made him decide not to admit it.

Brac went down on one knee and held out his arms to Claire.

'I am really sorry,' he said sincerely. 'Give me a hug and forgive me please.'

Claire looked at him with big round eyes.

'I forgive you,' she said softly but made no move towards him.

'But I don't,' Lilian said in mock anger. 'Not until you cook Claire a nice meal.'

Brac got up.

'Very well, I will make young Miss Claire the best meal in the whole world,' he agreed with a smile.

He disappeared into the woods again.

Still trying to hide his smile Brighton called, 'Adri, you can come out of the bushes too!'

He knew Liam and Nelson were very close as well but didn't call them.

Adri stepped into the clearing.

'Hello, I'm Adri,' she said to Claire.

Claire just gave a small wave in Adri's direction.

'This is Claire,' Lilian introduced her.

Adri came over and took Claire's hand.

'Will you please help me gather wood for a fire?' she asked.

The younger girl nodded and they set off.

Lilian came over to Brighton.

'I saw you smiling at Brac's little trick,' she said as she punched his rock hard shoulder.

'It was funny,' Brighton defended.

'No it wasn't. The poor girl is already scared out of her wits and then Brac made it worse. All we need now is for Mischief to put in an appearance. The poor girl will probably die!' Lilian complained.

'Mischief isn't anywhere near them right now,'

Brighton answered as he used his sense to find the big cat.

'That's good. We can introduce Claire to him later,' Lilian replied.

'No, we won't,' Brighton said quickly.

'Why not? He's a part of our little group,' Lilian argued.

'But she isn't,' Brighton said flatly.

'Bri, we can't send her back to Avarya. We don't know what Richard will do to her,' Lilian pleaded.

'I know, but she's not staying with us either,' Brighton replied.

Lilian knew why Brighton was being stubborn. The memory of Michaela and Joshua was still very fresh.

'Then what do you suggest?' she asked gently.

'I don't know yet,' Brighton admitted.

The two girls returned with their arms full of wood. Adri quickly arranged it on the ground and asked Brighton to light it. Claire clapped her hands when the tiny bolt of white energy jumped from Brighton's hand onto the wood.

'That's pretty!' she exclaimed.

'And I still think it's the best use for his talent,' Lilian joked.

Brac reappeared carrying a small deer.

'Your food will be ready shortly, milady,' he said to Claire while bowing deeply.

She giggled behind her hand.

Brac turned to Brighton and said, 'I know it's too much for us but maybe that cat of yours will finish the rest.'

'He will. I don't think he's hunted in days. We're always feeding him. He is getting lazy and fat,' Brighton replied with a smile.

Adri helped with the food as usual. She was getting extremely good at preparing very tasty meals with little to work with.

Chapter 20

JUST BEFORE SUNSET Brighton called Brac, Liam and Nelson together.

'I'm going to have a quick talk with Claire and then we leave. I want to slip into the city tonight,' he told them.

He went over to where the women were sitting next to the river.

'Claire, where would I find the group that wants Richard out of Avarya?' he asked.

Claire explained to Brighton where her house was.

'My mother's brother also lives there. He will know who to contact,' she told him.

Lilian saw the three hunters waiting.

'You're going now, aren't you,' she said to Brighton.

'Yes, darkness will be our best ally,' Brighton replied.

'Are you taking Mischief?' she asked.

The cat still hadn't shown himself since Claire got

there.

'If a fight breaks out it would be useful to have him near but I would much rather he stay here and protect you and the girls,' Brighton said.

Lilian didn't ask to go with them. She knew Brighton would never agree. He was determined not to put her in any more danger.

'Be careful please,' she said.

They hugged tightly before Brighton turned and disappeared into the woods followed by the three hunters.

'I love you,' Lilian whispered with tears in her eyes.

*****

Brighton and Brac sat with their backs against the wall of a house. Things were going well. They managed to enter Avarya unseen. Earlier he touched the other three men with a small amount of healing energy to hide them from the Dark Ones.

Liam and Nelson were truly like ghosts, even in the city. Brighton only had to point towards a roof or hiding place where he felt a presence and they silently took care of it. So far nobody was killed, simply knocked unconscious and bound. Brighton knew the men wouldn't hesitate to kill the defenders if they had to, he just hoped it didn't get that far.

According to Claire's directions they were very close to her house.

Brac tapped his arm. That was the signal that everything was clear. Brighton snuck around the corner, Brac following.

They passed Claire's house. Brighton sensed four people inside, three of them talented. At the next corner they hid again and waited for Liam and Nelson. The two hunters caught up with them quickly. Brighton pointed to a rooftop just down the road and held up three fingers. The hunters nodded and disappeared into the night.

After a while a very faint whistle reached their ears. Brac tapped his arm again. The men continued moving through the city like this until they were almost at the house where Brighton sensed Richard.

'Stay here,' he whispered the Brac.

'Will you be alright?' Brac whispered back.

'Yes, there are only four of them and Richard in the house,' Brighton replied.

He weaved an energy barrier around himself and stepped out in the street. The hunters already took care of the archers on the roof so there was no immediate danger.

He walked up to the house where Richard was hiding, opened the door, and simply walked in. The four Dark Ones were sitting around a table talking. It took a moment for them to realize who had just walked in. Before any of them could move four tiny bolts of pure energy shot from Brighton's body. All four were dead before they knew what hit them, each of them with a neat hole straight through their heads.

Brighton walked to the bedroom where he sensed Richard. Again, he simply entered. Richard shot up from the bed he was lying on.

'Hello Richard,' Brighton said as he shot a bolt of healing energy at the man.

It entered Richard through the chest. Richard lifted his hand but nothing happened. He shouted for the Dark Ones he believed were still in the kitchen.

'They are dead,' Brighton said. 'Sit down before you join them.'

Richard tried again to summon his black energy link but nothing happened.

'What have you done to me?' Richard blurted out.

Brac, Liam and Nelson stormed through the door. They heard Richard's scream and thought something must have gone wrong.

'Go get Claire's uncle,' Brighton told them.

Brac gestured for the other two to do as Brighton asked but he stayed behind. Brighton knew the Dark Ones would use their sense to detect intruders but Liam and Nelson were still invisible to their talent. The three holding Claire's uncle hostage had no chance against two men who were like ghosts.

Brac retreated to the kitchen to guard the door.

'So, Richard, I believe you wanted to talk to me,' Brighton said mockingly.

Richard was still looking for a way to get out. He decided that the only way was past Brighton. Putting his shoulder down, he stormed. Brighton absorbed the blow easily.

Richard was a small man and not very strong, he hardly moved Brighton's large muscular body. He stepped back and tried again but this time Brighton's fist found his face.

Richard went down hard.

'It looks like you don't want to talk,' Brighton mocked.

He lifted his fist again.

'Wait, I do want to talk,' Richard quickly blurted out but said nothing further..

'Talk, I'm listening,' Brighton prodded.

Richard got up from the floor and sat down on the bed.

'Why do you hunt me?' he asked.

'Why did you try to kill me at the palace?' Brighton countered.

'That was Seth, I had nothing to do with it,' Richard defended.

'That's not true. You used your energy link on me the same as your brothers and sisters. All of you tried to kill me,' Brighton said.

'I'm sorry, that was a mistake. But you must

understand why we did that. You are a threat to the order we've created and upheld for generations,' Richard said quickly.

'Order? You ruled through fear and intimidation. You forced your will down on the people. That's wrong! The people should decide their own fate. Who gave you the right to decide? Were you chosen? No, you simply took control because you could,' Brighton shouted at him.

'You don't understand what you're doing,' Richard argued. 'People need leaders. If you take the leaders away, there will be chaos. There has been no war or unrest as long as anyone can remember. We keep the peace and uphold the law.'

Slowly he slid his hand under the blanket.

Brighton laughed sarcastically.

'You uphold your own law and make slaves out of people who cannot defend themselves. You've ruled long enough, it's time for a change.'

'Can't we strike a bargain? You and I will rule together,' Richard tried.

Brighton leaned a little closer and said softly, 'I promised your mother I would send all her children to her. You're the last one alive. I never break my promises.'

'Please don't kill me,' Richard pleaded.

Suddenly he pulled a large knife from under the blanket and lunged forward. Brighton easily deflected the onslaught downward and to his left, but Richard turned the blade up and cut Brighton deep on his left forearm.

Richard stepped back quickly and tried using his energy link again but still it did not respond. Before he could lunge again a heavy blow landed just under his right arm. Ribs broke with a sickening sound.

Brighton looked at his arm.

'Still trying to kill me,' he said. 'Now you will give me

the energy I need to heal this.'

A white energy link slammed into Richard's head. Brighton slowly stole Richard's energy and let it flow to his injured arm. Before Richard's eyes the cut stopped bleeding and then closed.

'What are you?' Richard asked through the pain.

Brighton answered by bringing his fist down on Richard's face.

*****

Liam jogged up to Lilian just after sunrise.

'Brighton asks that you join him in Avarya,' he said.

Lilian, Adri and Claire immediately jumped up and followed Liam back to the city.

Mischief was sleeping at Lilian's feet.

He also got up and followed Liam.

Strangely, Claire was not afraid of him at all.

The young hunter stopped and said to Lilian, 'I'm not sure if Brighton wanted the panther to come.'

Lilian put her hands on her hips and said, 'You tell him to stay then.'

Liam looked at Mischief and decided he would rather not.

He set off towards Avarya at an easy pace since he didn't know how fast the women could run.

'Is Brighton all right?' Lilian asked while they jogged.

'Yes, we've established a safe zone with the help of Charles, Claire's uncle. I'm taking you there,' Liam answered.

Lilian tried asking more questions but Liam didn't answer. His task was to get the women safely into the city and he concentrated only on that. They stayed off the main road and instead entered the city using a narrow pathway between the houses. After a few turns Liam stopped and knocked on a door.

Brac opened, knife ready. He quickly ushered them in

and closed the door. Mischief flopped down on the floor and fell asleep instantly. Brighton rushed over and put his arms around Lilian.

'I'm glad you're safe,' he whispered.

'And I'm glad you're safe,' she whispered back.

Her eyes took a moment to get used to the dim light. Richard was sitting on a chair, hands and legs bound. His nose was obviously broken and his left eye was swollen shut.

Claire rushed into Charles' arms.

'I thought I would never see you again, little one,' he said, tears rolling down his cheeks.

Claire couldn't speak, she just cried against his chest.

Charles looked at Brighton and said, 'I can never thank you enough.'

'Actually, we have to thank Claire,' Brighton replied. 'Without her none of this would have been possible.'

Claire smiled at him through her tears.

Lilian was still looking at Richard with loathing in her eyes.

'What is the plan now?' she asked.

'We take him to the market and let the people decide his fate,' Brighton said.

'And the Dark Ones?' Lilian asked.

'We've taken care of fifteen already. I will handle the rest,' Brighton replied.

He didn't tell her that there was at least another thirty-five Dark Ones in the city.

Brac put his hand on Brighton's shoulder.

'We should go now before too many people are out of their houses,' he said.

Brighton agreed. He touched everyone with a small amount of healing energy to hide them from the Dark Ones.

He did the same with Richard, not enough to heal his wounds but enough to hide him.

'Stay here,' he said to Lilian, Adri and Claire.

'No, I'm coming too. I can help,' Lilian said defiantly.

Brighton smiled at her.

'Stay close to me then,' he said.

As he walked past Mischief he scratched the cat's head.

Mischief opened his white eyes.

'Look after Adri and Claire,' Brighton told the cat.

Mischief let out a deep growl and returned to his nap.

Brac cut the rope around Richard's leg and yanked him up. Everybody except Mischief, Adri and Claire left the house.

Brighton took the lead. Every so often he would stop and point to a house or an alley. Liam or Nelson neutralized the threat every time with ease. They reached the market without any incident and hid in a narrow alley between two buildings.

There were already many people in the market.

Brighton let a bit more healing energy flow into Richard to make sure he didn't regain the use of his talent anytime soon.

'Wait here,' Brighton said to the group.

He scanned the area for Dark Ones. When he was sure there were none close by, he pushed Richard in front of him into the open. They walked to the centre of the market where hawkers used some tables to display their goods.

Some people were staring at them. Brighton climbed on top of a table dragging Richard with him.

'People of Avarya,' he shouted.

More people turned and looked.

'People of Avarya,' Brighton shouted again. 'Today you will decide your own fate.'

People started running and shouting, scurrying to fetch friends and relatives. Soon people were streaming into the market from every entrance.

Brighton waited until there was no more room for anybody before he spoke.

'People of Avarya,' he shouted again. 'Today you will decide whether you want to live under the oppression of the Supremes or be free forever.'

Shouts of "The White Demon" and "The Saviour" came from the crowd.

One man in front shouted, 'But the Supremes are powerful. How can we oppose them?'

Brighton pointed to Richard.

'This is Richard, last of the Supremes. If he had any power don't you think he would have used it by now?'

He held out his hand. A ball of pure white energy as big as his fist jumped from his palm and danced above his hand.

The crowd gasped and stepped back.

'I have power but I don't force my will down on the people like the Supremes have done for countless winters,' he shouted.

Brighton converted the energy into fire and shot it up in the air.

The crowd was stunned. They watched the fireball disappear in the clouds.

Another voice shouted, 'Are you the one who killed the Supremes?'

'Yes, I am,' Brighton answered. 'But only after they tried to kill me. I wanted to be rid of this gift so that I can marry the woman I love and live in peace.'

He explained that a People's Council was being formed in Zedonia and that no talented person will be allowed to serve on the Council.

'Will you serve on the Council?' another question came from the crowd.

'No, I am talented,' Brighton answered. 'Someone needs to represent your city, but before we get there, you, the people of Avarya, need to decide what to do with Richard.'

The crowd was silent for a moment and then shouts of 'Kill him' and 'Cut his throat' rose up.

A man jumped onto the table next to Brighton.

'He should be banished,' the man shouted.

A big cheer went up from the crowd. They simply wanted Richard gone and didn't care how it happened.

The man turned to Brighton.

'It's decided,' he said.

'What is your name?' Brighton asked.

'Lars. I'm a hunter,' the man replied.

Brighton addressed the crowd again.

'Who wants Lars to represent Avarya on the People's Council?'

Another big cheer erupted.

'Well Lars, you are now officially Avarya's representative. Go to Zedonia and seek out Graham the baker,' Brighton told him.

He turned to Richard and said quietly, 'Run, I'm coming for you.'

Richard jumped off the table and ran out of the market. Brighton used his sense to find out where Richard was going. Richard took the road that went past Carmen and Brighton's old house.

Brighton got off the table and walked over to his group.

'That went better than expected,' he commented.

He felt a little bad for deceiving the people about Richard's talent.

'Why do you think Lars was so quick to stop the crowd from killing Richard,' Lilian asked.

Brac answered, 'He is a hunter like me. We respect life. Killing is only done when it's necessary. What I want to know is where all the Dark Ones went?'

'They are gathered just outside the city near the house I used to live in. Richard is heading for them as we speak,' Brighton answered.

'How many?' Brac asked.

'More than thirty,' Brighton replied.

Brac whistled.

'Can you handle that many?'

'Probably not. Are you willing to go with me?' Brighton asked him.

'You know I am,' Brac answered.

Liam and Nelson also voiced their agreement.

'Me too,' Charles answered.

'Why don't you go fetch Adri and Claire? Take them to your house,' Brighton suggested.

Charles looked relieved as he agreed and left.

'Remember, we do not have to kill the Dark Ones,' Brighton reminded them. 'If they surrender we will do them no harm. I'm only after Richard.'

When there was no argument Brighton turned and headed for his old house.

Lilian's small hand found his. He looked into her blue eyes.

'I suppose you will not stay here where it's safe?' he tried.

Lilian gave him a look that answered the question.

'Please just stay close to me,' he told her.

'Always, my love,' she replied sweetly.

When they were almost at the far end of the market panic broke out on the other side. People were screaming and running in all directions. The group turned and looked to see what was going on.

Brighton smiled.

'I didn't think Mischief would stay away for too long,' he said.

The big black cat was strolling through the market place as if it belonged to him. He didn't take any notice of the panic around him; his white eyes were fixed on Brighton.

Brac chuckled.

'If I didn't know any better I would say that cat knew when you were about to put yourself in danger. He always seems to be around when things are about to get rough.'

Brighton laughed and said, 'It does seem that way. Let's go, Mischief will catch up.'

*****

Richard sat down carefully on the ground holding his broken ribs.

'Supreme Richard, what happened?' a Dark One asked.

'That boy surprised me but I got away,' he lied.

'What are we going to do now?' the Dark One asked.

'The plan stays the same. He will come for me and walk into a trap. He cannot possibly fight all of us and win. We have strength in numbers,' Richard replied.

'But he has already killed so many of us and he still lives,' the Dark One argued.

Richard got up and glared at the man.

'How dare you argue with me?' he said as he lifted his hand.

His talent was still not responding but the bluff worked. The Dark One fell to his knees and begged for his live. Richard dropped his hand.

'Next time I might not feel this generous,' he told the man.

He turned to address the other Dark Ones.

'As soon as Brighton appears, rush him,' he instructed.

One Dark One stepped forward.

'I will not take part in this any longer. It's gone on for too long,' she said.

More Dark Ones joined the woman.

'We're going back to Avarya. Perhaps the people will forgive us for all the wrong things we've done and let us live. Kill me if that's what you wish,' the woman said.

She turned and started walking followed by twelve others. The other Dark Ones looked at him expectantly but there was nothing Richard could do.

'We don't need them. There are still more than twenty of us here. Brighton cannot stand against that many,' he said.

A murmur spread through the remaining Dark Ones.

'Is something wrong, Supreme Richard?' one man asked.

Richard ignored the man and said, 'Make a fire right here. Bring me some wet branches and then get into position.'

The Dark Ones scrambled to get into the bushes. Richard remained standing in the middle of the road. Since he couldn't use his sense he didn't know how long Brighton would take to get here.

The wait was not long. Brighton, Lilian and Brac appeared over the small rising.

'Brighton,' Richard called. 'Can we talk?'

The small group stopped about fifty paces away.

Brighton shook his head.

'The time for talking is over, I have a promise to keep,' he shouted back.

Brighton sensed the Dark Ones in the forest. There was also a large group of untalented people some distance towards Avarya. Brighton assumed they simply gathered to talk about the day's events. He ignored them and focused on the immediate threat.

If it's a fight they want, it's a fight they will get, he decided.

Richard tossed a few wet branches on the fire sending large columns of smoke into the air. Brighton wondered about that for a moment but then decided to ignore it.

He shouted as loud as he could, 'To all the Dark Ones hiding in the forest, surrender now and I will not harm you. Fight me and you will die. I've just met thirteen talented people on the way here. They surrendered and are now under my protection. The people of Avarya will allow them to live in peace for as long as they don't use their talent.'

One man stepped out from behind a tree and faced Brighton.

'I surrender,' he said.

Before anyone else could speak Richard's black energy link slammed into the man's head.

His talent had returned. The man's lifeless body flopped to the ground.

'Get him!' Richard shouted as he sent the energy link towards Brighton.

Dark Ones rushed out of the bushes towards Brighton and his group. Two fell almost immediately, knives sticking out of their throats. Liam and Nelson stepped out of the forest between the Dark Ones. More Dark Ones fell before they realized there were two attackers in their midst. As per Richard's orders they didn't stop, they simply ignored the two hunters and continued running. A black form leapt out of the woods. Mischief ripped through three Dark Ones before they were ten paces up the road.

Brighton did not block Richard's link, he allowed it to enter his head but stopped Richard from draining his energy.

You cannot win this fight entered into Richard's head.

I'm not trying to; I just need to keep you busy so the others can kill you, his thoughts travelled back to Brighton.

Brighton used his sense. Hundreds of people were running in their direction. He realized that the smoke was a signal for them to attack.

'Clear a path to Richard,' he shouted at Brac and Lilian.

Brac stormed forward, throwing-knives flashing through the air. More Dark Ones fell. Mischief leapt for another Dark One from behind. The man spun around, knife in his hand, just before Mischief crashed into him.

They tumbled to the ground, Mischief's powerful jaws

closing around the man's throat but then let out a loud yelp as the blade slid between his ribs and pierced his lung.

Brighton concentrated on the energy link between him and Richard. He could not allow Richard to break it since that would leave him free to attack the rest of the group. Lilian's black energy link touched a Dark One, then another and another. Corpses were strewn everywhere, only two Dark Ones remained alive. Both changed course and ran into the woods. Liam followed one and Nelson set off after the other.

Brighton reached Richard. He slammed his fist into the Supreme's broken nose. Richard's head snapped back, he lost concentration on the energy link. Brighton quickly touched him and let some healing energy flow into him.

He grabbed Richard by the shirt and yanked him up.

'Just kill him,' Brac shouted.

'No,' Brighton replied.

'Why not?' the hunter cried.

'There are hundreds of people coming this way. I think they are loyal to Richard,' Brighton said.

Brac turned around and looked towards Avarya.

'Well, this is going to be an interesting fight,' he muttered getting two more throwing-knives ready.

'There will be no fight if I can help it. Get behind me,' he said to Brac and Lilian.

The first of the attackers came into view. They did not stop. War cries were shouted as they approached, spears and knives held high. Brighton threw Richard on the ground in front of him.

His talent connected with the forest. He sent a thick bolt of pure white energy into the Supreme.

Richard burst into flames. In moments there was nothing but ashes left on the ground. Richard was gone.

I kept my promise, Evangeline, flashed through

Brighton's mind.

The attackers in front slid to a halt causing the ones at the back to crash into them. People went down in a mess of tangled arms and legs.

Brighton hoped this would discourage them but they got up, retrieved their weapons, and charged again. Arrows flew from the back of the crowd. Brighton threw up a wall of white energy blocking the arrows.

The attackers had almost covered the distance. Bolts of energy shot from Brighton's body into the ground a few paces in front of them. He used so much energy that the ground itself caught alight.

This display of raw power finally discouraged the attackers. Some fled into the forest while others threw down their weapons and fell to their knees. Brighton drained the energy from the fires putting them out.

'Why do you attack us?' he shouted at the crowd.

'Richard told us to,' a voice came from the back.

'Richard is dead. You don't have to do as he says anymore,' Brighton shouted back.

'But he said you would kill us if we didn't kill you first,' another voice shouted.

'You saw what I just did. Don't you think you would all be dead already if I wished it so?' Brighton shouted.

It was a bluff. He was very close to his limit. He hoped the crowd would fall for it, Carmen always said he was a bad liar. It looked like they did.

'I won't kill innocent people,' Brighton shouted.

'Are you letting us go?' a man in front asked.

'Yes, there has been enough violence. Go back to your families and live in peace from now on,' Brighton answered.

Slowly the people turned and started walking back to Avarya. None of them bothered to pick up their weapons.

Brighton sighed with relief.

'Could you have killed them all?' Brac asked.

'No, my body is very close to its limit again,' Brighton answered.

Lilian stepped closer, concern in her eyes. Brighton put his arm around her.

'I'm all right, don't worry. I just need to rest a bit,' he assured her.

'Your old house is not far, let's go there,' Lilian suggested.

Brighton noticed Mischief lying on the ground in a pool of blood.

'Oh no,' he whispered.

He rushed over and knelt next to the panther. Mischief's breathing was shallow and made a gurgling sound.

Brighton checked his body quickly. He found the knife still sticking out of Mischief's ribcage.

'I'm going to pull this out and try to heal you,' he told the cat.

Quickly he pulled the knife clear and tossed it away. He put both his hands on the wound. He gathered as much energy as he dared from the surroundings and let it flow into Mischief.

'I hope it's enough,' Brighton said right before he blacked out.

Chapter 21

THE HOUSE WAS exactly as they left it.

Brac, Nelson and Liam carried Brighton to the house first and then went back for Mischief. When both were settled inside the men went outside and sat down on the porch.

Lilian came out after a long time.

Brac got up, offered her his chair, and asked, 'How are they?'

Despite the tears in her eyes she smiled a thank you and said, 'Brighton is resting comfortably, he will be fine. I'm not sure about Mischief. Would you mind staying until Brighton wakes up?'

'We will stay as long as you need us to,' Brac replied.

Addressing Liam she asked, 'Please fetch Adri. She is probably worried sick.'

Liam nodded and set off towards Avarya.

Carefully Brac asked, 'Do you think it's over?'

'The Supremes are all dead. Any Dark Ones still foolish enough to think they still rule will soon join them. Yes, I think it's over now,' Lilian replied.

'Good, now you and Brighton can settle down here and raise a family,' Brac commented.

'No, not here. I want to live in Four Mountains,' Lilian replied.

'Where is that?' Brac asked.

'From here it is two weeks travel west. The real name is Clareton,' Lilian explained.

'I've never heard of it,' Brac replied.

'It's the most beautiful town I've ever seen,' Lilian mused.

'If it's that far west it must be close to the boundary,' Brac worked out.

'Actually, it's in the mountains itself. Thinking about it, I wonder why Clareton exists. There is nothing of real value and it's very hard to get there,' Lilian replied with a frown.

Brac shrugged his shoulders.

'Maybe some people wanted to get as far away from the Dark Ones as possible. They may have travelled until the mountains became impassable and settled there,' he offered.

'Maybe,' Lilian echoed, not convinced that it was the real explanation.

They talked for a while until Liam and Adri walked up to the house.

'Please tell me what happened, I think Liam is deaf and mute,' Adri complained.

Liam just smiled.

Lilian relayed the events of the day. Although Adri shared Lilian's concern for Brighton and Mischief, she was pleased that the ordeal was finally over.

'Now we can all live here and I will take care of the babies,' she said with a big smile.

Lilian shook her head.

'I was just telling Brac that both Bri and I want to live in Four Mountains,' she replied.

'Fine, I'll come there with you,' Adri replied.

'Wouldn't you rather stay here? There are lots of handsome young men around, you can find a good husband,' Lilian said.

'I'm not interested,' Adri replied. 'Besides, you will need me around to look after the twins.'

Brac's eyes went wide.

'Babies? Twins?,' he gasped.

'Yes, I'm pregnant,' Lilian confirmed with a wide smile.

'You and Brighton will make wonderful parents,' Brac said.

*****

For a while life was quiet.

Brac and his men stayed for a while but eventually went back to Brasten.

People walking past the house to the river recognized Brighton and stopped for a quick chat or to bring them some food. Soon everybody knew where they lived and the visits became more frequent. Nobody was hostile towards them.

Lilian asked a few times when they would be travelling to Zedonia again. Brighton knew she was anxious to get married and go live in Four Mountains. He told her that the People's Council probably had a lot to deal with and performing marriage ceremonies would be a very low priority for the time being. Lilian accepted the explanation although she suspected there was another reason why Brighton was so reluctant to go.

He knew that she was tired of all the travelling and wanted to give her time to recuperate.

*****

Time passed quickly and soon Lilian could no longer hide her growing belly. Brighton thought it was very funny to lie with his head on her stomach and act as if the babies were speaking to him. He often relayed long amusing tales the twins were supposedly telling him. This never failed to bring a smile to Lilian's face. She knew he would be the best father any child could ever hope for.

Brighton used his sense often to check on the babies. He could feel their energy growing inside Lilian. One day he asked if she wanted to know their sex. Lilian excitedly said that she would.

'A boy and a girl,' Brighton told her.

Lilian cried against Brighton's chest and choked out, 'That's perfect.'

Brighton could still not understand why women cried when they were happy.

Adri still stayed with them and insisted on doing most of the housework and cooking. One day after Brighton nagged her for hours to let him help she bluntly told him that she would rather eat rocks than his cooking and promptly chased him out of the house. He didn't take offense; his cooking was pretty bad at the best of times.

Early one morning there was a knock on the door. Brighton looked at all the food stacked on the table.

'This is getting ridiculous,' he said as he got up.

'The people are simply trying to display their gratitude,' Lilian smiled.

'I know, but it's gone on long enough. Even Mischief can't finish all the food they keep bringing. Look how fat and lazy he is getting,' Brighton replied looking under the table at the sleeping panther.

The big cat was quite content with staying close to the house. He seldom disappeared for more than a day at a time.

Lilian knew Brighton was complaining because he hardly ever got a chance to go hunt these days, there always seemed to be more than enough food in the house.

Brighton opened the door.

Brac stepped inside. He had a grave look on his face.

'Brighton, you need to come with me to Zedonia,' he said.

'Good morning Brac,' Brighton said sarcastically.

'I'm sorry,' he apologized for his lack of manners.

'Good day Brighton, Miss Lilian, Miss Adri,' he greeted.

Lilian greeted him back and asked, 'How are you?'

'There is big trouble in Brasten and Zedonia. We need you,' Brac said flatly.

Brighton immediately started packing a rucksack.

'When I needed you, you came. Now I will do the same for you. Fill me in on the way,' Brighton said.

Lilian and Adri also started packing but Brighton stopped them.

'We won't be gone for long. You can stay here if you want,' he said.

Lilian knew he was concerned about her pregnancy.

'Where you go, I go my love. Don't worry about the babies. The three of us will be fine,' she said as she packed more stuff in her rucksack.

'And if I don't go poor Lilian won't have any decent company,' Adri commented.

Brighton smiled. He didn't really expect that they would be happy staying here alone but wanted to give them the chance anyway.

'It would be best if Miss Lilian stayed here,' Brac interjected.

'I'm coming with,' Lilian replied.

'I really think…' Brac tried again but Lilian interrupted him.

'Brac! Stop arguing,' she said irritably.

He had a pained look on his face but didn't argue any further.

It took only a few more moments for them to get ready.

Brac looked at all the food on the table.

'Where did this come from?' he asked.

'The people just keep bringing it. Everybody seems to think they have to feed us. Help yourself,' Brighton replied.

Brac grabbed some food and stuffed it into his rucksack.

'I'm ready,' he said.

Mischief was instantly awake and followed them out.

*****

They travelled fast. Brac didn't say too much until they were well clear of Avarya.

'Things seem to be peaceful here, I don't want anybody to hear about the trouble,' he explained.

'So what's this all about?' Brighton asked.

'Do you remember the five Dark Ones that surrendered when you were in Brasten?' Brac asked.

'Yes, they promised never to use their talent again,' Brighton answered.

Concern crept into his mind.

'Did they? Are they stealing energy again?' he asked quickly.

'Not as far as I know, but that didn't stop the people from killing them,' Brac answered.

Brighton was confused.

'Why did the people kill them if they didn't do anything wrong?' he asked.

'It wasn't really the people themselves. The High Council decided...' Brac started.

'The High Council?' Brighton interrupted.

'Yes, that's what the People's Council is called now,' Brac replied. 'The High Council decided that the world must be cleansed of all talented people. They gathered hundreds of expert hunters and divided them into groups of five. They are called the Justice Squads. They hunt down talented people and kill them,' Brac explained.

'Now I understand why you wanted me to stay behind,' Lilian said to Brac.

Brighton shook his head.

'No, I'm glad you came with. The safest place for you will be with me,' he said to her.

Brac didn't seem comfortable.

'These men are experts at killing. Do you remember my men? They are all dead,' he said slowly.

Brighton's jaw dropped.

'Liam and Nelson too?' he gasped.

Brac nodded.

'But...but...those two were like ghosts! I didn't think anyone could get close to them!' Brighton exclaimed.

'I'm the only one left. I barely escaped with my life,' Brac choked out.

He cared very much for his men. Their deaths were a big blow to him.

'Why did these Justice Squads kill your men? They were not talented,' Brighton asked.

'The squads kill anyone they suspect of being talented or may have assisted talented people in the past. We were protecting everybody in Brasten including the five former Dark Ones, that's why they came after us,' Brac answered.

'That's a pretty vague connection between your men and the former Dark Ones,' Brighton argued.

'Any connection or reason will do. The squads don't ask too many questions. Suspicion alone will sign anybody's death warrant,' Brac answered.

Brighton was still not convinced that Brac's men were

killed simply because they were suspected of protecting former Dark Ones.

'Brac, there must be another reason your men were killed. How do you know it was because the squads suspected you of protecting the former Dark Ones?' he asked.

'I...uh...got the information from one of the squads,' he answered uncomfortably.

Lilian didn't understand.

'How did you get information from them? Did you just walk up to a squad and politely enquire?' she asked.

'Well, not exactly Miss Lilian. I...uh...' Brac stammered.

'Brac killed the squad that came after him. There was probably some form of torture involved to extract the information,' Brighton explained to Lilian.

Brac nodded, eyes cast downward.

'I'm not proud of it,' he said softly.

Brighton looked at Brac intently.

'That's not the whole story, is it?' he asked the hunter.

Brac looked into Brighton's eyes.

He realized it would serve no purpose to hide anything.

'No. I did get another small bit of information. Another reason we were hunted is because we helped you,' he replied softly.

Lilian's hand shot to her mouth, her eyes filling with tears.

Brighton put his hand on Brac's shoulder.

'Brac, I'm so sorry,' he said softly.

'It's not your fault. It's the High Council that has become power hungry. They want to rule like the Supremes did,' Brac replied.

'And I simply handed them all the power they wanted,' Brighton said through clenched teeth.

'That's not true my love,' Lilian said gently. 'Your

idea was that the People's Council will serve the best interest of the population. It's not your fault things turned out this way.'

Brac didn't want to upset them any further but there was more he needed to say.

'It gets worse. When the squads kill someone they don't bury or burn them. Next to the roads leading into towns there are poles with the victim's heads on them. The bodies are left on the ground to decompose. Nobody is allowed to remove it.'

Lilian could not believe what she was hearing.

'That's ridiculous! Why would they do that?' she gasped.

Brighton understood what was going on.

'Fear and intimidation,' he said. 'The High Council saw how the Supremes ruled for so long. Now that they are in power, they're doing the same thing. They don't know any better.'

Brac agreed.

Brighton got a determined look on his face.

'There is only one thing to do. I caused this, I will fix it,' he declared.

Although Brac didn't hold Brighton responsible for any of this he knew Brighton would probably see things that way, that's why he went to him. There was no one else anyway that could possibly do something about the situation.

Brighton turned to Adri. She had been walking quietly behind them.

'Adri, this will get dangerous. It might be best for you to go hide somewhere until it's all over,' he said.

'I'm coming with you. Besides, I'm not helpless,' she said holding up her bow.

It still had the blade fitted on the one end.

Brighton and Adri had been practicing with the bows, not just to shoot but also how to use the blade effectively in a close combat situation.

Brighton nodded and then faced Brac.

'You don't need to travel all the way to Zedonia. You informed me of the situation, your job is done,' he said.

'I have a score to settle with the High council. I'm going with you,' Brac said.

Lilian asked, 'I thought you had a family in Brasten? Shouldn't you get them to safety first?'

Softly Brac answered, 'I had a wife and two daughters.'

Lilian thought that Brac was referring to his men when he said he had a score to settle but now she understood.

Brighton was hoping Brac could give them a bit more information.

'How far have these squads travelled? We haven't seen any of this in Avarya,' he said to Brac.

'The furthest I've seen them was just south of Brasten. They are working their way through all the small towns and villages in the area. Eventually they will reach Avarya and beyond,' Brac replied.

'Once they're done with a town, do they simply move on to the next?' Brighton asked next.

'At least one squad is left in every village, more in the bigger towns and cities. They simply take over a house and demand food and drink be brought to them. The High council passed a law that the general population should provide for them since the squads "protect" them from Dark Ones,' Brac answered.

Brighton recognized the idea as his own. He had given it to Graham when they first spoke about the former palace staff being used as messengers. The idea had been twisted and was now made into a law to suit the High Council and their minions.

'Once all the suspects in a town have been executed, what do these squads do there?' Lilian asked.

'Another function of the squads is to uphold the law. This is left almost entirely to the discretion of the squad commander. Most of them are vicious, bloodthirsty men so you can imagine the things that are going on. They simply take what they want and claim it as payment for their "protection services". Food, drink, clothes… young girls,' Brac said with tears in his eyes.

Lilian was about to ask how he knew this but clamped her mouth shut when she remembered that he had two young daughters.

Instead, she softly said, 'I'm sorry.'

Brac just nodded, the tears now rolling freely down his cheeks.

They walked in silence for a while.

Brighton's mind was racing. He muttered something to himself.

'Did you say something my love?' Lilian asked.

'I was just wondering why the squads haven't reached Avarya yet,' he replied.

Brac cleared his throat and said, 'I think it might have something to do with you.'

'Me? Why do you say that?' Brighton asked with a frown.

'First, the fact that you were the one who ended the Supremes' rule is still fresh in everyone's memory. Second, the story of how you handled the crowd that attacked us outside Avarya spread quickly. I think the squads are simply scared of you.'

Brighton got a wry smile on his face.

'I never wanted anyone to be scared of me but this could be an advantage to us,' he said slowly.

He suddenly looked down the road.

'Someone is coming. We should avoid people for now,' he said.

Brac immediately lead them into the forest.

'How many?' he whispered to Brighton.

'Seven men and one woman,' Brighton whispered back.

'Not a squad then. Probably just travellers,' Brac

concluded.

'True, but I would still like to avoid contact,' Brighton replied.

*****

For the next few days they stayed clear of the roads. Travelling through the forest was a lot slower but Brighton was determined not to have a chance encounter with a squad. It took them six days to get close to Brasten.

Brighton had a quick word with Brac.

'I don't think there is anything to be gained by going into town. Can you lead us safely around?'

'Yes I can, but it will take a lot longer,' Brac answered.

'I'm not too concerned about that, as long as we stay hidden for now,' Brighton replied.

He was constantly using his sense to detect danger. So far he was sure they passed two squads already. The temptation to intercept these squads and kill them was almost too much for him.

The little group carried on travelling. Ten days later they were on the outskirts of Zedonia. They were hiding in some thick undergrowth.

'Where will I find the High Council?' Brighton asked Brac.

'They've taken over some shops in the centre of town. The walls between these buildings were knocked out to create one large hall. This is only a temporary arrangement though. The Council is having a sort of palace built where there will be a hall for meetings and rooms for their families,' Brac answered.

'Where?' Brighton asked.

'At the top of the hill in the middle of the city,' Brac answered.

Brighton shook his head. That was right on top of the old Supremes' palace he destroyed.

'What are you planning my love?' Lilian asked.

'Well, first I want to go talk to them. Maybe they will see reason and stop this madness,' Brighton answered.

'And if that doesn't work?' Lilian pressed.

'I don't really know. Let's see what happens and make our decisions accordingly,' Brighton answered.

Brighton quickly scanned the area with his sense. When he was happy there was nobody close to them he stepped out of the bushes. The others followed, including Mischief.

'Stay here boy. You will cause panic and that's the last thing we need,' Brighton said to the cat.

Mischief hung his head low but did not follow the group.

'It still amazes me how that panther listens to you,' Brac said.

Adri smiled and said, 'Yes, next Brighton will be teaching Mischief to shoot a bow and cook supper. Soon they will have no more use for me!'

Lilian gave Adri's shoulder a little squeeze and said, 'Even if you didn't cook so well we would still love you.'

Brac chipped in, 'Don't believe that. They only love you for your food.'

Brighton didn't join in the light-hearted banter; he was focused on what to say to the Council.

They made it to the town centre without incident.

Brac pointed out the entrance to the makeshift hall.

Brighton walked up to it and entered. The inside was well lit and beautifully decorated. A guard stopped them just inside the door. Brighton towered over him.

'The High Council will see petitioners tomorrow. Come back then,' the man said as he put a hand on Brighton's chest.

Brighton thought about simply pushing past the man but decided that he wanted to avoid any violence if possible.

'We have urgent business to discuss with the Council,' he said to the guard.

The man shoved Brighton backwards.

'The High Council is busy. Leave before I have you arrested,' he said angrily.

Brighton was taken aback a little.

'Touch me again and I'll break your arm off,' he threatened. 'Now step aside so I can enter.'

The guard took a step backwards. Brighton's sheer size scared him but he was under orders not to let anyone in. He was uncertain what to do. Brighton didn't wait for him to make up his mind. He pushed the man out of the way and entered the hall.

'Stay close,' he said softly to the others.

At the far end of the hall was a large table with five chairs behind it. There were people sitting on all five chairs, deep in discussion. Brighton recognized three of the five, Graham, Lars and Garth. Smaller tables were neatly lined up along the walls also with chairs behind them. Roughly half the chairs were occupied.

Nobody noticed the group at first; everybody seemed focused on their own conversations. Guards in uniform were standing behind the chairs. Brighton quickly counted them, twenty-five in total.

He boldly walked through the hall towards the big table.

Graham looked up briefly and said, 'We're not seeing anyone today. Come back tomorrow.'

Brighton kept walking until he was less than ten paces away from the big table. Lilian, Adri and Brac took up position right behind him.

'You will see me!' Brighton stated in a loud voice.

The conversations died down and everybody looked up.

Graham got up slowly and said, 'Brighton, I did not recognize you.'

Brighton wasn't in the mood for small talk.

'What is going on here?' he asked.

'The High Council is having a meeting, not that it's any of your concern,' Graham answered.

'Not my concern?' Brighton said, fighting hard to stay calm.

'Yes, that's what...' Graham tried but did not get to finish.

'You're having useless meetings and outside your Justice Squads are stealing other people's property, raping young girls and murdering anybody they feel like,' Brighton growled.

Graham's expression did not change.

'The Justice Squads work under our orders. They...'

'Your orders?' Brighton shouted. 'Did you order them to rape young girls? Did you order them to murder innocent people?'

Graham's face turned red with anger.

'Because of your previous service to the High Council I will forgive you this indiscretion. Don't ever interrupt me again,' he snarled at Brighton.

'As I was saying, the Justice Squads uphold the law. The people will provide whatever they need as payment...'

'The law?' Brighton shouted, his anger boiling over. 'There is no law anymore. Those thugs do as they please. You are doing the same thing the Supremes did! You rule through fear and intimidation!'

'Brighton, I'm warning you. Don't...' Graham started but Brighton stormed forward and smashed his fist down on the table.

'No, you have this backwards. I'm warning you. Stop this madness or I will,' he growled at Graham.

Graham took a step back. He was clearly not used to anyone challenging him or speaking to him in this manner.

'Guards, arrest these people!' he shouted.

Without taking his eyes off Graham, Brighton

shouted, 'Touch any of us and it will be the last thing you ever touch!'

The guards looked at each other uncertain what to do. All of them had already realized exactly who Brighton was. They were unwilling to go up against him but also knew they dare not defy Graham.

Brighton turned around and walked towards the door. His little group followed close behind.

'You have one day to sort this out. I'll be back tomorrow,' he shouted over his shoulder at Graham.

'Arrest them now!' Graham shrieked.

One guard, a burly man, stepped forward and put his hand out towards Brighton.

'You are hereby arrested…'

Without stopping Brighton grabbed the outstretched hand and twisted it violently. The man's wrist broke with a loud pop that echoed through the quiet hall.

None of the other guards had the courage to try, they stepped back and let Brighton's group pass.

Chapter 22

Brac led the group deep into some very thick forest. The last thing Brighton wanted was to battle hundreds of the Council's guards.

For the moment it would be better to hide.

'This looks good,' he said to Brac.

They were in a tiny open space between some thick undergrowth and many large trees.

Brac agreed.

'It will be hard for them to find us here,' he commented. 'But I'm going to take some precautions anyway.'

He disappeared into the bush. Brighton and the two women settled down to wait for nightfall. They had to make do with cold food since Brighton didn't want a fire to give away their position.

A while later Brac returned.

'Nobody will get close to this place without us

knowing,' he said confidently.

'I'll use my sense anyway to scan the area from time to time,' Brighton said.

'I thought you might do that, but you also have to sleep at some point. I've set up my own "sense" to warn us when intruders are coming,' Brac said with a wink.

'How did you do that?' Lilian asked.

Brac smiled and said, 'There are all kinds of things that will make a sound when you step on it or walk through it; dry twigs, leaves, sand and pebbles. Nothing and nobody can get here without making some sort of noise.'

Brac sat down and accepted some of the cold food Adri offered him.

Brac, Lilian and Adri spoke about unimportant things for a while. Brighton was deep in thought; he didn't even hear their conversation. Nobody really wanted to discuss what had happened earlier but they were all curious as to what Brighton was planning.

Eventually Lilian looked at Brighton.

'What do you think will happen tomorrow?' she asked.

'I don't know,' Brighton sighed. 'I'm hoping that the members of the Council will see their mistakes and rectify them.'

Everybody knew there was almost no chance of that happening. Lilian knew that Brighton had already decided what to do should the Council persist in their ways. He was going to remove them from power just as he did with the Supremes.

'How are your defences against arrows and spears these days?' Brac asked.

'I'm getting better at it. I practiced a few things while we were living in Avarya,' Brighton answered.

Adri punched his shoulder and said, 'Probably because you were bored seeing as I didn't allow you in the kitchen.'

It brought a small smile from Brighton.

Twigs snapped not far from them.

'It's Mischief,' Brighton said quickly.

Brac had a wide smile on his face.

'See, not even the demon cat can get here without us knowing it,' he said proudly.

Brighton was glad Brac was with them.

'I think we should go to sleep. Brac, you take first watch, I'll relieve you at midnight,' Brighton said.

'You will need to be well rested tomorrow. I'll take the second watch so you don't have to break up your sleep tonight,' Brac suggested.

Brighton didn't argue, what Brac said made a lot of sense.

*****

The next morning Brighton was awake before sunrise. Lilian was still sleeping so he didn't move. Just as the sun started rising, she woke up.

'Good morning my love,' she said in a sleepy voice.

Brighton got up on one elbow and kissed her forehead in reply.

She smiled and said, 'I had a wonderful dream. The twins were born and we were living in Four Mountains.'

Brighton smiled at her. There was nothing he wanted more.

He stroked her stomach softly. Lilian lifted her head and gave Brighton a long, tender kiss.

Adri, who had been watching them, pulled a face and said, 'Stop it. That's the reason your stomach is getting so big.'

Lilian giggled and said, 'Yes, I suppose you're right.'

All of them got up.

Brighton walked to where Brac was sitting on a rock.

'Any disturbances?' he asked.

'Nothing,' Brac reported.

Brighton spoke quietly to Brac.

'I want you, Adri and Mischief to stay here today. I would have liked Lilian to stay as well but I probably have a better chance of convincing this rock to get up and walk,' he said.

Brac chuckled a bit.

'No problem. I'll keep Miss Adri out of harm's way. Just promise me if you pick up some trouble you will run straight for this spot. Miss Adri, Mischief and I will make anybody that dare follow you very sorry,' he agreed.

'We will, thank you,' Brighton smiled.

He was thankful Brac didn't argue.

Convincing Adri will probably be a different story.

Deciding there was no point in putting it off he walked over to her.

'You're staying here with Brac today,' he said to her.

'No way, I...' she started but a quick shake of the head from Lilian made her swallow her words.

'Fine,' she said folding her arms.

Brighton gave Adri a quick hug and said, 'Thank you for not arguing again.'

He held out his hand to Lilian.

'Let's go. I want to get there early,' he said to her.

*****

Graham walked into the hall.

He stopped so abruptly that Lars bumped into him.

'What...' Lars started but then also saw what Graham was staring at.

Brighton was sitting behind the big table at the other end of the hall. Lilian was seated to his left. There was not another chair in the entire hall that was whole.

'Please come in,' Brighton called to them.

Graham slowly walked into the hall followed by Lars and the rest of the High Council members.

Graham finally found his voice.

'What have you done? How dare you come in here and desecrate the High Council like this?' he shrieked.

One of the Council members ran out.

Moments later guards started pouring through the door.

'…twenty-three, twenty-four….' Brighton counted.

When it seemed no more guards would come in Brighton said softly to Lilian, 'Thirty-one guards.'

'This is going to get very interesting,' she muttered.

Graham stormed forward screaming, 'Arrest them! Hang them!'

'Let's talk,' Brighton suggested.

Graham kept screaming as the guards rushed forward.

Brighton pointed at the leader. The man dropped his spear and clutched his chest with both hands. He dropped to the floor, stone dead.

Brighton pointed at the next man. He was hoping this would discourage the guards but they kept coming. Brighton concentrated hard. All thirty guards dropped to the floor instantly.

Lilian whispered, 'How did you do that?'

'I'll tell you later,' Brighton whispered back.

The Council members where stunned. Most of them ran for the door. They crushed each other trying to get out of the hall. Finally only Graham and Lars remained.

Lars had a panicked look on his face.

Graham was glaring at Brighton.

'Come forward, let's talk,' Brighton said to them.

Lars started walking but Graham stood dead still.

'I am the first member of the High Council. I will not be ordered by anyone,' he said defiantly.

'Graham! Do as he says before he kills us,' Lars urged him.

Graham ignored the plea.

'You can come closer willingly or I could make you come closer,' Brighton said calmly.

Graham turned his back on Brighton and took a step towards the door. A small white energy ball, no bigger than a man's hand, hung in mid-air blocking his way. Graham stopped, carefully reached out, and touched it. He screamed in pain as the pure energy instantly burnt the skin off his hand. He retreated quickly holding his injured hand.

Lilian knew Brighton had been practicing to use his gift but this left her speechless.

Is there anything he can't do? she wondered in amazement.

The energy ball moved closer to Graham forcing him to retreat further.

Lars ran to the big table. He fell to his knees and started begging Brighton to spare their lives.

Graham tried to go around the white ball but it blocked his way every time. Still it kept coming at the Councillor.

He turned to face Brighton.

'All right, I will talk to you,' he blurted out.

The little white ball disappeared.

'Then come over here, I don't feel like shouting,' Brighton said.

Lilian looked at him carefully. He showed no signs of strain. This display of raw power frightened her a little.

Graham came over and stood in front of the table.

'You broke all the chairs. Where will I sit?' he said to Brighton.

'You will stand,' Brighton replied.

Graham looked unhappy about this but didn't argue.

'What do you want?' he asked Brighton.

'I told you yesterday: Stop the madness or I will,' Brighton said calmly.

'Madness? I don't know what you mean,' Graham

exclaimed.

'You know exactly what I'm talking about. The People's Council was formed to serve the best interest of the people. No more Justice Squads, no more palace on top of the hill, no more ridiculous laws,' Brighton answered.

'We can't just call off everything we've started. A lot of hard work has gone into creating law and order and getting out from under the Supremes' rule. We struggled long and hard for this, I will not let it go to waste now,' Graham complained.

'You did not do any of that, I did. It was me who brought an end to the Supremes and I will do the same with this preposterous "High Council" of yours.'

'But...you can't...' Graham stuttered.

Brighton slammed both hands down on the table so hard the wood cracked straight through.

'Enough arguments! It's clear you are not willing to do what has to be done. Fine, I will. Lars, go fetch all the members of your council. Be quick, I'm losing my patience,' Brighton screamed.

Lars ran out as fast as his trembling legs could carry him.

Graham sank to the floor still clutching his burnt hand.

'What are you going to do?' Graham asked.

'Kill all of you and take command,' Brighton said flatly.

Graham started whimpering.

'Please Brighton, give us a chance. I see now that we were wrong. I will personally see to it that things change,' he begged.

'No more Justice Squads?' Brighton asked.

Graham shook his head.

'They will be recalled today,' he promised.

'Every one of the Justice Squad members must be put on trial. Let the people decide what their punishment should be for the horrible crimes they have committed.'

'Done,' Graham agreed.

'What about the law? Will it be fair to everyone?' Brighton pressed on.

'Yes, yes, we will discuss everything in the open so that the people can have a say. I will also stop the building of the palace.'

'The hunt for talented people will stop immediately,' Brighton said.

It wasn't a question but Graham nodded anyway.

The first of the Council members started drifting into the hall. They huddled against the far wall in fear. Brighton looked around the hall.

'Let's do this in the town centre where everyone can see,' he said.

The Council members left the hall again and gathered in the town centre.

Graham came out followed by Brighton and Lilian. By now most of the Council was present. Brighton pushed Graham forward.

'Tell them,' he instructed.

Graham slowly relayed everything he and Brighton spoke about. He outlined the changes that will be made and gave instructions for certain things to be done immediately.

When he was finished Brighton said, 'Good. I will be back often to check that you're keeping your word.'

'Yes, of course. We will keep the promises and serve the people,' Graham quickly reiterated.

Brighton took Lilian's hand and set off towards their camping spot. Just before they left the town centre, he turned around and called Graham over.

'Who performs marriage ceremonies now?' he asked the Councillor.

'Anyone on the council can but Faye normally does it, why?' Graham answered.

'She will perform the ceremony for Lilian and me

today. Send her over here, we'll wait,' Brighton said.

'But the law….' Graham started.

He smiled an apology.

'Forgive me, I will fetch her immediately.'

*****

Lilian looked radiant.

'You're a miracle worker,' she whispered to Adri as she gave the young girl a quick hug.

Adri wiped a tear from her eye and said, 'Don't forget your flowers.'

Lilian smiled as she took the beautiful blue and white arrangement from Adri. The two women stepped into a small clearing next to the river.

Faye was facing them but Brighton had his back turned.

He started looking over his shoulder but Faye quickly said, 'It's not allowed.'

Brighton smiled and returned to staring at the ground.

Brac was on Faye's left side also facing Lilian and Adri.

Lilian stopped behind Brighton and put her hand on his back.

'Brighton, I come to you willingly. This is my choice,' she said formally.

Brighton turned around, looked into her eyes and replied, 'Lily, I come to you willingly. This is my choice.'

Adri quickly went to stand on Faye's right side.

Faye smiled nervously.

'Brighton and Lilian have chosen to be here. This is of their own free will. Can anybody dispute that?' she said to nobody in particular.

She felt a little silly performing a wedding ceremony with only two people next to her. Normally there would be at least twenty or thirty people next to and behind her witnessing this.

Adri and Brac spoke together, 'We cannot dispute this. Let these people be wed.'

Faye looked at Brighton.

'Brighton, today you take Lilian to be your wife. You will love her, protect her, honour her and never have desire in your heart for another.'

'This is my promise,' Brighton replied.

Faye turned to Lilian.

'Lilian, today you take Brighton to be your husband. You will love him, protect him, honour him and never have desire in your heart for another.'

Struggling to control her voice Lilian replied, 'This is my promise.'

Silence fell over the little gathering. Faye poked both Adri and Brac in the ribs.

'Oh, sorry,' Adri squeaked.

Together they said, 'We witness this union.'

Brighton scooped Lilian up in his arms and gave her a long passionate kiss.

'Well, that's unusual,' Faye commented.

'But does not affect the ceremony,' she quickly added when Brighton looked at her worriedly.

Formally she said, 'Brighton and Lilian are now joined as one. This bond cannot be broken.'

Brac stepped forward and shook Brighton's hand vigorously.

'Congratulations young man.'

He gave Lilian a small kiss on the cheek.

'Congratulations Miss Lilian.'

Adri gave Lilian a tight hug. She stretched out her arm and pulled Brighton closer. He put his big arms around both of them.

'I'm so happy for you both,' she managed to say past the lump in her throat.

Faye coughed nervously.

When Brighton looked at her she carefully asked,

'May I go now?'

'Yes and thank you for your services, we appreciate it,' Brighton said to her.

*****

'How many?' Graham asked impatiently.

'Only the four of them,' Faye answered.

'Are you sure?' Graham pressed.

'Yes, I did not see anybody else,' Faye confirmed.

Graham sat down in his chair.

'So it's still only the four that were here yesterday,' he mused.

Most of the Council members had returned to the big hall.

'Brighton is powerful, I think we should leave them alone,' Lars said nervously.

'Coward!' Graham snapped at him.

'The boy might be powerful but everybody has a weakness,' he shouted at nobody in particular.

'What could be his weakness?' Lars asked. 'He killed more than thirty guards with a mere thought. He is invincible.'

'No, he is not. When I was first elected to be the leader of the High Council, Brighton was there. He killed three Dark Ones with his bare hands,' Graham replied.

Everybody knew Graham was not elected as their leader, he had simply assumed the position, but nobody argued.

'Even more reason to fear him. It would be best to just do as he says,' Lars argued.

Graham had an evil smile on his face.

'That day he showed us that even the most powerful person in the world is still human. A knife through the heart works on anybody. For now we will play by his rules but one day he will be sorry. Brighton is going to die, I will see to that,' he snarled.

Lars was still not convinced that this was the best course of action but didn't argue any further.

Graham got up and addressed the Council.

'Travel to every city, town and village. Gather all the Justice Squads and bring them here,' he ordered.

'What are you planning?' Lars asked quietly when Graham was seated again.

'We're going to put them on trial just as Brighton ordered,' Graham said.

A little smile crept across his lips.

*****

The newly weds strolled hand in hand into the centre of Zedonia. It had been fourteen days since their wedding.

Another trial was taking place. They stood for a while and watched the proceedings. As with all the others, the members of this Justice squad were sentenced to an undefined period in a prison camp. At the first trial, Graham suggested that their lives be spared. He argued that perhaps they could be imprisoned in a special camp outside the city and be taught the value of human life.

Brighton agreed with this.

Construction of fences around the prison camp just outside Zedonia had already started. After some time in the camp these men might learn to respect life and they could be set free to join the community again.

The former council hall had been hastily converted into a makeshift prison. Brighton stuck his head through the door, and saw that there were five more Justice Squads, who arrived the day before, and were now awaiting trial.

The couple walked closer to where the trials were being held.

Lilian didn't like watching the trials.

'Brac once said that hunters respect all forms of life. How come these men are such cold blooded killers? They were hunters once,' she asked Brighton.

'That's what power and greed will do to a person. Look at Graham. He was a simple baker when we met him. Having too much power twisted his morality,' Brighton answered.

'I've seen enough. It looks like the Council is keeping their promise. Do you want to leave?' he said to Lilian.

'Go back to camp or leave Zedonia?' she asked hopefully.

'Leave Zedonia. It's time we get a house built in Four Mountains,' he said patting her belly.

Lilian smiled and nodded enthusiastically.

'Let's go pack up and get going,' Brighton suggested.

The couple turned around and headed out of town.

'Aren't you going to tell the Council we're leaving?' Lilian asked.

'No, they can work it out for themselves,' Brighton answered.

He was still a little worried that they might revert back to their old ways as soon as he was gone. Better to make them think he might return at any moment.

Brighton tried to stroll at a leisurely pace but Lilian pulled him along.

'Come on, why are you walking so slowly?' she complained.

'I'm not. It's you that's running,' he defended.

Lilian slowed down slightly.

'I don't want to stay here longer than is absolutely necessary,' she explained.

Brighton already knew that. Over the last few days she asked often when they were going to depart.

'We won't be travelling today anyway, it's already too late,' he said to her.

She looked disappointed but didn't argue. Brighton was correct; they wouldn't get far before sunset.

Their camp was quite a far way out of town. Brighton insisted on staying in the woods. He was still concerned about the safety of the group. Brac was in his element in the forest and Mischief could stay close to them so it suited everybody.

*****

Graham was in a good mood. Brighton and his followers were seen travelling towards Brasten around midday.

'Lars, come here,' he shouted.

Lars came running from where he was overseeing a Justice Squad trial.

'Stop that stupidity. Get these men to the training camp,' he ordered.

'But…' Lars started.

'Do as I say!' Graham shouted.

'Yes Graham…I mean High Councillor Graham,' Lars stuttered.

Graham walked into the hall.

'Everybody out,' he screamed.

As the Justice Squads made their way out he pulled a fierce looking man aside.

'Lars will take you to the training camp. When you get there, kill him,' Graham instructed.

The man responded in a deep voice, 'As you wish High Councillor Graham. What about the rest of the Council?'

'Do as we discussed,' Graham replied.

*****

The group travelled fast. Brighton didn't see the need to hide any longer so they used the roads. When they neared Brasten, Lilian carefully enquired from Brac whether he would be staying there.

'There is nothing for me here. I would like to continue on with you, if you'll have me,' Brac replied.

'Of course! We will be more than happy if you travelled with us,' Lilian assured him.

The travellers didn't spend any time in Brac's hometown or Avarya, there was no need. More days passed and soon they were standing in the clearing where Brighton used to bring the goats more than six winters before.

'So many good memories here,' Lilian mused.

Brighton smiled and said, 'Yes, this is the place where I fell in love with you.'

He looked around.

'Does that look like a good place for a house?' he asked pointing to the western side of the clearing.

'Yes, that would be wonderful,' Lilian replied happily.

'So, where is the town?' Adri enquired.

'Just up that path,' Lilian replied pointing to the north.

She got a serious look on her face.

'I suppose I should go and see my parents,' she sighed.

Lilian had never had a good relationship with her parents, especially her mother.

'I'll go with you,' Brighton offered.

'Thank you,' Lilian said gratefully.

'Why don't you do that and we'll set up camp?' Brac said.

He didn't bother telling Brighton where the camp would be, he knew Brighton would use his sense to find them.

Brighton and Lilian walked towards town while Adri and Brac looked for a good camping spot. Brac didn't like being in the open so he insisted that the camp should be in the woods. Adri didn't care, as long as it was close to the river.

They found a spot that pleased them both.

*****

Brighton knocked on the door and stepped back. Lilian knew Martha was home, she sensed the older woman. Lately Lilian hardly used her sense; she preferred to think of herself as a normal person.

The door swung open.

'What do you want?' Martha barked.

'Hello mother,' Lilian said.

Martha staggered back.

'Get away from me!' she shrieked.

'Mother, it's me,' Lilian said softly.

'Get away!' Martha shrieked again.

'Where is father?' Lilian sighed.

'Dead. Now leave before you bring more trouble into this house!' Martha screamed as she slammed the door.

Brighton gently pulled Lilian away.

'I'm sorry,' he said to her.

'Don't be, she never loved me anyway,' Lilian answered.

'I wonder why?' Brighton mused.

'Think about it. I'm Seth's daughter. How did that happen?'

Realization hit Brighton.

'Oh, Seth must have…' Brighton trailed off.

'Yes, raped my mother,' Lilian finished for him.

They walked away from Lilian's old house.

'I'm sorry about Markus,' Brighton said.

'He didn't love me either but at least he was kind,' Lilian replied.

Brighton put his arm around her and pulled her close.

'You know I love you more than anything in the world,' he said.

'I know,' Lilian smiled.

They walked through town back to the clearing.

'Brac and Adri are over there,' Brighton said pointing towards the river.

'Let's go and see the place where our house will be, before we join them,' Lilian suggested.

Brighton took her hand and led her west towards the trees.

'I was thinking we could build it just between the trees over there. That way we will have shade but also a very good view of the clearing,' Brighton said excitedly.

'That will be great! We could watch the twins play in the clearing from the porch,' Lilian said.

'Porch?' Brighton asked.

'Yes, I want a porch to sit on,' Lilian demanded playfully.

'Yes dear,' Brighton said with a wide smile.

*****

The men worked hard to get the house finished before Lilian gave birth to the twins.

Lilian invited Adri and Brac to stay with them once it was finished. Adri eagerly accepted but Brac gently declined the offer.

'When we're done with your house, we'll build one much deeper in the woods for me,' he said to Lilian.

Brighton urged Brac a few times to get started on his own house but the hunter refused. He insisted that Lilian must have a proper house by the time the twins are born.

One evening, just as the house was almost finished, Brighton and Lilian were lying on the grass. Adri was in the house cooking. She insisted that the kitchen be finished first so she could make proper food for the working-men.

'We should go have supper,' Lilian said to Brighton.

'Do we have to? I would prefer to stay here,' Brighton said sleepily.

'I'll go get the food and bring it here,' Lilian offered as

she sat up.

Brighton also sat up and said, 'No, I'll go fetch it.'

'Thank you, my love,' Lilian smiled.

'I can imagine how difficult it must be for you to move around now. You're almost as big as the house,' Brighton teased her.

Lilian pulled a face at him. She didn't mind the teasing.

Brighton got up and set off towards the house.

'BRI!' Lilian screamed.

In an instant Brighton was kneeling next to her.

'What's wrong?' he asked, concern filling his mind.

Lilian was holding her bulging belly.

'Your children have decided it's time to meet their father,' Lilian said through clenched teeth.

'What? It's time? Oh no, oh no! What do I do?' Brighton screamed in a panic.

'First you calm down, and then you go call Adri,' Lilian said calmly.

'I'm not leaving you here!' he replied, still in a panic.

'Bri, I'll be fine. Now go,' Lilian said as calmly as she could.

Brighton jumped up and turned towards the house. Adri was already running towards them.

'Adri, we need you!' Brighton shouted.

Adri didn't answer until she was close.

'Yes, I know. I heard your girlish screams,' she replied dryly.

'What do we do now?' Brighton shouted.

'Stop shouting,' Adri said.

'Sorry,' Brighton whispered.

'Good, now carry Lilian to the house,' Adri instructed.

Carefully Brighton picked up his wife and carried her as gently as he could to the house.

'Amazing, isn't it?' Adri said to Lilian.

Lilian smiled despite the pain and nodded at Adri.

'What's amazing?' Brighton asked.

'You,' Lilian answered.

'Me? Why?' Brighton frowned.

'You ended the Supremes' hold on the world, faced off against numerous Dark Ones and even more untalented people without any fear but childbirth scares you senseless,' Lilian answered still clenching her jaw against the pain.

'I'm not scared, I'm just concerned,' Brighton defended.

'He's scared,' Adri said to Lilian.

They reached the house. Brighton stepped inside and carefully put Lilian down on their bed. Since none of the bedrooms were finished yet they were all sleeping in the kitchen.

'Go get Brac,' Adri instructed Brighton.

Brighton shook his head.

'I'm not leaving Lilian.'

'Brighton, I need Brac here,' Adri said as she pushed the big man towards the door.

'I'll be back as soon as I can,' Brighton said and ran out.

He ran as fast as his legs would carry him.

'Brac! Brac!' he kept shouting as he ran.

Brac had made a camp for himself some distance into the woods.

Before Brighton got there, Brac heard his screams. He ran towards the younger man.

'What's wrong?' he shouted while he was still some distance away.

'Lilian is in labour,' Brighton shouted back.

Brac broke into a dead run. Brighton started jogging back until Brac caught up with him. When he heard Brac right behind him he started running hard again.

Getting back to the house felt like ages to Brighton.

He burst through the door.

'I'm back. Brac is here too. Are they born yet?' he stammered.

'No, it's far too early for that,' Adri replied.

'What do we do now?' Brighton asked as he paced from wall to wall.

'You're not doing anything,' Adri responded.

'And Brac? What do you want him to do?' Brighton asked still pacing up and down.

Addressing Brac, Adri said, 'Take him outside and keep him calm. I will call you if we need anything in here.'

'Certainly Miss Adri.' Brac replied.

Brac took Brighton by the arm.

'Come my friend,' he said gently.

Although Brighton was far stronger than Brac, he didn't resist. He realized that he was probably just going to be in the way. Brac lead the young father-to-be outside. He sat on the ground and gestured for Brighton to do the same. Obediently Brighton sat down.

'Brac, you had two children. What was it like when the first one was born?' Brighton asked.

'Nerve-racking,' Brac answered.

'And the second time?'

'Nerve-racking,' Brac said again.

'You're not helping much,' Brighton complained.

'Look, this is not something we can help with. All we can do is wait and let nature take its course,' Brac offered.

Brighton got an idea.

'I can help. I can give Lily some healing energy,' Brighton said as he started to rise.

Brac caught his arm.

'Brighton, don't. This needs to happen naturally.'

Brighton sat down again. He knew Brac was correct.

The men waited outside for a long time. Close to midnight Adri came out of the house.

'Is everything all right?' Brighton asked fearfully.

'Your children and wife would like to see you,' Adri

said with a wide smile.

Brighton stormed up to the house but caught himself just before the door. Slowly he entered.

Lilian was sitting up on the bed. She was holding two tiny little bundles, one in each arm. The babies were wrapped in small blankets. Brighton carefully sat down on the bed.

'Bri, meet your son and your daughter,' Lilian said proudly.

All Brighton could see were two small faces sticking out.

Gently he stroked their cheeks.

'Our little angels' he said as a tear rolled down his face.

'That's the first time I've ever seen you cry,' Lilian said tenderly.

'I'm not crying,' Brighton said quickly as he wiped the tear away.

'Don't worry, I won't tell anyone,' Lilian teased.

Brighton could see that she was exhausted. He touched her leg and slowly let some healing energy flow into her. She realized what he was doing and smiled a thank you.

'We need to think of names,' she said to him.

'That's not something I'm particularly good at. What about Velvet and Mischief,' he joked.

Lilian pulled a face and shook her head.

'I have names in mind but you must tell me if you don't agree. The girl can be called Clarissa, after your mother, and the boy can be Thomas,' Lilian said.

'That's perfect,' Brighton whispered.

He looked at the tiny faces again.

'May I hold one?' he asked.

'Of course, they are your babies too,' Lilian laughed.

Brighton leaned over and gently took little Clarissa.

There was a soft knock on the door. Brighton got up and opened it.

'May we come in?' Adri whispered.

She knew the twins were probably sleeping and did not want to wake them.

'Yes, please do,' Brighton said softly.

When Adri and Brac were inside Brighton whispered, 'I would like you to meet Clarissa and Thomas.'

Brac looked at both babies.

'They are beautiful. It's a good thing they take after their mother,' he teased Brighton.

He slapped Brighton on the back.

'Well my friend, from now on you will have very few moments to yourself. Welcome to parenthood.'

Chapter 23

THE DAYS SEEMED to fly past. Brighton and Brac continued to work on the house. The plan was to have one big bedroom on the north side and two smaller ones on the south. One evening after supper they were sitting outside on the grass. Lilian had little Thomas in her arms and Adri held Clarissa. Brac got up, thanked Adri for the supper, and strolled off to his camping spot. Adri insisted that he ate with them every night.

'The twins can go into one of the small rooms with us right next door. That leaves the big room for Adri,' Brighton said to the women.

Adri immediately shook her head.

'I will take the room next to the children. You and Lilian will have the big room,' she countered.

'That would be unfair to you,' Brighton argued.

'Why?' Adri asked with a frown.

'Because the twins will wake you up every night,'

Brighton answered.

'I don't mind. In fact, I would love to take care of them so you and Lilian can have some time for yourselves,' Adri replied.

Brighton looked at Lilian for help. She just shook her head, she knew that look on Adri's face. Arguing with the younger woman was the same as hitting your head against a tree when she was in this mood.

'But why?' Brighton asked in exasperation.

'So that you and Lilian can make more little bundles of joy like these two,' Adri said with a sly smile.

Brighton didn't know what to say.

Lilian reached out and touched Adri's arm.

'Thank you,' she said softly.

Lilian and Adri got up and went inside to put the sleeping babies down in the cribs Brighton had built.

'Adri, why do you insist on taking care of us?' Lilian asked softly.

'The first reason is that you and Brighton have given me a life. If it weren't for Brighton I would still be in the palace. By now Seth probably would have raped me several times,' Adri said.

'You have no debt to us,' Lilian whispered.

'I know. The second and biggest reason is that I love you both very much,' Adri continued. 'I feel like you're my sister and Brighton is my older, very overprotective brother.'

Lilian had tears in her eyes.

'You know I think of you as my sister,' she choked out.

The two women hugged each other tenderly.

Brighton poked his head through the door, saw what was going on, and quietly retreated.

'Women,' he mumbled as he walked away.

He spotted Mischief sleeping not far away.

He sat down next to the panther and started stroking his soft fur.

'I have to convince Brac to come live here. I'm outnumbered but at least I still have you,' he told the cat.

Mischief opened his completely white eyes. He got up, stretched his powerful body, and headed for the house. Adri had just come out. She was holding something out to Mischief.

Brighton smiled and shook his head.

'Traitor!' he called after the cat.

*****

The men finished the house and a small cottage deep in the woods for Brac. The cottage had only one bedroom and a kitchen. Brac joked that they shouldn't have bothered with the kitchen; he was never going to use it anyway.

'Not that I'm complaining. Miss Adri is probably the best cook in the whole world. Look how fat I'm getting,' he said patting his belly.

'She is a wizard in the kitchen,' Brighton agreed. 'And also very good with the twins. Sometimes I think she's an angel sent to look after us.'

Brac chuckled, 'You're probably right.'

They were working in the vegetable garden not too far from the house. Brighton decided against keeping goats. There was more than enough small game around to provide them with all the meat they needed.

He looked towards town. Three men were approaching. Brighton instantly recognized them. It was John, Brent and William.

'This ought to be fun,' Brighton mumbled.

'Who are they?' Brac asked leaning on his spade.

'Three bullies who used to terrorize smaller kids in the village. I wonder where Garth is,' Brighton replied.

'Garth from Brasten? What would he be doing here?' Brac asked with a frown.

'No, not him. The one I'm referring to was the leader of this little group. I broke his nose one day,' Brighton explained.

'I see,' Brac said.

He held the spade in front of him.

'Relax, I don't think they've come for a fight,' Brighton said.

The three men reached them.

'Good day Brighton,' John greeted.

'Good day to you,' Brighton greeted back.

'I'm John, this is Brent and William,' John said to Brac.

'Brac,' the hunter replied.

'What can I do for you?' Brighton asked.

'Well…uh…we've come to ask something,' John replied.

'Ask, I'm listening,' Brighton prodded.

'I…um…we were wondering if you would let us work in your vegetable garden,' John blurted out.

He was clearly uncomfortable.

Brighton was taken aback slightly.

'Why?' he asked.

'Everybody seems to be struggling with their crops except you,' John said sheepishly.

'If it is food you need we will be more than happy to share,' Brighton replied.

'Thank you, but we don't feel it is right just taking it. We would prefer to work in return for some food,' John explained.

'I see,' Brighton said.

This was a surprise.

'Let me think about it and discuss it with Brac. Come back tomorrow.'

All three said a quick thank you and retreated back to town.

'Well, that was interesting and slightly disappointing,' Brac commented.

'Why are you disappointed?' Brighton asked with a

smile.

He already knew what Brac was going to say.

'I was hoping for a good fight. It's been a while and I'm getting restless,' Brac answered trying to look serious.

He was actually enjoying the peaceful life.

'I'll fight you if that's what you want,' Brighton offered.

'No thank you, I'll rather take on a thousand men armed to the teeth,' Brac quickly laughed.

*****

That evening Brighton told Lilian and Adri about John's request.

'It sounds like a good idea,' Adri said.

Lilian agreed, she didn't mind giving the food away but it was probably better if the men worked for it.

Brighton was not convinced, he didn't trust John's motives.

'I have to protect you, Adri and the twins,' he said to Lilian.

'What about Brac?' Lilian asked.

Brighton frowned and said, 'Brac can take care of himself.'

Lilian laughed and said, 'No, I meant he can also protect us. Besides, we're not entirely defenceless.'

'And we have Mischief,' Adri chipped in.

'True,' Brighton said slowly.

'Give them a chance,' Lilian said to him.

Brighton was still not sure.

'The timing is a bit bad. I wanted to go to Avarya for some string, arrow heads and blades,' he replied.

Brac finally raised his opinion.

'Then it would actually be a good thing if the three men started working here. They can look after the crops while we're gone,' he said.

'We? No, if we're going to do this I need you to stay behind and keep those men in line,' Brighton said quickly.

They spoke about it for a while longer.

Finally Brighton said, 'Fine, we'll give them a chance but only if Brac agrees to stay here when I go to Avarya.'

Reluctantly Brac agreed.

*****

John, William and Brent came back early the next morning. When Brighton told them that he would give them a chance they immediately got to work. Each got a small piece of ground to work on. Brighton and Brac taught them how to prepare the ground, how to plant new vegetables and when to water the plants.

A few days later four more young men arrived asking for work. They all insisted on doing Brighton and Brac's share of the work as long as the two guided them.

Although Brighton enjoyed working in the garden himself, he agreed and took the role of supervisor with Brac assisting him. The vegetable garden expanded so much it covered almost a quarter of the clearing.

More people came asking for work. Brighton didn't turn anybody away and soon the entire clearing was turned into a small farm complete with goats and sheep.

Brighton made frequent trips to Avarya accompanied by two or three men every time. They took their surplus goods to the city and traded it for other things like implements, leather, clothes and shoes.

Some of the women made big rucksacks for them to help carry their goods to and from Avarya.

On one such a trip Brighton was joined by John.

As they entered the city Brighton said to John, 'I'm

going to Joseph. Meet me back here.'

John nodded and went his own way. Brighton knew there was a particular young lady John wanted to visit. He kept going towards the centre of town.

'Hello Joseph,' Brighton greeted cheerfully, as he entered the store.

The old shopkeeper ran over and slammed the door shut.

'Come, let's go to the back,' he nervously suggested.

'What's going on?' Brighton asked still smiling.

Joseph pulled Brighton along by his shirt and said, 'They are looking for you.'

'Who?' Brighton asked.

Joseph pushed the younger man through the backdoor into the alley behind the store.

'The army,' he answered.

Brighton's mind was racing.

'What army?' he asked.

'King Graham's army. Actually they are called "The Royal Peacekeepers",' Joseph replied.

Brighton was speechless for a moment and then rage flooded his mind.

'King Graham? The Royal Peacekeepers?' he asked struggling to control his anger.

'Yes, King Graham. We only heard about this a few days ago. The Royal Peacekeepers came into town, declared Avarya part of the Kingdom and started house to house searches for you and your wife,' Joseph explained.

'How do you know they're looking for us?' Brighton asked.

'They are circulating physical descriptions that match the two of you,' Joseph explained.

Joseph only met Lilian once but he never forgot how beautiful she was.

'It could be someone else,' Brighton tried.

'It's you, I'm sure of it. What I want to know is why

are they calling you a demon and your lovely wife a witch?' Joseph asked.

'We're the last of the talented people; they will never stop hunting us. I made a mistake by letting Graham live but I will rectify that,' he said softly.

*****

Brighton sat on a rock next to the road. It wasn't the exact spot he was supposed to meet John. He had walked a little further up the road to where the forest was thicker. He sensed a large group of people coming his way. John was with them.

Soldiers marched up the road and headed straight for Brighton. They were all wearing brown trousers and red shirts. One soldier was dragging John along. The young man's eyes were swollen shut, his nose broken and he had numerous cuts on his arms and chest. It was clear that they tortured him to find out where Brighton was. The soldier shoved John to the side.

'You can be glad you told the truth,' he sneered at John.

A big man, obviously the squad commander, came to a halt right in front of Brighton. Two fierce looking men took up position just behind him. Brighton estimated that there were about a hundred soldiers in the squad.

'Under orders of King Graham you are to be arrested and brought to Zedonia. If you resist we will kill you on the spot,' he loudly announced.

'You're welcome to try,' Brighton said calmly.

The commander turned to his two lieutenants and said, 'Arrest him. Be careful, he is very dangerous.'

Both men drew the longest knives Brighton had ever seen out of scabbards and stepped in front of the commander.

'What are those called?' Brighton asked casually pointing at the knives.

'Swords,' the commander barked.

'Swords? That's interesting. And you think these swords will help you arrest me?' Brighton asked mockingly.

One of the lieutenants pointed the sword at Brighton's face and said, 'Get up or I'll run you through.'

Brighton spoke to the man like a parent would speak to a naughty child, 'Don't point that thing at me, you might get hurt.'

He pushed the point of the sword to the side and stood up.

The lieutenant thrust the sword at Brighton's chest but the big man was ready. He swayed to his left letting the sword go past and grabbed the man's forearm. With a single, powerful twist he broke the man's arm at the elbow. Quickly he slid his hand down and caught the sword by the hilt just as the man dropped it.

'Thank you,' he said as he flipped the sword the right way around in his hand.

The other lieutenant took a big round-arm swing at Brighton.

Brighton blocked the weapon with his own, stepped inside the man's attack, and brought his knee up. It took the man in the stomach, knocking the wind out of him. Brighton stepped back as the man doubled over. He dropped the sword and brought his fist up from his hip. Brighton felt the man's nose break under the heavy blow. He tumbled backwards, blood splattering everywhere.

Stepping back the commander drew his own sword and pointed it at Brighton.

'Stop or we will kill you,' he said in a high pitched, panicky voice.

Brighton leaned forward and said, 'You saw what happened to the last man that pointed a sword at me. Are you sure you want to do the same?'

The commander stepped further back until he was

between his soldiers.

'Kill him,' he screamed at the men.

Brighton held his hands open, palms forward and slightly away from his legs.

Small bolts of lightning started jumping from the trees behind him to his fingers.

*****

'Miss Lilian! Miss Lilian!' the young girl shouted as she was running towards the house.

She was still more than two hundred paces away when her eyes went wide and she tumbled forward.

Lilian saw an arrow protruding from her back.

'Take Clarissa,' she quickly said to Adri.

The younger woman took the baby from Lilian and put her in the crib next to Thomas.

Adri noticed some time before that the babies slept better when they were close to each other so Brighton had built a larger crib to replace the two smaller ones.

Lilian stepped down from the porch where she and Adri were feeding the children. She didn't see anybody so she used her sense. The attacker was hiding between some trees towards the east of the farm.

Lilian's black energy link slammed into his head. She drained him instantly of all his energy.

She didn't sense anybody except the farm workers around so she walked towards the corpse. Brent and two other men accompanied her.

They saw what had happened to the young girl. The group reached the trees. Lilian walked straight to where she knew the attacker's corpse was. He was on his back, dead eyes staring into the sky. The first thing she noticed was his red shirt.

'That's a bad colour if you want to stay hidden in the woods,' she mumbled.

Brent stepped closer and asked, 'What happened?'

'He killed little Maria so I killed him,' Lilian replied.

'How?' one of the other men asked.

Lilian didn't answer.

She concentrated on casting her sense as wide as possible.

'More men are coming this way. They are through the pass already,' she told the three farm workers.

'What should we do? Judging by what just happened I don't think they're simply coming for a visit,' Brent replied.

'Get everyone into the woods and hide. Don't try to fight these men, they look well armed,' Lilian replied looking at the corpse again.

His bow was lying next to him. A very long knife in a sheath and two short spears were strapped to his belt.

She turned around and hurried back to the house.

'Bring the twins, we're going to Brac's house,' she said to Adri.

She called Brac over, told him what had happened and asked him to accompany them to his house.

'I will stay in the woods close by in case the men find the trail to my house, that way I can warn you,' he said.

'I'll use my sense constantly so I'll know if they are coming towards us. Rather stay with us please,' Lilian replied.

She knew Brac couldn't go up against that many men alone, she wanted him out of harms way.

They quickly gathered some things and set off towards Brac's little cottage.

*****

Brighton picked up a sword. He held it to the commander's throat.

'Run back to your King and tell him I'm coming for him,' he growled at the man.

The commander turned and started running but

tripped over a corpse. He got up and carefully stepped through the corpses that littered the road. All of the soldiers had neat round holes where their hearts used to be.

'Are you alright?' Brighton asked John.

'Nothing that won't heal quickly,' John replied through broken teeth and bleeding lips.

Brighton helped him up. He started healing John's wounds.

'That's fine, thank you,' John said as he pulled away slightly.

He was not comfortable at all with this.

'I can heal all of it, just let me know,' Brighton offered.

'Let's get going,' John said trying to change the subject.

'Can you run?' Brighton asked.

'Yes,' John replied and set off at a fast jog towards Four Mountains to prove it.

Brighton smiled and jogged after him.

When he caught up he asked, 'Didn't you want to say goodbye to your lady friend?'

'No, that witch is the one that betrayed us,' John spat.

It was obvious that the girl told the soldiers she knew someone close to Brighton and that's why they tortured John to find out where he was.

After jogging for a while John slowed and said to Brighton, 'I'm struggling to see. Would you mind healing just my eyes?'

Brighton smiled and put his hand over John's eyes. He let more healing energy than was necessary flow into the young man.

'Is that better?' he asked as he removed his hand.

'Yes, thank you,' John replied and started jogging again.

They jogged in silence until John slowed down.

'Sorry, I'm getting tired,' he said.

They came to a halt and Brighton said, 'I could give

you energy to run longer and faster. I once made it from Avarya to Brasten and back in three days.'

John looked at him to see if he was serious.

'Three days?' he gasped.

'Yes and on the return trip I had Brac and two other men with me. We all ran hard for a day and a half without stopping. You and I could do the same,' Brighton replied.

John shook his head.

'Sorry Brighton, I'm not comfortable with this magic of yours. I would rather not do that,' he said.

Brighton understood.

He would never force anyone to accept energy from him.

'Magic doesn't exist. What I'm doing is simply manipulating energy,' he explained.

John shook his head.

'Still sounds like magic to me. I couldn't see much but the way those soldiers died was certainly not natural,' he argued.

Brighton nodded and said, 'You understand I'm going to run as fast as I can.'

'Go ahead, I'll follow and join up with you there,' John said.

Chapter 24

―――

FOR FIVE DAYS Brighton ran non-stop.

As he reached the farm, he slowed to a walk. The crops were all trampled, the animals slaughtered and their house was burnt down.

He used his sense. There were people hiding in the woods. He recognized all of them as farm workers. When he sensed Lilian, the twins, Adri and Brac he sighed with relief.

He smiled when he felt Mischief's energy.

They were all at Brac's cottage.

'Clever,' he mumbled as he started jogging.

He felt Lilian using her sense. He knew she already felt it when he used his so she knew he was coming.

Halfway to Brac's cottage she came running. She flew into his arms and hugged him as if she would never let him go.

'I'm here now, don't be afraid,' he said gently.

She stepped back and looked at him with a frown. He was short of breath and drenched in sweat.

'Why are you so tired? Did you not take energy from the surroundings?' she asked.

'I did for the first four days. Today I ran using only my own energy,' he explained.

Lilian was still confused.

'Were you worried about the amount of energy you took? Did it take you close to the limit again?' she asked, concern clearly evident in her eyes.

'No, but I didn't want to push too far. I had no idea what was going on here, if anything, so I wanted to make sure my body could handle large amounts of energy if need be once I got here,' he answered.

Lilian relaxed a little.

'So, what did happen here? I see the farm is destroyed,' Brighton asked as they started walking hand in hand towards Brac's cottage.

'Scores of heavily armed men came here. Little Maria tried to warn me but their forward scout shot her in the back. I killed him for it,' Lilian replied.

'What were they wearing?' Brighton asked.

Lilian didn't understand why that was important but answered anyway.

'The one I killed wore brown trousers and a red shirt. I didn't actually see the rest, I tracked them with my sense,' she recalled.

'The Royal Peacekeepers,' Brighton mumbled.

'The what?' Lilian asked.

'The Royal Peacekeepers. It's Graham's army. Or King Graham as he calls himself now,' Brighton said with disgust in his voice.

Lilian already knew the answer to her next question but asked anyway.

'And what is the purpose of this army?'

'To hunt us. We are the last of the talented people,' Brighton said flatly.

Just after the twins were born, Brighton realized that he did not sense the talent in either of them.

He reasoned that since his talent was counteractive to Lilian's it must have had a permanent effect in their children, leaving them with no form of the talent at all.

'Bri, there was more than a hundred men here. How many do you think Graham has?' Lilian asked.

'Well over five thousand. Do you remember the Justice Squads and the prison camp they were sent to? It has been turned into a training camp. Graham planned it from the start. I can't believe I was so blind!' Brighton replied softly.

But I will not make the same mistake twice, he thought.

Lilian stopped and turned to face him.

'Wait, how do you know all of this?' she asked suspiciously.

'I killed a squad just outside Avarya. Everyone except the commander. I got some answers from him before I sent him running to his king,' Brighton answered.

'Why did you let the man go? He is going to report to Graham where he saw you! You should have killed all five of them,' Lilian berated him.

She assumed Brighton was referring to one of the old Justice Squads. He didn't correct her.

'I know, but Avarya is far to the east. The squad that came here didn't see you, did they?' he replied.

'No, we came to hide here long before they reached the farm,' she assured him.

'Good, that gives us a bit of time. Graham's army will search the forest around Avarya first. It will take a long time before they get here again,' Brighton replied.

'And that's why you let the commander go,' Lilian said in understanding.

They reached the cottage. Everyone was standing outside waiting for them. Adri had Thomas in her arms and Brac was carrying Clarissa. The old hunter would never admit it but he loved playing with the babies. He often fed them sweet berries when he thought nobody was looking. Of course both Adri and Lilian knew but they didn't say anything.

'Did you run into trouble?' Brac asked casually.

He knew Brighton was only due back in seven or eight days. The fact that he was here could mean only one thing.

'Just a little but I took care of it. It seems like there were problems here too,' Brighton answered.

'Just a little,' Brac echoed Brighton's words.

A knowing look passed between the men. Both knew the trouble was far from little.

Lilian took Clarissa from Brac. It was time to feed the babies so the women went inside the small cottage.

Brighton led Brac into the woods a little and spoke in a soft voice.

'Did you get a look at the men that came here?' he asked.

'No, Lilian didn't want me to go close. She used her sense to track them. They went straight to town,' Brac answered.

Brighton knew that the soldiers probably destroyed the town looking for them. Sadness washed over him.

'I will fix this,' he said mostly to himself.

'What are you planning?' Brac asked.

He knew the look on Brighton's face.

'The first priority is to get the women and children to safety. Let's concentrate on that for now,' Brighton answered.

'Where would they be safe? Graham's troops are looking everywhere, even in this remote part of the world. There is nowhere we could hide for long. Sooner or later they will find us,' Brac sighed.

Brighton pointed to the west.

'We will cross that mountain,' he said flatly.

Brac's eyes went wide.

'That's impossible. Nobody has ever crossed the

western boundary. Besides, beyond it is only darkness,' he gasped.

Brighton shook his head.

'I think it looks the same on the other side of the mountain as it does here. If I'm correct there will also be people there,' Brighton answered.

Brac looked at Brighton closely to see if the younger man was serious.

'I think all that energy you take from the forest has melted your brain,' he finally said.

Brighton didn't take notice.

'Think about it. Why does this town exist? You think people came here to get away from the Dark Ones and that's a good theory but I don't think it's the whole story. If I wanted to get away from the worst evil in the world I wouldn't stop here, I would keep going. I would have liked to have a seemingly impassable mountain between me and the evil I'm running from. My theory is that some people felt this place was far enough and settled here while others kept going,' Brighton explained.

Brac wasn't convinced.

'If there are people why haven't you sensed them?' he asked.

'It's too far. From here, it's more than half a day's travel to the foot of the mountain. After that it's at least another day to get to the top and who knows how far you have to go to reach the other side,' he explained.

'Here is something else to think about. Have you ever wondered why there are roads between the towns and cities?' he asked the older man.

'That's a really odd question. Roads are there so that we can travel on them,' Brac replied with a frown.

'Yes, I know that, but why are the roads so wide? Everybody walks, there should only be narrow trails. Someone built the roads like that for a purpose,' Brighton continued.

Brac thought for a while and said, 'I've never thought of it that way. It seems the roads were built for something larger to travel on.'

'Exactly!' Brighton exclaimed.

'But what could be large enough to need a road that wide to travel on?' Brac asked.

'I don't know,' Brighton admitted.

'Even if I'm wrong and there is nobody on the other side it doesn't matter. I've had enough of people and their greed. If we could go live where there is nobody else around, it would suit me just fine,' he said.

'I support that my friend,' Brac agreed.

The men walked back to the cottage. Lilian was still trying to feed Clarissa but the little girl was being difficult. She was simply not interested in the boiled vegetables. Adri had the same problem with Thomas. Without asking, Brac took Clarissa from Lilian. He produced a red berry from his pocket and held it in front of her. Clarissa immediately grabbed the berry with her tiny hand and attempted to shove it in her mouth. Most of it squashed against her cheek leaving red juice dripping down her face. Brac pulled another berry from his pocket and helped her get it in her mouth. Thomas saw this and held his arms out to Brac making little whimpering noises. Brac gave him a small red berry. Thomas had more success with shoving it into his mouth. Brac sat down next to Adri and kept feeding the twins the red berries.

'No wonder they won't eat their food,' Lilian complained.

She didn't really mind all that much. She knew Brac loved the children with all his heart and this was his way of showing it.

Brighton didn't sit down. He knew convincing the women to cross the western boundary was going to be difficult.

Before he could speak Lilian said, 'I think we should

leave. Our presence is putting everybody here in danger. I just don't know where we should go.'

'But I do,' Brighton said.

'Where? I can't think of any place that will be safe for us,' Lilian said.

Brighton took a deep breath and said, 'Across the western boundary.'

Adri's head snapped up.

'What? Have you lost your mind?' she exclaimed.

'That's what I said,' Brac mumbled.

More clearly he said to the women, 'Just listen to Brighton, I support him.'

Adri looked at him sideways.

'So you've also gone mad?' she asked.

Brac chuckled. He thought this was the reaction they were going to get.

Lilian surprised them both.

'I think it's a good idea, assuming we make it to the other side,' she said.

Brighton nodded.

'I believe we can. If I have to blast a hole straight through that mountain that is also fine by me, but we cannot stay here any longer,' he said.

*****

Graham's anger reached boiling point. He pulled out his sword and stepped closer to the man kneeling in front of him.

'It's simple. You take a sword and run him through,' he screamed as he waved his blade in the air.

He pointed his sword at the kneeling man and thrust it forward. The sharp blade easily entered the man's chest and pierced his heart.

'See. Nothing to it,' he screamed at the ten squad commanders behind the kneeling man.

He pulled his sword free and tossed it to a girl behind

him.

'Clean that,' he instructed.

The girl tried to catch the sword but only managed to cut her hands on the sharp edge. She dropped the sword with a little cry. Graham turned around slowly.

'What did I say about dropping my sword?' he asked the young girl.

'I'm sorry King Graham,' the girl stuttered as she picked up the sword with her bleeding hands.

Graham stepped closer. He slapped the girl hard on her right cheek. She barely managed to keep her balance as her hand shot up to her face.

'One more time and you will be very sorry,' Graham threatened.

The girl took a deep bow and then rushed off to get the sword cleaned up.

'Where was I?' Graham asked as he turned back.

'Oh yes, I was explaining how easy it is to kill that boy,' he answered his own question.

Graham and his entourage were on their way to Avarya. News had reached them that Brighton had been seen there on a number of occasions. Graham was tired of getting news that was fourteen days or more old so he decided to go to Avarya in person. The commander of the squad Brighton killed met the royal party less than a day's travel outside the city. Graham was in the process of giving ten new squad commanders their orders when the man ran up to the camp.

Pointing to the dead commander Graham said, 'This monkey wanted to gain my favour by arresting Brighton and bringing him to me. Is that what I ordered?'

'No King Graham,' the ten commanders answered.

'What are my orders?' Graham asked.

'To kill Brighton and the witch,' the ten voices came as one.

'And do you understand these orders?' Graham asked sarcastically.

'Yes King Graham,' the answer came immediately.

'Then go do it!' Graham screamed.

The ten commanders scrambled to get out of Graham's sight.

Graham walked back to his chair. A young woman, Ashley, occupied the chair next to his.

'Why do you want Brighton dead so badly?' she gingerly asked.

Graham sighed.

'You're not very clever, are you?' Graham sneered at her.

Ashley dropped her eyes and softly said, 'No, I'm sorry.'

Graham grabbed her by the chin and yanked her head up.

'Well, at least you're pretty,' he said in a softer tone.

Ashley nodded and tried to force a smile.

Graham sat down and started talking slowly, 'I'll explain it one more time. Brighton is the only man who can challenge me. As long as he lives I will always be the second most powerful man alive.'

Ashley frowned.

'But you are not talented. How can you be the second most powerful man?' she asked.

Graham rolled his eyes and said, 'I am king. I command an army of more than five thousand men. With these new squads added the count is now well over six thousand. Does that not sound powerful to you?'

Although Ashley didn't think this made Graham powerful she still nodded.

Graham and Ashley had been married for a short while. Graham spotted her in Zedonia one day and her beauty captivated him. She was a tall slender girl with long dark hair that reached halfway down her back.

Her skin was dark and her eyes looked like big black grapes. Graham immediately decided he had to have her but, unfortunately, he was already in wedlock for more than twenty winters.

The following day Graham's wife was found floating face down in the river.

Five days later Graham married Ashley.

'I have to attend to the other commanders. Just sit there and be quiet,' he instructed her.

He waved his hand and a pageboy ran off. He returned quickly followed by five commanders. The serving girl also returned holding Graham's sword in her bandaged hands. He snatched the sword from her and inspected it. When he was satisfied that the sword was clean he waved the commanders forward.

One by one they nervously came forward and reported that their squads had been unsuccessful in tracking Brighton down. Graham asked each of them a few select questions before waving them off.

More commanders came before him with nothing to report. Graham's mood slowly got darker and darker as the day wore on until the commander that raided Clareton stood before him.

'What do you mean there was nobody in town?' Graham snapped at the man.

The man nervously answered, 'It was like nobody lived there, King Graham. Everybody was gone.'

Graham frowned.

'What did the houses look like? Were they in good condition or in ruins?' Graham asked the nervous commander.

'They looked normal, like there should be people living there. We also saw large vegetable gardens and a lot of goats and sheep just outside the town. It was definitely a farm where a lot of people worked,' the commander answered quickly.

He smiled a little, happy that he could answer

Graham's questions.

'So where do you think the people went?' Graham prodded.

'I don't know, King Graham,' the commander answered, his small smile quickly disappearing.

'Did you send a forward scout?' Graham continued the interrogation.

'Uh…yes I did,' the commander stuttered.

He didn't like where this conversation was going.

'Bring him here,' Graham ordered.

The commander didn't move.

'Well…um…I can't. We found him dead in the woods not far from the farm I mentioned.'

'And how did he die?' Graham asked the nervous man.

'I don't know, King Graham. He seemed to be untouched except for a black mark on his forehead,' the man answered.

By the way Graham looked at him he knew he was in deep trouble.

Although the king still spoke calmly, his face was going redder with each passing second.

'And how do you suppose that happened?' he asked.

'Um…I…uh…don't know,' the commander stammered.

Graham looked at Ashley and said, 'I am surrounded by idiots.'

She started smiling but then remembered their earlier conversation. He was obviously referring to the commander on this occasion but the comment stung her.

To the commander Graham said, 'Go fetch your lieutenants.'

The man rushed off immediately. The squads camped quite a far way from the royal party so it took the commander some time to return.

When the three men were standing in front of

Graham, he slowly got up and walked closer.

'It's been only two winters and already everybody seems to have forgotten how the Dark Ones used to kill,' he said looking from face to face.

The men all had their eyes cast downward.

'Who do you think killed your forward scout?' he asked the three men.

The commander looked up and said, 'I'm sorry King Graham, I made a mistake. If you will allow me I will take my squad back to Clareton and search until we find Brighton and his witch.'

Graham answered by pulling his sword and running the man through.

'No, I will not,' he said to the dying commander.

He pulled his sword free and tossed it backwards.

'Clean that,' he ordered.

When he didn't hear the sword falling to the ground again he smiled.

'That serving girl is more clever than you,' he said to the lieutenants.

Neither of the men answered.

'The entire squad should be executed but since I am a generous king, I will spare your lives,' Graham continued.

He pointed at the one lieutenant.

'You are now squad commander. Go back to Clareton and search until you find Brighton and the witch,' he instructed.

Both men quickly took a deep bow and rushed off.

'Rather you than me,' the lieutenant whispered to his new commander.

'Thank you,' the man replied sarcastically.

*****

Brighton looked up.

'I don't think we can climb that,' he said to the others.

He was carrying a sleeping Clarissa in his arms. They had travelled west through the forest until they stood at the bottom of a sheer cliff going up hundreds of paces.

'Let's camp here,' Brighton said.

'It's only midday, shouldn't we try to find a way around,' Lilian asked.

'You wait here, I'll go look,' he suggested.

Brac wasn't interested in going with. He had Thomas in his arms and was feeding the little boy berries again.

Brighton handed Clarissa to Lilian and set off in a southerly direction. Clarissa woke up and immediately started whimpering. Adri produced some berries from her pocket. As soon as Clarissa saw the little red treats, she held out her arms to Adri.

'You two are stealing my children away,' Lilian complained good-naturedly as she handed the baby to Adri.

Brighton returned a while later.

'There might be a way up a little south of here but it looks dangerous. I'm going to look north for a better route,' he said and jogged off again.

It was close to sunset before he returned.

He had a big smile on his face.

'I found a way not too far north from here,' he said.

'Why did you stay away so long if it's not far?' Lilian enquired.

'I had to make sure it wouldn't be a dead end so I went up the mountain quite far,' Brighton explained.

'Does it look like we will be able to cross the mountain on that route,' Lilian asked.

'We'll certainly make it almost to the top. I don't know what awaits us there,' he answered.

The group settled down for supper and went to bed soon after that. Brighton didn't think they needed to stand guard since he didn't sense anybody around but them.

'Besides, Mischief is here. He will keep watch for us,' Brighton reasoned.

Brac looked at Brighton, down at the sleeping panther and back at Brighton again.

'If you say so,' he said shrugging his shoulders.

Chapter 25

———⁎———

EARLY THE NEXT morning the group started their climb up the mountain. Brighton set a very easy pace. He didn't want anybody to slip and hurt themselves. If it did happen he could heal the wounds but it was best to avoid injury altogether.

Brighton took the lead followed by the two women while Brac and Mischief brought up the rear. They agreed to take turns carrying the twins.

'Would you like me to carry Clarissa?' Lilian asked Brighton.

'No, I'm fine thank you,' he answered.

Adri didn't bother asking Brac. She knew he would not hand Thomas over even if she begged or threatened not to give him food. Secretly she was thankful for that since she was getting very tired.

The ground levelled out somewhat and Brighton decided to stop for a while. The babies were getting hungry and he wanted to scout ahead a little anyway. Lilian and Adri sat down to feed the twins while the men went further up the mountain. So far the woods were rather thick but as they climbed higher, it thinned out a lot.

After climbing for a while Brighton stopped and looked back.

'Look, you can see the town from here,' he said.

Brac squinted and said, 'You have good eyes!'

Brighton also squinted and said, 'There seems to be a lot of people down there, and they are all wearing red.'

'Graham's army?' Brac asked.

'I think so. I wonder what made them decide to wear red shirts. If they had been dressed in brown I never would have spotted them,' Brighton commented.

He used his sense to find out how many soldiers there were.

'This is not good,' he muttered.

'Let me guess, they're coming this way,' Brac said.

'Yes, more than I can count,' Brighton replied worriedly.

'They will never find our trail, I've made sure of that,' Brac tried to reassure Brighton.

'I don't doubt your ability but it looks like they are simply searching everywhere. Sooner or later they will reach the mountain.'

'Do you think they will find the break in the cliff? You said you were lucky to have spotted it,' Brac tried.

'There are thousands of men down there; someone is bound to stumble across the path I found,' Brighton replied.

'Then we should fetch the women and get going,' Brac suggested.

The two men immediately started walking back to where they left the others.

When they got there Lilian pulled Brighton aside.

'Adri is tired but won't ask you for help. Talk to her

please,' she whispered to him.

Brighton quickly told the women what they saw and then said to Brac and Adri, 'I know you don't really want me to give you energy but we need to travel fast now. For the moment, we have a good lead but they might realize we have gone into the mountain. They will then pick up the pace to try and catch us.'

He held his hands out. Wordlessly Adri and Brac put their hands in his.

After a few moments, Brighton said, 'There, that should be good enough for now. Tell me when you get tired again.'

'I will,' Brac said quickly.

He wasn't tired to start with but he played along for Adri's sake.

'Me too,' she said.

They quickly gathered their things and set off again.

*****

Brighton looked up at another cliff hundreds of paces high.

'This is ridiculous,' he muttered.

To the others he said, 'Let's keep going. We will find a way around this one.'

It was past sunset already and they desperately needed to find a good camping spot. A very cold wind was howling around them. Brighton made sure Clarissa was covered properly and set off again.

Trying to set up camp where they were would have been dangerous. The slope of the ground was far too steep. One of them could easily roll down in their sleep and be seriously injured or killed.

The group continued on next to the cliff.

Mischief was about twenty paces ahead of him. Brighton could only just see his black form in the gloomy light.

He looked back to see how the others were doing. When he looked ahead again, Mischief was gone again.

'Mischief!' he called.

The cat's head appeared briefly out of a bush and then disappeared again.

Brighton rushed forward. There was no chance that bush was big enough to hide a panther Mischief's size.

When he got to the bush he smiled.

Turning back to the others he called, 'Mischief found a cave!'

Without waiting for them to catch up, he entered the cave. The small opening was hidden by thick bushes, and was only just big enough for him to fit through it.

Just past the entrance, the cave opened up into a much bigger space.

'Where are you?' Lilian's voice came from outside.

Brighton pushed the bushes away. The group was standing right in front of the entrance but didn't see it.

'In here,' he said.

Adri jumped with fright and almost lost her footing but Brac's hand quickly steadied her.

'Don't do that!' she snapped at Brighton.

'Sorry,' he said trying not to laugh.

Everybody went inside.

'Well, this is quite a find,' Brac commented.

'Thank Mischief. I never would have seen the entrance.' Brighton said.

'Good boy,' Adri said to the cat as she scratched his ears.

Inside the cave it was quiet; the bushes in front of the entrance blocked most of the wind.

'Can we make a fire?' Adri asked.

They brought some food but it needed to be cooked.

Brighton thought for a moment and said, 'Let's move deeper in, that way there is no chance of the soldiers seeing the fire in the night sky.'

Brac looked at the bush covering the entrance.

He didn't think a small fire could be seen through that, but understood why Brighton was cautious.

The group moved a bit further into the cave.

'This should do. Brac, help me gather some firewood please,' Brighton said.

The men went out into the cold wind again and started looking for dead wood.

'The soldiers found the break in the cliff. I feel them coming up the mountain towards us,' Brighton said to Brac.

The hunter looked worried.

'I'm sure our trail is well hidden but an experienced tracker might just find us.'

Brighton tried to keep the worry out of his voice.

'They can't travel at night either. We have until morning to think of something.'

Brac didn't answer.

He knew Brighton would fight should they be discovered, he just didn't know if Brighton would survive.

The men returned to the cave carrying a few pieces of wood.

'Only a small fire and we're killing it as soon as we're done,' he said as they put the wood down.

Adri had supper done in no time.

The twins were fast asleep on a little bed Lilian made for them. Brac had fed them the last of the berries in his pockets.

'You know you will have to find more of those. They will not be happy with just vegetables anymore,' Lilian told him.

She seemed to have reached a compromise with the twins: If they ate enough vegetables, they were allowed some of those sweet red berries.

Brac put another spoonful of food in his mouth and nodded.

As soon as supper was finished the women got up to

wash the dishes.

'No, don't,' Brighton stopped them.

'Bri, we have to get the plates clean,' Lilian complained.

'We need to save the water we have. I don't know if we're going to find water again this high in the mountain,' Brighton countered.

Lilian didn't like putting dirty dishes back in the rucksacks but she understood Brighton's argument.

She and Adri wiped the plates and pots clean with leaves as best they could and packed it away.

'As soon as we reach water, you two are washing the dishes,' Adri said, wagging a finger at the men.

'As you wish my queen. Shall I draw you a hot bath?' Brac teased her.

Brighton looked intently at the last flame dying out.

Without taking his eyes off the glowing embers he said, 'Give me some more wood please.'

Brac shoved a dead branch into Brighton's outstretched hand.

'What happened to killing it when we're done?' he muttered.

'Keep quiet, the fire will keep us warm,' Adri whispered urgently to him.

'You may have all the heat in this body, my queen,' he teased her again.

Adri quickly scooted close to Brac.

'That's fine by me. Put your arms around me and start sharing,' she said to him.

Brac obediently opened his arms and Adri shifted as close as possible to him.

'Thank you, you're my hero,' she said through shivering lips.

Brac closed his arms around the young woman. He immediately got a frown on his face. Adri was burning up.

Brighton had the flames going again.

Lilian leaned closer to him and softly said, 'Thank you for keeping the fire going. It looks like Adri is really suffering in this cold.'

'Huh...oh, yes...heat. That's good,' Brighton said absentmindedly.

Lilian frowned at him.

'You didn't do it for Adri?' she asked.

He looked up.

'Do what for Adri?' he asked with a frown.

'The fire. Didn't you do that because Adri is cold?' Lilian asked with a frown.

'Uh...well no, not really,' Brighton said.

He was staring intently at the flames again.

'Then why did you?' Lilian asked.

'Look at the flames,' he said.

Brac and Lilian looked into the fire. Brac noticed that Adri didn't lift her head to look; she seemed to be asleep already.

Brighton waited a moment for them to have a good look then asked, 'What do you see?'

'Fire,' Brac said dryly.

It didn't look like Brighton heard.

'Look at the flames. See the way they are leaning towards the cave entrance?' he asked.

Lilian looked close and said, 'Yes. Why does this interest you?'

'There is air moving through the cave, that's why the flame is constantly leaning towards the entrance,' Brighton explained.

'It's just the wind outside,' Brac said.

'No, listen. The wind had died down,' Brighton countered.

Brac listened for a moment and said, 'You are correct, I can't hear the wind anymore.'

Lilian shook her head and said, 'I still don't understand why this is so interesting.'

Brac answered, 'If there is air moving through the

cave it means there is another entrance further on.'

Understanding washed over Lilian.

'I see. And you're thinking we can go through the mountain rather than over it,' she said to Brighton.

Brighton nodded and said, 'I'm going to have a quick look further into the cave. Stay here.'

'Uh...Brighton,' Brac started.

'Yes?'

'Before you go, don't you want to take a quick look at Adri please?' Brac asked.

'Sure, what is the problem?' Brighton replied.

'It's not really cold in here but she said she was freezing. The funny thing is, her body is burning up,' Brac told him.

Brighton gently shook Adri's shoulder.

'Adri? Adri?' he said.

She didn't wake up.

Brighton cupped her cheek in his hand.

'You're right, she is very warm. We should check her for injuries,' he said to Brac.

The hunter got a panicked look on his face.

'I...um...I'm not...uh...well...it's not that I don't want to, it's just...' he stammered.

Lilian smiled at him and said, 'Relax, I'll do it.'

She quickly laid out a blanket on the ground and said, 'Put her down here.'

Brac carefully laid Adri down.

'It's not that I'm unwilling, you understand. I will do anything for Miss Adri, but...' he tried to explain.

Lilian smiled and finished for him, 'I understand. You're a gentleman.'

Brac nodded sheepishly.

'Now turn around so I can check her for injuries,' Lilian said to both the men.

They walked a few paces into the cave.

'Can you sense anything?' Brac asked Brighton.

Brighton knew he was referring to the soldiers.

'They are still coming up the mountain,' he answered.

Brighton also sensed the plants and animals in the direction they came from, above them and in the direction they will be travelling. What he didn't tell Brac was that the energy seemed to just stop some distance ahead of them.

Lilian called them over.

'She has a scratch on her left arm. That's all I can find,' she reported.

Brighton kneeled next to Adri. He put his hand over the scratch and tried to heal it, but nothing happened.

Putting both his hands over the wound, he let more healing energy flow.

'Something is wrong,' he muttered.

No matter how he tried, he could not heal the wound.

'Perhaps I should try something else,' he said.

He touched her again and let a tiny amount of her energy flow into him. A sharp pain shot through his hand.

'Her energy feels…strange,' he said.

'Strange? What do you mean?' Lilian asked.

'I can't explain it. It's not normal,' he said.

Lilian stuck out her hand and said, 'Let me feel.'

Brighton quickly stopped her.

'No, as soon as I took a small bit from her my hand started hurting. I don't know what's going on but I don't want you to also get sick,' he explained.

'May I look at the wound?' Brac asked.

Brighton lifted Adri's sleeve for Brac to see.

He took a long look and said, 'It looks like this was caused by a darkweed.'

Neither Brighton nor Lilian had ever heard of a darkweed.

Before they could ask Brac continued, 'It's an extremely poisonous plant with sharp thorns. One scratch will kill a person.'

Lilian's hand shot to her mouth.

'No! Are you sure?' she gasped.

'Well, I've never seen it for myself but from the look of the scratch, yes, I'm sure,' Brac answered.

Although Brighton didn't feel calm, he forced his voice to be soft and even, 'If you've never seen this, how can you be so sure?'

'My father taught me about them. He never saw it either, his father taught him. In fact, it is believed that darkweed has been extinct for many generations. Our family, and a few others, kept the knowledge alive by passing it on from father to son.'

'Why?' Brighton asked.

'Darkweed is very tough to kill. If you try to burn the bush, it explodes. Any tiny fragment that comes into contact with the ground will sprout a new bush. Cutting it down has the same effect, tiny fragments fall to the ground and soon there is more darkweed than you started with.'

'So how do you kill it?' Brighton asked.

'Darkweed doesn't like growing in the same ground as Avrilias. It's a small purple flower named after a lady, Avril, who discovered that the little flowers somehow kill the darkweed. Avrilia seed was collected and sowed everywhere in and around the darkweed bushes.'

'Ok, so we know how to kill the bush. What about Adri?' Brighton asked.

'I honestly don't know what will happen to Miss Adri. You must understand, I'm giving you information that is centuries old. For all we know I only have a tiny bit of the original knowledge. I do know that feeding a victim Avrilias, or their seeds, has no effect. Once the poison is in the blood it cannot be removed,' Brac replied.

He was trying very hard to hide his sadness but Lilian could see it in his eyes.

She touched his arm and said, 'If there is one man that

can cure this, it's Brighton.'

Brighton looked at Brac and said, 'Tell me everything you know about this darkweed.'

Brac thought for a moment and said, 'The only other thing I know is that the bush was named after the Dark Ones. Just like them, the poison will suck away all your energy. Depending on the amount of poison that entered the body it could take anything from a day to five or six for the victim to die.'

Brighton waited for Brac to continue but the hunter remained silent.

Eventually Brighton asked, 'How sure are you that this is in fact a darkweed scratch?'

Brac stepped closer and pointed at the area around the wound, careful not to touch it.

'Look at how the skin has turned black around the scratch. That part of her arm has already died. Soon the rest of her body will look the same. I'm sure this is a darkweed scratch,' he said confidently.

Brac stepped back.

'Anything else?' Brighton asked hopefully.

Brac started shaking his head but stopped.

'There is a story about a Dark One that stole the energy of an infected person. I don't know if there is any truth to it but apparently the Dark One died a few days later. His whole body had turned black,' he said.

Brighton thought for a moment and said, 'That makes sense. When I took some of Adri's energy just now, it felt...wrong, like it was poisonous.'

Softly Lilian asked, 'Does this mean you will also get sick now?'

'I don't think so. I immediately channelled the bad energy into the ground,' Brighton replied.

Brac looked at Brighton hopefully.

'Is there anything you can do for Miss Adri?' he asked softly.

'I'm not sure. I've healed wounds before but I don't

really know how to do this. I'm going to try everything I can though,' Brighton replied.

*****

'How many?' High Commander Tristan growled.

'Fifteen dead and another twenty two infected. The healers say that the infected ones will die soon,' the commander in front of him replied.

'This is one of Brighton's tricks! I will kill that boy if it's the last thing I do!' High Commander Tristan shouted.

'Uh...excuse me High Commander but I don't think Brighton had anything to do with this,' the commander said nervously.

Tristan glared at the man. The commander didn't know if that meant he should keep quiet or share his information with the High Commander. He decided silence was the safest.

Tristan leaned forward in his chair.

'Well? Are you going to make me beat it out of you?' he boomed.

'No High Commander, sorry High Commander,' the man quickly apologized.

He relayed what one of his men had told him about darkweed.

'I've never heard of it. Is your man trustworthy?' Tristan asked when the man finished.

'Yes High Commander, I've known him all my life,' the commander replied.

'And this darkweed will kill anybody including those cursed Dark Ones,' the High Commander prodded.

'According to my source, yes, it will,' the commander answered quickly.

Tristan smiled and sat back in his chair.

'Gather the best archers we have and bring them

here,' he instructed.

*****

The group slept for a while before travelling deeper into the caves. Brac had made two torches from thick branches and some cloth. The cloth was coated in a paste made from specific leaves he had collected outside.

'This way it will burn longer,' he explained.

Brighton didn't want to wait for morning. The soldiers were getting closer with every passing moment.

He insisted on carrying Adri, he didn't want the others coming into contact with the poison.

Brac and Lilian carried the twins and a torch each while Mischief followed at the rear.

Brighton laid Adri down and stepped away.

'Every time I give her some healing energy it seems to just disappear into her body. She isn't getting any better. In fact, the infection is spreading faster now,' he said worriedly.

'How can that be?' Lilian asked.

'I don't know. The poison seems to feed off any form of energy. It looks like I may have made the situation worse by trying to heal her,' Brighton replied.

'How long?' Lilian whispered past the lump in her throat.

'A day, maybe slightly more,' Brighton answered honestly.

'Can't you think of anything else to try?' Lilian asked, tears rolling down her cheeks now.

'You know I will try everything I can think of, my love,' Brighton softly answered.

'Yes, I know,' Lilian choked out.

Brac didn't attempt to speak. He didn't trust his voice.

'Let's keep going for a while, maybe I will think of something else,' Brighton suggested.

He didn't tell the other two that his right hand felt like it was on fire.

Gently he picked Adri up and set off again.

*****

Brighton estimated that they had travelled for about another half a day. So far, the cave was high and wide enough for them to walk comfortably.

Adri was close to death. Her breathing was shallow and uneven.

Brighton sank to his knees.

'Bri, what's wrong?' Lilian asked.

Brighton couldn't hide it any longer.

'The poison is in me,' he replied without looking back.

Lilian handed Clarissa to Brac and rushed forward.

She held her torch close enough to see his face and lifted her hand to feel his temperature.

'Don't,' he quickly snapped as he pulled away.

'I don't know if you can also catch this by touching me,' he said in a softer tone.

Lilian pulled her hand back. Unsure of what to do next she just stared at Brighton.

Brighton put Adri on the ground, stood up and turned so he could face both of them.

'This poison feeds off energy. The more I get from the plant life above us the quicker it spreads. There is only one way to rid both Adri and me of this,' he said.

'So you have a solution?' Lilian asked hopefully.

'Yes and I don't have the strength to argue with you about it,' Brighton answered.

'Argue? Why would I argue?' Lilian asked with a frown.

'I need you two to keep going without us. You have to get further away from me than what the plants above us are,' Brighton answered.

'Why? How is that...'

Lilian stopped as realization washed over her.

'No!' she shouted at Brighton. 'I will not allow you to do that!'

'It's the only way, my love,' Brighton said calmly.

'No!' Lilian screamed again, her tiny hands clenched into fists.

Brac looked from face to face.

'Would someone mind telling me what's going on?' he asked.

'Bri wants to kill himself and Adri. Talk to him Brac!' Lilian answered harshly.

Brac frowned and said, 'It doesn't seem like the best solution. I thought you were trying to save yourself and Miss Adri?'

Brighton nodded and said, 'Yes, that is the idea.'

'You will need to explain this,' Brac said calmly.

'If I'm close to death my instinct for survival will take over. My body will draw energy from any available source to stay alive,' Brighton explained.

'So you won't die. That sounds good to me,' Brac replied.

'No, I will die. Eventually the energy around me will be used up and the poison will kill me. I don't think it will go that far though, my body will fail long before it reaches that point. If I try to fight the poison I will end up dying slowly and painfully,' Brighton said calmly.

Brac was starting to understand.

'Because of all the energy that will flow through you. So this leaves you with no options,' he surmised.

'There is one option. I will gather all my energy and send it into the ground. That way the poison will be out of me completely. My spirit will go to the afterlife. Hopefully I can maintain a link to my body for long enough to return to it,' Brighton answered.

Lilian shook her head and said, 'It won't work.'

'Why do you say that?' Brighton asked.

'Because you will be keeping your body alive from the spirit world. That means you are not really dead and the poison will not leave you,' she argued.

'Technically my body will be dead. My spirit will simply keep a link to it so that I can return,' Brighton explained.

Brac couldn't believe what he was hearing.

'This is a very dangerous theory. Isn't there something else to try first?' he said to Brighton.

'It's not a theory, I've done it before,' Brighton replied.

'How many times?' Brac asked.

'Once,' came the reply.

'And you feel confident that you could do this again?' Brac asked.

'No, but there is no other way,' Brighton replied.

Brac nodded with understanding.

'Fine, let's say this works, how does it help Miss Adri?' he asked.

'I will drain all her energy before I send mine into the ground. The poison will leave her too,' Brighton answered.

'And how does she come back to life? She is not talented like you,' Brac said.

'I will bring her back as soon as I have returned to my body,' Brighton explained.

Before Brac could ask the question on his lips, Brighton spoke again.

'I've also done that before, with him,' he said as he pointed to Mischief.

'And me,' Lilian said softly.

'Yes and you,' Brighton smiled at her.

'Then how come your talent stayed behind in Mischief and not in Lilian?' Brac asked.

'I channelled energy from Carmen to Lilian that time, I did not have any of my own to give her like I did with Mischief,' Brighton replied.

Brac shook his head in amazement.

'One day we're going to have a long talk about all of this but for now I think we should do what Brighton is suggesting,' he said.

Lilian knew it was the only chance Brighton and Adri had to survive but she didn't like it one bit.

'Lily, my love, this is the only way. Now go please and take Mischief along,' Brighton said softly.

Lilian took Clarissa from Brac and stared walking away with Brac following.

She stopped for a moment and without looking back she said, 'If you don't come back to me, I will go to the spirit world myself and fetch you.'

Brighton smiled and said, 'I love you too.'

He used his sense to track them.

When they were far enough away he said to Adri's still form, 'Let's do this.'

He took her hand and concentrated. Adri had very little energy left. As soon as Brighton started draining it from her, a sharp, shooting pain travelled through his entire body.

Brighton fought against the darkness that threatened to overcome him. When he felt no more energy coming from Adri he concentrated on his own.

With one last burst of willpower he sent everything he had left into the ground.

Chapter 26

———⚜———

BRAC AND LILIAN walked in silence for a long time. Brac knew she was getting tired but it didn't look like she was going to stop soon.

'Miss Lilian, would you mind if we stopped for a rest?' he said carefully.

Lilian nodded. She handed Clarissa to Brac and spread out a blanket on the ground for the babies. Brac put the twins on the blanket and sat down next to them.

'Sit down for a while,' he suggested.

Lilian wordlessly sat down.

'Do you think Brighton's plan will work?' he asked her.

'I don't know,' she whispered.

'When did he bring you back from the spirit world?' Brac pressed on.

'In the palace. Seth killed me,' she answered.

'Brighton is certainly a very special person,' Brac commented.

'Was,' Lilian said.

'What do you mean was?' Brac asked.

Lilian looked at him, her eyes filled with tears.

'Oh, I see,' Brac said softly.

He realized that Lilian must have been using her sense and knew that Brighton and Adri were dead.

*****

'Ah, this is a welcome surprise. Young Brighton has come to visit us my love,' Evangeline said to Robert.

Brighton got up from the ground.

'Hello Evangeline, Robert. I'm glad to see you two are back together. Now if you will excuse me I have to return to my body,' he said to the couple.

'Not so fast young man. Why do you assume I will let you go?' Evangeline said quickly.

'Let me go? I didn't think I needed your permission,' Brighton replied.

Evangeline smiled at him and said, 'I am in charge here. Nothing happens without my permission.'

Brighton didn't want an argument so he quickly said, 'With your approval I would like to return to my body now.'

'I'm afraid that's not going to happen. You've already returned to the living once, I cannot send you back again.'

Brighton clenched his jaw.

'Evangeline, I need to go back,' he said as calmly as possible.

'I'm sorry Brighton, I will not help you,' Evangeline replied.

'Evangeline, don't do this please. I helped you and Robert be together again. Does that not count for something?' he said trying to keep the panic out of his voice.

'We thank you for that but it does not get you any favours with me,' she answered calmly.

Brighton tried again, 'I have to get Lilian, Brac, Adri and the children to safety before...'

He suddenly stopped. Nobody knew what he was planning and perhaps it was better that way.

'Before what, Brighton?' Evangeline prodded.

'Uh...before Graham's army finds them,' Brighton finished.

'Brac and Lilian can make the journey without you, and Adri is with me already,' Evangeline argued.

She looked at the young man closely.

'You were going to say something else; I can see it on your face. Tell the truth!' she scolded.

Brighton thought for a moment. He suddenly didn't see the harm in telling Evangeline his plan.

What was she going to do about it anyway?

'As soon as I get the others to safety I will go back and remove Graham from his position,' Brighton answered honestly.

What he didn't tell her was that he planned on simply killing Graham and taking over as king.

He was tired of people abusing power, especially when he helped those people gain the position and power they held.

'Why?' Evangeline asked.

'To fix my mistake,' Brighton sighed.

'And what would that be?' Evangeline asked.

'I'm the one that defeated the Supremes and put the People's Council into place. They were greedy and power hungry and I could have stopped it, but I didn't. I gave them another chance and now Graham has made himself king. He has to be stopped and...' Brighton's voice trailed off.

'You think it is your duty,' Evangeline finished for him.

'Yes, I caused all of this and I have to fix it,' Brighton said.

'No, you don't. It's not your fault people are what they are,' Evangeline said gently.

When Brighton did not say anything she continued, 'Remember, nobody is born evil. If you try really hard you can see the good in anybody.'

Brighton looked into her eyes.

'Why are you telling me this? You said I can't go back again,' he said despondently.

Very softly Evangeline whispered to Robert, 'Wait for it. Just a few more moments.'

Brighton's eyes suddenly went wide.

'There it is,' Evangeline whispered to her husband.

'Wait, you didn't send me back last time, I went by myself,' Brighton told Evangeline.

She didn't argue the point, instead she said, 'Brighton, if you are not careful your power will destroy you.'

'It won't, I am in control,' Brighton replied.

Evangeline didn't answer. She just stood with a worried look on her face as Brighton's spirit started fading away.

'You were right, he is very clever,' Robert remarked.

Just as Brighton's spirit was almost gone, his voice reached the couple's ears.

'I'm taking Adri with me.'

Robert turned to his wife.

'It wasn't very nice deceiving him that way, you know,' he accused.

'I had to. If he knew he could return immediately I wouldn't have had a chance to talk to him,' she defended.

With a sigh she added, 'I just hope he understood what I was trying to say to him.'

'You did have a talk with Lilian when she was here, didn't you?' Robert asked.

'Yes, I did. Because Brighton loves her with all his

heart, he has no defence against her. If he loses his way she will have to kill him,' Evangeline answered.

*****

Lilian lost count of how many times she had used her sense while they travelled through the cave. She berated herself once again for not practicing more so that the range could increase. She didn't know if she couldn't sense the other two because they were still dead or simply because her sense didn't reach far enough.

'I want to rest a bit longer,' she said to Brac.

They had been resting far longer than Brac thought was necessary. He knew Lilian was hoping to sense Brighton and Adri coming towards them.

'I think we're close to the other side of the mountain. We should go look why you can't feel any life beyond that line you spoke about. When Brighton comes we will have some valuable information for him,' he suggested.

Earlier, Lilian had told him it felt like there was a line that separated life and death just up ahead. She could feel some plant life above and in front of her but after a certain point there was simply nothing.

'Fine, let's go,' Lilian sighed and got up.

They walked until they saw daylight ahead of them.

'It looks like we've made it through,' Brac commented.

Mischief leapt forward and raced for the light.

'I'm glad to see I'm not the only one who was getting tired of this dark cave,' Brac chuckled.

He was trying his best to get a conversation going with Lilian to get her mind off Brighton and Adri. Lilian didn't respond, she seemed to be in her own little world.

The two carried on walking until they stepped into

the late afternoon sun.

Brac closed his eyes and faced the sun.

'Ahhhh, that feels so good,' he sighed.

Mischief was rolling around on the ground making soft growling noises.

'Brac, look at that,' Lilian interrupted Brac's moment of ecstasy.

Less than a hundred paces beyond the cave entrance was a line of thorny bushes. It stretched north and south for as far as the eye could see and was at least twenty paces wide. The ground sloped downwards until it reached the line and then levelled out. Beyond the bushes was just open ground where nothing grew. Far in the distance, Lilian could make out what she thought to be some trees.

'So that's why it feels like there is a line that separates life and death,' she whispered.

'Because there is,' Brac commented dryly.

His eyesight was not nearly good enough to see the forest in the distance. Lilian didn't think her sense would reach all the way there but she tried using it anyway to find out how far the trees she saw on the horizon were.

'Brighton!' she screamed as her head snapped around.

'I assume your husband is coming,' Brac said calmly.

'Yes, he is alive!' Lilian shouted.

She gave Brac a tight hug with her free arm.

'And Miss Adri?' Brac asked carefully.

'Yes, she is coming too,' Lilian exclaimed excitedly.

Brac slowly let out a sigh of relief.

'That's good,' he said in a calm, controlled voice.

It was not how he felt. His insides were all knotted up since they left Brighton and Adri behind in the cave.

Excitedly Lilian said, 'Let get some food going. Those two will be hungry when they get here.'

She looked around for some firewood. There were no trees, just a few bushes and small plants.

Lilian quickly spread out a blanket on the ground and put Thomas down.

Brac put Clarissa down and said, 'I'll go look for some wood.'

'No,' Lilian said quickly. 'I will. It looks like I might find some dead wood in those thorn bushes down there.'

'But…' Brac started.

'Brac, please, it will give me something to do. Look after the kids, I will be back soon,' Lilian said with pleading eyes.

Brac smiled and nodded. He loved playing with the twins.

Lilian walked down to the line of bushes that seemed to separate life and death. She spotted a few dead ones slightly to the south.

'Not really good firewood but it will have to suffice,' she mumbled to herself.

As she stuck out her hand to break off some dead branches, Brac's voice reached her ears.

'Miss Lilian! Stop! Stop!'

She pulled her hand back and looked around.

Brac was running towards her screaming and waving his arms.

'Stop! Stop!' he kept shouting.

Lilian held her hands in the air so that Brac could see she wasn't doing anything.

He skidded to a halt right in front of her.

Grabbing her hands and looking intently at them, he asked breathlessly, 'Did you touch the thorns?'

'No, I didn't. I was about to break off some dead wood when you started throwing your little tantrum,' Lilian said irritably.

Brac turned her hands around a few times inspecting them carefully.

'Let's step away from these bushes a bit, shall we?' he suggested.

The two walked a few paces back towards the cave entrance.

'Why are you getting yourself in a twist about a few dead branches?' Lilian asked.

'It's not the branches I'm worried about, it's the thorns and what could be on them,' Brac answered.

Lilian put her hands on her hips and said, 'Brac, what could possibly…'

She stopped and looked at the thorn bushes.

'Oh, I see. It is darkweed,' she said in understanding.

'It could be. I've never seen it so it's difficult for me to make a positive identification. I think it would be clever to stay away from it just as a precaution,' Brac replied.

'Yes, you're right,' Lilian agreed.

They walked back to where the twins were playing on the blanket. Mischief was lying between them. Clarissa was trying her best to remove his ears from his head and Thomas was pulling on his tail. The big panther seemed not to notice, it looked like he was fast asleep.

When Thomas saw his mother coming, he started crawling towards her. Lilian scooped him up and tickled him a bit.

'Your father is almost here,' she said happily.

Thomas started whimpering.

As soon as Clarissa heard her brother, she joined in.

'You two are always hungry,' Lilian said to them.

Brac walked off and inspected the bushes around them. At the third bush he found what he was looking for. He picked a handful of berries and went to sit down on the blanket.

'Who wants berries?' he said to the twins.

*****

Brighton and Adri stepped out of the cave.

'I will never complain about the hot sun again,' Adri said.

Lilian flew into Brighton's arms. Neither of them said anything, there was no need.

Brac stepped closer to Adri.

'Miss Adri, so nice to see you healthy again,' he said awkwardly.

Adri flung her arms around his neck and planted a kiss right on his lips.

Brac didn't know what to do.

Adri stepped back, a little embarrassed.

'Sorry, I am just very glad to see you…uh…everybody again,' Adri apologized.

'It's quite all right, I'm happy to see you too,' Brac smiled at her.

Brighton and Lilian stepped closer. Brighton had both the children in his arms. He looked at the thorn bush line and the dead ground beyond it.

'Now I see,' he muttered to himself.

To the others he said, 'I wonder why there is such a wide piece of seemingly dead earth here. I can feel life beyond it. Thick woods, lots of animals and even a few people.'

'Brac says the thorn bushes down there are darkweed,' Lilian offered.

Brac quickly corrected Lilian's statement, 'I can't be sure of it, I just wanted to be careful.'

'That's a good decision,' Brighton agreed.

He handed the children to the women and said to Brac, 'Let's go have a look. We will need to find a way through.'

The men walked off towards the thorn bushes.

'So, what happened after we left you?' Brac asked.

'Nothing much, it all worked out exactly as I planned,' Brighton answered.

He was still mulling over Evangeline's words and wasn't quite ready to share it with anybody.

Why did she try to defend Graham? he thought.

Brighton could not imagine seeing any good in

Graham no matter how hard he tried.

When they reached the thorn bushes Brighton looked at Brac.

'How will we know if this is in fact darkweed?' he asked the hunter.

'Honestly, I don't know,' Brac answered.

Brighton thought for a moment and said, 'The only thing we know is that darkweed explodes when it's burned. That will be the way to test these bushes.'

Brac didn't like the idea at all.

'If it is darkweed and it does explode, don't we run the risk of someone getting infected again? A fragment could easily pierce the skin,' he argued.

Brighton shook his head and said, 'Everybody will hide in the cave while I send a small amount of energy into a bush to set it alight. We should be safe enough up there.'

Brac still didn't like the idea but he couldn't think of anything else.

'Let's go do it then,' he agreed.

*****

The group moved some distance back into the cave.

'This should do,' Brighton said.

He turned around and headed out again.

'Where are you going?' Lilian asked.

'I have to set fire to the bushes,' he answered as he turned back to face the others.

The men had already explained Brighton's plan to the women.

'Can't you do it from here? You can sense the bushes, just direct the energy towards them,' Lilian argued.

'And how will we know if they explode or not? Someone has to watch what happens otherwise the exercise is pointless,' Brighton countered.

Before anybody could say anything he quickly added,

'And I will be doing that alone.'

Brighton expected arguments but instead he was greeted only by silence.

He headed towards the cave entrance again. Standing just outside the opening he gathered some energy from the plants around him. A small ball of energy jumped from his hand and raced towards one of the smaller thorn bushes.

The bush caught fire immediately.

Brighton watched closely as it burnt. Small popping sounds started coming from the bush.

'Not exactly an explosion,' he muttered.

He turned around and called for the others. They joined him at the cave entrance just as the fire was dying down.

'There were no explosions but I did hear some popping sounds. It's not enough to say definitively that those bushes are in fact darkweed but I think we should stay clear of them just in case,' Brighton told them.

'We need to find a way around,' Brac mused.

'Yes, but that's going to be a slight problem. These bushes go in both directions as far as my sense can reach,' Brighton answered.

'So we can't go around them and we can't go through them. I don't see another option. We will have to turn back and face the soldiers,' Brac said worriedly.

'No, we will go through,' Brighton replied.

'How are we going to do that?' Lilian asked.

'I'll burn a pathway for us tomorrow,' Brighton answered.

They retreated to the cave to set up camp.

*****

The next morning when Lilian woke up, Brighton wasn't next to her. She looked around the cave but he was nowhere to be seen. Using her sense, she felt him and Brac about halfway down to the line of thorn bushes.

'Adri, are you awake?' Lilian called softly.

When the younger woman didn't reply, Lilian crawled over to her.

She gently shook Adri's shoulder and said again, 'Adri, are you awake?'

Sleepily Adri said, 'No.'

Lilian frowned and said, 'If you're not awake, how come you're talking to me?'

Adri opened her eyes.

'I was having such a nice dream until you interrupted it,' she complained.

'Really? And who was this dream about?' Lilian asked with a smile.

'I was in the most beautiful forest with….uh….who says the dream was about a specific person?' Adri asked indignantly.

'It's all over your face. Could it be a certain older gentleman?' Lilian prodded.

'Lilian! Brac is far too old for me!' Adri immediately started arguing.

'I never said his name, you did,' Lilian pointed out.

'It's obvious you were referring to him,' Adri defended.

'Why do you say he is too old for you?' Lilian asked.

'He must be twice my age, maybe more! I could be his daughter,' Adri replied sharply.

'What does that matter?' Lilian asked, still smiling.

'Well, I suppose…' Adri started.

She quickly looked around.

'Where are the men anyway?' she asked hoping to distract Lilian.

'Just outside the cave,' Lilian replied.

Adri was relieved that Lilian didn't continue the awkward conversation about Brac.

'You and I are still going to talk some more about a certain man and your feelings for him,' Lilian said as she got up.

Adri sighed. She didn't really think Lilian would just let it go.

They picked up a baby each and stepped out into the crisp morning air. It looked like Brighton and Brac were involved in a serious discussion.

'Morning,' Lilian called to them.

Brighton looked up, waved briefly, and continued talking to Brac.

'That looks serious,' Lilian muttered.

They walked down and joined the men.

'We should at least try to hide our trail,' Brac said heatedly to Brighton.

'And what would that help? The soldiers will find it no matter what we do. A burnt pathway through these bushes will be a dead give-away, whether I do it here or way over there,' Brighton argued.

'True, but doing it right here will make it too easy for them. We should pick a direction and travel at least a day before we attempt to get through the bushes. The soldiers won't know which way we went so they will have to split their forces in two to cover both directions. Besides, we might just come across something that we can't see now, something that will make it easier to get across,' Brac argued.

'And what about our trail? They could follow it to find out which way we went,' Brighton made his next point.

'I will hide our trail and lay a number of false ones. Not even their most experienced tracker will be able to say for sure which way we went,' Brac countered.

Brighton thought for a moment before saying, 'I still think it is a waste of time but I understand your point. Which way do you think is the best?'

'North,' Brac immediately answered.

'Any particular reason why?' Brighton enquired.

'It looks like there is more plant life that way. If we're lucky we might come across some water,' Brac explained.

'Good thinking Brac. Let's get going,' Brighton replied.

*****

They travelled until well past sunset. The line of thorn bushes remained unbroken. The next morning Brighton decided to keep going north until they could find a place where the thorn bushes were not so wide. They continued until midday.

'This looks like a good place,' Brighton said looking at the line of bushes.

It was about ten paces wide, easily the narrowest they had seen in the last two days.

Brighton led the group up the slope. He used his sense to find out whether the soldiers were catching up to them.

'It looks like Graham's men haven't found the cave entrance yet,' he said to the others.

'That's a stroke of luck,' Brac commented.

Brighton looked north.

'And we may have just had another. There seems to be a break in the thorn bushes further north,' Brighton replied.

This brought smiles to everyone's faces, they were all nervous about burning a pathway through.

'It's about a day and a half's travel,' Brighton said as they started walking again.

Chapter 27

HALFWAY THROUGH THE next afternoon they came across the break in the bushes Brighton had sensed.

Brighton slapped Brac on the back and said, 'Remind me never to argue with you again.'

The group was standing on the edge of a stream about fifteen paces wide. It came out of the mountain and lazily flowed straight through the line of thorn bushes.

Brighton didn't want to waste any time.

'Come on, we can rest later,' he said as he stepped into the waist deep water.

Nobody followed him. When he looked back, he saw why.

The women were sitting on the ground unpacking their rucksacks and Brac was picking berries from a nearby bush.

'We're not camping here, there is still a lot of daylight

left,' Brighton said to them.

'Better to camp here than in the middle of that dead ground,' Brac replied.

'We need to keep going, we might even make it to the forest by nightfall,' Brighton argued.

He knew there was no chance of that happening but felt they shouldn't waste good travelling time.

Brac pulled a face and said, 'So much for never arguing with me again.'

Lilian held out the plates to Brighton.

'Remember what Adri said when you wouldn't allow us to wash the dishes back in the cave?' she asked.

'No,' Brighton tried.

'Of course you do. Now wash these and don't forget the pots in your rucksack,' Lilian replied.

Brighton realized he had already been outvoted. They were not going to travel any further for the rest of the day.

He stepped back onto dry land, took a deep bow, and said, 'As you wish, my queen.'

Lilian smiled at him as he took the plates from her.

'Thank you, my love,' she said sweetly.

Adri quickly added some more instructions, 'When you're done, take Brac and look for some firewood. Don't rush back though, Lilian and I want to get the twins clean and then have a bath ourselves.'

Brighton got a naughty smile on his face.

He leaned over, gave Lilian a small kiss, and said, 'Perhaps I should stick around for that.'

Adri put her fists on her hips and quickly snapped, 'No you won't.'

Lilian also had a naughty smile on her face as she said to Brighton, 'I'll help you look for wood. Brac can help Adri bath the twins and maybe even wash her back for her.'

Adri's mouth was hanging open. She looked from face to face not knowing what to say.

Brac stepped closer and said seriously, 'Perhaps that is not such a good idea. Miss Adri would certainly like some privacy when she is bathing.'

'Oh, I don't know. I'm sure she wouldn't mind a certain someone washing her back and keeping her company,' Lilian teased some more.

'Lilian! Stop it!' Adri gasped.

Brighton laughed and said, 'I think I should get going on the dishes. This conversation is getting dangerous.'

Brac quickly went back to searching for more berries.

'Lilian, how could you?' Adri whispered.

'How could I what?' Lilian asked innocently.

'Suggest that Brac come bathe with me?' Adri replied.

'I didn't. I said he should wash your back and keep you company,' Lilian answered still trying to act innocent.

It was all she could do not to burst out laughing looking at Adri.

The younger woman had a look of complete and utter horror all over her face.

'Keep me company? I know what happens when Brighton "keeps you company",' Adri snapped.

For a moment Lilian was tempted to tease Adri some more but she decided against it.

Getting a serious look on her face she said to the younger woman, 'Adri, I'm not suggesting you give yourself to Brac but please keep an open mind. If you and Brac have romantic feelings for each other you owe it to yourself to explore that.'

*****

The next morning Brighton had everybody out of bed very early.

'I'll go first. Lily, you follow with Thomas. Adri, you bring Clarissa and Brac will carry the rucksacks,' Brighton told the others.

He handed out walking sticks he had carved the night before.

'Keep your balance with these. If you happen to slip, bend your knees immediately and try to fall backwards onto your bottom. You should rather fall into the water than try to regain your balance and risk stumbling into the thorn bushes,' he instructed.

He waded into the water holding a handful of long thin branches he had also cut the night before. Taking it one step at a time, he prodded the bottom of the stream with his walking stick. Every time he felt a deep hole, he stuck one of the branches into it and left it there. Brighton was hoping this would help avoid someone stepping into an unseen hole and twisting or breaking an ankle.

When he reached the other side of the thorn bushes he turned around and said, 'Lily, carefully enter the water. Stay in the middle of the stream and avoid the branches I've placed.'

Slowly Lilian stepped into the icy water. She also prodded the bottom of the stream with her walking stick before every step.

Brighton waited in the middle of the stream watching her closely. He was ready to throw up an energy barrier in case Lilian slipped and fell towards the thorn bushes.

Without any trouble Lilian and Thomas reached Brighton on the other side. Brighton helped her out of the stream.

'Adri, your turn,' Brighton called.

Adri mimicked what she saw Brighton and Lilian do. She and Clarissa reached the other side also without any trouble.

'Brac, call that lazy panther before you come through, please,' Brighton called to Brac.

Brac called Mischief but the cat refused to budge. He was sitting a good twenty paces from the river watching the people.

'Mischief, come here boy,' Brighton tried.

Still the big cat didn't move.

Brighton threw up his arms and said, 'Brac, you come through then I will go back to fetch him.'

Brac nodded and stepped into the water. He reached the others without mishap. As soon as he was out of the water Brighton went back for Mischief.

No matter how much Brighton asked, coaxed, threatened or begged, the big cat would not enter the water.

'I can't believe this! You will take on dozens of armed men but a little bit of cold water scares you!' Brighton said in exasperation.

He got out of the water and walked over to Mischief.

'You big baby,' he scolded the cat.

He put his hand on Mischief's big head and said, 'Come, I will go with you.'

Reluctantly the cat got up and walked to the water with Brighton. Slowly, as if it was the most painful thing on earth, Mischief entered the water.

'Good, now go to Lilian, I'll walk right here next to you,' Brighton instructed.

They reached the narrowest and deepest part of the stream. Mischief's claws could not find any grip on the slippery rocks below and he started skidding forward into the deeper water. In a panic, the big panther tried to climb onto Brighton's back.

Brighton lost his balance and fell towards the thorn bushes. Instinctively he threw up an energy wall between himself and the thorns.

'Bri!' Lilian shouted.

Brighton regained his balance and called back, 'I'm fine.'

He pushed Mischief into the deeper water forcing the cat to swim. They reached the others without further incident.

'What happened? Are you hurt?' Lilian asked in a slight panic.

'Mischief bumped me into the thorns but I put up an energy barrier to protect myself. See, I'm fine,' Brighton said holding out his arms for her to see.

Lilian looked at his arms.

When she couldn't find any cuts or scratches she breathed a sigh of relief.

'See, I told you. Now let's start walking so we can get to that forest, I'm uncomfortable in such a dead place,' Brighton said looking at the barren ground ahead of them.

The group set off towards the forest in the distance.

'Brighton, why didn't you simply put an energy barrier around us so we could walk through the thorns?' Brac asked.

'First, it would have left the same tell-tale trail as burning a pathway. Second, a barrier like that is difficult to maintain, it takes a lot of energy,' Brighton answered.

Brac nodded his understanding.

*****

High Commander Tristan followed four archers into the cave. He was in a terrible mood; it took his soldiers far too long to find the entrance.

'Are all your arrows coated in darkweed poison?' he asked the archers.

'Yes High Commander,' they answered as one.

'Good, shoot anything that moves,' he instructed.

Slowly they crept forward, the archers' bows ready and Tristan's sword drawn.

'It looks like they camped here,' one of the archers observed.

'How long ago?' Tristan asked.

'More than a day, maybe as much as three days ago,'

the man answered.

'Are the trackers sure they didn't come out of the cave again?' Tristan asked.

'Yes, High Commander, they are sure. Brighton's group must have gone deeper into the cave,' the archer answered.

Tristan didn't like this at all.

Although the cave was large inside, it still felt like the walls were closing in on him.

As the five men crept further into the cave Tristan started sweating more and more.

'Do you think this cave goes all the way through the mountain?' Tristan asked one of the archers.

'Yes High Commander, it does,' the man replied.

He started explaining about the flame movement on the torches but Tristan cut him short.

'So it's likely that Brighton and his witch have already gone through to the other side?' he asked.

'Yes, High Commander, I believe that is possible but...'

Again, Tristan cut him off.

'And we know there is only darkness on the other side of the boundary. This would mean they are already dead,' he said mostly to himself.

The four archers looked at Tristan, waiting for his orders.

'Keep going, perhaps they are just around the next corner,' he commanded.

The archers all turned their backs on him and slowly started creeping forward again. Tristan pulled a long knife from his belt with his left hand. Silently he stepped closer to the archers. With the sword he ran one man through from behind, the knife in his left hand plunging deep into another man's back.

Quickly Tristan yanked the sword free. Before the other two men could react the sword flashed through the air. The sharp blade sliced through one man's neck with ease. Wide eyed the last archer watched as the disembodied head tumbled towards the ground.

He lifted his bow but it was far too late. The point of Tristan's sword took him in the throat. Tristan twisted the sword hard to make sure the man had no chance of survival.

The man sank to his knees as Tristan pulled his sword free.

Quickly he checked the others. The man who took the knife in the back was still alive. With one quick slash his head was also separated from his body.

Tristan headed back towards the cave entrance. Just before he stepped out into the sunlight again, a thought entered into his head. He made a shallow cut on his right forearm.

Holding his bleeding arm close to his body, he walked out of the cave. As soon as his men saw him, they rushed to his side.

He refused any assistance. Instead, he held his bloody sword high and shouted, 'Brighton and his witch are dead!'

A cheer rose up from the men.

One of the squad leaders asked, 'What happened?'

'We found them hiding inside the cave. They killed the archers but didn't count on my skill with the sword. I killed them both. Brighton did manage to cut me but it is not serious,' Tristan shouted holding up his injured arm.

One of the other commanders turned to a soldier and said, 'Take word to King Graham: High Commander Tristan has found and killed Brighton and the witch.'

*****

Brighton stopped about a hundred paces from the edge of the forest.

'Someone is watching us,' he said to the others as he

slung his bow from his shoulder.

He sensed four people in front of them, at least twenty more some distance to the north-west, and a whole town full of people just beyond them. There was also another form of energy close by that felt like four large animals.

Brighton suddenly felt the temporary energy of an arrow speeding towards them. He didn't do anything; he knew the arrow was going to fall short. The others all got a fright when the arrow hit the ground a few paces in front of them.

'You could have warned us,' Lilian complained.

'I could have but then your reactions wouldn't have been genuine. Remember, we don't know how these people feel about the talent. It's best we hide it for now,' Brighton answered.

He had already spotted the man who shot at them, sitting high up in a tree.

Brac looked at the arrow and said, 'Not the friendliest greeting I've ever seen.'

Brighton stepped forward and plucked the arrow from the ground.

'Let's greet them back,' he said as he brought his bow up.

He nocked the arrow, took aim, and let it fly. It hit the tree trunk about an arm's length above the man's head. The man quickly pulled the arrow free and shot it right back at Brighton. This time the arrow hit the earth between Brighton's shoes. Brighton plucked the arrow from the ground again and sent it back the way it came.

'You missed!' the man howled when the arrow flew past him.

'Really?' Brighton shouted back.

The man looked around. His eyes went wide when he saw the arrow pinning a large snake to a branch behind him.

'Lucky shot,' the man shouted at Brighton.

'If you say so. Why don't you come down here so we can meet properly?' Brighton called back to him.

Quickly the man scrambled out of the tree. Four men emerged out of the woods. One was carrying a longbow and the other three had some very strange looking weapons in their hands. It looked like a bow turned horizontal with a handle at the back.

'Stay here,' Brighton said to the others as he started walking towards the four men.

Brac decided the instruction was meant for the women and followed Brighton. They stopped about ten paces from the four men. The strange bows were pointed straight at Brighton's chest.

'Good day strangers,' Brighton greeted with a big smile.

'That's quite an assumption. You have three loaded crossbows aimed at your chest. In my opinion it's not such a good day for you,' the leader of the four replied.

Brighton put his bow down on the ground, pulled his knife from his belt and put it next to the bow.

'We come in peace,' he said as he stepped back from his weapons.

Brac also pulled his knife out, put it next to Brighton's weapons, and stepped back. Brighton knew the hunter had a few more blades hidden in his clothes.

'That's not very clever. Now you are on the wrong side of my crossbow and you're unarmed,' the leader commented.

Brighton smiled and said, 'It seemed the right thing to do since you are also without weapons.'

The four men looked at each other in confusion.

'What do you think this is?' the leader asked waving his crossbow in the air.

Brighton took a closer look and said, 'Well, it's a "crossbow" as you've pointed out but it doesn't look very dangerous.'

The leader had a very confused look on his face.

He turned to one of the men and said, 'Patrick, shoot at that tree. Let's show this barbarian what formidable weapons these things are.'

The man called Patrick took aim at a nearby tree and pulled the trigger. Brighton was already concentrating on the bolt in the crossbow. As soon as it left the string he removed all the temporary energy from the projectile. The bolt barely flew two paces before falling to the ground.

Patrick's eyes went wide.

'How...what...' he said as he looked at his crossbow.

Brighton smiled and said to him, 'Yes, it does look like a formidable weapon, as long as the enemy is not more than two paces away.'

The leader of the group snapped at Patrick, 'Did you load it properly?'

Patrick quickly snapped back, 'Don't insult me Clark!'

He quickly picked up the bolt and reloaded the crossbow. Taking aim again, he pulled the trigger. The bolt dropped harmlessly to the ground again.

Patrick looked at the crossbow from all angles.

'It must be broken,' he stammered.

Clark took aim at the tree and squeezed the trigger on his crossbow. Again, the bolt simply dropped to the ground.

'It looks like yours is broken too,' Brighton commented.

Brac understood what was happening. He had to concentrate hard not to burst out laughing.

Clark and his men all took a few steps back.

'Don't move!' Clark said threateningly.

'Or what? You're going to use your crossbows on us?' Brighton mocked.

Clark tried to sound superior, 'There is still four of us and only two of you.'

Brighton stepped forward and retrieved their weapons. He handed Brac his knife back, slid his own into his belt and slung the bow over his shoulder.

'So what now? Are we just going to stand here and threaten each other all day?' he asked.

Clark didn't know what to do or say.

'Look, take your time to decide, I don't mind. If I could just ask one favour, please, could we get the women and children into the shade? It's terribly hot out there for them,' Brighton said to the man.

Clark looked past Brighton at Lilian, Adri and the twins.

'Um...yes, that would be in order,' he agreed.

Brighton turned around and called to the women, 'These men have kindly allowed us to move into the shade.'

Lilian and Adri walked closer. Mischief got up from where he was lying behind them and lazily wandered closer. Panic broke out between Clark's men when they saw the panther. All of them ran for the trees.

'Relax, he won't hurt you,' Brighton called after them but they kept running.

Brac rolled his eyes and said to Brighton, 'Great, now they are probably going to fetch more men. You shouldn't have made fun of their weapons.'

'Perhaps not, but the looks on their faces were rather amusing,' Brighton said with a smile.

Brac also smiled.

'Yes, it was. What is the plan now?' he asked.

Brighton shrugged his shoulders.

'To be honest I haven't really thought past crossing the boundary. I suppose we should find a place to build a house again,' he said.

The women reached them.

'What was that all about?' Lilian asked.

'They panicked when they saw Mischief,' Brighton answered.

He used his sense to find out if the men were still running. A very surprised look crossed his face.

'Amazing,' he breathed.

'What?' Lilian asked.

'Use your sense,' Brighton told her.

She did as Brighton told her and also got a surprised look on her face.

'Yes, that is amazing,' she agreed.

Brac threw his arms in the air.

'Wait, let me use my sense quickly. Mmm, yes, that is amazing,' he said sarcastically.

'Sorry,' Brighton laughed. 'Not too far from here I sensed four large animals. It seems the men have now climbed on top of these animals and are riding them,' he explained.

'Riding on top of animals?' Brac asked suspiciously.

'Yes, it seems that way,' Brighton answered.

Brac looked at Brighton closely to see if he was joking.

When it looked like he was serious Brac said, 'Well, that's something I would like to see.'

*****

Brac got his wish sooner than he thought. They were camped in the forest a short walk from where they met Clark and his men.

'We're getting some company,' Brighton announced.

He sensed roughly twenty men all on top of those large animals coming towards them.

'Mischief, go hide,' Brighton told the big cat.

The panther quickly disappeared into the forest.

Brighton continued using his sense.

'They are surrounding us,' he told the others.

He didn't really want to get involved in a fight but got ready none the less.

An elderly man rode into the camp. He dismounted and walked closer leading the animal by two leather straps.

'Good day to you,' he greeted everyone as he came to

a halt a few paces away.

'Good day,' Brighton greeted back.

The man smiled and said, 'First, let me warn you that there are a number of crossbows aimed at you right now, so please don't make any sudden moves.'

Brighton smiled back and said, 'You seem to be a suspicious lot. Have no fear, we come in peace.'

The man laughed a little and said, 'I am not afraid but you should be.'

Remembering his first meeting with Brighton, Brac mumbled, 'He obviously doesn't know you.'

The old man stepped a little closer and held out his hand, 'I'm Joel Finderson.'

Although Brighton didn't like this form of greeting, he took Joel's outstretched hand anyway. He already knew that Joel was not talented.

He shook the man's hand and said, 'Brighton. This is Brac, Lilian and Adri. On the blanket are our twins, Thomas and Clarissa.'

Brac couldn't contain his curiosity.

'Why do you have two names?' he asked Joel Finderson.

'I don't. My name is Joel and my surname is Finderson,' came the confused reply.

'Surname? What's that?' Brac blurted out.

Joel's mouth hung open.

'Clark was right, you are barbarians from across the boundary,' he gasped.

Brighton was getting irritated with being called a barbarian.

'It would seem that you are the barbarians. We come here in peace and thus far we've only been treated with hostility. Tell your men to lower those crossbows immediately. If they accidently shoot someone in this group I will personally make every last one of you sorry,' he growled at Joel.

Joel was taken aback slightly by Brighton's

aggression.

He waved his left hand in the air.

'There, the crossbows are lowered. Not that I think you could make good on that promise but you do have a point about our hostility,' he said.

Brac just shook his head and smiled.

'If only they knew,' he whispered to Adri.

To Joel he said, 'You still haven't told me what this surname thing is.'

'It's my family name. Every family has one,' Joel answered.

'Why?' Brac asked.

'It's to signify which family you belong to and helps identify a person. There are a few men named Joel in our community but only one Joel Finderson,' he explained.

'I see,' Brac said.

While they were talking Brighton had been looking at the animal Joel had with him.

'What kind of beast is this?' he asked Joel.

'It's a horse. Now I know you are barb…uh…from the other side,' Joel answered.

Brighton got up and walked closer. He noticed the animal was nervous, probably because it could smell Mischief.

'Do you mind?' he asked Joel as he stuck his hand out towards the horse.

'I don't but he might. This one has a nasty streak in him. He bites,' Joel answered.

Brighton put his hand on the side of the horse's head and let a tiny bit of energy flow into the animal. The horse immediately calmed down.

'You're magnificent,' Brighton whispered to the horse.

He turned to Brac.

'Do you still have some of those berries the twins like so much?' he asked.

Brac produced some berries from his pocket and

handed them over. Brighton offered the berries to the horse. Eagerly the animal gobbled up the sweet treats.

'You certainly are a natural with horses,' Joel remarked.

His face got serious.

'Tell me, why are you here?' he asked.

'We are looking for a place to build a house and live in peace,' Brighton answered.

'And what is your arrangement?' he continued.

'Arrangement? What do you mean?' Brighton asked.

'Are you all brothers and sisters? Are you married?' Joel explained.

Without thinking Brighton answered, 'Lilian and I are married and Adri is our little sister. Brac is a very good friend travelling with us.'

'Why did you cross the boundary?' Joel asked next.

Brighton had to think quickly. He decided to keep some of the truth in the story.

'We don't agree with some of the King's new laws and decided it was time to seek out a new place to live,' Brighton answered.

Joel seemed to accept the answer without thinking too much about it. He looked over his shoulder and whistled. A few moments later Clark came running into the campsite. Joel quickly and quietly spoke to the younger man.

'But they are barbarians and they had a black panther with them! I think the big one is a wizard. Our crossbows won't fire when he is around,' Clark argued heatedly.

'Clark, mind your manners!' Joel snapped at the younger man.

'But father...' Clark tried again.

Joel held up his hand for silence.

He turned to Brighton and asked, 'Are you a wizard, young man?'

Brighton laughed and said, 'Everybody knows

wizards don't exist. No, I am not a wizard.'

Turning back to Clark, Joel said, 'Satisfied? Now do as I told you!'

'Yes father,' Clark sighed.

He quickly walked back into the forest.

'Please forgive Clark, he is highly superstitious. He gets it from his mother. I've told Clark you are no danger to us and he must send the men back to their patrols,' Joel explained.

Brighton briefly used his sense. Joel was telling the truth, the men around them started moving away.

'With your permission I would like to stay a while and talk. As far as I know nobody has ever crossed the boundary,' Joel said to Brighton.

'You're welcome to stay. I have some questions for you too,' Brighton said.

Joel quickly fired off the first question, 'According to legend the other side of the boundary is inhabited by demons with black blood in their veins. Is this true?'

Brighton pulled his knife and made a small cut in his finger.

He showed Joel the blood and said, 'No, we are not demons and our blood is not black.'

Joel asked a few more questions to which Brighton gave careful answers.

Eventually Brighton started asking some questions. The others chipped in with some questions of their own from time to time. The group gathered some valuable information about how things worked on this side of the boundary.

The land was divided into three kingdoms: The Mountain Kingdom where they currently were, The Northern Tribes and the kingdom of Erostan, which was the biggest. The Northern Tribes and Erostan were currently in a war.

When Brighton asked why, Joel shrugged his shoulders and replied, 'I think it's because they have nothing better to do.'

East of the boundary, where Brighton's group came from, was called the Dark Land. Since the Mountain Kingdom protects the rest of the world from the Dark Land, the other two kingdoms agreed that nobody may invade this land. This pact is still being honoured centuries after it was made.

A wide river far to the west separated The Mountain Kingdom from Erostan and a low mountain range was the border with The Northern Tribes. There was no definitive border between Erostan and The Northern Tribes. Joel thought this was possibly the reason for all the wars between the two kingdoms.

Joel also explained the use of money, books, reading and writing, how horses are tamed, wagons, horse carts, crossbows and many more things.

Brighton started understanding more and more what the Supremes had done.

Joel eventually asked, 'How come there was no development where you're from? It seems like time was standing still!'

Carefully Brighton answered, 'The previous kings and queens deliberately did that. They were convinced that any form of development or advancement would threaten their rule.'

'Which previous king?' Adri asked with a frown.

'King Seth, Queen Amber and their predecessors,' Brighton quickly replied.

'Oh, them!' Adri said.

Brac and Lilian also understood what Brighton meant. The legend of demons with black blood obviously referred to the Supremes and the Dark Ones. It was important not to give Joel any reason to start believing in the legend.

Joel looked ready to leave.

He got up and said, 'Before I go, just one last question: If you came over the boundary, how come you are so far south?'

Brighton was not certain he understood correctly.

'Don't you mean so far north?' he asked.

'No, I meant south. The pass is a good five or six days by horse north of here,' Joel replied.

Brighton's eyes went wide.

'There is a pass to the north? We didn't come that way. We came through a cave about two days south of here,' he explained.

This time it was Joel's eyes that went wide.

'The cave of the demons? This just gets more and more amazing! I have to go now but I would really like to hear that story. I just assumed you came through the pass and slipped past the garrison somehow,' he said shaking his head.

'Garrison? What is that?' Brighton asked.

'At the pass there is a fort where two hundred men are stationed permanently. It is their job to make sure none of the demons from the other side get through,' Joel explained.

Before anybody could ask another question Joel quickly said, 'I really have to go. If I get home late for supper one more time I will be in some serious trouble!'

He bid everybody a good night, mounted his horse, and rode off.

'Well, that was interesting,' Brac said.

Brighton had a big smile on his face.

'Remember I asked you about the roads quite a while ago? Now we know why those roads are there. There used to be horse carts and wagons. I think the Supremes deliberately destroyed anything that could promote development so that they could stay in power forever,' he said to the others.

Brac wasn't convinced.

'There are no horses were we came from. What did the people use to pull these wagons you think existed?' he argued.

'The Supremes killed all the horses. Think about it: If people realized that a horse could be tamed and ridden, it would not take long for them to also think of building wagons. No horses meant no wagons and that halted progress,' Brighton explained his theory.

Brac conceded the point but Lilian still had one more question.

'What would be the purpose of halting progress?' she asked.

'Like I said, to rule forever. If the population were allowed to develop, it stands to reason that eventually better weapons would be invented like those crossbows. I think those things could do some serious damage to a person. Better weapons, like the crossbows, would have meant the people could stand up against the Supremes,' Brighton answered.

'Just look at what has happened recently,' he continued. 'Graham has created an army and already they have better weapons than the simple knives we're used to. The soldiers I killed all had swords.'

Slowly Lilian nodded her head. Adri didn't take part in the conversation. As usual, she was more concerned with making sure everybody got a good meal.

'Our food supply is running very low. Brighton, please go see if you can get a small deer or some rabbits. Brac, go with him and find us some beans or any other type of vegetable,' she asked the men.

Brighton immediately rose and picked up his bow. He gave Lilian a quick kiss and set off towards a deer he sensed not too far away. Brac followed him but not before he had a look back and caught Adri staring at him. He flashed a quick smile and disappeared into the woods.

'And some berries for the twins,' Lilian called after him.

When Adri was certain the men were out of earshot, she carefully asked Lilian, 'What does it feel like when you're in love?'

For a moment Lilian was tempted to tease Adri again but she quickly decided to give the younger woman a straight and honest answer.

'Every time you see the other person it feels like there are a thousand butterflies in your stomach. Every moment you spend together is a moment you remember and treasure forever. The simplest touch is pure ecstasy. When you kiss it feels like the whole world is standing still,' Lilian answered from her heart.

'Is it still like that for you and Brighton?' Adri asked wide-eyed.

'After a while the butterflies don't come anymore and you get used to each other's touch. It does not mean we're not in love anymore, it just means that it has been replaced with something much deeper and more meaningful. My heart does not belong to me anymore, it belongs to Brighton. I did not ask for anything in return, I gave it freely. Brighton did the same, he gave his heart and his love to me without expecting anything in return,' Lilian answered.

'And what does it feel like when you...uh...you know...' Adri asked uncomfortably.

'Make love?' Lilian asked.

Adri nodded.

'That is something you have to experience for yourself. The only advice I can give you is to wait for the man you really and truly love before you consider it. If you're lucky and you get a gentle, caring lover like Brighton it will be the most wonderful thing in the world,' Lilian answered.

Adri smiled and gave Lilian a big hug.

'Thank you. You are the best big sister anyone could ever hope for,' she whispered in Lilian's ear.

Lilian got a sly smile on her face.

'So, little sister, is there some reason you asked these questions?' she asked innocently.

Adri's face went a little red.

'Uh...no...not really,' she stammered.

'Looks to me like there is a reason and he is searching for vegetables at the moment,' Lilian teased.

Adri got a pensive look on her young face.

'Well, maybe. In the cave when Brighton brought me back from the spirit world all I could think of was to see Brac's face again. Does that mean I'm in love with him?' Adri replied.

'Only you can answer that,' Lilian told the younger woman.

Chapter 28

JOEL RETURNED EARLY the next morning. After a quick greeting, he sat down and with a serious look on his face started talking to the group.

'You will have to be very careful. Rumours have started in town about four demons that crossed the boundary. I am ashamed to admit that my own son is the one spreading these ridiculous stories,' he said gravely.

Brighton thought for a moment and said, 'We don't want to make any trouble. Perhaps it's best we move on as quickly as possible.'

Joel shook his head.

'You are going to run into this kind of trouble no matter where you go. I have a better idea: Less than half a day's travel west of the garrison that guards the pass to the Dark Land is a town called Fenton. My sister and her husband live there. I will take you to them and explain the situation. They will help you become part of the community,' Joel suggested.

Brighton thought about it for a moment before he said, 'That sounds like a good plan but why would you do this for us?'

'You look like good people. There is no reason you should be shunned because of silly superstitions. Besides, it is our belief that all good deeds get rewarded in the afterlife,' Joel answered.

'Thank you Joel, you're a good man,' Brighton replied.

'There are a few things you will need. First, here is some money,' Joel said as he pulled five gold coins from his pocket and held it out to Brighton.

'Joel, I couldn't possibly take your money,' Brighton objected.

'Take it, you will need it,' Joel said as he placed the coins in Brighton's hand.

'Thank you. Someday I will repay this,' Brighton said gratefully.

Joel waved it off.

'Now remember, ten silver coins make one gold coin. Twenty five bronze coins are equal to one silver coin,' he reminded them.

Brighton nodded as he put the money in his pocket.

'Next, you will need a surname. Brighton, since you and Lilian are married and Adri is your sister, you will all have the same family name. Brac will have to choose something else,' Joel advised them.

Brighton had no idea what a good surname would be.

Joel saw the uncertainty on his face and quickly said, 'I'm assuming the towns in the Dark Land have names. Where do you come from?'

'A place called Four Mountains. No wait, the real name is Clareton,' Brighton answered.

'That's a good surname. Brighton, Lilian and Adri Clareton,' Joel declared.

'And don't forget Thomas and Clarissa Clareton,'

Lilian added.

Brac smiled and said, 'I guess that makes me Brac Brasten.'

'Brac Brasten. That's funny!' Adri giggled.

Joel got up and said, 'You should get going as soon as possible. The road to Fenton is a short walk to the west.'

Brighton didn't like the idea of travelling on a road; he preferred to stay hidden in the woods.

'We'll travel through the forest,' he told Joel.

Joel shook his head and said, 'It will arouse suspicion. Everybody uses the roads, you should too.'

Brighton saw the logic in what Joel was saying so he didn't argue any further.

Joel climbed on his horse and said, 'I'll catch up with you later.'

'Well, let's pack up and go,' Brighton sighed.

*****

They were only travelling for a short while when Joel joined them again. He was driving a wagon pulled by a big, strong looking horse. His own horse was following behind; its reins tied to the wagon's railing.

'A good friend of mine agreed to lend us his wagon for the trip to Fenton,' he said cheerfully as he stopped next to the group.

'That's kind of him. I'm getting tired of all this walking,' Lilian replied as she climbed on.

Brighton handed Thomas to her then held Clarissa so Adri could climb on. As soon as the women and children were settled, they continued the journey. Brac and Brighton walked next to the wagon while Joel drove.

'Brighton, you and Brac should join me up here. I'll teach you how to use the reins,' Joel invited them.

Brac immediately shoved Brighton towards the

wagon and said, 'You go first.'

'Why? Are you scared?' Adri teased him.

'I prefer the term "careful",' Brac played along.

Brighton hopped onto the front seat of the wagon.

Joel handed him the reins and said, 'Treat the horse like you treat a woman. If you're harsh and demanding you will only make trouble for yourself. Be gentle and they will do almost anything for you.'

Brighton laughed and looked back at Lilian.

'Is that true my love?' he asked her.

She fluttered her eyelids, pouted her lips, and said, 'I'll do anything for you my love.'

Mimicking Lilian, Adri also fluttered her eyelids and said, 'Oh Bri, I'll do anything for you.'

This brought a roar of laughter from Brac.

Adri turned to him, fluttered her eyelids some more and said, 'You too Brac Brasten. Your wish is my command!'

Brac doubled over with laughter.

'I might just hold you to that Adri,' he stammered between laughing fits.

Adri looked at Brac closely and said, 'That's the first time you didn't call me "Miss Adri".'

Brac stopped laughing and quickly said, 'I'm sorry Miss Adri. I didn't mean any disrespect.'

She smiled at him and said, 'Please don't apologize, I like it when you call me Adri.'

Brac gave her a smile and echoed her earlier words, 'Your wish is my command, Adri.'

*****

For the next three days, the group travelled without any trouble. Both Brighton and Brac quickly learnt how to drive a wagon and even took turns riding Joel's horse. Brac looked uncomfortable on the animal but Brighton was a natural. Joel didn't even have to give him instructions; he simply climbed on and instinctively knew what to do.

Lilian also learnt how to ride a horse but Adri decided it was far safer on the back of the wagon.

'You're a big baby,' Brac laughed at her.

'That may be, but when you fall off that animal and break your neck don't come crying to me,' Adri retorted.

Brighton and Lilian were walking behind the wagon.

Quietly, so that Joel couldn't hear, Lilian asked, 'Can you sense Mischief?'

'No, the last time I felt his presence was two days ago. Just before he went missing, I did sense another animal close to him. I can't be sure but it felt a lot like a female panther,' Brighton replied.

With a wide smile Lilian said, 'Mischief found a girlfriend. That's good; he is a wild animal after all and needs to be with his own kind.'

'I know, but I will miss him. He must have decided we're safe now and it's time to get on with his own life,' Brighton sighed.

Lilian picked up her pace and hopped onto the wagon to check on the twins. Adri and Brac were feeding them berries again.

'Did they eat their vegetables?' Lilian enquired.

'Uh...yes,' Brac answered avoiding eye contact.

Lilian looked at Adri but the younger woman also refused to look her in the eye.

'You two are a bad influence on my children!' Lilian complained.

'Yes mother,' Brac and Adri replied together, looked at each other, and burst out laughing.

'Maybe I should go relieve Joel,' Brac said when he caught his breath.

He climbed to the front of the wagon.

Holding out his hand he said softly to Joel, 'Feed the twins this, they will love you forever!'

Joel looked down at the red berries in Brac's hand. He handed Brac the reins, took the sweet treats, and climbed to the back.

Brighton untied Joel's horse from the back of the wagon. Before he hopped on, he checked the hooves and reins like Joel had taught him. Quickly he caught up to the wagon.

Brac gestured for him to come closer. When Brighton was next to him, he checked to see if Joel was paying attention. Seeing that the old man was far too busy buying the twins' love with berries he pointed down the road.

Brighton nodded and held up eight fingers. He gestured towards Joel.

Brac caught his meaning and said, 'Joel, there seems to be people in the road up ahead.'

Joel quickly jumped up and peered down the road.

'Stop,' he said softly.

When Brac didn't bring the wagon to a halt immediately Joel repeated the instruction more urgently. Brac finally got the horse to respond and the wagon stopped.

'Joel, do you know these people?' Brighton asked calmly.

He could see the fear on the old man's face.

'Yes, everybody knows them,' Joel whispered.

'Who are they?' Brighton prodded.

'A gang of robbers,' Joel replied.

'Are you sure? They could simply be some travellers,' Brighton tried.

Joel shook his head.

'No, look how they have deliberately blocked the road. Their intention is to stop anyone that comes past and rob them,' Joel explained.

'Should we turn around?' Brac asked.

Brighton already knew it wasn't an option but he kept quiet.

It was Joel that answered, 'They probably have four or five men behind us cutting off the escape route.'

Brighton knew it was four, he sensed them long ago.

'Stay here, I'll go have a look,' he said to the others.

Joel started protesting but Brighton had already swung the horse around and went back the way they came. As he rode past the wagon, he leaned over and grabbed one of the walking sticks. He kept using his sense, partly to find the four men behind them and partly to make sure the others were not closing in.

A short while later he returned.

'There were four men behind us,' he announced.

Brac just smiled, he knew the four men wouldn't be bothering them any time soon.

'Did you…' Lilian started but Brighton cut her off.

'Their heads are going to hurt for a long time,' he said wagging the walking stick in the air.

'Now let me go and have a talk with those gentlemen,' he said pointing to the men in front of them.

'You're built like an oak tree but going up against eight armed men is just stupid,' Joel protested.

'I'll be fine,' Brighton answered as he rode off.

He stopped about twenty paces before he reached the men and dismounted. He tied the horse to a tree and casually strolled forward.

'Good day gentlemen,' he greeted with a smile.

The leader of the gang looked puzzled.

'The line between bravery and stupidity is a thin one. It seems you just crossed it,' he growled at Brighton.

Brighton ignored the comment and said, 'My friend seems to think you are here to do us harm. I cannot believe this so I decided to come ask.'

Still the leader looked a bit confused.

'I'll tell you what, leave your money, the horses and those two women with us and we might let you live,' he replied.

Brighton fished a gold coin out of his pocket and

flicked it at the man.

'That is all the money I have, we still need the horses and if you touch the women it will be the last thing you ever touch,' he said softly.

'You're definitely stupid! Can't you see you're outnumbered?' the leader spat at Brighton.

Still smiling Brighton said, 'We have a long journey ahead of us. Let us pass and I won't hurt you.'

The men all burst out laughing.

'Hurt us?' howled the leader. 'You've lost your marbles!'

Brighton shrugged and said, 'Last chance.'

The leader lifted a long curved sword and pointed it at Brighton.

'Just because you're so arrogant I will make you watch as I take those two women,' he snarled.

The walking stick flashed through the air. In a single motion Brighton knocked the sword sideways and landed a crushing blow on the man's temple. He dropped the sword and staggered back holding his head.

Brighton moved forward. He danced through the men like a shadow. Every time someone thrust a sword in his direction it was just a little too late. He avoided the sharp edges with ease while his walking stick found its mark with every swing. Men went down howling in pain, some holding their heads and others clutching at their knees and elbows. In mere moments Brighton was the only man standing. He pushed the end of the walking stick down on the leader's throat.

'Give me a reason not to kill you,' he growled at the man.

'Please, I beg you,' the man sobbed.

Brighton pressed down on the stick until the man was struggling to breathe.

'If I ever see you again, I will kill you,' he said softly.

Without waiting for an answer he turned around and

walked back to the horse. He sensed one of the men get up and charge forward. An arrow sped past his head. The assailant instantly dropped to his knees clutching at the arrow in his throat.

It was Adri who shot with such deadly accuracy. Brighton untied the horse and walked back to the wagon. Brac was sitting on the front casually scratching under a fingernail for some imaginary dirt with a knife. Brighton gave Adri a little wink and a smile as thanks for her assistance. She smiled back at him and put the bow down.

'Shall we go?' Brighton suggested.

Joel looked from face to face. Nobody looked the least bit worried or flustered.

As Brac got the wagon going again Brighton asked, 'Joel, what are marbles? That fellow seems to think I've lost mine but I'm sure I've never even had any.'

*****

The group reached Joel's sister's house without any further trouble. An elderly couple was sitting on the porch.

'Nicky, Peter, how good to see you again!' Joel called from the wagon.

He jumped off and rushed into his sister's arms.

'It's good to see you too, big brother,' Nicky said as she hugged him as tight as she could.

Brighton was slightly surprised that Joel was older than Nicky; she looked much more frail than he did.

Joel looked Peter square in the eyes.

'So, Peter, have you made my little sister pregnant?' he asked with a serious face.

Without batting an eyelid Peter answered, 'I'm still trying but you keep barging in here!'

The two burst out laughing and gave each other slaps on the back.

Joel remembered why he was there.

'Nicky, Peter, I want you to meet some friends of mine.'

He introduced Brighton, Lilian, Brac and Adri to the older people. Nicky and Peter were both immediately besotted with the twins. Without asking they each took a baby and started making funny noises and faces at them.

'What are their names?' Peter asked.

'Clarissa and Thomas,' Lilian replied with a smile.

'Beautiful names for beautiful children,' Nicky replied.

Brighton tugged on Joel's shirt and softly asked, 'Joel, what was that about Peter making Nicky pregnant? Aren't they a bit old for that?'

Joel laughed and said, 'Peter, tell Brighton about the first time we met.'

Peter sat down and gestured for the others to do the same.

As soon as everybody was seated he said, 'When Nicky was eighteen and I was thirty three we fell in love. One day, when we thought we were alone in Nicky's parent's house, things got very passionate. We were in Nicky's bedroom, naked as the day we were born when Joel walked in on us. He was furious! The first thing he screamed at me was "Have you made my little sister pregnant?". A few months later it transpired that Nicky was in fact pregnant. Her parents didn't want anything to do with us; they said we had brought a terrible shame over their family. Joel had seen how much we loved each other and he organized for us to get married and come live in Fenton. Ever since then he always asks me the same thing when we see each other: "Have you made my little sister pregnant?"'

Brighton had trouble believing that Peter was fifteen winters older than Nicky; they looked roughly the same age to him.

Lilian leaned over to Nicky, and asked, 'How many children do you have?'

The old woman's smile disappeared as she said, 'We had one but he died at a very young age.'

'I'm sorry,' Lilian replied.

'Don't be, it was long ago. Just promise me you will look after these two little angels well,' Nicky replied.

Lilian nodded and smiled at the older woman.

With a serious look on his face Joel said to Peter and Nicky, 'I've come to ask you a big favour. Brighton and his group are from the other side of the boundary and they want to make a new life for themselves here.'

Peter quickly waved his hand in the air and said, 'Say no more Joel, they are welcome in our house.'

Brighton was taken aback by how quickly Peter made up his mind.

'Aren't you going to ask if we're demons?' he said to Peter.

'No need. If Joel calls you a friend, then I call you a friend,' Peter replied.

'That's very kind of you,' Brighton replied.

Nicky got up and told Lilian and Adri to follow her.

She went inside and showed Lilian a room.

'You, Brighton and your gorgeous children may have this room,' the old woman said.

She showed Adri another room and said, 'You and Brac can share this one.'

Adri started saying that it won't be appropriate but Nicky cut her short.

'I was a young woman once, I understand the desires of the heart,' she said with a wink.

'But Brac and I are not a couple,' Adri protested.

'He certainly wished you were,' Nicky observed.

'Well…I…uh…he is too old for me,' Adri stammered.

'Peter is fifteen winters older than I am and we still love each other very much after almost fifty winters of marriage,' Nicky countered.

Poking a finger at Adri she added, 'You're wishing right now that you and Brac were a couple, I can see it in your eyes. Stop denying what both of you so obviously want!'

Lilian didn't try to hide her giggle.

Adri looked at her with pleading eyes but she quickly said, 'You won't get any help from me, I agree with Nicky.'

Adri poked her head through the door.

'But there is only one bed,' she argued.

'Yes I know,' Nicky said as she walked away.

*****

Lilian fell asleep in Brighton's arms with a smile on her face. For the first time since Seth took her away from Four Mountains all those winters ago, she felt like her life made sense again.

Slowly she opened her eyes.

'Don't be alarmed Lilian,' a gentle voice said to her.

Lilian looked around. She was sitting on a fallen tree in a clearing much like the one she and Brighton used to play in when they were kids. Evangeline was standing close by.

Quickly Lilian got up. Panic shot through her mind.

'Where am I? Am I dead?' she whispered.

'No, you're not dead but I needed to talk to you,' Evangeline answered.

Lilian thought for a moment.

'Am I dreaming?' she asked.

'Something like that. I don't have a lot of time. It is very difficult to maintain a link to your mind from the spirit world so listen carefully: When you died we had a brief conversation before Brighton pulled you back to the land of the living. Do you remember?' she started.

'Yes, I do,' Lilian replied.

'Good, so you know that I'm worried about Brighton.

He has become very powerful and it's threatening to destroy him. You have to be the voice of reason when that happens,' Evangeline said.

'I don't understand. Is his talent going to kill him?' Lilian frowned.

'That's possible but I don't think so. He knows the limit of energy his body can handle. I am far more worried that the power will destroy the good person that he is,' Evangeline answered.

Lilian shook her head in confusion.

'What do you mean?' she asked.

'My children were sweet, innocent and caring when they grew up. Robert and I taught them to respect life and be kind to others. When Seth realized what the talent could do for him, he became evil almost overnight. He convinced his siblings that they were better than everybody else and that they could rule forever if they wanted to. Having that much power corrupted the good that was in them. I didn't see it until it was too late. Seth killed me, imprisoned his father and they ruled through fear and intimidation. It took someone far more powerful than them to end this rule of terror. Brighton will go the same way as my children if something is not done.'

Lilian looked at Evangeline with disbelief in her eyes.

'Bri would never become evil. He is the kindest, most loving person I know,' she argued.

Patiently Evangeline continued, 'He has already forced his will down on the people simply because nobody could stop him. Look what happened in Zedonia with Graham and the High Council. Brighton didn't like the way they were doing things and he forced them to change it.'

'What they were doing was wrong. Brighton simply tried to rectify that,' Lilian countered.

'Who put him in charge? Why does he decide what is right and what is wrong? Yes, the High Council, and particularly Graham, turned out to be less than perfect but that was not for Brighton to fix. If the population didn't like their leaders they should have been the ones to do something about it. Graham and the High Council were normal people; they did not have any special talent or power to force their will down on others. Brighton does and he is becoming used to the fact that nobody can deny him. Do you think Graham wanted to change his ways? No, but through a brutal show of power Brighton forced him. Do you think the population all agreed with the idea of a People's Council? No, some didn't but who was going to stand up to Brighton after he showed everybody how powerful he is,' Evangeline explained.

Lilian simply didn't believe that Brighton would ever become evil. Evangeline didn't give her a chance to argue.

'You are the only one that can stop Brighton. He has given himself to you unconditionally. He has no defence against you. Drain his energy and drive a knife through his heart, it is the only way to make sure he stays dead.'

'What? No! I will never kill my husband. Besides, I have also given myself to him unconditionally so I have no defence against him either,' Lilian screamed.

'That's why you have to be quick about it. Don't hesitate, drain his energy and put a knife in his heart,' Evangeline repeated.

'No!' Lilian screamed again.

She woke up to the sound of her own screams.

Quickly she sat up. A look out the window told her it was morning already. Brighton was nowhere to be seen. She used her sense but couldn't feel his energy anywhere.

Adri stormed into the room.

'Lilian, what's wrong?' she asked breathlessly.

Lilian didn't answer. She concentrated on finding

Brighton with her sense.

'Lilian, what's wrong?' Adri repeated.

Lilian looked at the younger women with tears in her eyes.

'Brighton is gone,' she said.

'Gone where?' Adri asked.

'I'm not sure,' Lilian lied.

She knew exactly where Brighton was going and she had already decided to go after him.

Chapter 29

―⋅⋅⋅―

LILIAN QUICKLY SHOVED things into her rucksack.

'Adri, look after the kids for me please,' she asked the younger woman.

'Yes, of course I will but where are you going?' Adri asked.

'I'm going after Brighton,' Lilian answered.

'But you said you didn't know where he went,' Adri countered.

'I have a good idea,' was all Lilian said.

Adri decided not to argue, it would have been useless anyway. Brac stepped into the room and put his arms around Adri from behind.

'Good morning,' he whispered in her ear.

Adri smiled and leaned back against him.

Lilian caught the little interlude.

'If I wasn't in such a hurry, I would tease you two,' she said with a small smile.

'Where are you going?' Brac asked.

'Brighton is on his way back to the Dark Land. I'm going after him,' Lilian replied.

'I'll accompany you,' Brac said immediately.

'No, stay here,' Lilian quickly snapped.

In a softer tone she said, 'Sorry, I mean you should stay with Adri now that you two have finally admitted your feelings.'

'Will you be alright?' Brac asked.

He was torn between going with Lilian and staying with Adri.

'I'll take Mischief with me,' Lilian said.

It was a lie since she couldn't feel the panther's energy anywhere, but it seemed to satisfy Brac. He obviously assumed the big cat was still hiding in the forest nearby.

'Why did Brighton go back?' he asked.

'Probably to kill Graham,' Lilian replied.

She finished packing and headed for the door. Brac still wanted to ask more questions but Lilian didn't give him a chance. She walked out to the porch where she knew Robert and Nicky were sitting.

'May I borrow one of your horses please?' she asked Robert.

'You may have one. Last night your husband paid me a golden coin for a horse, when a good one is only worth two silvers. I owe you at least another four horses,' Robert replied.

'Thank you,' Lilian said as she headed for the stables around the back of the house.

Moments later she appeared again leading a big stallion. Adri and Brac were on the porch with the older couple. Each of them had a baby on their hip.

Lilian quickly gave the children each a kiss and a hug before she set off towards the boundary.

For three days, Lilian made the horse run as fast as he could. She knew it was probably going to kill the animal but she felt she had no choice. The guards at the pass had tried to stop her but she simply kept riding ignoring their shouts of "demons" and "darkness". As soon as she was through the pass, she set a course for Zedonia guessing that Brighton was also heading that way. She knew it would be impossible catching up with him, he was probably keeping his horse running by feeding it energy from the forest.

The horse stumbled under her.

'I'm sorry I'm doing this to you,' she apologized.

She brought the horse to a stop and dismounted.

'I think there is a river just up ahead, we can stop and rest there,' she told the horse.

A short while later they reached the river. She knew that it was madness to try and carry on without resting so she found a well-hidden spot and settled down for a while.

*****

Brighton watched from his hiding place. Graham and a young pregnant woman were walking at the front of a large column of soldiers. Brighton immediately decided that the woman and Graham's evil offspring must die. He used his sense to find out how many soldiers there were. There were at least ten squads, each with more than a hundred men. For a moment he thought he felt a familiar energy behind him. He ignored it and concentrated on the soldiers.

Graham turned to the young woman and slapped her hard in the face. Brighton couldn't quite hear what was going on; all he caught was 'stupid girl'. He had an almost overwhelming urge to strike Graham down immediately but decided against it since that would ruin his plan.

They were fairly close to Zedonia, no more than two days travel on foot. There was a small clearing between Brighton and the road. Brighton was making his way towards the city when he sensed Graham and his soldiers nearby. He had changed his course a little to intercept them. It was a stroke of luck since Brighton preferred to face Graham and his army in the forest where there was an abundance of energy available to him.

They were almost at his hiding place. Brighton got up and stepped out of the undergrowth. He walked to the middle of the clearing. Some of the soldiers saw him but took no notice. Brighton spread his arms slightly. Small bolts of lightning jumped from the grass to his fingers.

This caught the attention of a squad leader. He rushed forward and spoke urgently to Graham. The king stopped and turned to have a look. His eyes went wide as he immediately recognized Brighton.

'Graham, it's time to face justice!' Brighton shouted.

He spread his arms wider. Thick lightning bolts started jumping from the trees into his body. The power around him was intoxicating. It surged through him making him feel invincible.

'You are supposed to be dead! Tristan killed you!' Graham shouted back.

'Nobody can kill me,!' Brighton sneered.

The soldiers started retreating in fear.

'Stand your ground! Archers, take aim!' Graham ordered.

He knew the arrows were coated in darkweed poison. Even if the arrows didn't kill Brighton a tiny scratch would be good enough.

Ashley quickly retreated into the woods on the other side of the road.

'Release!' Graham shouted.

Brighton felt rather than saw hundreds of arrows

flying towards him.

He smiled. After this day nobody was ever going to challenge him again. A wall of pure white energy rose from the ground. As the arrows passed through it they burst into flames and were reduced to ash instantly.

'I will not be challenged, I am immortal!' Brighton screamed into the air.

Be careful, the power will destroy you, flashed through his mind.

Some soldiers threw down their weapons and fell to their knees. Desperately Graham tried to get them to attack but nobody moved.

'Attack! Kill him!' the king shouted repeatedly.

Brighton walked closer.

'They won't attack me. They know real power when they see it,' he said to Graham.

Be careful.

Brighton stopped a few paces from Graham.

'Now you will die,' he said as he lifted his hand.

The power will destroy you.

'Bri, what's going on?' a familiar voice came from behind him.

Brighton spun around.

'Lily! What are you doing here?' he exclaimed.

'I've come to stop this madness,' she replied.

She looked ragged.

'Lily, wait for me in the forest, I won't be long,' he said.

'No, you must come with me now,' Lilian replied.

'Lilian, I don't have time to argue. Do as I say!' Brighton snapped at her.

He turned around and faced Graham again. A white energy link slammed into Graham's head. The king immediately sank to his knees, pain clearly evident on his face.

'Brighton, stop it!' Lilian shouted.

Slowly Brighton started draining Graham's energy

making him twist and turn in pain on the ground.

'Can your king do this?' Brighton screamed at the soldiers.

More soldiers threw down their weapons and fell to their knees.

A black energy link slammed into Brighton's head. Confused he turned and looked at Lilian, severing the link to Graham.

'What are you doing?' he asked.

'Stop this madness or I will,' she threatened.

'How? Are you going to kill me?' Brighton asked.

'If I have to. The world does not need another Seth. Let these people sort out their own leadership problems,' Lilian answered.

'They can't be trusted to do that. I am taking control now,' Brighton answered as he turned his back on Lilian.

Be careful, the power will destroy you, Evangeline's warning rang in his ears again.

You were wrong Evangeline, I am in complete control of my talent, Brighton thought.

'Bri, please!' Lilian pleaded.

Tears were starting to run down her cheeks.

'You're also talented. We can rule forever. Is that not the reason we got this power in the first place?' Brighton said without looking back.

Lilian dropped her hand and the black energy link disappeared.

'Today I am a widow. The good person that was my husband died. Enjoy ruling forever by yourself,' Lilian said softly.

She turned around and started walking away.

The power will destroy you.

Still Brighton didn't understand. He stepped forward, grabbed Graham by the throat, and pulled him up on his feet.

'Nobody will ever challenge me again!' he screamed

as he drained the king's energy.

Lilian had intended to keep walking but when she reached the trees, she stopped and turned back.

Graham's lifeless body flopped to the ground. Brighton spread his arms. Pure white lightning bolts jumped from everywhere into his body.

'Who disputes that I am king now?' Brighton shouted at the soldiers.

Softly Lilian said, 'I do,' as her black energy link slammed into the back of Brighton's head.

She didn't hesitate, instantly she drained Brighton's energy.

Desperately Brighton tried to reverse the link but he couldn't, he was powerless against her.

The energy was almost too much for Lilian to handle.

Brighton dropped to the ground.

*****

Brighton looked around him. He immediately knew he was back in the spirit world.

Evangeline stood not to far away.

'So, you are back for a third time,' she said softly.

'Uh...yes...how did this happen?' Brighton stammered.

'Lilian killed you', Evangeline said flatly.

'No! She would never do such a thing!' Brighton screamed.

He knew Evangeline was right but could not face the truth.

Evangeline did not respond, she simply stood looking at the young man.

Brighton concentrated but could not feel a link to his body.

'I...I can't go back,' he whispered.

'No, it seems your wife is a widow and your children will never know their father,' Evangeline replied.

'But...but...', Brighton stammered.

'You threw away the most important thing in life because you thought you were immortal. You became even more power hungry that the Supremes or Graham ever was and it destroyed you, just as I warned!' Evangeline scolded him.

'I simply wanted to fix my mistakes,' Brighton defended.

'Everybody makes mistakes. Just because you are the most powerful human that ever lived does not make you perfect,' Evangeline answered in a softer tone.

'But why did you or Lilian not just tell me? Why did Lilian have to kill me?' Brighton whispered.

Evangeline did not answer. She saw the realization in Brighton's eyes.

When he finally spoke, his voice was barely more than a whisper.

'She loved me enough to make the biggest sacrifice of all. She gave up her love for me to stop me from becoming another monster like her father was.'

'Yes, and it is love that will save you this time. Concentrate on Lilian. Find her and remember the love you shared,' Evangeline said.

Brighton closed his eyes. He could see Lilian standing in front of him wearing one of her white dresses. Her long curls were neatly tied back, decorated with small pink bows.

Slowly he reached for her hand.

*****

One of the soldiers grabbed a spear and came forward.

'Stop!' Lilian shouted as she ran towards her husband's corpse.

More soldiers picked up their weapons.

Lilian flung herself over Brighton.

'Stay back, I will kill you all!' she screamed.

'I don't think you can,' one soldier said as he lifted his sword.

'Stand down,' a soft female voice came from behind him.

All the soldiers immediately lowered their weapons and bowed their heads.

'I am Queen Ashley,' she introduced herself to Lilian.

Lilian didn't answer.

'Don't be afraid, nobody here will harm you,' Ashley said.

'But my Queen...' one soldier started.

'I will not allow any more killing. My husband did enough of that,' Ashley cut him off.

The soldier stepped forward.

'These people are talented like the Supremes were. We cannot allow them to live,' he said.

'Who are you to decide? They have as much right to live as any of us. Now give us some space please,' Ashley replied.

The soldier did not back off.

He came closer with his sword raised.

Three men stepped in front of him.

'Are you disobeying our queen's orders?' one man asked.

The three soldiers pushed the man backwards.

'We'll take care of this Queen Ashley,' the one man said over his shoulder.

Lilian looked up at Ashley.

'May I have a knife please?' she asked.

One of the soldiers quickly stepped forward and held a knife, hilt first, towards Lilian. She took it and placed the sharp point over Brighton's heart.

'I'm sorry my love, I have to do this,' she said softly.

'Please don't,' Brighton whispered.

Lilian's eyes went big. She scrambled back, scraping her hands on the rough ground. She was so shocked she did not even feel the cuts or notice the blood trickling through her fingers.

'Bri, you're alive!' she exclaimed in surprise.

'Yes, I am,' he confirmed as he sat up.

'But I killed you. I drained all your energy,' Lilian stammered.

'Yes, you did, but it was also you who brought me back from the spirit world,' he answered.

He slowly got up and held out his hand to Lilian. She stared at him with big eyes but didn't take his hand.

'I am ashamed to admit that I was wrong. Evangeline tried to warn me that the power will destroy me but I misunderstood. I thought she meant it would kill me but now I know what she was trying to say. I almost destroyed our love because I became obsessed with power,' Brighton said softly.

He turned towards Ashley and went down on one knee.

'Queen Ashley, I am Brighton of Clareton. I promise my allegiance to you. I will defend your honour and your kingdom until the day I die. Do you accept my service?' he said solemnly.

Ashley was a little unsure of how to respond so she simply said, 'Yes, I accept.'

All the soldiers also went to one knee and repeated Brighton's words.

Ashley raised her voice so everybody could hear, 'I accept your service and thank you for it.'

When nobody got up she added, 'And you may get up now.'

Brighton got up and looked at Lilian. She was still sitting on the ground.

'Lily, my love, I cannot begin to tell you how sorry I am. How can I ever thank you for showing me my mistake?' he said softly.

'Love the children and me like I know only you can,' she whispered.

'I promise,' Brighton replied as he helped her up.

Gently he cupped her hands in his and let a little bit of energy flow. Instantly the cuts on Lilian's palms closed.

Brighton pulled her close and whispered, 'I will never hurt you again.'

Lilian hugged him so tight he thought she might squeeze the breath from his lungs.

'Are you trying to kill me again?' he joked.

Lilian jumped back and stammered, 'I'm so sorry Bri, Evangeline said...'

'You did the right thing. I will tell you later exactly what happened but first there is something else I must do,' he cut her off.

He turned to Ashley and said, 'Are you aware that you are pregnant?'

Ashley's eyes went wide.

'No, I wasn't aware,' she gasped.

'I'm assuming it is Graham's child,' Brighton said.

Ashley nodded, uncertain of how she felt about the news.

'Remember, your baby is not evil just because his father was. Teach him kindness and fairness. One day he will be king, you have to prepare him for that,' Brighton advised her.

Ashley smiled and nodded again.

'With your permission, my Queen, I would like to return to my family,' Brighton said solemnly.

Ashley smiled and said, 'Yes, sure. I mean, permission granted.'

Brighton held out his hand to Lilian.

'Shall we go my love?' he asked.

She took his hand and said, 'I hope you still have your horse. Mine died this morning.'

*****

Lilian sat on the horse while Brighton led it.

They had been travelling for a few days and were close to the pass that would lead them back to The Mountain Kingdom.

When they reached a river Brighton stopped.

Lilian swung her leg over the horse's neck and held out her arms towards Brighton.

He reached up and put his big, powerful hands on her small hips.

Effortlessly he lifted her from the horse's back.

He gave her a long kiss before he put her down.

Lilian looked at the river.

'Are you thinking what I'm thinking?' she asked with a sly smile as she stepped back and started unbuttoning her dress.

Printed in Great Britain
by Amazon